Nekomancers

Soul Purrtectors

By
Mel Tokken

Guardian of Ni Series

This book and the greater series are dedicated to all the four-legged family I have had support me through out my life. Without you I would have been lost to the darkness.

Special thanks to Marley and Leia who insisted in having a paw in every part of the writing and editing process.

Contents

Prologue - Lucky Cat	Page 4
Chapter 1 - Purrfect Love	Page 8
Chapter 2 - Purrpose	Page 11
Chapter 3 - Paws For Reflection	Page 24
Chapter 4 - The Purrfect Plan	Page 44
Chapter 5 - Mischief Of One	Page 49
Chapter 6 - CATastrophe	Page 58
Chapter 7 - Scratch That	Page 67
Chapter 8 - Scaredy Cat	Page 75
Chapter 9 - Gatto Go	Page 80
Chapter 10 - Little Rascars	Page 90
Chapter 11 - Felino Remorse	Page 97
Chapter 12 - Purrder & Found	Page 107
Chapter 13 - CAT, Classic Autism Therapy	Page 118
Chapter 14 - Haute Kottur	Page 129
Chapter 15 - Domesticated Abuse	Page 142
Chapter 16 - Body Pawsitive	Page 159
Chapter 17 - Hisstory Repeats Itself	Page 174
Chapter 18 - Bite The Hand	Page 181
Chapter 19 - CATholic	Page 197
Chapter 20 - CATechism	Page 214
Chapter 21 - CATerwauling, Fowl Play, & Mad Dog	Page 232
Chapter 22 - Repurrcussions	Page 256
Chapter 23 - Get To The Pointer	Page 268
Chapter 24 - Moving Furward	Page 283
Chapter 25 - Let Sleeping Dogs Lie	Page 302
Epilogue - CATatonic	Page 309

PROLOGUE
Lucky Cat

    The night before this one had revealed a moon wrapped in a halo, but the day had been pleasant and mostly clear. The Daimyo had almost canceled his excursion, but his advisors insisted that tradition be respected despite the ramblings of monks about ominous omens. Naotaka had spent most of the early afternoon occupied with takagari. His goshawk, Jinsoku, had bested two geese, but they had yet to come across a swan which would have been the most desirable prey. Their hunt had brought them close to Gotokuji temple. Although Naotaka thought the title of 'temple' was a bit grandiose for something that was no more than a run down hut. However, he still had to try to respect the Buddhists. Buddhism condemned takagari due to its ideology against killing, but Naotaka enjoyed the sport. As a warrior, takagari gave him an outlet for his more militaristic inclinations. Personally, he didn't care much about the objections of peace-loving monks, but since the temples were land owners, he had to respect their opinion.

    It seemed that prey somehow knew the Buddhist lands were sanctuaries. They would always flee to the safety of the temples when pursued. Not that their retreat mattered much anymore. The intermittent clouds had been helpful to conceal his raptor during the hunt, but the weather was turning and heavy rain would make the sport detrimental to Jinsoku. Nevertheless, Naotaka would still need to tread carefully in this territory. The Shogunate could be volatile. Currently, Naotaka was in the Shogun's favor because of his part in the Siege of Osaka. He was rewarded with his family's headship and their holdings at the fief of Annaka, but favor could be fleeting. The siege of Osaka was the result of a shift in favor. The Shogun even beheaded his daughter's eight year old son. Though technically the child was the child of a concubine, he was still favored by the Shogun's daughter, but even that could not save him from the wrath of the Shogunate. Naotaka was certainly not taking any chances that might jeopardize his new found favor. There was also the familial problem that Naotaka's new position caused. The Ii family headship originally was the right of Naotaka's older brother Naokatsu. His brother would never officially go against the order of the Shogun, but Naotaka did not currently have an heir, so he was always looking over his shoulder to guard against surreptitious attacks orchestrated by his brother.

As the sky continued to grow more and more menacing, Naotaka's hunting party decided to call off the game and seek shelter. As they were near the temple, Naotaka sent a delegation to seek permission for them to stay at Gotokuji until the storm passed. Unfortunately, the delegation did not return before the sky decided to open and release a deluge. Naotaka sought refuge under a large maple tree just off the road. He was relatively dry thanks to the shelter of the tree, but he could not shake a strong feeling of impending doom. At that moment he regretted his decision to occupy his afternoon with takagari and was consumed with the desire to be back at his castle in Hikone. Out of the corner of his eye, Naotaka caught a flash of something. This was it. His brother had sent assassins and Naotaka had sent a good number of his Samurai to the temple. He instinctively reached for his katana, but before he could draw his blade he saw the source of the movement. On the road, sitting out in the open, getting drenched by the rain, was a cat. The cat looked to be mostly white with bursts of color around the eyes and ears, but it was hard to tell with the discoloration caused by the dampness of the fur. The cat just sat there, staring at Naotaka. Their gaze met and a sense of calm washed over the Daimyo. His earlier fear was instantly replaced with the overwhelming desire to pet the cat. Being overly affectionate with animals was not one of Naotaka's virtues. He appreciated animals that could provide a service, such as Jinsoku, but had never really been fond of felines. However, in this instant, Naotaka wanted nothing more than to run to the oddly calm cat in the storm. As he fought with this peculiar desire, the cat slowly lifted a paw and seemed to beckon to him. Without making a fully conscious decision, Naotaka found himself walking into the rain to approach the cat, which made no effort to move from his spot in the middle of the open road. Naotaka's ensemble followed after him into the rain, perplexed by his behavior. As Naotaka knelt down beside the cat, who never moved except to follow Naotaka's movements with his eyes, a loud crash knocked the Daimyo to the ground. His people ran to his aid but were confused and frightened by the unexpected event. Naotaka looked back to the source of the sound and was horrified. The tree that had moments before been his shelter was now split in two and both parts were on fire despite the heavy rain. A large branch now occupied the place he had been standing. Had he not pursued the cat, both he and his entourage would have been crushed. He looked back at the cat. The cat met his gaze for just a moment, then gracefully stood and made his way to the temple. Naotaka needed no more encouragement. He ordered his group to follow the cat. They were met halfway by his Samurai, along with a monk from the temple. Naotaka asked the monk if they could stay and rest and the monk obliged.

Inside the temple Naotaka and his group were given every hospitality the monk had to offer. As they drank tea and listened to the sermons, the cat quietly made its way to the pagoda overlooking the garden and began to bathe itself. Another cat quietly approached and sat next to him. She was graceful and confident. Her presence had an air of dominance contained in a delicate package. "We are *not* supposed to interfere in political matters." Her tone was soft but authoritative. "I have done no such thing" he replied. "Did you not just prevent the death of the Daimyo from that lightning strike?" Her question was not really a question nor an accusation. Her energy betrayed her tone. She was fond of her fellow guardian and despite her position, she always found herself being lenient to him. "Ki-Ang. I really don't see how you are going to avoid an official inquiry this time." She paused and eyed him warily. He seemed not at all bothered with the idea of an official sanction. "Ki-Ang, what are you up to?" "I am not up to anything. My job is to guard the soul light of my human. No more. No less." he replied in the pauses between his licks. "Your assignment is the monk, not the Daimyo." she said, slightly irritated that he would not even pause his bath for such an important conversation. "Ama-gi, I have only done the things necessary to protect the well-being of my assignment's soul, as per training." Ama-gi eyed Ki-Ang suspiciously. Under the weight of her gaze he paused his bath and looked at her. "My human was in danger of losing his purpose. The lack of support from the community has driven him to the brink of emotional collapse. He was about to forsake everything he dedicated his life to because of hunger and despair. He could barely afford to eat with the meager amount of donations to the temple, yet he has always shared what he had with me. I did not save the Daimyo from certain death, I have brought my human a benefactor and helped him accomplish his soul path of teaching and guiding his community in Dharma." From across the temple the cats heard the voice of Naotaka introducing himself. He continued "I am the Daimyo of Hikone, Koshu prefecture. I have followed your cat for shelter but have received the gift of your sermon. My eyes have been opened and this will be the start of something new. This must be Buddha's will." Ki-Ang resumed his bath and Ama-gi just stared at him in awe. "You sly fox!" Ki-Ang halted mid lick and raised his hackles. "I am no such thing and how dare you equate me to some filthy canine?!" Ama-gi just laughed and flicked his nose with her tail. "So you saved a feudal lord, possibly altering the political structure of the region for generations to come just to bring in donations to your human's temple and help him shine his light? It was a bold move. Do you really think that your reasoning will get you off the hook with … you know who?" She instinctively lowered her voice when referring to her superior. "For fluff's sake Ama-gi. You are second in command, you can use their name. And yes. I feel my actions were more than justified. I didn't just strengthen my human's light, I kept it from being taken over by the darkness. I would have altered anything in heaven or earth to keep that from happening." They both paused at the sound of "shu-shu-shu" being carried by the wind. Ki-ang stopped his bath and stood with a stretch. "Good talk, but if you will excuse me, my human beckons." and with little more he sprang from the shelter of the pagoda and sprinted in the direction of the sound. Ama-gi watched him for a while. "You are dedicated, I'll give you that. But one day your passion is going to get you into trouble." A streak of lightning lit up the sky and with it Ama-gi vanished.

CHAPTER ONE
Purrfect Love

She wore a silky pink ruffled jumpsuit, one that, in another time, was a 1940's negligee. However, it had since been repurposed as a child's silky pajamas. The silk which used to gently caress the skin was now soaking wet and clinging to almost every part of the child's body. The girl slowly sat up in her bed, pushed her hair away from her face and fell into yet another coughing fit. Her mom brought over a machine and a handful of tubing and sat down beside her. "Mom, can BT sit with me while I do my breathing treatment?" she pleaded, her eyes sunken in and her lips a pale shade of blue. Her mom nodded and left the room, returning shortly with a small bundle of gray fur. She placed the kitten on the bed and the girl gently scratched his head. The kitten looked up and his eyes locked onto a dangling strand of hair. With all the determination of a fierce tiger, he reached out and batted at the dangling menace. The girl tried to laugh but the attempt triggered another coughing fit. Her mom quickly filled the nebulizer with medication and turned on the machine. The kitten jumped at the unfamiliar sound and fluffed himself up, quickly backing into the girl's lap and making the most ferocious "Phffft phffft" sound he could manage. With one hand the girl scooped up the kitten into her arms and with the other she gently grabbed his tail and brushed the end to the tip of his nose. This was enough to make him forget the scary sound and turn his attention to his newly identified foe. The girl couldn't help but smile and was quickly reprimanded by her mother. "Asha, you have to keep your lips on the mouth piece so you can get all the medicine into your system." Asha nodded and tried to focus on the treatment but the restless bundle of fur in her arms had other plans. Since the day they brought him home from the shelter, he seemed to be fascinated by absolutely everything. Nothing could distract him from his mission of exploring and identifying everything in his new domain. Nothing except his little girl.

They had only been together for a couple days but he loved her more than milk. He didn't remember much about his real mom, only that when he finally opened his eyes, his mom left and never came back. He had been completely alone in the cold cement cell. There was a bowl with strange mush and a towel, but it was noisy and he was always afraid. That was until he saw her. He wasn't sure why, but he felt safe when she peered through the bars at him. He ran the first time she tried to touch him, but curiosity coaxed him back to the bars where her little hand was attempting to squeeze through. When she softly stroked his fur he got a feeling of love and safety that he hadn't known since blindly curling up next to his real mom. The memory of their first meeting was still clear.

"Oh mom! We have to help him! Look at his little broken tail!" she said with tears in her eyes. "Ok. But bottle feeding a baby kitten is a lot of work and we can't keep him forever." Her mom knew this answer wasn't entirely what the girl wanted to hear. "But look, he loves me!" she cried as she scratched the kitten's ears through the bars of the cage. "He does love you and we will help him until we can find a forever home for him." "BUT-" the girl tried to interject but her mom stopped her and explained "If we help him, we will have to find him a different forever home or we won't be able to help other kitties who need us." The little girl looked sad but that sadness evaporated when she looked at the little kitten in the cage in front of her. "Ok, but I'm gonna love him so much until we find his new mommy. Can I call him BT for broken tail? It's cute and it sounds like he should be in a boy band." The girl giggled at her cleverness and her mom nodded. The shelter attendant opened the cage and handed the kitten to the little girl. They had been practically inseparable from that moment.

The girl's mom shut off the nebulizer and put it away. She returned with two cold, damp rags. Asha settled into bed and BT curled up on her stomach. Her mom placed one rag on her forehead and the other over her neck. Asha inhaled sharply when the rags were placed. "It's cold." she protested. "I know, but it will help keep your fever down." her mom explained. BT suspiciously eyed the rags. He left his spot to cautiously sniff the rags and tentatively bat and the one on her neck. "It's ok BT. It doesn't hurt." Asha said as she pet him reassuringly. The kitten still didn't seem convinced but gave into the petting and laid down on her chest which rumbled with congestion and slowly rose and fell with significant effort. "Can BT sleep with me?" Asha asked. "He can sleep with you until I have to feed him in a couple hours. But no playing. You need to rest." Asha looked happy but exhausted. She nodded in agreement and closed her eyes, still lightly stroking BT on her chest. He was already asleep.

CHAPTER TWO
Purrpose

As BT listened to the rhythmic rasp of Asha's breath, he found himself drifting off. When he opened his eyes, he was no longer snuggled with his girl on her bed, he was in a place unlike anything he had ever experienced in his short life. He didn't have any idea how to even describe it, but for some reason he felt safe. He stood up and noticed the ground ripple beneath his paws. He lifted his paw to lick off the water, but there was none. He looked at the ground which seemed to be both there and not there. It was black, but he wasn't in darkness. Flashes of color happening at varied speeds bathed the area in light. It was like a rainbow split into a million colors and they were dancing in and out of existence to different songs. There were spots that sparkled and moved. BT couldn't help himself when he saw a particularly sparkly dot. He crouched into an attack position. That sparkly dot wasn't going to get away from him. His little hind legs prepped for the pounce, wiggling to one side then the other. He was completely focused on his sparkly nemesis until he noticed a figure in the distance. He released his pounce pose and tried to see what was coming his way. BT thought about puffing himself up just in case the thing coming toward him was a predator, but the closer it got the more his fear seemed to evaporate. He felt the same way he did when his girl held him. Warm. Protected. Loved.

As the figure approached, BT was struck with the sheer wonder he felt. The figure began to take the shape of a large cat. It was the brightest shade of pure white he had ever seen or even imagined. Its long fur seemed to gracefully flow with a mind of its own, almost as if they were under water. BT couldn't tell if the figure was walking or floating. The closer it got the less he could pull his gaze away from its hauntingly marvelous eyes. One of its eyes was blue. The color one might see in the depths of an Alaskan glacier. The other eye was the pure gold like you would expect to see at the core of the sun and it seemed to shine just as bright. Part of BT wanted to look away. It was as if staring directly at something so pure was somehow wrong or disrespectful, but he couldn't help himself. His gaze was like a tractor beam pulling this glorious creature towards him and he didn't want to miss a moment. In their presence, BT felt warm and supported. It was like he had no memory of anything but love and happiness. He wanted to run and hug it but reverence held him in place. As it circled him BT could smell freshly baked bread. The glorious creature gently bumped their forehead against BT's and licked him. "Welcome home Ki-Ang." Their voice was like a warm hug. It was powerful like a wave crashing against the shore but still as gentle as the fluff of a dandelion. BT closed his eyes for a moment to take in the majesty but when he opened them again the cat was gone and another approached. This cat was a stranger but somehow eerily familiar. It was like it was something BT was trying to forget but still couldn't place or fully remember. This new cat sat next to him. She was sleek and muscular. Her fur was dark, almost black, with a reddish hue like burnt cinnamon. Her face was slim and long and her ears seemed just a bit too big for her body. Her eyes were bright green with a slight tinge of gold. Her expression was stern and regal but BT had to suppress the urge to laugh. Perhaps it was the slight cross of her eyes that diminished her foreboding expression but BT felt it best to keep his amusement hidden. "Did you get what you needed Ki-Ang?" She looked at BT expectantly, but he didn't understand. "A-are you talking to me?" he asked her with his head slightly bowed in reverence. "Don't be cheeky. Of course I am talking to you. I would like a progress report. That is if it isn't too much trouble." Her words did nothing to hide her irritation. BT was confused and a bit scared. "I don't know who you are or what you want, but I would like to go back to my family now... please." The female cat crinkled her nose, which made the small strands of white crumple together in a patch. "Ki-Ang, I don't have time for this. You know how dire these times are and we have already wasted too much time on your little R&R side quest." BT was becoming distraught. This was too much for his little kitten brain. He just wanted to go back to cuddling his girl. Maybe if he closed his eyes really tight and then opened them again he would find that this was just a weird dream. He squeezed his eyes together as tight as he could manage and then opened them as quickly as he could. As the light spots faded he saw two large bright green eyes with a tinge of gold staring at him. "Ki-Ang what is going on? Recovering from Samsara never takes you this long." BT was in a panic. He turned and ran from this strange cat asking the confusing questions. She stood as if to pursue but BT closed his eyes and willed his little legs to carry him as far away as they could, but when he opened them he found himself running toward the cat. He passed by her and continued in the other direction, but inexplicably he found himself again running toward her. She pounced on him and bit the fur on the back of his neck lifting him up with his little legs still trying to run. BT shouted "No! Put me down. I have to get back to my girl! She needs me and I need her! Put me down! Let me go!" The calming voice he heard earlier echoed through his mind and body, instantly calming him. "Ama-gi, put him down. He hasn't yet released his previous life. Something keeps him holding on and no matter how much you try, you cannot force him to let go." Ama-gi dropped BT and looked at the white cat. The panic in her eyes betrayed her "But we need him to-" Ama-gi's objection ceased immediately. "Forgive me. Of course. I just don't understand his situation at all. Ki-Ang is one of our best Kahu. We can't afford for him to get distracted now, of all times." For a moment Ama-gi thought she saw a flash of worry on the white cat's face, but she must have been wrong. Dingir was Teacher, revered by all Kahu, timeless, omnipotent, powerful beyond measure. No way could anything ever worry such a powerful being. Ama-gi pushed the thought from her mind. Dingir curled their body around BT who had clenched himself into a small ball of fur. "Precious, be calm. You are safe." Despite his fear, BT relaxed in Dingirs' presence. He blinked open his eyes. Dingir waved their tail over the ground before BT "Look. What is it that you see?" BT looked at the ground before him and his reflection materialized. "I see me." Dingir brushed their tail across BT's face. "And who are you?" Dingir asked with a bit of a chuckle. BT looked again. He saw his long, somewhat scruffy fur. He studied how the white on his face came together in a sort of snow cap on his forehead. He licked his paw and tried to smooth out the dark grey fur that covered his eyes and ears. He flicked his tail and noticed the distinct bend that earned him his name. He couldn't remember how he broke his tail, but maybe it was something he didn't want to remember. Dingir waited patiently as BT examined his image. "I'm just me. I live with my girl. I am protecting her from the sick. He wants to come and steal away her breath, but I am standing guard to keep him from stealing it. I am going to be brave and strong." BT tentatively looked up at Dingir "May I go back to my girl now. She really needs me. I shouldn't have fallen asleep. I promise I won't do it again. I will keep her safe." Dingir nuzzled BT. "Sweet boy. Think back to the last thing you remember." BT closed his eyes and thought carefully. "I remember defeating the cold blooded monster attacking my girl's throat." BT opened his eyes and on the ground before him he saw himself back at his home. He saw himself struggling to pull the washcloth from Asha's neck and then replacing it with his own body. "That's me but how-" Dingir interrupted "Perhaps you should just watch for a bit longer." BT stared at the scene unfolding before him.

    BT felt every strained inhale and exhale. He felt worried. Some part of him told him that there was something very wrong with his girl. He tried to stay awake so he could fight anything that might threaten her, but he found himself struggling to keep his energy up. All of a sudden his head felt ten times heavier than it should and he found himself fighting for every inhale. The girl's mother entered and picked him up. Her expression was one of concern. She took him into the bathroom and turned on the shower. Steam began to fill the small area. He felt her lift his lips and press on his gums but he found it hard to focus and he kept drifting in and out of consciousness. Everything was black, then the light returned and someone was squirting sweet liquid into his mouth. He tried to swallow but didn't have the strength. Blackness faded in. He knew he had to get back to the light. He had to fight. Light returned and he heard his girl's mom crying and talking to someone. "I don't know what happened. He seemed completely healthy a few hours ago. Is there any way the vet could get him in now? Can I take him to an emergency hospital? I don't know what to do to help him." Blackness returned. He was being held, but he couldn't open his eyes. He tried to meow but only a weak squeak escaped. He had to get back to his girl but his body wasn't cooperating. All of a sudden his body went rigid then completely numb.

  When he opened his eyes again BT was back in the embrace of the white cat. He looked up at them. "Did I… did I.." BT gulped "die?" Dingir said nothing but looked at the ground in front of BT and then stood. BT followed their gaze back to his reflection. The ground rippled and his image began to change from the small snow-capped kitten to a much more regal creature. His small round face morphed into a strong triangle shaped face with strong features. His fur changed from scruffy to long and silky, appearing even mane-like under his chin. His ears were tall and seemed to sprout their own fur. His color was almost silver with hints of brown and the faintest of tiger stripes. As he stared into his own eyes, they changed from a muted hazel to a striking gold with green around his pupils. He had just a hint of white on his muzzle which gave him a distinguished look. As the image before him began to consolidate, so too did his memories. His life as little BT began to fade and his memories from before began to return. "My apologies, Teacher. I lost myself for a moment. I had forgotten how powerful the illusion of incarnation can be." Ki-Ang bowed his head in reverence. "You must never diminish the power of Samsara on a soul's path. Illusion is real to those within it and awakening cannot be brought about by force." Dingirs' eyes were piercing and Ki-Ang was glad that they were a force for good rather than Darkness. "Thank you Teacher." Ki-Ang always found himself at a loss for words in their presence. "Ki-Ang, you must always honor the path, both yours and that of those you protect. Now there is much work to be done and Ama-gi is eager to get you to Kanunuru after your journey." Without another word Dingir was gone.

    Ama-gi was standing in front of Ki-Ang with squinting eyes. She cocked her head to the side, "You aren't going to make me scruff you again, are you?" "I'm back to the old me again, if that's what you mean, but if you really want to bite the scruff of my neck I would make time for that." He slinked past her and flicked her with his giant fluffy tail. She rolled her eyes and pranced up beside him. "Well, at least I know you are back to your old self. How are you feeling?" Before he could answer she pulled ahead and blocked his path. "I mean how are you really? You had me worried. We can't do this without you." He felt a bit irritated with her for hounding him, but one look in her eyes convinced him that she was truly concerned. He stopped, "Honestly, Ama I don't know. I entered Samsara because I felt empty. I was missing… something. I could not remember what it was we had been fighting for. There is always a mission, an assignment, an objective. I lost sight of what it was we were trying to accomplish." Ama-gi looked confused, "We are fighting for-" Ki-Ang stopped her "I know. I know what our mission is, but I just didn't feel it." Ama-gi closed her mouth and backed away from him. "I really don't understand, but the important thing is that you are back. Did you find what you were looking for?" Ki-Ang closed his eyes and tried to remember his life with the girl and her mom. What had he been looking for? It all came rushing back. The love, the warmth, the safety. The feeling of complete, unconditional acceptance. That was what he needed. That was what was missing from his mission. It is hard to save something one does not fully comprehend. He opened his eyes and saw Ama-gi waiting patiently. The feeling of love that was so strong a moment ago began to fade and he felt trapped in a desolate wasteland without it. That was his purpose, to help everyone he could to find their way to that feeling. To help souls find their way to that light. "Love, Ama. That's what I was looking for. Remember the last time you were truly loved?" He paused in anticipation of an answer. Ama-gi shifted uncomfortably. "I have our mission. That is enough for me." Ki-Ang flicked his ears back for a moment, then shook his head. "Then we probably shouldn't keep the mission waiting." They started on their path again when Ama-gi stopped and began sniffing around Ki-Ang's face. He stayed still, tucking in his chin and closely watching her movements. "What?!" he finally blurted out. "What about the darkness?" Ama-gi's eyes searched him, looking for some sign that his mission was not as successful as he claimed. Kahu must always be alert and not take anything at face value. Ki-Ang flipped his tail back and forth in irritation. "I'm not proud of what happened, but even we can slip. After centuries of battles I was exhausted. I had no more will to fight. I lost focus for only a moment-" His words seemed light but the guilt and pain were still very much weighing on him. He had been reminded of why he chose to be Kahu, but he could spend centuries more winning battles and still not forgive himself for his one forfeiture. The pain was real and intense, but Ki-Ang's memory was still fuzzy. He knew he had failed, somehow, in some way, but when he tried to find the source of that pain he could only see darkness. That pain etched in his features worried Ama-gi, but it was better than the indifference she had seen before. Perhaps her best warrior was not a casualty of this war as she had previously thought. "I believe you." She tried to sound more reassuring than she felt. They had to move forward before it was too late, but was it worth having Ki-Ang's help or was he just going to be a liability? The first step was Kanunuru. If Ki-Ang could face his actions and not be manipulated again, then there was hope that he could lead the charge like they so desperately needed him to.

Ama-gi led Ki-Ang to a large atrium. The walls were made of grayish brown stone. There were no straight lines and vines clung to the walls in a growth pattern to show how they chased the light. Between the vines were large openings that let in beautiful rays of white, warm light. Above them was what appeared to be an opening but the light was so bright, he couldn't look directly towards it. Ki-Ang paused as he looked around and absorbed the beauty of this place. His memory was still a bit fuzzy, but he felt like he recognized this area. There were texts in different forms, books, scrolls, projections, stones, tablets, crystals, leaves, and recordings. Peppered around the atrium were panes of glass. They ranged in size, color, and thickness. The pieces of glass were as diverse as the cats staring into them. Ama-gi didn't wait for Ki-Ang to appreciate his surroundings and Ki-Ang had to scramble to catch up. They passed a very large Persian cat. The Persian paused from his task and acknowledged them "Ki! Bean dunky's since A las saw ye! Hou'r ye daein?" Ki-Ang stopped in his tracks as the large orange cat stared at him. "Sorry were you talking to me?" Ki-Ang asked, slightly embarrassed. "Are ye aff yer heid? Aye. A'm talk'n to ye." Ki-Ang stared at the strange cat feeling dumbfounded. He was sure that he was being addressed, but could not understand a word, if they were words, that he was saying. Perhaps he was speaking an ancient dialect that Ki-Ang had yet to recall or perhaps it was because this particular Persian's face was so flat and smushed. Luckily Ama-gi stepped in and saved him from needing to respond. "Sorry Nuska, Ki-Ang just returned. We have to meet with Ninimma as soon as possible." "A unnerstaun. Tha's whey he's up to high. Guid luck!" Nuska turned, flipping his giant fluffy tail in their direction and returned to his task. Ki-Ang watched as Nuska batted around a few sparkling orange stones with rune symbols on them. Ama-gi hurried on and Ki-Ang followed. "Was he speaking English?" Ki-Ang asked in a hushed tone. The Persian's ears were small and folded, but he didn't want to chance that his hearing was sharp. Ama-gi laughed. "Yes, of a sort. Nuska prides himself on his heritage. He is Persian and Scottish Fold." "Ah, so that was Scottish?" "That was pure Nuska. You two were quite close. You'll get used to his accent again soon." Ama-gi looked ahead and Ki-Ang took it to mean the conversation was over. He refocused on his surroundings. There were cats everywhere. All of them staring through the different panes of glass, but he could not guess at what they were staring at. Some of the glass pieces were not the least bit transparent. It all seemed familiar but his memory felt cloudy, like waking from a dream. Some of the cats were so focused they looked like statues. Others were crouched and making short chirping sounds. One black cat they passed spontaneously jumped up pressing both front paws on the glass, then just as quickly sitting back down, frozen with the exception of its tail flailing wildly. Ki-Ang couldn't stand it anymore. His curiosity was killing him, "What is this place? Is this Kanunuru?" Ama-gi didn't even pause, she just continued on, "This is the Library of Destiny." "That's not at all pretentious." he whispered, rolling his eyes. Ama-gi stopped and turned to face Ki-Ang, "These giant ears of mine are not just for making me look good you know. I don't choose the names, but I do respect them." she said with an irritated flick of her tail then quickly turned and continued on her path. Her answer did nothing to quell his curiosity. "What is all the glass for? What are they looking at?" he pressed. "They are for scrying. They-" A shrill voice interrupted, "They are *not* for scrying they are for seeing. Scrying is the act of divination. These panes of glass are mediums from which we can see the past, present, and the future. Therefore calling it scrying is a misleading simplification." A small, round, hairless cat approached them. She was as wide as she was tall, which really wasn't saying much as her little legs were unusually short. Her skin was oddly wrinkly for someone so round and it seemed to fall in bunches near her shoulders and ankles but looked stretched over her back and generous belly. She was mostly a pale pink except for around her nose which was an off-white. Her whiskers were uneven and kinked but in no way made her look any less fierce. Ki-Ang couldn't help but notice that her presence exuded strength and wisdom despite her rather small stature. Ama-gi took a deep breath, "Ah Ninimma. I see you are as pedantic as ever." Ninimma trotted over to Ama-gi. Her face looked angry, but her voice was soft and sweet, "Pendantry has nothing to do with it. I am the Keeper of Zikru. Words are important. If we allow words to lose their meaning then life will lose its meaning. Words give us power and order with subtlety and grace. Change a single word and you begin to write a different story. If I were to call you a soldier instead of a warrior I would strip you of your fierceness and replace it with duty. If I exchange the word companion with pet, I take away independence and loyalty and replace it with servitude and codependency. Words are magic and can create a world with only a breath." Ki-Ang admired her fervor but Ninimma's haughty attitude on someone with such short stature triggered an urge to be contrary that he just could not ignore, "But what about colloquialism?" Ninimma hissed then choked like she was clearing a fur ball. Which Ki-Ang thought would be quite funny since she was completely hairless. Her back was slightly arched and had she possessed a single follicle it would be standing straight up. Ki-Ang probably should have felt bad but the only emotion he felt was pure joy. This creature was so ridiculously cute when she was raging. "Ki-Ang! If I didn't pride myself on the accuracy and infallibility of the Zikru I would record that you consistently suffered from tapeworms! Colloquialism is provocative and exasperating. If two wrongs do not make a right, then a majority of wrongs certainly does not permit the misconstruction of language. You must be returning from a Ti as a feral." Ama-gi quickly put herself in between Ki-Ang and Ninimma and gently urged her towards a large pane of glass, the largest in the section. "Ninimma, Ki-Ang needs a Kanunuru for his last mission." Ama-gi was authoritative but kind and Ninimma automatically changed her tone from lecturing to business. Ki-Ang was beginning to feel frustrated. His memory was returning, but it wasn't fully clear and not understanding what was going on was frightening, not that he would ever admit that he was scared. Ki-Ang plopped his haunches on the floor and refused to move, "What does that word mean, Kana roo roo? What exactly am I supposed to be doing?" Ninimma was irritated and a bit perplexed, but she was never one to leave a question unanswered, she was more than happy to share knowledge. "Well. I'm not sure what game you are playing but if you insist on behaving like a new recruit, I suppose I have no choice but to educate you." Ninimma took a deep breath and Ama-gi tried to intervene, "Ki-Ang is just having a difficult time letting go of his last Ti in Samsara-" but Ki-Ang interrupted, "You are doing it again. I don't remember what those words mean. I remember the mission. I remember that we are fighting some sort of darkness and that my job is to keep that darkness from hurting humans, but I am still a bit fuzzy on the details and you are not explaining anything!" Ama-gi was angry and her body did nothing to hide this fact. Her large ears were pressed back against her head and her hackles, the hair on her spine between her shoulder blades, were raised and her back slightly arched. She didn't have time for this nonsense. She spoke against Ki-Ang's request for reassignment and she still believed that sending him to incarnate between missions was unnecessary and a reckless use of resources. She was beginning to feel like she was the only cat who truly understood the gravity of the situation. The Kahu were on the precipice of losing control of the war and no one seemed to be acting with any sort of urgency. Ki-Ang was too seasoned of Kahu to be wasting his time at this point in the campaign. Ama-gi tried to stay calm but her voice came out in a hiss, "Perhaps you could remember that you are a soldier and I am here as your superior and not your kitten-sitter! And perhaps you should-" a loud, high pitched "Ahem" cut her off. It was Ninimma's turn to calm the tension. "Perhaps I may interject?" Ninimma's question was not really a question but a command. "Ama-gi is the commanding officer, but I am the keeper of the Zikru." Ki-Ang opened his mouth to object but Ninimma cut him off, "the Zikru is the record of all Life. Past, present, and future. It is the knowledge of lifetimes of Samsara. And before you ask, Samsara is the experience of a life on earth. It is known as an incarnation, cycle of death and rebirth, transmigration, metempsychosis, Punjarnaman, karmic cycle, the-" a glare from Ama-gi convinced her to get on with it. "Right, well you get the idea. As Kahu, we act against the Gaudium Cleptes or the darkness that threatens to consume all life and steals the light or happiness from those in Samsara, leaving them to suffer in darkness, pain, and regret. Our mission is to protect and stoke the light in the souls of those assigned to us. Your last mission was particularly taxing and Teacher, in their infinite wisdom, assigned you to a short Samsara to help you process your fail- um derelicti- I mean um your uh nonfeasance." Ninimma's pale pink skin was beginning to turn bright red. "Look Nini, I know I messed up. I remember that part clearly, more than I would like to. But what am I doing here now? I just want to rest and when my memory has returned, I want to get my next assignment." Ninimma could never understand why others didn't value information like she did. Every grain of knowledge had unfathomable potential. Knowledge was a comfort, a weapon, joy, pain, opportunity, explanation. Knowledge is the very key to the Universe, but no one appreciated the nuance of the smaller details. Luckily, she was there to remind them, constantly. "My good sir, details hold the power of creation, but I agree that conciseness is desirable at this moment." Ki-Ang gave her a frustrated stare and flicked his ears. "Right. Moving on. Before you can get a new assignment, you must go through Kanunuru where you will examine your previous assignment and reflect on your triumphs and fail- um well one must reflect on one's areas of potential. During Kanunuru, we use these panes of glass known as scrying mirrors. Though I feel it necessary to point out that the term scrying was first used in 10th century Persia in regards to the Cup of Jamshid, which was the divination practice of gazing into a cup or pool of water. And Scrying itself is a term used to most commonly refer to divination practiced in Ancient Egypt and Babylon-" Ama-gi growled, "Kindly get on with it!" Ninimma squared her tiny shoulders and continued. "Right, moving on. As you might imagine, many Kahu were quite uncomfortable with the whole pool of water situation, luckily, scrying can be accomplished through any reflective surface. We use glass because it is something easily found in the majority of assignments. Here, we use glass as a screen to view past assignments, future marks, and as a way to check in with Kahu currently on the Earth plane. Before you can get a new assignment, you must review your previous mission with a senior Kahu to seek the truths learned. This is Kanunuru." Ninimma stood proudly. She loved nothing more than education. She opened her mouth to begin another lecture on the history of the Kahu but the icy glare from Ama-gi convinced her to save that for another time and she abruptly closed her mouth again. Ki-Ang took advantage of the pause "but didn't I just do Kanunuru with Teacher? I saw my last life as a kitten. It was very short. How much more reflection could I possibly do?" Ninimma snorted as she controlled her laughter. "Sorry." She composed herself and shook to realign her wrinkly skin-folds like an older woman smoothing out her dress. "Ki-Ang, there is a vast difference between a mission and a Ti. A Ti is a lifetime in Samsara. Those within a Ti have no recollection of any existence outside of their current Ti. They have no memory of Samsara or any of the truths of the Universe. When a soul is experiencing a Ti they are fully immersed in that experience and are fated to endure the earthly stimuli as if nothing else existed. Another way to enter Samsara is by Girru, which thanks to Nuska's Girru with an American Army General we now sometimes call Girru by their more-" Ninimma gave the most contemptuous glare at Ki-Ang, "-*colloquial* term, missions. Though I see no need to give in to the influence of one's peers on such a matter, but I digress. During a mission-" she said the word as if it was a bad aftertaste she was trying to rid from her mouth. "-Kahu retain all knowledge of their existence outside of Samsara. We enter Samsara as teachers or warriors or guardians. In such roles we can influence those within a Ti but cannot reveal sacred knowledge or force outcomes. The Ti you were just in was within Samsara and you were there as a soul not Kahu.

And may I say you were such an adorable little rescue kitten I could have just squeezed you half to-" Before Ama-gi could object Ninimma corrected herself and continued. "I know, I know. Moving on. Kanunuru is specifically for reflection on missions by Kahu. Now we must observe and analyze your last Girru- mission as Kahu." They approached the large piece of glass that was embedded in stone at a slight angle. The glass looked to be an abnormally large piece of rainbow obsidian volcanic glass. It was natural and showed no signs of tool marks. The edges were rough but the surface was smooth and had varying hues of purple, green, red, and yellow. Ki-Ang and Ama-gi positioned themselves directly in front of the glass. Ki-Ang could see his reflection. It was strikingly different from the little kitten he identified as, what seemed like, only moments ago. He felt an odd pang of loneliness at the thought of his former life. He missed his girl. He had never missed his human assignments before, though he had cared deeply for every one of them. He understood why those in Samsara were forced to forget their previous incarnations. Losing those you had loved and starting again was much easier if you couldn't remember them. The problem for him was that he did remember his girl and despite the fact that he was a hardened warrior and was determined to dedicate himself fully to his missions, he ached to be back in his former life and be embraced by those who loved him. He closed his eyes to force the image of his former life away. "So what exactly do I do? Burn some incense and speak the magic words?" he asked with more sarcasm than he intended. "Ha." Ninimma responded coldly and utterly unamused. "All words are magic. Their power varies based on the incantation. And I would advise against incense as most are toxic to cats." Ki-Ang looked at Ninimma confused, "Wait. Toxic? How can something be toxic here? Didn't I just die to get here?" Ninimma's skin twitched a couple times and it almost looked like she smiled. "Hold on. Did you just make a joke?" Ninimma didn't answer. She just trotted towards a nook with a very dark smokey quartz crystal. She jumped on the nook, which took a bit of wiggling to get her large body up so high with short legs. She scooted the crystal towards the ledge. Then looked up at Ki-Ang and knocked it off the side. Ki-Ang braced for the impact and shatter, but there was no crash. Instead he saw the crystal floating just above the ground. He glanced over at Ama-gi but she was unfazed. He looked back at Ninimma who had less than gracefully hopped off the ledge of the nook and was walking back to them with the crystal floating in front of her. Ki-Ang stood there completely in awe. There was so much he had yet to recall about this place and his life before. Ninimma must have seen the confusion and wonder on his face because she explained, "I am the Keeper of Zikru. Zikru is not only the story of all there is, but also the idea of everything, everywhere. In this place, the only limit to anything is the limitations of the idea that creates it. This particular idea was created by yours truly. I have spent a Ti or two living among the Mayans of Central America and I suppose it made an impression on me. I suppose I could have chosen a different method of object manipulation but I have been enamored with telekinesis since Shakuni in the Mahabharata, but I will save that story for another time." She placed the crystal in a perfectly shaped indentation in the stone next to the pane of glass. Ama-gi directed Ki-Ang's attention back to the glass, "Let's begin."

CHAPTER THREE
Paws For Reflection

The line was long but he had time before his presentation. He had spent most of the night making last minute tweaks to his slides and notes, but managed to perfect his handouts. He still wasn't confident that his slides were perfect, but he couldn't think of how to make them better. He was nervous, but excited. History was his passion and this presentation would be great practice for when he had to defend his thesis. He ran his lines over again in his head. "The first cat… No. The mother of all cats… No. The progenitor of domestic felines. Yes. That was it. DNA marks Felis Silvestris lybica as the ancestor of domesticated cats and evidence from Poland dated 4,200 to 2,300 BCE is the earliest evidence of-" Gideon paused in his thought to survey the line. To him, it hadn't seemed to move at all. He saw the hold up. A group of three guys had joined the two girls that were one person ahead of him. They were too busy talking to notice that the line had moved. Gideon cleared his throat but they didn't pay him any attention. He tried again, a bit louder. Still nothing. Again Gideon fake coughed to try and get their attention but the fake cough triggered a real coughing fit and he had to dig in his bag for his inhaler. This finally got the guys' attention. They looked at him disgusted, "You sick dude?" Gideon still hadn't caught his breath so he just pointed at the empty gap in front of them. The guy that seemed to be the head honcho cracked his neck, never breaking eye contact with Gideon, "Chill dude. We don't want you to die before you get your coffee." Another of the guys chimed in "Dude, this guy isn't a coffee drinker. Look at him. He is probably getting an earl grey latte." The guys erupted in laughter high-fiving each other in a smug, self-congratulatory ritual made comical over the years by generations of pretentious, narcissistic so-called alpha males. The guy's mock British accent led Gideon to believe the guy had never actually heard a British person speak, but he just rolled his eyes. He was by no means a tough guy, but he didn't consider himself a geek by any definition. He was passionate about history which led to him being bullied mercilessly throughout elementary and high school, but college was different. The first year was a bit rough, but he was finally around people who shared his passions in an institution that valued intelligence over popularity and sport. There was still a social hierarchy, but he felt like he fit in more than any other time in his life. He even joined the cross country team for a few years. He was far from considering himself an athlete, but he was certainly more fit than he was in high school. Unfortunately some guys had a hard time giving up their high school glory days and failed at any kind of mental progression past the prom king phase. Gideon shook the thoughts from his head. He needed to focus on his presentation. He resumed his mental recitation. What seemed like ages passed. An alarm on his watch snapped Gideon back to the present moment. The line had not moved and he only had thirty minutes left to get his coffee, make it across campus, and set up. He looked at the front of the line. The guys from before were still at the counter. The two guys with the girls had ordered but the third guy, the leader of the pack, was attempting to flirt with the barista. He had taken off his football jacket to reveal a red tank and was showing off his muscles under the pretense of asking what tattoo she thought he should get. The girl directly in front of Gideon was complaining under her breath and the barista looked as if she was being held at knife point. Gideon looked at his watch in hopes it might make the delay vanish, but the man-child at the counter didn't wrap up the conversation, he instead leaned over to touch the barista's hair and ask her recommendations for drinks. Gideon, being a PHD student, was the oldest person in line, so he felt obligated to speak up and his temper was beginning to rise. Gideon felt like screaming but decided to take a more diplomatic approach, "Excuse me, but can you hurry up and decide or step aside? Classes are going to start soon." The guy at the counter stopped mid sentence but did not turn to look at Gideon. Under his red tank, his yoke tightened and almost seemed to lift like the hackles of an animal. He snapped his head to both sides making a horrible cracking sound like a war cry of a primitive beast. In high school that sound would have been followed by Gideon being stuffed in a locker or dumpster or something of the sort, but this was college so despite the conditioned flight response, Gideon squared his shoulders and lifted his chin in defiance. The guy at the counter turned slowly. It was like the entire coffee shop could feel the abrupt increase in tension and what was just a lively and loud meeting place had been silenced, or perhaps the blood pumping loudly through Gideons veins had drowned out all other sounds. For a moment, Gideon saw the familiar death stare that he saw all the time in bullies growing up, but it was only for a flash. The guy gave a large insincere smile, "My bad dude. Wouldn't want you to miss out on your tea govna." His friends made jeering noises and fist bumped their buddy. Gideon clenched his book bag tighter, but didn't say anything else. After a few more minutes Gideon was finally able to place his order. The barista smiled at him and when she was sure the other guys weren't paying attention she leaned over the counter and said "Thanks. He was really creeping me out but I didn't know how to get rid of him. Your drink is on me." She handed Gideon back his reusable tumbler, now filled with hot coffee. At the milk station, Gideon added a bit of cream. It was much more pleasant in the coffee house with the loud wanna-be alpha males gone and excitement was beginning to creep back into Gideon's morning. He loved talking about history and this morning he would not only have a captive audience, it would be his fellow history students who might even appreciate his lecture on the recent discoveries on the origin of feline domestication. He tightened the top of his tumbler and headed for the exit.

The sun was bright compared to the inside of the coffee shop and Gideon had to shield his eyes. All of a sudden the ground was no longer beneath his feet. He instinctively dropped his coffee and brought his arms up to brace his fall. The ground met him quicker than his arms could protect him and he smacked his chin on the concrete. Gideon blinkingly looked around only to be unpleasantly surprised by the sight of the three guys and two girls from earlier. The guy in the red tank pulled his foot back from under Gideon's legs, "Oops, sorry dude. Looks like you *ripped*. Get it? Ripped, cause you lost your tea." The guy erupted into laughter at his own joke and the other guys followed suit along with the two girls a moment later. Gideon's handouts had spilled from his bag and the tank top guy stepped on them before picking one up. "Yo, this guy has papers about cats. Dude really is a homo." Gideon stood up to face his attacker, "You know research shows that people with hidden same-sex desires are the most likely to show hostility toward gay individuals or traits they associate with nontraditional or seemingly feminine qualities." The guy looked confused but tried to hide it. He was so used to getting his desired reaction from people, that someone standing up to him was completely unexpected. One of his buddies chimed in, "Yo, I think he just called you gay." Tank top guy's face began to turn the same shade of red as his shirt but before he could react a woman rushed to Gideon's side. She was petite and somewhat plain. She was wearing a Beatles Abbey Road t-shirt with baggy jeans that were at least five sizes too big and cinched at the waist with a leather belt. Her long brown hair was pulled back into a messy bun with some unruly strands sticking around her face. She stood directly in front of tank top guy and looked at Gideon, "You know Gideon, I know you are ready to kill it at your presentation, but I didn't think you would actually draw blood." She grabbed some tissues from her gigantic beach tote turned book bag and pressed them against Gideon's chin that had begun to drip blood onto his shirt. She then turned to the still steaming tank top guy and snatched the handout paper from his hand, "Thanks for helping him up and getting his things. It's so nice to see students helping each other around campus but you should probably get going before you are late to whatever class it is you take." The guy and his entourage were not pleased, but the presence of more people encouraged them not to take the interaction further. The guy retreated, putting his arm around his friend's girl and walking off, the others trailing behind him. The woman picked up the rest of Gideon's papers and handed them back to him. Gideon finished cleaning up his face then took the papers and carefully placed them back into his bag. "You didn't have to do that. I had everything under control." The woman placed a hand on her hip, "I am sure you did, but what's wrong with accepting a little bit of help from a friend? A more correct response would be, 'Thank you Cass. I appreciate the help and the use of the last of your tissue. I hope I can repay you one day' or something along those lines." Gideon looked at her with the most sarcastic smile he could muster given the pain from the gash in his chin. "Thank you Cassandra, you are a modern day Hatshepsut. What would I ever do without you." Cass smiled and bowed deeply, "I live to serve." In her bow she noticed Gideon's tumbler in the grass by the walkway. She scooped it up as she stood, "Wow, it must be your lucky day! Your coffee barely spilled at all. How tight did you twist this lid Maximinus Thrax?" Cassandra had been Gideon's friend for the past 3 years. They took the same Master's in History course and were both still in the department for their PhDs. It took Gideon a while to work up the nerve to talk to her but they had so much in common that friendship was inevitable. He had yet to find the courage to tell her he had feelings for her, but just being around her was enough for him. He loved that they had their own private humor based on obscure historical facts. She appreciated his weird obsession with ancient Mesopotamian Civilization and he liked that she was happier around dusty ancient texts than she was around people. He had heard some shallow girls making fun of the way she dressed and because she was a bit curvier than society deemed appropriate but to Gideon she was perfection. Cassandra just stood there staring at him. Which made him realize he had yet to respond to her and had just been staring at her like a love sick puppy for longer than was socially acceptable. He tried to cover, "Sorry. Um my mind is on my uh my uh presentation." As if on cue, his watch beeped again with a fifteen minute warning. Cassandra sighed. She wished he would just hurry up and find the courage to blurt out his feelings, but apparently she would have to wait a bit longer. She gathered the rest of Gideon's things. "Then we better get to the presentation before they start without you, professor." For just a second Gideon beamed. He wasn't a professor yet but one day soon…

***

Before Gideon could get the door all the way open Cassandra pushed past him. "Where is he? I brought some canned chicken. He should celebrate with us. I brought him a toy too." She pulled a stuffed black and white toon cat from her bag. "I stuffed it with catnip. He's gonna love it! Silvestr. Here kitty. Where's the puddy tat?! Come here puddy tat." Gideon grabbed the toy from her with his free hand, "Why do you keep buying him these things? His name has nothing to do with the cartoon. Did you not listen to my presentation at all? His name is not Sylvester it is-" She cut him off and did her best to mimic his voice, "Silvestr, short for felis silvestris lybica the wild cat that is the progenitor of domesticated felines. I did listen to your presentation and the other thirty or so times you have told me, but I like the cartoon. Besides, I know it irritates you and you are cute when you are perturbed." She yanked the toy back from his grasp and continued around the house making a loud 'psspsspss' sound. Gideon carried the pizza to the living room and then went to the kitchen to grab two beers. Cass was already there with a large can of chicken. Gideon felt a twinge of jealousy for his cat. He wished Cass would buy him presents and light up the same when she saw him, but at least the cat was a good reason for her to stop by often. Gideon made a pouty face, "You love Silvestr more than me." He didn't mean to use the word love and for a moment he couldn't breathe. He waited for her reaction and what he feared would be a rejection, but she didn't even pause as she opened the can, "That's because he is cuter than you." At the sound of the opening can, a lanky, scruffy looking cat stood from his resting place on top of the fridge. He stretched and promptly jumped down onto the counter. He was not a cute cat by normal standards. His fur was a pale grey on his body that faded into a dark grey down his legs and on his face. His fur was curly, but only enough to look messy and was slightly matted in places despite Gideon's effort to brush him. He had bald spots in some places where the matted fur had to be cut out. His whiskers were bent and broken. Gideon wasn't sure he should be offended or proud that Cass thought his cat was cuter than him, but he was leaning towards proud. He never considered himself an animal person. His parents wouldn't let him have as much as a goldfish growing up and he had always considered having a pet to be just a bit dirty. Silvestr changed all of that. He thought back on when he first got Silvestr…

  Gideon had finished his last class of the day and had a few hours to waste before heading home. His roommate would be making dinner and Gideon preferred not to be there as his roommate was particularly chatty when cooking. He started walking toward the campus cafe when he noticed one of his classmates, a girl named Cassandra, kneeling by the dumpsters at the back of the building. He was curious but hesitated to approach her. He heard an odd sound and saw Cassandra inch closer to the trash without standing up. He walked up behind her and she turned and pulled him down next to her. It was not at all what he was expecting and he opened his mouth to protest but she used one hand to cover his mouth and the other to press a finger to her lips. Gideon was slightly horrified because her hand had just been rummaging in the trash and was now over his mouth, but the warmth of her touch and the smell of her fruity hand cream made it a rather pleasant experience. She gestured with her eyes and he followed her gaze. Huddled next to a slightly torn bag of trash was a kitten about the size of a fist. The thing was hideous. Its fur was dirty, matted, and missing in spots. Lying next to it, where it had spilled out of the hole in the trash bag were the corpses of two kittens with a similar look. Gideon deduced that someone had thrown the kittens into the bag alive and then tossed it against the side of the dumpster and only the one survived. Cassandra slowly put her hand out towards the kitten and spoke softly, "It's ok baby. I'm not going to hurt you. Come here." She made a kissing sound that scared the kitten and it arched its back and made the harshest hiss it could manage which sounded like a toddler attempting to blow a raspberry. Gideon slowly removed his backpack from his shoulder and pulled out the turkey sandwich he couldn't finish at lunch. He pulled off a sliver of meat and threw it towards the kitten. It landed a few inches away, but the kitten wouldn't budge. He tore off another piece and tried to toss it closer but ended up throwing it onto the kitten's face. The scruffy ball of dirt flipped backwards and knocked the offending debris off its face, but rather than fleeing it attacked and bit its foe. The look of shock on the kitten's face made Gideon smile. The kitten paused for only a moment and then greedily devoured the rest of the deli meat. Then, as if it had a mind of its own, the kitten's nose began to twitch and lead it to the other piece of meat thrown earlier. When it reached it, it grabbed it with both front paws and started to growl as it ate it as fast as it could. Cassandra quietly giggled and Gideon looked at her. She was completely focused on the kitten. He couldn't believe how incredibly gorgeous she was. She turned to him and caught him looking at her, "Do you have any more? I think I can catch him if he gets a bit closer." Gideon nodded silently and tore another piece off his lunch. His aim was better this time and he tossed the meat a few feet in front of where they were kneeling. The kitten was suspicious but its nose began to twitch and it rushed towards the food. Gideon tossed a few more pieces and the kitten got closer and closer. Cassandra slowly removed her jacket. When Gideon went to throw another piece she grabbed his hand. She moved his hand to extend the food in front of them without dropping it, then she slowly inched away. The kitten looked at Gideon and took a tentative step. It was leery of the new circumstance, but was so hungry it couldn't help but creep closer. Just as it extended its neck to reach for the food Cassandra swooped in and scooped up the kitten with her jacket. Gideon was just as surprised as the kitten and fell back onto the pavement, Cassandra gasped and said "Oh my goodness! Are you ok?!" Gideon started to reply but she continued "You poor baby. What kind of monster could do such a thing? People are disgusting! Don't worry little one, I've got you." The kitten was responding with half-hearted hisses but Cassandra wasn't loosening her grip. Gideon stood and she turned her attention to him. "Thanks. We make a good team. I'm Cassandra." He knew her name. He had known her name since her presentation on the influence of the Ramayana on Indian Culture. More than that he had been in love with her since she laughed at his Karl Marx tea joke. "I'm Gideon". He had imagined what he would say to her for so long but at that moment he could hardly find the breath for even an introduction. He prayed she wouldn't ask him anymore and at the same time prayed that she would never stop talking to him. The kitten in her jacket had settled down and stopped hissing and decided to break the silence with an off key yowl. They both looked at the kitten, neither knowing exactly what to say next. Cassandra spoke first, "I think he is still really hungry." Gideon grabbed the remainder of his lunch meat and held it near the kitten's mouth who briefly pulled back but then devoured it so quickly it almost took Gideon's fingers as well. Gideon flinched and then tried to make conversation to hide his embarrassment, "Do you think he is ok? He looks like he could have mange. What if he has fleas?" Cassandra looked concerned, "He definitely needs to get looked at by a vet, but I drive a moped and can't drive and hold him. You wouldn't happen to be free and willing to go with me? Would you?" In his head Gideon screamed yes but on the outside he just shrugged and said "Yeah, no problem."

After a quick check up at the emergency vet and some food and fluids, the kitten was given a clean bill of health. The vet tech explained that the kitten was a breed of cat called a LaPerm cat. She said there was a breeder in the area and if the kittens didn't turn a certain color by the time they were eight weeks old, the unscrupulous breeder would dispose of them and usually not in a humane way. They reported the incident to animal control but due to high shelter numbers they couldn't accept the kitten. Gideon sat with Cassandra in the room while the tech went in search of a contact list for local cat rescues. "Poor little guy." Cassandra sighed. "He is so little and no one wants him. It breaks my heart. I wish I could keep him, but I live in the dorms." She let out another big sigh. Gideon was entranced. If he had been in love before, he completely worshiped her now. He watched how she looked at that little kitten with such affection and felt a bit of jealousy creep up his spine. He couldn't take it anymore. He would do absolutely anything to see her again and it looked like fate was giving him that opportunity, "I can take him." Cassandra looked up at him with surprise and delight, "You would do that?" "I would do anything for you" Gideon thought. "Yeah, sure. But I don't know anything about taking care of an animal, especially a kitten. You seem to be really good with it. He can stay with me if you could help me figure out how to take care of him." Cassandra looked down and for a moment a small smile graced her features. She had liked Gideon from the first moment she saw him in their class together, but had gathered that he was not a very social person. She had tried to speak to him before but, despite her outgoing nature, lacked the confidence to approach him directly. This seemed like a dream. Of course she would help him. What could be a better excuse to see him than checking on the kitten. She stroked the kitten who had fallen asleep in her lap, "I could help you, for sure. It will be nice to be able to see this guy more." She looked up and their eyes met and Gideon knew today was just a beginning.

Silvestr finished his chicken and made his way into the living room. He made a big show of jumping onto the coffee table and weaving his way through empty bottles. He paused to sniff at the pizza box and bat at a few dropped toppings on the table before jumping in between Gideon and Cassandra. Silvestr's fur was much thicker than it was when he was a kitten but he was still bare in some spots from the mats. Cassandra and Gideon were happily chatting away about the presentations from earlier that day. Cassandra was being particularly complimentary about Gideon's poise and flow for his presentation. Silvestr took his time looking at the pair. It was so obvious that they deeply loved each other but neither had the nerve to express their feelings, "Humans!" Silvestr thought. "They have such capacity for great love and intelligence but complicate things more than necessary. If only they were honest and open with each other and themselves instead of manufacturing problems where there are none just to feed their own fear." Silvestr flicked his tail in frustration. Obviously, it was up to Silvestr to once again light the fuse. He had already done so much for Gideon that he was beginning to feel like a parent and not Kahu. When Gideon couldn't decide on a topic for his thesis, Silvestr helped with hints like pushing certain books off the shelves and being himself an inspiration. "The guy is a history major for fluff's sake. How could he not be in awe of all the historical contributions of cats?" Silvestr would never understand how humans could be so species-centric, but he was getting off mission. Gideon had the potential to be a strong presence for light and good, but he was so afraid of everything that he was smothering his own power. Silvestr was making progress. The unconditional love of a cat can help anyone build confidence, but it was time to implement an aggressive strategy, one he had been planning since he first appeared as a kitten. It was time for operation-life mate. "Oh my purr, it is finally happening. Nuska has rubbed off on me. I'm even thinking in cliche military speak" Silvestr quickly licked his paw and brushed it across his head and face to wipe the thoughts away. He had to focus. Gideon did well on his presentation, but even so his confidence was still lacking. Cassandra was a great influence on Gideon, but even she had trouble expressing how she felt. They really were a perfect match. Even if they hadn't both told Silvestr over pets and ear scratches how much they cared about the other, he would be able to tell just by seeing how they looked at one another. The moment was now. Silvestr jumped in between them head butted Gideon's arm and then plopped down on the cushion. "He really loves his dad." Cassandra said as she gently scratched Silvestr's chin. "Not just me. You're like his mom." Gideon froze, wide-eyed as he realized what he said. Cassandra smiled, "We are pretty good parents then." A strand of hair fell out of her bun and came to rest over her eye. Without thinking Gideon reached up and tucked it behind her ear. She looked up and their eyes met. "Mission accomplished." Silvestr thought.

***

The next few months seemed to flash by. Everything was going perfectly to Silvestr's plan. Gideon was happier than he had ever been. There was no way the Darkness could touch him now. He practically generated his own electricity, he beamed so much. Cassandra spent more time at the house than Gideon's roommate did and she and Gideon were planning on moving in together when the school year was over. Gideon had high hopes for his life after graduation. He planned to get a job as an Archivist at whatever museum would have him and then start a family with Cassandra. They had talked about marriage but decided it was too soon to think like that while they still needed to focus on school. The plan to wait didn't faze them in the least. They spent every free moment together, which wasn't too different from when they were friends except now they could openly show their affection without fear of rejection. Silvestr even found himself getting a little bit jealous as he was usually the one receiving all the attention that they couldn't show each other. He couldn't remember the last time Cassandra brought him a toy or fed him extra treats. He even thought about getting back at them by peeing on the bed, but Silvestr was here to do a job and being petty was not part of it. Things had been going so well that Silvestr had completely forgotten to check in. He was reminded of this duty when a delivery driver came to the house and rudely tapped on the window Silvestr was sunning himself by. The man was quite brawny but didn't come across as overtly macho. He had a full, bushy beard that was mostly brown with patches of ginger and just a peppering of grey. His hat was tight on his head and pressed on his ears making them look almost folded. His eyes were dark and kind with their fair share of crow's feet wrinkles and eyebrows as bushy as his beard. Silvestr blinked through the sun to stare at the man and gave a few thumps of his tail to convey his displeasure at the rude interruption. The driver didn't even have a package to deliver. The man stuck his face right up to the glass causing a greasy smudge where his cheek assaulted the pane. "Ah Su yer nae deid. A tot ye fer deid. Alright pal? Tatties o'wer the side? Ye got paralysis of ye galluses? Be'er git flitting." The man's voice was deep and thick like a stew. With another couple of taps and a two finger brow salute the man was off. Silvestr rolled his eyes and stretched onto his back. "Message received Nuska." Silvestr got up and moved closer to the window. He focused all his attention on the glass. He noted how the sun beams were visible and almost solid. He focused without blinking until an image began to form in the glass, an image only visible to him. A dark furred feline with overly large ears appeared. "It's been months and you can't even be bothered to provide a short check in or status update?!" Ama-gi was fuming, but he liked that about her. Nothing was ever half way with her but she never stayed angry long. "There's nothing to report. Everything is going according to plan. The target's light is strong and there is no sign of Darkness or dimming. I am planning to stay until he graduates and gets settled, but then I feel that my mission will be complete." Silvestr was so confident he almost came across as cocky. He had been doing this work for centuries, or was it millennia? Ama-gi's unamused tone brought him back to the moment, "Very well. But you still have to check in. I don't have the cat-power to be sending you reminders." Silvestr brushed off her instruction, "Did you really have to send Nuska? Don't you think he stands out a bit too much?" He was fond of Nuska but even in feline form he was big and bulky. "Yes, it had to be Nuska. No one else wanted to do it. You know how much we hate taking human form. Human females are supposed to be hairless. It is completely disgusting and unbearable walking around without any body hair whatsoever. It's exposing and indecent." Ama-gi shivered at the thought but straightened up as soon as an irritated Ninimma walked up next to her, "I think being hairless is liberating and beautiful, but I can't be bothered to take human form every time you slack off on your duties." Ninimma huffed. She continued, "I have aligned the details so that the Ni can successfully apply for the Archivist position as you requested. Now if nothing else is required of me I am going to retire and groom my lovely *hairless* body." Ninimma glared at Ama-gi then flicked her tail and waddled away. Silvestr cringed for Ama-gi. "It's ok Ama. I get what you were saying. I don't like human form either. Humans are so clumsy and they hardly ever land on their feet. It's very uncomfortable." Keys jiggled in the door and the knob turned. "Sounds like my report is over." Silvestr looked towards the door but Ama-gi called back his attention, "Ki-Ang. Don't let your guard down. This Ni has a strong light but that can be turned to Halqu if you are not careful." Ama-gi's words were heavy but Silvestr wasn't worried, "I'll check in once more before I reach completion of the Girru." Gideon walked in and looked at Silvestr staring out the window making funny little chirping sounds. "What are you doing buddy? Do you see a bird? You tell that bird." Gideon chuckled. "Gotta go" Silvestr said in a rush then turned and lazily jumped down and strolled towards Gideon.

***

Cassandra was sitting at the table with three books sprawled open around her, trying to take notes. Silvestr was doing his best to cover all three books with his body and still keep the ability to attack the point of her pen as she moved it. She lifted and moved his tail to read the next line of the text when Gideon came bursting through the door. He made so much noise that Silvestr puffed up like fresh cotton candy and flung himself from the table for a safer location, knocking two of the three books off the side. Cassandra had flipped the pen in her hand and had it poised to use as a weapon. "Woah, Cass! Don't edit, I'm unarmed." Gideon laughed at her defensive position. "Don't tempt me. After all, the pen is mightier than the sword." The side of Gideon's mouth twitched up in a grin, "Puns aside, I have news!" Cassandra put the pen down and began picking up the her books and began returning them to their previous state, "So I gathered. What is so important that you came bursting in like the Koolaid man?" Silvestr had returned to the kitchen at the sound of Gideon's voice but was still partially puffed up. Gideon dropped his belongings on the table and took a dramatic pause, "I got it." Cassandra was still flipping through one of the books, "You got wha-" She dropped the book which sent Silvestr scurrying out of the room again. Cassandra grabbed Gideon's hands, "You did?! You got it?!" Gideon was so excited, he was practically vibrating, "I got it! The Archivist position! They were impressed by my interview and they said Professor Beck gave such a glowing recommendation that they are willing to take a chance. Can you believe it? I thought they would turn me down because I lacked experience, but they said that they were willing to work with me! Cass, I can't believe it!" Gideon seemed to be holding back tears but Cassandra had no such hang ups and was bawling openly. "Oh Gideon, I am so proud of you! When do they want you to start?" Gideon hugged her, "The position is contingent on me successfully defending my thesis. I start in six weeks, provided everything goes well." Silvestr peeked around the archway from the living room. He saw Cassandra and Gideon hugging and immediately interceded to get his share of the affection. As Gideon scratched his ears and chin, Silvestr smiled internally and thought "Ninimma really came through. Everything is perfect. One more month or so and Gideon will be set as a beacon of light and I can go home." A twinge of sadness hit Silvestr. He had become very fond of Gideon and Cassandra. He would miss them a lot, but he was a warrior and it was up to him to protect those who would act as guiding lights to others. Without this, the world was in danger of being out of balance and having chaos and darkness reign. Silvestr chuckled to himself. It all sort of seemed like a cliché, but then again the battle between good and evil was as timeless as the universe. What was the origin of creation if not the ultimate battle of light versus dark. Be it religious text or the big bang theory, everything always begins with the creation of light to keep the darkness at bay.

***

The time seemed to whizz by in a stress tsunami. Gideon was in a panic preparing to defend his thesis and the more he prepared the less prepared he felt. The deadline just kept barreling towards him like a freight train full of explosives. Finally the day was upon him. He had hoped that his parents would at least call to wish him luck, but the day that had weighed so heavily on his mind was absent from theirs. Gideon brushed off his disappointment and straightened his tie. Cassandra was waiting for him in the kitchen with a coffee from his favorite cafe and food from their favorite breakfast spot. She had really wanted to cook him breakfast, but she was a horrid cook and could barely manage to cook scrambled eggs without burning them or leaving them runny. She wanted today to be perfect. Gideon was a bit overwhelmed by her thoughtfulness. Silvestr was already circling the table meowing for a bit of sausage. On the outside he didn't seem to care that today was perhaps the most important day of Gideon's life, but on the inside Silvestr was beaming with pride and confidence in his human. Gideon sat at the table and Silvestr rubbed against his legs. Gideon worried about stray cat hairs on his pants ruining his appearance, but Cassandra seemed to read his mind, "I put a lint roller in your bag in case you notice any hair. I know Silvestr is rooting for you today." Gideon smiled and pet Silvestr. The cat's nonchalant attitude helped to calm Gideon and he was feeling more confident than nervous. Today was the culmination of so many choices, some Gideon regretted and some he would make again a million times over. He had to consciously fight the feeling that he was afraid and would never amount to anything. He worked hard to get to this day. Cassandra had done her dissertation defense two days prior and, of course, passed with flying colors. He knew she was brilliant so it wasn't a surprise.

She barely batted an eye at the challenge. He was a bit jealous and felt slightly more pressure to succeed. He would feel absolutely horrible if Cassandra passed with no problems and he failed or had to redo the defense. He was proud of her, but at times he questioned his manliness in the relationship. He wanted to be the one who protected and cared for her, not the other way around. However, today he indulged in a bit of pampering. After he finished his breakfast, he kissed Cassandra and headed for the door. She grabbed his bag and followed after him, "Don't forget this. Deep breath. You've got this. I made reservations at Tablemono at six for celebratory sake bombs. Good luck!" and she pushed him out the door. Silvestr stretched and made his way to the bedroom where he would not be disturbed. He made his way over to the window and found a sunny part of the ledge. He focused on the glass and tapped it a couple times with his paw. A round hairless cat appeared with a brown cat with medium length fur and a slight pattern. The new cat was small but was still taller than Ninimma, though she had him beat when comparing widths. Silvestr appraised the stranger. Even though it was just a projection, the newbie seemed to squirm at the attention. Ninimma spoke first, "Try not to terrify the new recruit on his first day. Ki-Ang this is Maahes, Maahes this is Ki-Ang. He is one of your seniors, scratch that, everyone is your senior. Anyway, Ki-Ang is currently in a Girru where he is responsible for guiding and protecting a human named Gideon Chance. This human has a strong light and can be a force for good and help the humans better their civilization which helps keep the chaos at bay. We call humans like this Ni because of their bright aura." The large kitten bowed his head respectfully, "Thank you teacher." Ninimma turned bright pink and was flustered, "Oh oh oh my I Uh don't mention it. And just call me Ninimma, we call Master Dingir 'Teacher', so reserve that title for them alone. I'm just a humble Keeper of the Zikru." Ninimma giggled and, catching herself, promptly returned her attention to Ki-Ang. "Maahes will be your contact here from now on. Ama-gi would like you to help train him so he can start a Girru soon." Maahes looked at Ki-Ang and did his best to keep his voice from shaking. "Thank you for taking the time to teach me sir. I have heard so much about you. You are a legend in Bit Nisirtisu." Ninimma interrupted, "Oooh I just get chills every time someone mentions the academy. Did you know that Bit Nisirtisu means 'treasure house' in ancient Sumerian? I love that the original Keeper of Zikru named our place of learning 'Treasure House' because knowledge is surely our greatest treasure." Maahes looked at her and tilted his head. "Wow. I didn't know that. I am much more comfortable with ancient Egyptian than I am with ancient Sumerian. I had planned to learn more, but by the time I started working with the humans Sumerian had become obsolete. Thank you for teaching me such an interesting fact!" Ki-Ang groaned which brought the others' attention back to him. Ki-Ang shook his head, "Look newbie, don't encourage her. If you show interest in her random facts then you will never get anything done." The kitten looked down in embarrassment, "Yes sir. Sorry sir. But sir my name is Maahes. In Bit Nisirtisu they called me 'Heads'. At first I thought it was because I was smart. You see I have always been top of my class. My teachers said it was because I take after my mom Sehkmet and she is brilliant and fierce, although I don't think I am that fierce. I am brave enough, but nothing like my mom. Anyway I thought that's why they called me 'Heads' but it turns out that they called me 'Heads' because I am a Manx. You see, Manx cats don't have tails and they thought it was funny to call me 'Heads' because I don't have a tail. Its referring to the human tradition of the coin toss, but their joke wasn't really accurate as the tradition started in Rome and was actually 'Head or Ship' because Roman coins had a head on one side and a ship on the other, and it wasn't 'head or tail' until the late 1600s in England but then the tail reference wasn't actually a tail just the opposite side of the coin from heads. And it doesn't really make sense that they would use the term to insinuate that I don't have a tail, because Manx cats do have tails, we just have a genetic mutation that causes our tails to be stunted, but I had a great uncle on my father's side who was Manx but had a full length tail. He would flick others on the nose with it to brag and-" Ki-Ang couldn't take it anymore, "Ok *enough*!" The kitten stopped speaking abruptly and crouched down, almost cowering. Ki-Ang instantly regretted the harshness of his tone and tried to redirect. "For fluff's sake Ninimma, he is like a not-so-mini version of you." Maahes kept his head down but raised his eyes, "I'm sorry sir, I have a bad habit of babbling when I am nervous." Ki-Ang felt even worse for snapping at him. "It's ok kid. I won't call you 'Heads', I'll call you Bob." Maahes looked at him confused, "But sir I am not a bobcat-" one look from Ki-Ang stopped him mid sentence. "Yes sir. Bob it is sir." Ki-Ang flipped his tail. Despite his irritation, he could tell that he was going to like this kitten. Ki-Ang addressed Ninimma, "Anyway, I am contacting you to request the completion of this

Girru. All the pieces are in place and Gideon has his dream job and will soon start a family, everything that his soul desires this Ti. I am confident that this is enough to keep his light protected for the remainder of his Ti." Ninimma looked impressed but worried. Ki-Ang had only been with Gideon for a few years but the Gaudium Cleptes had been after him for most of his life. She wasn't convinced that a few years under the protection of Kahu would be enough but Ki-Ang was the expert. "Ok Ki-Ang. I will check with Ninlil on the status of Gideon's destiny. If she gives her approval I will schedule your exit from this Girru." Ki-Ang was feeling accomplished. He had been with Gideon for four years and was just about done with his mission. He was sure that that had to be some kind of record in a direct placement like this one. "Thanks Nini. I will wait for your contact. Now if you will excuse me, my humans are going for Japanese food to celebrate and they always bring me their leftover sashimi. Ah, just the thought of it makes me miss my Girru in Gotokuji." Ninimma looked cross and mumbled under her breath "Braggart. He knows we don't have food in this realm. Leave it to him to rub it in. Oh, I miss the taste of fish. Signing off!" and with one last glare, the image of Ninimma and Maahes vanished.

***

The group triumphantly raised their glasses. "Doctor" they all said in unison. Gideon was in awe of his own accomplishment. He had been dreaming of this moment since he was a child and now he could hardly believe it was his reality. Not only did he finally have his doctorate and the most perfect job, he had the woman he loved with him, who seemed more elated of his victory than he was. Every time he looked at her, Cassandra had the biggest smile he had ever seen and her joy was contagious. Just being there with her in his moment of glory was intoxicating. He was pleased that his colleagues were celebrating with them, but Gideon only had eyes for Cassandra. After they had eaten their fill, Cassandra stood up and clinked her chopstick on her tea cup. "I would like to say something. I don't really know how to say this but here goes nothing. It's not a leap year and I'm not Irish, but I thought I would shake things up. Gideon Diggory Chance, oh excuse me *Dr.* Gideon Diggory Chance ... will you marry me?" Their group of friends practically exploded with energy but everyone stayed silent looking at Gideon. He felt a bit uncomfortable. He loved

Cassandra and definitely wanted to spend the rest of his life with her, but as much as he tried to push the feeling down, he felt a bit bitter at what he felt was her emasculating him. He gulped and silently chided himself for allowing his father's voice inside his head to darken what should have been a completely beautiful moment. Gideon decided to lean into it. He crossed his ankles and folded his hands together, bringing them up to rest on his cheek. In his most effeminate voice and with an over exaggerated eyelash flutter he answered "Why, I thought you'd never ask!" Cassandra laughed and cried simultaneously. Gideon stood up and embraced her, giving her his most affectionate kiss yet. Their friends erupted in cheers and applause.

 The next day Gideon and Cassandra talked about their wedding plans. Neither of them wanted a big wedding and they decided it would be best to just have a small ceremony at the court house so that they could start their new life together as Gideon started his new job. Gideon wanted to call his parents, but Cassandra was against it. Gideon had a strained relationship with his mom, and him and his dad always fought. Cassandra didn't want an argument with his parents to sour the happy occasion, but she wasn't about to do anything that would put her in between Gideon and his family. Cassandra had her own familial problems, but the things Gideon had told her about his parents, his father in particular, had made her blood run cold. Gideon's father had never physically abused him, but his words were stones and daggers that left wounds that may never heal. Gideon had even stopped talking to his parents completely for a few years when he enrolled in college. Gideon's father did not agree with his choice of major. Gideon Sr. was a lawyer and had always expected his son to follow in his footsteps. He had tried to use money as a way to control Gideon, but that tactic only caused the divide between them to grow. But despite all the abuse, and the hatred Gideon harbored, deep down he still desired his parents approval. He refused to acknowledge it, but young Gideon hiding beneath the pain, emotional scars, and building anger desperately wished to be good enough for a single kind word from his father. Gideon picked up the phone and tentatively dialed putting the call on speaker phone. A woman answered, "Chance residence, Eloise speaking." Gideon found that his voice was sticking in his throat but pushed it out the best he could, causing it to break slightly. "He-hello mother. It's Gideon." There was a short pause, "Oh. Oh Gideon. We weren't expecting your call. We were just about to leave for brunch. What is it that you need? I suppose we could spare a few moments, will whatever you need take long?" Gideon felt dejected but tried to hide it. "I just had some good news to share. Is father around?" The woman paused again and seemed to be silently deciding what her next words would be. "Oh I suppose I could go and fetch him." She poorly covered the phone's receiver and spoke to someone else in the room, "Gideon, your son is on the telephone. Do you want to speak with him or should I tell him we are leaving?" Cassandra could see Gideon's pain at the rejection written on his face and posture. She clenched her fist but said nothing. They could hear the woman put down the phone and move across the room. There was a quiet argument but neither Gideon or Cassandra could make out the words. Finally the woman came back on the line, "Gideon, your father is on the other receiver, what did you want to say?" Gideon's father didn't even bother to greet him but Gideon could hear the click of the second receiver and he could hear him breathing. Gideon knew he had made a mistake and wanted to hang up, but it was too late to back out now. "Mother, Father, I was calling to tell you some good news, well, great news actually. Things are going really well for me. Yesterday I passed my thesis defense so I am officially finished with my doctorate." He paused but no congratulatory remarks came so he awkwardly continued. "Also, I am going to start a position as an Archivist at the Yale Peabody Natural History museum and if I do well I can work my way to Curator and help form an affiliated Babylonian Collection." Gideon again paused for some sort of reaction but still nothing was said. He continued, feeling a bit desperate, "But the best news of all is… I am engaged. … to Cassandra." There was another long pause and finally Eloise spoke up. "Cassandra? Is that the girl with the wild hair from your master's graduation picture?" Cassandra unconsciously touched her hair. Gideon sidestepped the hair reference, "Yes, Cassandra has been studying in the same department." Gideon's father finally spoke, but slightly under his breath. "Oh good, two of them with ridiculous degrees." Gideon clenched his jaw but his mother interjected before he could respond. "And this position you mentioned, does it pay well?" Gideon was thankful for even the smallest interest in his work. "It isn't going to make me a millionaire, but the Archivist position starts at forty thousand a year and when I can make Curator I can expect around seventy thousand a year or possibly more." His mother seemed a bit more chipper, "Well that's not so bad. Your father's first job at his firm was around that much." "Eloise don't be an idiot. That was thirty years ago. It would be much higher in today's market. A silly museum job can't even compare to a prestigious profession like law, even if it is at Yale." Cassandra put her hand on Gideon's shoulder, partly to console and partly to keep him from lashing out. Gideon chose to try to de-escalate rather than make a snide comment back. "You're right. I won't be making as much as a lawyer, but the money is still good and I will be doing what I love." Gideon's father huffed and mumbled under his breath but was clear enough to be heard "What a waste of the Chance name." Gideon had had enough. Calling his parents was a mistake and an entire childhood of pain and disappointment flooded back. Gideon raised his voice practically screaming, "You're right a museum is no place for the Chance name. That's why I am going to take Cassandra's last name! To finally rid myself of your asinine expectations." Cassandra's eyes were wide with shock and his father tried to interject, but Gideon continued. "I'm sorry I interrupted your day. I just wanted to tell you that your good-for-nothing-son managed to get his useless degree and is now Dr. Good-For-Nothing. Now I can finally say that I have learned something. I have learned that *nothing* I do will ever be good enough for you and I will *never* call again." Gideon slammed the phone into the receiver as hard as he could. It took him a few attempts to hang it up properly and he could hear his father yelling even though his hand muffled the sound. At that moment Gideon really wished he could have slammed the phone into the base and continue slamming it down until he beat his father's painful words out of his brain, but he didn't want to break the phone. Instead all he could do was drop his head into his hands resting on the table. Cassandra didn't say a word, only draped herself over him in an awkward hug. The phone rang but Gideon ignored it. It rang again and Gideon ignored it again. Silvestr jumped up on the table and head butted the top of Gideon's head and then continued to rub his face on Gideon's head. This was not something Silvestr expected. He thought that Gideon had progressed past the need for his father's approval, but maybe the outburst was what Gideon needed to finally put it in the past. After a few minutes Gideon sat up and pulled Cassandra and Silvestr into his arms. "You two are all the family that I need."

CHAPTER FOUR
The Purrfect Plan

As the days passed, Gideon had completely moved on from the confrontational call with his parents. There was too much to do to prepare for the future to waste any time on the past. All their plans were progressing nicely. They had found a house to rent near Gideon's job, Cassandra had a few job interviews set up, and everything was packed and ready to move but most importantly Cassandra and Gideon had officially gotten married. They wanted to start their new life in Connecticut as a couple and it was easier to do the legal stuff like a marriage license and name changes now rather than have to change more documents later. They still planned to have a ceremony with friends, but for now they had too much to do. Their honeymoon consisted of a celebratory dinner and grocery store cupcakes on paper plates and champagne served in paper cups. This luxurious dessert was enjoyed sitting on the floor with a moving box labelled "kitchen supplies" as their table. Silvestr watched his humans laughing and enjoying themselves. He wanted to join in the affection, but he was confident that his mission would end soon and he didn't want them to be too attached to him. He had been slowly distancing himself to make the parting easier. His humans had noticed but they thought he was just stressed from the move. As he watched them feeding each other cake and reminiscing about their relationship, Silvestr began to wonder if he had truly been distancing himself to protect Gideon and Cassandra or if he was actually doing it for himself. Ki-Ang had been Kahu for almost 6,000 Earth years. He had lost count of how many Girru he had completed. Leaving his human was never easy, but he had become more indifferent over the years. In the beginning, he truly loved the humans he was assigned to, but the problem with loving someone and then parting from them is that a little piece of your soul stays with them. After 6,000 years Ki-Ang was feeling a bit empty. The result is that now he tried to keep some distance from his assignments. He cared for them and did his duty, but he did his best to stay emotionally detached. This Girru was different. Gideon had managed to connect with him. Maybe it was Gideon's isolation and dependence on their relationship or maybe it was Gideon's light and strength that caused Silvestr to feel more affection for him, and Cassandra, than he usually allowed himself. Whatever the reason, Silvestr knew that this parting would be difficult and he resolved to do what he could to lessen the pain.

***

Months passed. One day Gideon got home to find Cassandra waiting with dinner ready. He was surprised because she never cooks. She must have read his mind or his concerned facial expression because she answered his silent question. "My mom came by and helped me make dinner. She is visiting for a while. Don't worry, she's at a hotel." Gideon had only been at his job for a little over six months. He didn't think today was any kind of anniversary, but it wasn't out of character for Cassandra to surprise him. Cassandra's next words made him worry he did forget something important, "I wanted to cook you a special dinner, but I wanted it to be edible, so I asked her to help. We made a veal cutlet with oven roasted baby potatoes and a side of mixed vegetables including baby broccoli, baby carrots, baby corn, baby squash, and baby artichokes. Before we eat, I have a present for you." She brought out a smallish box wrapped in baby blue tissue paper and a soft pink ribbon. Gideon found that he could hardly breathe. He didn't want to say anything in fear that this might be a dream, so he just silently accepted the gift and began to unwrap it. Silvestr sauntered up to greet him but got completely distracted by the dropped ribbon. Gideon slowly opened the box to reveal a test stick with two solid pink lines. His brain completely disconnected from his body and he sat there, silent, looking into the box. Cassandra nervously bit her thumb. She was very excited, but didn't know how Gideon was feeling. They hadn't really discussed having children. They both wanted to be parents eventually, but with all the change, they weren't thinking about it at the moment. They hadn't even begun to plan their wedding ceremony yet. Gideon's silence was eating at her and she began to worry he was upset. His shout caught her completely off guard and she nearly jumped onto the table. "Yes!" He jumped out of his chair, his entire body vibrating in excitement. "Yes, yes, yes, yes, yes, yes! This is amazing! You are amazing! You're gonna be a mom. Oh my god, I'm gonna be a dad! We're going to have a baby! We have to make a nursery! No, this house isn't big enough. We need to buy a bigger house and then make a nursery. We're going to need a minivan. All parents have minivans. What are we going to name him? What if it's a girl? Will she like me? What are dads supposed to do with kids? Do I have to learn how to fish? I bet they are going to want a bicycle-" Cassandra interrupted before he got to prospective colleges. "Woah, slow down. Let's just start with getting through dinner. I'm so glad you are happy! I was worried because we weren't planning for a baby." Gideon couldn't speak anymore. He rushed to Cassandra and hugged her but then became acutely conscious of the fact that she was pregnant and arched his back to hug her without putting any pressure on her abdomen. Cassandra laughed and reached for a bag and handed it to Gideon. He reached in and it was his turn to laugh. He pulled out a cartoon looking black and white cat in a white bonnet and a diaper with an oversized safety pin. Cassandra smiled "that can be Silvestr's first gift to his little brother or sister." At his name, Silvestr looked up from where he sat near the table, his paw firmly on the pink ribbon, wagging his tail. "So the time to leave had finally come." he thought to himself and took the ribbon in his mouth and triumphantly headed towards the couch to stash his trophy under.

***

"What do you mean Ninlil won't approve Girru completion?!" Silvestr paced before the large window in the living room. Ama-gi sat stoic, following him with only her eyes. "Ninlil read Gideon's destiny and she still sees the Darkness. The Girru cannot complete until the danger is neutralized." Silvestr huffed, "I think Ninlil is losing her touch. Gideon is happy. He is even going to counseling to deal with his anger towards his father so he can be a better dad. He is successful at work. His relationship with Cassandra is better than ever. What more can I do here? Can you ask Ninlil to see exactly how the Darkness is still a threat?" Ama-gi sighed and rubbed her right eye on her front leg. "It doesn't work like that. Ninlil only declares destinies based on... well based on... Look I don't know how she does it but it never involves specific details. You know how all those seers are. Everything is vague or abstract based on their 'feelings' or 'readings'. We wouldn't have much of a job if they could tell us exactly how and when things would happen." Silvestr was irritated and at a loss for an effective argument. "But I've already been here six months longer than I was expecting. Cassandra is emotional and uses me as practice for the baby. Do you know how many times I have been 'swaddled'? She is smothering me! I am a warrior! I do *not* belong in a bonnet!"

Ama-gi snorted but kept her laughter under control. Most of Ki-Ang's colleagues had watched with extreme delight his many experiences being dressed up, swaddled, and held like a baby. Silvestr didn't particularly mind the bottle practice but the rest he found undignified and always endured with his ears firmly against his head. He would have wagged his tail, but it was usually securely confined by the swaddling blanket. Now anytime he heard a 'how to' video being played, he ran to the closest hiding spot. Ama-gi decided, against her deepest desire, to avoid telling Ki-Ang what a cute human baby he was and just bit her tongue. "Look Ama, I am being wasted here. There has not been any sign of darkness for quite a while. Even on my three am patrols, when darkness usually creeps in, there has been no sign of it. Gideon has even forgiven his parents and is working on rebuilding their relationship. I am confident that even if the Darkness appeared, the power of his light would protect him better than even I could. There has to be another Girru that would be a better use of my skills. I should be on the frontline fighting the darkness, not human sitting a Ni that is out of danger. Please Ama! I'm so bored!" Ama-gi didn't disagree with him. She also felt that as Kahu they should be on Girru where they could directly fight the agents of chaos. She didn't see much use in being so overprotective of certain humans, but her job was to protect. She was a warrior, she preferred when it fell to others to devise strategy and her job to follow their plans. "I will speak to Ninlil again. Even if she does still feel the threat, perhaps I can convince her to assign a different Kahu so you can be put to better use elsewhere." Her words weren't exactly what he wanted to hear, but they were better than sitting around waiting for old age. He did consider arguing but he heard a familiar baby video instructor's voice and he only had a few minutes to hide before he was subjected to another humiliating ordeal. He rushed a goodbye to Ama-gi and headed for behind the fridge.

***

After a few more weeks, Silvestr finally got the news he wanted to hear. Ninlil refused to deny the threat, but under Ama-gi's unrelenting requests, she did not object to the assignment of another Kahu. Ninlil told Ama-gi that she still had a foreboding feeling, but Ki-Ang was one of their best warriors and if he felt that he had done enough to set up Gideon's protection, then she could not justify the denial of a transfer. Ama-gi had told Ki-Ang that a new Kahu would not enter Girru until a few months after the baby was born. They agreed that the best timing for Ki-Ang to leave was right before the birth as Gideon would be so distracted that he wouldn't have time for grief. Ninimma arranged everything and informed Ki-Ang during his next check in. "Everything has been set into motion. I'm sorry to tell you, but you will die of kidney failure due to genetic predisposition to urinary tract infections. It will happen quickly so you shouldn't feel too much discomfort. Your replacement has already been chosen. You'll be happy to know that it is Maahes. He has been studying your Girru notes like they are a holy text. You will have time to brief him here before he enters Samsara. We are a bit short staffed here, so Teacher needs me to accept a short Girru. I won't be around to answer any of your calls because I will be on a mission. Did you hear that? I will be on a mission. An important mission too. See I can do important things on Earth too. Well I better go prepare for my important Girru. I have so many *important* things to do. Me." With a haughty shake of her puffed out chest, Ninimma was gone. Silvestr stared contently out the window. Finally, he was going to get back into the fight. Suddenly the hairs on his back stood up and he went from relaxed to fully alert. He surveyed the view from his window but saw nothing out of the ordinary. He jumped down and ran through the house, still nothing. He returned to the window and saw it. A single magpie on the fence. Silvestr crouched and began chanting. Before he could get through the first incantation, the bird flew directly to the window sill and landed to his right. It twitched its head to the north and then sharply to the south. It was too late.

CHAPTER FIVE
Mischief of One

This could not be happening. He had been so prepared. There had not been one sign of any kind of trouble. He had checked and double checked. Silvestr closed his eyes and prayed to Dingir that the bird was here for him but he knew that the timing wasn't right. He wasn't going to leave this Girru for another few months and the wing harbingers of death always appear within days of a soul's departure. He tried to finish his chant to ward off the creature but he was interrupted. Cassandra entered and saw Silvestr crouched by the window making a chirping sound at the bird. "No, no, no Silvestr. I know you want to get the bird, but you can't." She ran to him and scooped him up in her arms. "Leave that poor birdie alone. You'll scare her. You mean thing. What has she ever done to you?" Silvestr never took his eyes off the magpie and growled "Speak you winged fiend. Who do you seek? I am Ki-Ang, Kahu of Saa Dul-barag-gal-mah, The Garden of the Gods. I am the protector of all who dwell here. State your intent so that I might challenge the claim." Silvestr was squirming in Cassandra's arms and she was struggling to keep him under control. Suddenly, the resistance from Cassandra was gone and Silvestr flung himself at the window. He howled at the magpie "You will not attempt to take anyone under my protection or you will forfeit your life!" Silvestr repeatedly threw his body at the window, trying to scare off the intruder. The magpie flinched and flapped its wings a few times, but remained at the window. The bird finally spoke to Silvestr, "Why must you Feline Kahu always interfere with the business of Kur? My orders come directly from Lord Birdu who labors on behalf of Lady Ereshkigal, The High Queen of Kur. We are not your enemies. I am only a messenger sent to guide the departing soul." Silvestr hissed "*Lies*! You aid the Gaudium Cleptes and darkness spreads wherever you go. You shall not bring darkness here!" The magpie squawked and furiously beat his wings. "Foolish feline! How dare you equate me with the darkness! This soul's exit from Samsara was preordained and my task will be fulfilled as it has already been set in motion. We are no less Kahu than you!" The bird looked past Silvestr towards the place Cassandra had been restraining him. Silvestr looked back and saw Cassandra hunched over clutching her stomach, surrounded by blood. His eyes went wide and he leapt to her. She collapsed onto the floor and Silvestr knew he was too late, but he had to do anything he could. He remembered that Cassandra often left the kitchen window open on sunny days. He rushed to the window and sure enough it was open a crack. Silvestr furiously pushed his face and paws in the crack to force it open enough for him to squeeze through, but there was a stopper on the track and it was providing strong resistance. Still Silvestr fought. He frantically pushed and pulled and wiggled until his nose and mouth were cut and bloodied. Finally he worked it open enough to squeeze himself through but was slowed by the screen. He clawed his way through, ripping the screen to shreds. He didn't know which way to go. He hadn't been outside before. He desperately looked around and happened to see the older lady next-door in her garden planting a new tomato plant. He ran towards her meowing. Luckily, she recognized him. "Well hello there handsome baby. How did you get out?" Silvestr ran around in circles and then would start back towards the house, but the older lady wasn't getting his urgency. "What's the matter baby? Are you scared?" The woman went into her house and grabbed her phone, dialing Cassandra's number and watching Silvestr through the door. Silvestr couldn't stay still, he had to get help and this woman was moving too slow. He ran to the door and back repeatedly. Cassandra was not answering the woman's call. This caused her to suspect that something might be wrong. To Silvestr's relief she headed towards his house. She knocked on the door and rang the bell but there was no answer. Silvestr weaved himself between the old woman's legs then jumped onto the window sill where the magpie had been before. He pawed at the window and yowled. The woman made her way over to the window and peered in. Seeing Cassandra on the floor she gasped and immediately ran home to call emergency services.

  Gideon paced back and forth in the hospital waiting area. His mother-in-law was with him, but could not get him to sit. After what seemed like a lifetime, a doctor came out to speak with them. His expression was solemn and it worried Gideon more than the lack of news. He informed them that Cassandra had experienced a placental abruption. He explained that this was when the placenta separated from the uterine wall. He asked questions about Cassandra's habits, if she smoked, used illicit drugs, or engaged in dangerous physical activity. Gideon answered in the negative but his tone was short and angry. Cassandra's mom chimed in, "Doctor, Cassandra has been very careful. She wouldn't do anything that might harm the baby.

When she was young, I had two miscarriages, so she was scared that she might experience the same." The doctor responded "It is possible that the abruption was caused by genetic factors. It isn't unheard of for genetic anomalies to cause placental abruption at twenty-one weeks." Gideon interrupted and snapped at the doctor, "So what does all this mean? Are Cassandra and the baby going to be ok?" The doctor cleared his throat "As I explained, Cassandra has a grade three placental abruption which is severe. There was hemorrhaging and she has gone into shock. The fetus still has a faint heartbeat, but I do not think that the severity of the abruption allows for viability. I feel the best course of action is to force labor and ensure that Cassandra can be treated." Cassandra's mom started to cry but Gideon just stared at the doctor blankly. The doctor continued, "I need you to consent to the procedure and treatment plan. Since she is only at twenty-one weeks we can legally still choose this option. However if we try to stabilize her and the fetus and the abruption worsens, we would not be able to abort the pregnancy after twenty-four weeks, even if the fetus is not viable, unless Cassandra's life was endangered and by then it may be too late. Since Cassandra has not regained consciousness, it falls to you to make the decision. Given the severity of her current condition I strongly recommend you do not wait." Cassandra's mother collapsed into a chair but Gideon was resolute, "Do the procedure." Cassandra's mom whimpered and tried to object but Gideon cut her off. "Christine, it is my decision. I will not risk losing Cassandra to save a fetus. It will not kill my wife." Gideon was uncharacteristically cold. He turned back to the doctor and grabbed the consent forms. "Do whatever you have to do to save Cassandra."

  Back at the house Silvestr had found one of Cassandra's shirts and dragged it to the living room to a square of sunshine on the floor. He carefully positioned himself in the middle of the sunlight on the center of the shirt. He tucked his legs carefully beneath him and began to purr. He closed his eyes and focused on Cassandra. Her Ni was weak and the Ni of the baby was practically non-existent. He gathered all his strength and focused his purr to flood Cassandra's Ni with energy. It was exhausting and Silvestr found himself close to collapsing, but he had to continue. From out of nowhere he saw it. The Darkness had finally decided to show itself, but something was off. The Darkness seemed to be attacking the baby's Ni. Silvestr tried to refocus his protective energy on the baby, but when he did,

Cassandra's Ni rapidly lost energy. He had to choose one. He sent an urgent plea to headquarters, but received no response. He was alone. He had to choose, and quickly. He knew how much Cassandra and Gideon were looking forward to meeting their baby, but he also knew how vital Cassandra was to Gideon. The choice, difficult as it was, was clear. With all of his remaining strength he extended his protective energy throughout Cassandra's Ni, leaving the baby unprotected. The Darkness swept forth and consumed the baby's Ni causing it to go dark. In reaction Cassandra's Ni flared with a bright nova and Silvestr passed out.

  Cassandra could feel Silvestr purring on her chest. She tried to smile but just felt so incredibly tired. She tried to remember what she was dreaming about but everything just seemed foggy and confusing. She could feel that she was in bed but couldn't remember going to sleep. She remembered Silvestr stalking a bird… without warning the memory of severe pain flooded over her and her whole body seemed to wince at the recollection. She wanted to sit up in panic, but her body wasn't obeying her commands. Her baby. The pain she remembered as a sharp pain in her stomach and she fell. Was her baby ok? She reached to push Silvestr off her chest but he wasn't there. She blinked open her eyes. Instead of finding herself at home, she was assaulted by the view of a cold and sterile hospital room. Her mom was asleep in a chair across the room. She looked to her right and saw Gideon. He was staring straight ahead. His eyes were bloodshot and glazed over. He was holding her hand in his and she gave a gentle squeeze. He slowly began to register the touch and looked at her. There was no joy or relief. His expression was hard. She wanted to ask what happened, but seeing a coldness across his features made her terrified to utter any sound. She was used to seeing Gideon worry, but this look was nothing she had ever seen and it was chilling. Cassandra sat up a bit and took in her surroundings. Her mother was sitting next to a pile of tissues. Cassandra looked at Gideon and in his other hand was a toon cat with a tear soaked bonnet. She paused. Nothing. She could not feel anything. She reached up to caress her belly but winched as her hand brushed bandage covered stitches. "No! No, no, no, no, no, *no*!" she screamed in her head and a single tear ran down her face. She looked at Gideon who was simultaneously looking at her and through her. She forced her voice out in a broken whisper, "What… our baby….

is… is…. where?" She didn't even know what to ask. She wanted him to hold her and tell her that everything was ok, that their baby was fine or that this was just a bad dream, a side effect of her weird chocolate pickle pregnancy craving. The words were just not there. She instead pleaded with her eyes. Gideon just looked down and slightly shook his head. Everything in the room seemed to shutter and Cassandra cried out. She squeezed her eyes shut as strongly as she could manage but nothing could stop the deluge of tears that burst forth and burned paths down her cheeks.

***

After multiple surgeries and just over a week of observation, Gideon was allowed to take Cassandra home. Her mom agreed to stay with them until Cassandra was back on her feet. Even Gideon's mom offered to visit for a while to help out. When news got out about the tragedy, Cassandra seemed to have a never ending flow of condolences and support. Gideon on the other hand was expected to return to work and support Cassandra through her mood swings and depression. The first week they returned home Gideon was as attentive and loving as a husband should be, but as time went on, his patience and affection dwindled. One uneventful Thursday, Gideon returned home to find his mother-in-law packing to leave. She wanted to stay with Cassandra longer, but her husband needed help with the business and she had already been gone longer than expected. On her way out she looked at Gideon with worried concern, "Take care of her. She is hurting to her core and desperately needs your support." Gideon nodded and walked her to her taxi. When he came back into the house, he heard Cassandra crying in the bedroom. He went in to check on her and ask if she needed anything, but she just shook her head and continued crying. This was a ritual that they had been doing since she returned home. At first he would sit with her and stroke her hair, but nothing he did seemed to help, so now he would just leave her alone. He picked up Silvestr, who was laying across Cassandra's belly kneading the blanket, and left. He plopped down onto the couch with the cat still in his arms and began to forcefully stroke his fur. Silvestr was unaccustomed to such direct and ungentle attention, but something told him he needed to stay with Gideon. So he allowed the assault disguised as affection to continue, but he made sure to wag his tail in protest. "It has been a couple weeks, but she is still inconsolable. Nothing helps. All of our friends, family, even the neighbors have been by to offer her support and nothing helps. She is either crying, silent, or angry." When Gideon paused Silvestr meowed, hoping to distract him from his thoughts, but it only seemed to urge him on. "I love her, but I don't know what to do. Everyone tells me I need to be strong and be there for her, but what about me? I lost my baby too. No one seems to care about my feelings. No one brings me food or offers me comfort. Cassandra won't even look at me, not to mention hug or support me." The fur on Silvestr's back began to rise. His whole body tightened and he was suddenly on high alert. He quickly scanned his surroundings. Out of the corner of his eye he saw it. A shadow that wasn't there before. It began to move like it was a wisp of smoke. Silvestr locked his eyes on it, forsaking all other stimuli. The shadow smoke began to clump together and seemed to take some sort of form. Within the makeshift form Silvestr could see flashes of red, brown, and black. He could not blink for fear of losing track of the intruder. Why was it here now? Had Silvestr really been so blind to the surreptitious schemes of the Darkness? He had to do something before it could gather more strength, but his timing had to be perfect. If he acted before it had solidified enough to enter this world, his pounce would be ineffective, but if he waited too long, the entity could garner enough energy to elude his attack. If his attack failed and he lost track of it, then the consequences could be dire. He watched it as it pulled energy from its surroundings, the chief source being Gideon himself. Silvestr needed to put a stop to Gideon's negative thoughts and hateful musings, but he couldn't risk taking his eyes off the entity. Gideon continued his ramblings of self-pity, but Silvestr was fixated on his foe. Silvestr flung his tail wildly from side to side trying to release a little bit of his frustration so he would not pounce prematurely. This caught Gideon's attention and he asked "What are you doing? Why are you angry? Why does everyone seem to be angry with me?" but Silvestr would not be distracted. Gideon looked in the direction that Silvestr was staring in, expecting to see a bug or something, but he saw nothing. Gideon clenched his fist. "My cat won't even listen to me. No one cares how I feel." he thought to himself, squeezing his eyes closed to fight back tears. Silvestr saw a subtle spark at the center of the forming darkness and knew it was his moment. He sprang from Gideon's lap, inadvertently sinking his back claws through Gideon's slacks and into his thighs. Gideon cried out but Slivestr was already about his task. Silvestr flung himself into the invisible cloud of malice and flailed his front paws wildly. Gideon abandoned his anger momentarily and was perplexed by Silvestr's odd behavior until blood started to soak through his slacks. He cursed and made his way to the bathroom to treat his wounds. Silvestr did not notice as he was too busy scanning the room to confirm that his attack had destroyed his opponent. When he was finally satisfied that he was the victor, he noticed Gideon's absence and ran after him. When he approached the bathroom Gideon saw him and angrily pushed Silvestr out and slammed the door. Silvestr frantically pawed at the door and stuck his paws under it in an attempt to gain entry, but Gideon just yelled at him and told him to go away. Silvestr pressed his face under the door, trying his best to survey the area. From his limited vantage point, the bathroom seemed to be clear of danger for now. Silvestr decided that it would be safe to leave Gideon be and report the invasion to Barag. Ama-gi was not going to be happy.

Silvestr waited until his humans had gone to sleep before contacting Barag. To his dismay, Silvestr learned that no help was available. Maahes was the only one available to answer the call and he told Silvestr that it appeared as if the Darkness accomplished a coordinated attack. Maahes seemed confused and overly troubled. "Ki-Ang, there is something I just can't understand. I thought the darkness was mindless. I thought it was just a state of being that was the result of certain energies mixing, like fog. I mean I learned that The Darkness was like a virus. It could infect those left unprotected, but that it was in no way sentient. So how could the Darkness plan or coordinate?" Silvestr had been asking himself the same question. He had always known that given an opportunity, the Darkness would infect a host, but he had never seen the Darkness act independently. It had always required the assistance of a host to spread. However, Silvestr was not about to admit his ignorance, so he did his best to emulate Ninimma and provide an explanation. "I was taught the same and that had been my experience until now. However, even bacteria have the ability to be minimally cognizant and exploit their surroundings. Perhaps the darkness is evolving. From the beginning, the Darkness has been the main agent of Chaos. Many millennia ago, we openly worked with humans to restrain the forces of Chaos, which was considered the first evil. We managed to bind the Chaos but its shadow remained. Kahu have been working to keep that Darkness from spreading and gaining strength so that Chaos could not overturn the order of creation. We have been mostly successful in our task, but with more souls in Samsara, it has been harder to keep the Darkness from spreading due to the sheer number of hosts available to it. Perhaps the more it spreads and mutates, the more sentient it becomes. It could be that when it infects a host it takes more than just that host's energy. I suppose it is possible that along with using the host to multiply, it also becomes imprinted with useful qualities of the host. I'm not sure, but I know that this situation calls for a revision of our tactics." Maahes looked concerned, "What am I supposed to do? All the experienced Kahu are in Girru and Teacher has been occupied doing… whatever it is that Teacher does. How can I help?" Silvestr paused to scan his surroundings. Something was not right. He knew it was only a matter of time before the Darkness returned. Gideon's anger and pain were drawing it to him. He needed Silvestr now more than ever. Silvestr returned his attention to Maahes, "I need you to stop the completion of my Girru. I can't leave yet." Maahes looked troubled but didn't say anything. "What?! Just do whatever you have to do to keep me here." Silvestr snapped. Maahes bowed his head, "I- I- I'm sorry. I- I can't. You were so eager to leave, that Ninimma has already set your departure in motion. Your kidneys are already failing. You may be able to use your healing ability to stave off death for a few weeks, but it can't be reversed. I'm sorry." Silvestr cursed under his breath. "I should have listened to Ninlil. She had a foreboding and I ignored the warning. Very well, I will do what I can with the time I have left. It has already been planned that a Kahu would return a few months after I left, so I will just take that opportunity to return and fix my mistakes. I will stay with Gideon his entire lifetime if I must, but I will not let the Darkness have him. Contact me when Ninimma returns. Hopefully I can hold on until then." Silvestr ended the connection and began his patrol. That night Gideon seemed to be having nightmares and awoke frequently. This distress drew the Darkness to him like moths to a flame and Silvestr was kept on high alert, dispersing the materializing Darkness repeatedly. The noise of Silvestr's guardianship disturbed Gideon until he had had enough and grabbed Silvestr by the scruff, locking him out of the bedroom. Silvestr cried to get back in, desperate to protect his humans from the unseen threat, but it only prompted Gideon to lock him in the laundry room. Silvestr tried to use the involuntary confinement to his benefit by focusing on his purr in an attempt to heal himself enough to prolong his Girru. If he couldn't be in the room protecting his humans, this was the next best thing. Eventually, he fell asleep purring.

CHAPTER SIX
CATastrophe

    Two weeks of medical complications and depression had left Cassandra's household in disarray. She had no energy or motivation to clean. She refused to do laundry, go shopping, pay bills, or anything that she used to do. Gideon felt like a single dad taking care of a petulant child. Cassandra's depression would not let up and Gideon's repressed sadness had morphed into hurtful anger which was particularly triggered by Cassandra's depression. Both felt the other should be doing more to ease the burden either physically or emotionally. The chasm that was rapidly forming seemed impassable and neither Gideon nor Cassandra were in any type of state to build a bridge. Finally, Gideon had had enough. He returned home from work to find the sink full of dirty dishes, most with food that had barely been touched, cat vomit in two places down the hallway, wet soured laundry in the washer, crumpled up used tissues all over the living room and bedroom, and Cassandra on the couch, wearing the same sweatpants and hoodie that she had been in for the past week. The entire house had a pungent smell of rot. He tried, with little effort, to speak to Cassandra with a sympathetic tone, but he failed and his irritation came through with a dusting of hatred. "What did you even do all day?" Cassandra just got up and went into the bedroom, slamming the door behind her. Gideon thought about calling Cassandra's mom, but he knew she would just be sympathetic to Cassandra and blame him for not being a good husband, so he broke down and called his own mother. Even though she had offered her help earlier, Gideon's mother acted irritated with his request but acquiesced in the end. She agreed to stay for a week and help him get the household organized. She was not quiet about her displeasure that Cassandra was not keeping her household organized as she felt a woman was required to do. At first Gideon was a bit upset that his mother would be so harsh towards Cassandra, but it vindicated the part of him that also felt anger towards Cassandra, so though he would not agree with her insults of his wife, he also did not contradict them.

    When Gideon's mother, Eloise, arrived, she was mortified by what she saw. She even refused to stay in the house for the first three days because she said it was too disgusting to live in. Gideon felt that she was overreacting, but didn't argue.

She would come by during the day to clean, but refused to clean up after Silvestr referring to him only as "that disgusting beast". For the first time since her miscarriage, Cassandra's normal emotional state switched from perpetual sadness or indifference. Unfortunately, the new perpetual state was anger. Cassandra was not happy that Gideon asked his mother over without talking to her first. She was angry that Eloise was taking over and completely rearranging everything. However, above all else she was furious at how her mother-in-law was treating her and Silvestr while Gideon said nothing. Cassandra was not proud about how she had been living. It felt as if every part of her body was fighting her. On top of that her heart had been smashed into dust and despite her trying to find a silver lining, all she could see was darkness and pain. She thought she could turn to Gideon, and at first she could, but when she looked at him, all she could see was his expression when she told him she was pregnant. That image haunted her. Knowing how much he was looking forward to meeting their child and seeing the pain etched on his face now hurt her worse than her own pain. The only thought that occupied her mind was how much she wished the doctor would have saved her baby and not her. She would gladly, without a moment of hesitation, trade her own life for her baby's life. The more that thought occupied her mind, the more she began to feel resentment towards Gideon. He told the doctor to save her and not the baby. He should have known that she would have gladly given up her life for her child, but she never even got that opportunity. Gideon had robbed her of that choice, and he was again taking away her choice by bringing his mother in without any thought of how it might make her feel. Cassandra tried to push away the resentment that was bubbling up, but something was feeding it and at every turn unwanted thoughts plagued her. Despite the overwhelming urge to scream and throw whatever object was closest to her at Gideon and his mother, Cassandra managed to be as kind as the situation would allow. She even managed to thank Eloise for her help and acknowledged that her homemaking skills had been subpar. Cassandra tried to explain her emotional state but was cut off by Eloise, "Honestly Cassandra, I'm not interested in your excuses. All of us have gone through tough times but most of us manage to maintain our responsibilities and not blame our husbands or circumstances. I am just so disappointed in you. I really thought you were stronger." Cassandra bit her lip to keep from crying and screaming obscenities. As angry as she was with Gideon, she still could not believe that he came from this monster disguised as a woman. A fight was just too much for Cassandra to deal with so she just nodded and left the room. Behind her, she could hear Eloise, "See Gideon, she even refuses to take constructive criticism. All I am trying to do is help, like you asked, and she just turns her back on us. What kind of woman turns her back on her family? I knew that getting married so young and to that kind of girl was a mistake for you. You should have met a nice girl at our church like I suggested." Cassandra paused, hot tears burning her cheeks, and waited for Gideon to contradict his mother. No objection came.

***

Cassandra felt as if she was being besieged on every front. Her body was still recovering from losing her baby and emotionally she doubted she would ever recover. Gideon had stopped communicating with her almost completely. Apart from the occasional acknowledgement or request, it was like she was living alone. Although, in reality, Cassandra would have preferred being alone to being with this new Gideon. It was not just the absence of someone, it was the burden of longing for someone who is there but distant. And if all that was not enough, she had to be constantly on guard against passive aggressive attacks by her mother-in-law. In order to keep the peace, Cassandra was doing her best to follow the demands veiled as suggestions that Eloise constantly assailed her with. She even wore the horrendous, scratchy, pretentious outfits Eloise insisted on, but nothing was ever good enough. If the outfit was right, her hair was not. If she did her hair right, then Eloise would complain about her lack of basic makeup. What was worse was that nothing was ever a direct confrontation or insult. All comments were half-heartedly disguised as assistance. The only solace that Cassandra had was taking care of Silvestr as Eloise outright refused to have anything to do with him. Silvestr had been banished to the master bedroom, where Cassandra had followed for sanctuary. Silvestr was the only one around who seemed to empathize with Cassandra. He would spend as much time as he could curled up on or near Cassandra's belly and he would begrudgingly allow her to constrict him in a firm embrace when she cried. Cassandra was grateful for his affection and for the reminder of better times. Each time she thought she had reached her limit with Gideon and his mother, she would look at

Silvestr and remember the affection and bond her and Gideon had just a short time ago. She longed for that connection again and that desire fueled her resolve to weather the bad times. However, Cassandra was noticing, though doing her best not to acknowledge, changes to Silvestr's health. He had lost a noticeable amount of weight, was not as active, and what she originally thought to be fur balls were actually vomit. One morning she noticed a large sore in his mouth. As horrified as she was by the oozing sore, she was relieved to find a probable cause for the other problems. She knew she needed to get him to the vet as soon as possible, but when she called, the only available vet appointment time conflicted with one of her medical appointments. At dinner, Cassandra mentioned that she was going to cancel her medical appointment so she could take Silvestr to the vet when Eloise, out of character, offered to take him. "You shouldn't miss your appointment with your doctor for an animal." Eloise couldn't even offer help without betraying her disdain for poor Silvestr. Cassandra certainly couldn't see her being compassionate to a sick Silvestr at the vet's office. "Thank you for the offer, but I want to be there for him. Going to the doctor is scary for any of us and he doesn't understand like humans do." Eloise shot an exacerbated look at Gideon who audibly sighed. "I know you want to be with him, but you have to put yourself first. You need to stay on top of your follow ups with your doctor. Mother is completely capable of taking Silvestr to the vet. You need to be open to accepting help or you are going to overwhelm yourself again." Gideon was talking down to her like she was a child and her anger bubbled up her spine but at the same time, on the surface, it seemed like he was once again showing some sort of interest in her well-being. Perhaps she was being unreasonable. Silvestr wasn't normally skittish at the vet and it probably wouldn't be a complicated appointment to get medication for a mouth sore and they could always reach her if there were any problems. Eloise had suggested that Cassandra had been substituting Silvestr for the baby she lost and maybe it was the trauma that was causing her to be so overprotective. Was insisting on taking him herself really worth a fight? Just the thought of an argument was too exhausting so Cassandra relented, "I suppose you are right. I am just worried about him. That's all. Just please do whatever the vet thinks is necessary for him to get better." Cassandra excused herself from the table and went to check on Silvestr. Eloise cleared the table and started on dishes. Gideon sat alone at the table. He didn't understand why

Cassandra was being so difficult to get along with. He knew his mother was hard to deal with sometimes, but she was trying to help. He just couldn't understand why Cassandra refused to see that. When he was hurting, it wasn't Cassandra that came to his aid, it was his mother. He thought about how things had been before. He missed Cassandra, the old Cassandra. The Cassandra who laughed at his obscure jokes and rooted for his success. He missed the girl that was always there for him. Now every time he looked at her all he saw was an empty shell that once held his child. It was like when the baby died, the woman he loved did too. He tried to feel compassion, but all he felt was remorse with a twinge of resentment. With his mother's help Cassandra had been trying, but nothing seemed to fix her.

    Silvestr was exasperated. He wasn't allowed to leave the bedroom, so he was unable to perform any sort of effective patrols. The Darkness seemed to be multiplying like enchanted brooms. At least he was able to protect his humans as they slept, but even that was complicated. If he made too much noise, he would get locked in the laundry room. Then there was that woman. Silvestr didn't like Eloise at all. She drew in and spit out darkness like a broken vacuum. Silvestr desperately needed help, but was having a difficult time checking in. He needed a reflective surface for scrying. The problem was that in his banishment he had nothing of the sort. The bedroom window was covered in heavy blackout curtains and every time he tried to move them he got in trouble which led to laundry room prison. His access to the bathroom had been restricted because in a past scrying attempt, Silvestr had knocked over Gideon's cologne bottle. Silvestr had even attempted to use a cup of water, but in the attempt had stuck his head too far into the glass and knocked it over. Another crime that resulted in laundry room confinement. Failures of the past aside, today presented a promising new opportunity. Gideon had left his laptop at home, open. Carefully avoiding the keys, Silvestr got as close as he could and focused on his reflection. After a longer than usual wait, a frazzled Ninimma answered. Silvestr expected a chastising for not checking in and preemptively provided his excuse, "I'm sorry for not checking in soo-" Ninimma cut him off. "I'm afraid we don't have time for pleasantries. This place is chaos. We have lost fifty-three Ni in our area alone. Unfortunately, we are not alone. All of the other Kahu guarding the other quadrants have suffered blows. We've no idea where the Gaudium Cleptes is getting this surge of energy nor how they managed to coordinate. Perhaps it is all coincidence, but to say we were unprepared would be a gross understatement. I must warn you before anything can interrupt us. The Gaudium Cleptes is not solely targeting Ni. They have begun to infect Kahu within Girru. While you are on the Earth plane, you are vulnerable. I can't tell you how to defend against it because I- I don't - I don't know." Ninimma looked utterly defeated. A stab of fear threatened to overtake him. Ninimma was the Keeper of the Zikru. She knows everything. Though she can't clearly see the future, there is not a question she doesn't have the answer to. If she was ignorant on this, they all were flying blind. She was their compass and the idea of her spinning out of control was terrifying. Silvestr took a deep breath. Panic would help no-one. "Don't worry about me. I can handle myself. My concern is for my human. Things are getting out of paw. I can see him battling the Darkness, but every attempt I make to fortify his light is countered by overwhelming darkness. It isn't restrained to Ni. The Darkness is feeding off anything they can gain access to. I've noticed that their forms are becoming more complex. Before the Darkness would appear as a simple undefined globule but now they are taking distinct shapes, some even animal-like. The other night, I almost didn't catch the Darkness attaching itself to Gideon. It looked like a temporal spider. Had it not been dropping directly down onto Gideon, I would not have suspected anything. When I pounced it was revealed to be an almost solid shadow. I have never encountered anything like it. I will report back if I learn anything else." Ninimma was doing her best to pay attention, but the chaos behind her kept pulling her attention. "Good, good. Do what you can, but your time is very limited. Ama-gi is desperate for a strategy meeting when you and the other senior Kahu have returned." Before he could comment, Ninimma was gone.

***

The day of the vet visit had Cassandra worried. This was Silvestr's first trip to the vet since they moved and she was worried he was going to be overly anxious, but Eloise eagerly dismissed her concerns and pushed her out the door. Silvestr was also uneasy. He didn't want Eloise anywhere near him. Hearing that Kahu were no longer immune to the darkness made him much more wary of having a revolving door of darkness, like

Eloise, anywhere near him. He struggled against going into the carrier which certainly did not endear him to the already perturbed Eloise. The vet visit itself was fairly routine. He got quite a bit of attention because of his unique looks. He wasn't a fan of the blood draw or the means by which they obtained his temperature, but the vet techs were generous with the treats and he enjoyed them despite the sore in his mouth. Oddly, they didn't return him to the room after the blood draw. He wasn't horrified because it meant more time free of Eloise, but the different protocol managed to flag his attention. He found himself in a cold, hard kennel that wreaked of strong disinfectant. He was Kahu but despite his generous blessing of courage, he found himself fighting off waves of panic. Something felt off, but he couldn't identify what. It seemed like an eternity alone, but eventually the vet returned with a single tech. The tech's eyes were glistening and the furrow of her brow worried Silvestr, but she hugged and kissed him, so perhaps it was just residue from his earlier panic attacks. He was taken to another cold hard table and poked with another needle. Against his will his breath came in short gasps and his heartbeat quickened. His body knew something that his mind was not keeping up with. As quickly as it had begun, the panic was over. Silvestr felt more relaxed than he had ever felt. He involuntarily began to purr, but his mind was catching up. This was not right. He yearned for his humans. Fear began to grip his thoughts and his eyes darted around frantically, but his body just felt like it was melting into the table. The vet rubbed Silvestr's head, "I'm sorry buddy, but at least you won't have to suffer." A red flag like a flare went off in Silvestr's mind. "What is that supposed to mean?!" He screamed in his head. He tried to force his body into action, but it was no longer his own. The vet approached with a second needle, but despite his commands, his body would not move. As his veins dispersed the contents of the second needle, a fog came over Silvestr and he drifted off into the deepest sleep he had ever had.

    Gideon and Cassandra arrived home at roughly the same time. Cassandra was in a relatively good mood as her doctor had cleared her of the need for anymore regular visits. It felt good to be free of the constant reminder of her miscarriage. Now perhaps she could devote all her energy to healing and try to find some way to move forward. As Gideon went to the bedroom to put away his work bag, he heard a shrill "What?!" From the kitchen. He rushed in to find Cassandra backing his mother into the corner of the kitchen. She was so angry that he swore he saw literal steam shooting from her ears. He quickly put himself in between his wife and mother. "What is going on here?!" He didn't mean to shout but the energy in the room took him over. Cassandra gasped trying to get her composure but sobs took over the words, "She- at the vet- Silvestr-" Gideon turned to his mom to try to make sense of the scene. "What happened at the vet?" Eloise, frustrated that she had to pause from cooking, allowed her contempt to seep through her words, "She is completely overreacting like a crazy person. I did exactly what she asked me to do. I took the animal to the veterinarian. He said that the creature had kidney failure. He said you could try a bunch of expensive procedures like IVs, vitamin injections, or surgery to remove blockages, but all that would do was delay the inevitable. You two are dealing with enough without spending ridiculous amounts of money on a dying animal. I made the executive decision to end his suffering so you wouldn't have to deal with it." Gideon now understood Cassandra's rage. He screamed at his mother "How dare you make such an important decision without even consulting us?! How could the vet even do something so drastic without our consent?" Eloise brushed off his anger, "I told the vet the cat was mine. There was no need to involve the two of you in such a straightforward decision. I knew you two would get overly sentimental and end up making the wrong decision. Would it have been better to let you two spend your savings treating an untreatable disease? I did what I thought was best for both of you. I really don't understand why you are being so mean to me." Eloise started crying, which just enraged Cassandra more. "You do *not* get to play the victim here! You killed our cat!" Gideon put his hand up to try and calm her down. "Let's try to approach this rationally. Mother, you should have called us before doing that. Silvestr was a member of our family and at the very least, we were entitled to say goodbye. Cassandra, blowing up and screaming at mother will not bring him back. Just try to calm down." Cassandra was delirious with rage, "You are taking her side?! She murdered my baby without even asking what I wanted, but I guess like mother, like son!" Gideon lost his cool, "What is that supposed to mean?!" Cassandra shouted so loud her voice was breaking, "Our baby is dead! I didn't even get to say goodbye!" Cassandra didn't even know who she was shouting at anymore. The pain of losing her baby and her anger at Gideon's decision was overlapping her pain at losing Silvestr and her mother-in-law's thoughtlessness.

In her mind the two were the same. Cassandra could no longer hold back all the resentful thoughts that had been gnawing at her and she let her thoughts and emotions burst like an overburdened dam. The outburst was contagious, like watching someone yawn. Gideon found himself voicing bitterness he had never even allowed himself to think, let alone say. They both said things they instantly regretted, but things had gone too far and neither Cassandra nor Gideon could stop. A wrath had overtaken Gideon and the more they fought the more empowered he felt. Every hurtful word that cut Cassandra fueled that wrath and brought him a power he had never felt before, but it went too far. "If you were any sort of good mother, you would have been able to protect and give birth to our baby. Your brokenness and bad genes killed my baby. If I was married to anyone else, I would be a dad to a healthy baby. It is completely your fault! You can't even give me a child but I chose to save you anyway. You should be grateful!" Cassandra went white and no words escaped her agape mouth. A glaze settled over Cassandra's eyes and she just turned around and left the room. Gideon felt triumphant but empty. He turned to his mother for any sign of validation, but she only had an expression of shock. The food on the stove began to smoke and Gideon furiously grabbed it and threw it into the sink, breaking the handle off the pan and shattering the two glasses in the basin. Eloise jumped at the crash and quickly retreated to the guest room. Gideon was enraged. He defended his mother and became the target for Cassandra's fury only to be silently judged by her. He grabbed the car keys and barreled out the door, leaving a wake of destruction behind.

CHAPTER SEVEN
Scratch That

Silvestr opened his eyes and saw a bright light. He looked down and saw his paws standing on what appeared to be water. His reflection was completely different. Where he had once seen a dark grey muzzle peppered with what looked to be scorched whiskers, he now saw a large fur covered muzzle with long, thick, distinguished white whiskers. His body was no longer covered in swirls of thick, curly, somewhat lumpy fur, he was now covered by long, soft, dark grey fur with subtle silver tiger stripes. Ki-Ang hissed at his reflection. He was so angry with himself. He swatted the reflection which dispersed and then rapidly reformed. A young Manx with a round face tentatively approached him. "Master Ki-Ang, sir, they are requesting your presence for a strategy meeting." The young cat's defeated demeanor echoed the feeling of defeat that pained Ki-Ang. He shook his entire body in an effort to free himself of the guilt, but only managed to startle Maahes. Ki-Ang just pushed past him on his way to the Atrium. Maahes ran after him, "But sir the meeting!" Ki-Ang ignored him. He didn't have time for a meeting. He needed to see what was going on with Gideon and get back as soon as possible.

The Library of Destiny was still chaotic. Objects were flying through the air, a crystal here, an oversized scroll there, nothing was left in its usual place. Tufts of fur were scattered around the ground with some being dragged in the wake of all the flying objects. It was obvious that tensions were running high. Ki-Ang was practically on top of Ninimma before she noticed him. "You aren't supposed to be here. You should be in-" Ki-Ang didn't have time for a lecture. "I have my own tasks that need attention. What is happening to my human?" Ninimma was more frazzled than Ki-Ang had ever seen her. She did not appreciate his demanding tone, "You are not my only Kahu in crisis. I don't have time for this and I certainly do not want to be involved when Ama-gi catches you ignoring orders. Ask Maahes if you need help. I can't waste time on individual humans when my focus is better spent on discovering why the Guadium Cleptes have so drastically changed behavior." With her ears tightly pinned back onto her head, Ninimma turned sharply to leave. In such a state, Ki-Ang wasn't about to protest. Ki-Ang looked around for an unused scrying mirror but all were occupied. So he looked around for Maahes instead. He spotted the younger feline peering at him from behind a glass slab. "You aren't useful to me in hiding. Come here, tell me what has happened since I left." With his head down, Maahes approached. He didn't make eye contact. "The female was very angry about the manner of your passing and yelled at the Ni and the other female. I don't know what happened exactly, but during that argument the aura of the Ni changed. It is no longer white and gold, it is a swirling black and red with sparks of gold. When the argument ceased the Ni left and the female packed her things and left as well. She is refusing to return. I don't think you should return. The excessive amount of shadows around the Ni is something I have never seen before. Master Ama-gi doesn't think you, or anyone, would be able to pull him from the grip of the Darkness. She has already marked him as one of the lost ones." Ki-Ang was not about to give up and he was furious that Ama-gi would move on so easily. "Gideon is not lost yet. I made a mistake and I fully intend to correct it. What is the plan to introduce the next Kahu? I need to be briefed before I prepare for the departure." Maahes's eyes went wide, "But sir Master Ama-gi marked the Ni as Halqu and told me to cancel the planned Girru." Ki-Ang stopped what he was doing and stared directly into Maahes's still very wide eyes. "Did you?" Maahes paused with a terrified look, "Did I what sir?" Ki-Ang was allowing his frustration to be directed at his subordinate, "Did you cancel the Girru, try to keep up Bob, you are playing with the big boys now." Maahes was beyond frazzled, "Yes sir. I mean, no sir. I mean I know sir…" Maahes choked on his own words. Ki-Ang felt like swatting Maahes multiple times on the head, but realized his harshness was only adding pressure that Maahes obviously could not operate under. Ki-Ang jumped on a book that was floating by, bit it, and kicked it with both his back feet. An angry yowl from across the room encouraged him to let go and thankfully his anger had been sufficiently released and he found himself feeling much more calm. Maahes was still staring at him with large terrified eyes. Ki-Ang spoke as calmly as he could, "Have you canceled the next Girru with Gideon yet?" Maahes shook his round head, "No sir. Not yet sir." Ki-Ang felt calmer knowing his plans were not completely derailed. "Good. If you haven't canceled it yet, then I can still go." Maahes tried to object, "But my orders from Ensi Ama-gi-" Ki-Ang wasn't about to give up, "I am your direct superior and I am giving you new orders. Follow them and let me deal with Ama-gi."

***

Gideon sat alone in the dark. A bottle of whiskey securely in his hand. The floor around him was littered with beer bottles, two wine bottles, and a mostly empty bottle of brandy. On the coffee table there was an envelope that had been forced on him by a process server the Thursday before. Its contents were thrown on the table, wrinkled by where they had been crumpled and un-crumpled multiple times. The middle of the pages had the start of a small tear where Gideon had tried to rip them in half unsuccessfully. On the floor next to the coffee table were the glasses that Gideon had used for his alcohol prior to smashing them on the coffee table. He hadn't stopped drinking since he received the packet. He even used a sick day. At first the liquor helped him forget, but after three days he had gone through his entire collection of alcohol, including the cooking brandy, and the desired effect was starting to require more alcohol to achieve. Gideon stared at the papers littering his coffee table. The bolded words "Divorce Complaint" cut him like a knife. After their fight, Gideon returned home to find Cassandra gone. He tried to call her but she wouldn't answer. After multiple attempts, her friend finally picked up and told Gideon to stop calling. The following week Cassandra called him from her parents house to tell him she was moving out permanently. Gideon thought it was like speaking to a robot. She refused to meet in person to talk and ended up hanging up on him when he tried to pressure her into coming back. Gideon suspected that it was actually his father-in-law that hung up the phone and was determined that he could convince Cassandra to come back until he received the divorce paperwork. He spoke with a lawyer who told him that it would be simple, since Cassandra wasn't asking for anything. Gideon had left the office in a rage. The lawyer actually said he was 'lucky' and it had set Gideon off. Gideon had not stopped drinking since. A car passed by, lighting up the dark living room for a moment. The light passed over Gideon's face causing him to wince. He finished off the whiskey and went to the kitchen to find a new sedative. His search revealed a new problem, no more alcohol. Gideon flung the empty bottle at the trash can, missing it completely. It hit the cabinet and shattered. Gideon remained unfazed. He grabbed the keys and headed out.

Gideon had stocked up at the corner liquor store. He made sure he had enough of the high proof liquid pain reliever to last him the month. He was already becoming more sober than he liked, so he opened a can of beer and quickly finished it in the parking lot so he could be sufficiently numb by the time he got home. On the drive back Gideon was tormented by thoughts of Cassandra. He was desperate to get her back but furious that she would leave. He was lost in his thoughts when he was promptly snapped back into reality by the reflection of his headlights on a box in the road. Gideon slammed on his brakes, skidding to a stop a hair from the box. Gideon pounded his hands on the steering wheel and let out a string of obscenities. He got out of the car to go kick the box, but on his approach he heard something inside. He opened the box to discover a single kitten. The kitten was a smokey white, with splotches of grey on its head and back. The kitten's eyes were crusted with dried mucus and when it looked up at Gideon he noticed its third eyelids encroaching towards the middle of its eyes from the center. The kitten was malnourished and shaking but managed a weak mew. Gideon just stared at the kitten for a moment. It triggered so many memories. He remembered when he first found Silvestr with Cassandra. He imagined what she would say if she was there. She would scoop up the kitten and shower it with affection. Gideon's entire body tensed up and an overwhelming feeling of spite overtook him. He glared at the kitten, then coldly walked back to his car, leaving it behind in the box. He could hear the faint mews as he slammed his door shut. He aggressively shifted the car into reverse and backed away from the box in the road. After he reversed a few feet, he put the car into drive and began to turn the wheel, but something in him caused him to freeze. He thought about raising Silvestr and he remembered happy scenes when he laughed til his sides hurt watching Silvestr roll in the catnip Cassandra had brought. Silvestr had been the reason Cassandra and Gideon had gotten together and Gideon felt a pang of longing. He wanted to go back to those times, but as quickly as it came on the pang of longing was replaced with indignation. A voice from deep inside whispered that without the cat he would never have met Cassandra. If he had never met Cassandra he would not be in pain now. He spoke to himself "Even at the worst moments Cass still loved that cat. I make one mistake, I say *one* thing out of anger and suddenly she doesn't love me anymore. How does someone care for animals more than they care for their husband?!" Gideon pounded on the steering wheel and let out a scream. He could feel all his hatred and fury crawling up his spine like magma forcing its way to the surface. He thought it was going to explode through the top of his head, but instead it sparked a thought. A wicked, disgusting thought. At first, Gideon pushed it out of his mind and started to roll the car forward, angling to go around the box, but he stopped. A hardness had come over him. He reversed again and straightened out the wheel. With his foot on the brake he revved the engine. He floored the gas pedal aiming the car directly at the box. He gritted his teeth and released the brake. The sound of the box being crushed beneath the wheels brought a sense of satisfaction to Gideon. Something inside him cried out with a sort of mutated joy. While he had expected to feel some sort of regret or remorse, all he could feel was an all consuming emptiness. No pain. No anger. No sadness. Just dark, cold, emptiness and he liked it.

***

Ki-Ang again found himself staring at his reflection in the waterless pool. "Why am I here?" His entire body ached in memory of his last incarnation. Even the echo of the pain was excruciating, but the pain in his heart screamed the loudest. "That didn't just happen. Gideon could not have just-" Ki-Ang had died many times. Most of the time he knew it was coming. Never had he died at the hands of the Ni he was sent to protect. Never. The plan for the Girru placed Ki-Ang directly in Gideon's path. Gideon was supposed to see him and be flooded with happy memories, encouraging him to apologize to Cassandra and she would come back and help him raise their new kitten. Everything would have been fixed and Ki-Ang would have been able to disperse the Darkness and protect Gideon for the rest of his life and next lives if needed. Ki-Ang could not understand what happened. "Gideon is a good person. He loved me and would always rescue a defenseless being in need. He might not be an animal person, but he would never purposefully harm anyone. There must have been a mistake. Gideon was probably going to his car to get something to pick me up in and a different car accidentally ran over the box. That must have been it." Ki-Ang was speaking out loud to himself so he was startled to get a reply. "I'm afraid that wasn't the case. The Ni you were assigned to has been overtaken by the Darkness. That is why I marked him as Halqu. There is no saving him. He is a host for the Darkness which will create such a yearning for malice that he will have no choice but to feed it with acts of maleficence. It will become like a drug and he will only be at peace when the Darkness has been satiated. That soul is lost. It is time now to move on and attempt to rein in the chaos of the Guadium Cleptes." Ama-gi spoke with such little feeling that it enraged Ki-Ang, "How can you be so frigid?! I won't give up on him. I can't!" Ama-gi's fur was standing on end. His remark hurt her, but her pain expressed itself as a cold anger. "You were given direct orders, which you ignored. Thanks to your little jaunt down to Earth on a mission I expressly revoked permission for, the Ni you were supposed to protect was given the opportunity to give himself over to the Darkness completely. If it had not been for your rogue stunt, it might have been possible to send a Kahu later when his emotions had cooled to provide a path to redemption, but as you well know, once a soul has given itself over to the Darkness, it cannot be redeemed. I could see that tempers were too high to soothe at the moment, hence why I gave the order to cancel the Girru. I don't make decisions lightly and I am sufficiently detached from the situations I am trying to solve. You on the other paw were short-sighted and emotional and acted out of desperation and pride. Your actions resulted in a strong Ni being commandeered by the Guadium Cleptes. You basically handed a dangerous weapon over to the enemy! I would send you to a tribunal if we weren't in such desperate times." Ki-Ang was in no state to hear her. He was reeling from heartbreak and the residue of physical pain from such a traumatic death. He was close to hysterical. "So do it! Send me to a tribunal! I don't care! I don't care about anything anymore! Why are we doing any of this?! I spent four years with Gideon. He was supposed to love me and be strengthened by that love, but one disastrous event and all of the effort of the past four years goes up in smoke. The love he was supposed to have for me meant *nothing*! The love he was supposed to have for Cassandra meant *nothing*! You're saying that all my effort to save Gideon did more to turn him to darkness than protect him from it?! Why do we even try? It would be better to just leave the humans to their own devices and deal with the fallout. Why kill ourselves, literally, to protect souls who are just going to throw it all away at the first hint of tragedy?!" Ama-gi tried to speak but Ki-Ang wouldn't even pause to breathe. His voice was becoming desperate and shrill. Ama-gi kept trying to raise her voice to intervene but all attempts were matched or outdone by Ki-Ang in volume and intensity. Suddenly a loud crack of lightning broke through the noise and was reflected in the water-like surface. The sound silenced the cats, the pattern still burning in their eyes. They both bowed their heads. Dingir gracefully sauntered towards them. While Ama-gi's face reflected the panic and worry she felt, there was no trace of emotion in Dingir. They were calm and exuded a contentment felt not only by them but radiate to Ama-gi and Ki-Ang. Even with the soothing presence of Dingir, Ki-Ang was still discontented. He was hurt. His mission, which had always been his source of purpose and drive, seemed inconsequential. If he couldn't even manage to protect one soul in modern times, then how talented of a Kahu could he really be? He had protected souls in times of famine, plague, even genocide and had never experienced such a failure. Gideon had everything. Yes, he had experienced a tragedy. The loss of a baby would crush anyone, but he was still alive. He still had Cassandra. He still had his dream job. Cats lose kittens all the time. Sometimes they are even forced to kill their own kittens to prevent the kittens' suffering. Losing someone you love is always hard, but one must go on and Ki-Ang could not understand how one moment of loss could have derailed everything they had worked so hard to create. Gideon's life had a purpose. How could he give it all up just because a couple bad things happened? He just wanted to scratch some sense or perspective into Gideon. However, Gideon wasn't here, a fact which left Ki-Ang feeling fragmented. Dingir said nothing but Ki-Ang felt as if they were staring at him with expectation. He felt the need to answer the unspoken question. "I can't do this anymore. There is no point. I have spent centuries in Girru protecting humans with powerful Ni in a never-ending attempt to defeat the Darkness and as a result of one misstep, the Darkness has become more powerful than ever before. That is centuries of planning, struggling, exertion, all made irrelevant in a single Girru. Now I am expected to start all over again. I don't have anything left to give." Dingir nodded with understanding, "Your passion has been great and a fire that burns with such intensity can quickly run out of fuel. You must choose your own path, but I would humbly suggest that before you turn away from the Kahu, you spend a short time in Samsara for a Ti or two. When weaving the tapestry becomes overwhelming, it can help to spend some time feeling the individual threads. Letting those threads speak to you, helping you the see where each piece belongs." Despite the calming influence of Dingirs' presence, Ama-gi was crawling out of her skin with restlessness. She had so many problems to attend to. "Why did everything have to fall apart on my watch?" she thought. She could no longer hold herself back, "With all due respect Teacher, now is not the time for Ki-Ang to pause for reflection. He is a warrior and we need all paws on deck if we are going to combat the schemes of the Darkness." Dingir looked at Ama-gi with a soft laughter in their eyes. "The Kahu and your humans are so alike. You are both so goal oriented. As your soul ascends you will learn that higher reality is not so linear. It is not only the destination that is important but the journey. You are so focused on reaching the peak of the trail that you are overlooking the wild flowers around you." Ama-gi was not in a mood for parables, "I will enjoy the flowers when the danger has been contained." Dingir rubbed their face against Ama-gi's. "You are the most tenacious feline I have had the pleasure of knowing." Ama-gi was frustrated and allowed herself to think, "Why are the higher beings always so vague and nonchalant? Why couldn't they just give clear and concise instructions instead of pussyfooting around?" Dingir answered like Ama-gi had spoken out loud, "Our purpose is to support and love those under our care, not to control or instruct you. Just like your humans can be guided but never pushed, We are here to bolster you on your journey, not carry you. A teacher must only guide their pupils to knowledge, not provide answers." Ama-gi felt the sting of being humbled by her mentor, "Forgive me Teacher, I was insolent." Dingir showed no sign of being perturbed, "I am not chastising you dear Ama-gi. I encourage you to find your path, just as I encourage Ki-Ang to find his. You must follow your heart and act in a manner true to yourself. Likewise, you must step back and allow Ki-Ang to discover his own path." Ama-gi tried not to let her irritation show, "Very well. I will tell Ninimma to prepare a Ti." Ama-gi could have sworn she saw a sparkle in Dingirs' eyes as the beautiful white Angora spoke, "There is no need. I will take care of everything myself. Ki-Ang will follow me". Ki-Ang nodded and just like that they were gone.

CHAPTER EIGHT
Scaredy Cat

Ama-gi sat in the Hall of Receiving at a complete loss. She did not understand Dingirs' logic but knew better than to question the teacher. Everything Dingir did had purpose and Ama-gi respected that, but she didn't know how to handle the crisis before her. She was Kahu and could see further and understand deeper than those on the Earth plane, yet she was still far from the enlightenment of the elders. Even the elders did not know everything. Ninlil was an elder and could read destinies, but she did not write them. As Teacher, Dingir had all the answers but never did they use their knowledge to influence or wield power. They may have greater authority or understanding, but in the higher realms it seemed like the more enlightenment a being had, the less attachment they had to the lower realms. Dingir always tried to explain that the elders were there to guide and protect, but not control. That it was important to let beings learn and experience truth for themselves, but Ama-gi hadn't quite reached that point in her enlightenment. In her heart she felt that those with greater strength and understanding were obligated to protect and guide those in their care. She thought that as guardians they should create and enforce strict rules for the benefit of the Earth realm. She didn't see the benefit of letting beings learn for themselves when the answer could be provided for them. As much as she tried to grasp the concept of free will, her core refused to release the idea of using force in the pursuit of order. Ama-gi was a warrior and although she was not the sole leader of the Kahu, she was in charge of the Kahu operations in her quadrant. It fell to her to handle the current catastrophe. She was proud that they had such faith in her, but it terrified her that she might not live up to their expectations. She was a creature of habit and routine and the current predicament was neither. The Guadium Cleptes were not behaving how they were supposed to behave. She was a skilled warrior who was accustomed to countering every move the Darkness made, but in the current situation it was like the Darkness started playing a new game and she did not know the rules or even the objective. She just didn't know what to do. "How do you play chess with someone playing Chinese checkers?" She asked herself aloud. A small voice answered, "I'm afraid now is not the time to be playing games." Ninimma looked discombobulated. Despite the lack of fur there was an unkempt look about her, like when someone awakens from a deep sleep. There was a heaviness to her that had nothing to do with the generous curves of her body. "We have another problem." Ama-gi's heart fell into her stomach and she felt as if the weight of the universe was becoming too heavy. Her legs felt like they were buckling beneath her, but she could not let the other Kahu see her struggle. She squared her shoulders and allowed a hardness to overtake her. "Ninimma, no theatrics, just tell me the issue so we can resolve it." Ninimma nodded absently, "Iksuda is refusing his Kananuru and says he won't do another Girru." Ama-gi closed her eyes and took a deep breath. "Another one?" she thought. Iksuda was the seventh Kahu to return with their spirit broken. She had already been forced to send her senior Kahu, the Kahu she desperately needed strategizing by her side, into Girru to replace those the Darkness had affected. She didn't understand what was happening. Kahu were supposed to be impervious to the Darkness. She had heard tales of her Canine Kahu counterparts or the detestable Avian Kahu succumbing to the influence of the Guadium Cleptes, but Feline Kahu were better than that. They were not burdened by the same attachment to humans as Canine Kahu and they certainly were not as morally corrupt as the Fowl messengers of the Underworld. Ama-gi must have been lost in her thoughts because Ninimma made a small show of clearing her throat and staring at Ama-gi expectantly. Ama-gi cleared her head. Now was not the time for questioning, it was the time for action. "Take me to Iksuda. I will talk with him." Ninimma shrugged, "I doubt talking will help as I have already tried to convince him to change his mind. Talking certainly didn't have an effect on the others, but you are the boss." Ninimma's words weighed on Ama-gi more than she would ever know. In that moment she desperately wished that these times were not occurring on her watch, but she knew that all she could do was decide what to do in such times. The one thing she knew for certain is that she would never decide to accept defeat.

    They found Iksuda cowering in a crevice under one of the far scrying mirrors. Maahes was desperately trying to coax him out, but having no luck. Maahes was grateful to hand the task over to Ama-gi. Ninimma and Maahes quickly scurried off to their next tasks. Ama-gi crouched to look Iksuda in the eyes. The color of his fur was dull and the texture was coarse. She had never seen Kahu look so frazzled in the Higher realm. Everything in Barag was luxurious and vivid. Everything had a bright vibrancy to it, except for recently. All the seven Kahu who had returned wounded by the Darkness had an insipid way about them. It invoked the thought of a muffled symphony playing out of tune. That diluted energy seemed to stifle everything in their direct surroundings. Even Ama-gi, though she considered herself impervious to such influence, felt a sense of indistinct malaise. Before Ama-gi could speak, Iksuda hissed "Don't say anything. You won't change anything. I won't go back. I can't. Humans are the personification of evil. We can't save them. I won't save them. They deserve everything coming to them." Ama-gi was shocked by the venom in his voice. "What happened?" Ama-gi tried to sound compassionate but her annoyance was hard to suppress. Kahu knew that the experiences of the Earth plane were transient at best and all suffering there was nothing more than the flutter of a butterfly's wings. The Feline Kahu prided themselves on their ability to detach from the Earth plane. Attachment had no place in enlightenment. Iksuda wedged himself further into his crevice, "Please, don't. I don't want to talk about it. I can't. Don't make me go back to Samsara. Send me to Kur, I don't care. Even the Underworld is better than that place." Iksuda's entire body shuddered and in spite of her annoyance Ama-gi felt pity for him. As much as she wanted to hiss and swat at him she could not deny that, at that moment, his fear was beyond repair. "I won't send you to Kur, though you do deserve it for shirking your duties. Go to Dingir. They will wish to speak with you. I have more pressing concerns than your chastisement." Ama-gi turned away. Iksuda slowly slinked out of his hole and staying as low to the ground as possible he sprinted to the next hiding place on his way to meet with Dingir. Ama-gi was glad to have him gone. Fear is contagious and morale was already low without adding more. She intended to keep the fact that they were down another guardian a secret. More pressure would not help. In order to keep this desertion classified, Ama-gi would need to handle Iksuda's next Girru herself. Ama-gi sent a quick thought to Ninimma to meet her for Iksuda's Kanunuru.

Ninimma saw Ama-gi and looked around for Iksuda. "I see you are alone. I don't wish to say I told you so but Ni iqbu kanu anna zae." Ama-gi glared. Ninimma was always right but she would never give her the satisfaction of saying it aloud. "We agreed not to speak the old tongues. It is too confusing for those going to Girru to hear Sumerian in spirit and the current Earth languages in Samsara." Ninimma crinkled her nose, "Such a pity.

The old tongues were so elegant. I don't see why I can't use Sumerian with you. You don't go to Samsara anymore. You haven't since you took over for Inanna." Ama-gi looked down. She missed her mentor. Inanna had chosen to return to Samsara to continue her Bodhisattva role. Ama-gi still got to see her on her return but she missed working side by side with her. Inanna was one of the beings that formed the Kahu and Ama-gi tried to emulate her in everything she did. She really wished she could turn to her for guidance now, but as Ninimma had pointed out, she was alone. "Circumstances necessitate that I return to Samsara." Ninimma looked uncomfortable, "This is your second Girru this century. Sag Du are not supposed to enter Samsara, they are supposed to stay in Barag and lead the rest of us. That is why you have the title of Ensi. You are our leader. This isn't how things are done." Ama-gi didn't like being compared to others. Deep down she felt like she was not worthy of the title bestowed upon her, but she knew Ninimma didn't mean it as a criticism. Ninimma was all about tradition and observance of routine. Ama-gi shared her appreciation of order. However, with their adversaries changing so much, she had no choice but to evolve as well. Inanna trusted her to make the right choices and Ama-gi trusted Inanna, even if she didn't trust herself. "Someone must complete the Girru assigned to Iksuda. We cannot lose anymore Ni. There is not much I can do here until we know more about this change in the Darkness. I am sure I can resolve the threat to this particular Ni in a short amount of time. Ninlil predicted that the threat to the Ni is transient and could be avoided altogether if I am careful." Ninimma was still uncomfortable, but she wanted to be supportive. "You are powerful. I am sure with your protection the Ni will be beyond reproach in no time. I will prepare everything." Ninimma turned to leave but Ama-gi stopped her. "There is one more thing. I need to see Iksuda's last Girru. Something caused him to break down like I have never seen him do. Iksuda was a warrior. He has faced darkness in all forms across time, all over the world. I need to know what shook him so deeply that he has turned his back on us and the humans." Ninimma nodded and walked over to a nearby shelf. She knocked a scroll off the ledge and floated it to the scrying mirror. When she placed the scroll on the altar it opened and she whispered "Kanunuru". The stone lit up and absorbed the scroll. Ama-gi approached the mirror and placed both her front paws on the altar. She had to know what was destroying her warriors. These were not green kittens. These were experienced guardians with a strong passion for protecting their humans. She could not fight an attack she didn't understand, but part of her was afraid to face it.

CHAPTER NINE
Gatto Go

Maria took her plate and freshly opened beer and sat at the rusted patio table on her back porch. Her apartment was small and always smelled of mold and cigarettes despite everything she did to clean it. The back patio was not any better, but at least it felt less cramped. She could hear the traffic, a loud television attempting to cover the sound of the neighbors domestic dispute, police sirens, and what Maria told herself was a car backfire, but she knew it was probably gunfire. She could smell the cigarette smoke from her neighbors mixed with the distinct smell of burning plastic indicating that someone nearby was smoking crack. Maria spent more money than she wanted to on canned air fresheners to try and keep the smell out of the room she shared with her son. She was thankful that her son Ray was already asleep. She had been living in South Central Los Angeles for seven years. She came to the United States in hopes of finding a safe place and opportunity for a peaceful life. The trip across the border had been hard but she was lucky. She knew that a lot of the coyotes who got others over the border would hold them until their family back in Mexico paid a ransom. Maria had no family, so she was forced to work off the debt herself. She shuddered at the memory. She would still be working to benefit the coyote that brought her here if he hadn't been killed in an ICE raid. She was not deported because her child had been born on US soil, but she was only given temporary leave to stay and was supposed to hire a lawyer to help her get a visa, but she could barely afford to survive. Lawyers are expensive and as much as she wanted to do things the right way to be an American citizen, she just couldn't afford it. Maria always dreamt that one day she would be able to save up and finally get a green card, but life is no dream. She was at the mercy of her employers who took advantage of her undocumented status and made her work long hours for hardly any pay, if they decided to pay her at all. She couldn't open a bank account and had to hide her money around her home, but the apartments she could afford came with regular break-ins. Things were hard, but she had to keep going. All she wanted was to protect her son so he might be able to escape the soul-sucking poverty and violence that had always been her life. Since she was born in Monterrey, Mexico, she had been forced to fight for survival. Her mother was the abandoned daughter of a prostitute who survived by working for the cartel. Working for them was both a salvation and a death sentence. It kept her mother and her alive until her mom angered her cartel member boyfriend, Maria's father. The man killed her mother right in front of her, but had just enough of a shadow of paternal devotion to spare Maria. She was lucky enough to be taken in by a local shop owner. He taught her to work hard and keep her head down and just happened to have a cousin who was a coyote. As bad as things were for her in America, it was still a hundred times better than living under the daily threat of the cartel. The sound of the beating going on next door reminded her of the violence she endured at the hands of the coyote and his crew. She unconsciously touched the scars on her arms and winced. Maria probably wouldn't have survived if it wasn't for her son. When she learned she was pregnant, her first thought was to kill herself. She didn't want to start a new cycle of suffering, but before she got the opportunity to act on her inclination, the baby started to grow. The first time she felt him kick changed everything. It awoke a fierce maternal desire to protect and from that moment on she was single-minded in her quest to save her baby from the nightmares of her past. His birth saved her. It was like the wounds from her past miraculously healed and even though they left scars, the pain was only a distant memory. She lived for him. Every hardship was the price of his freedom. A price she would gladly pay. He would be the first Solíz to crawl out of the muck and make something of himself rather than just surviving. That dream kept her going.

    Maria sat and fantasized about the life her son would one day have. She imagined him going to college like a fancy American man, getting a good job, meeting a nice girl, settling down in a house that he bought with his good job's generous salary. She thought about herself teaching her six grandchildren how to make tamales on La Noche Buena. Her thoughts were interrupted by a faint meow. She looked down and saw a tattered-looking young cat. She was surprised to see a cat in her apartment complex as the neighborhood had many loose pitbulls who normally kept the stray population, both cats and other dogs, down to nothing. Her heart was overcome with empathy for the kitten. She saw a determination in its eyes that reflected her own. Life had not been kind to this gatito and that she could intimately understand. Maria bit off a generous piece of her pollo asado and tossed it to the kitten. As it greedily gnawed on the chunk of meat, she looked it over. The cat was dark brown in color with a faint hint of darker stripes and some random splotches of tan. Maria deduced that it would probably boast a more vibrant color scheme if not matted with dirt and what looked to be car oil mixed with blood. The cat had obvious wounds but none that looked too severe. When it was finished with the chicken, it moved slightly closer and meowed again. Maria smiled and answered with a portion of her tortilla. It didn't take long for the cat to join her at the table. Maria didn't have much to share, but she had experienced charity in her life and firmly believed that, if presented the opportunity, a human being was required to offer aid. This seemed like that kind of opportunity. She took a final bite of her meal and pushed the plate towards the cat. The cat wasted no time in digging in. Perhaps she imagined it but she could have sworn that she saw the cat nod a 'thank you'. When the cat was finished it jumped off the table but stayed close, licking the missed food off its muzzle. Maria picked up the plate and went inside. As she was washing the dish she could still see the cat sitting near the table. She felt like it was watching her. She quietly went into her room. The neighbors had finally stopped fighting and it lent a sort of peace to the neighborhood. The angry car horns and sirens had become a type of lullaby over the years. As she was getting ready for bed she heard dogs barking. It sounded fairly close to the apartment and she found herself incessantly thinking about the little cat. She knew how it must have felt. She remembered being in a similar situation.

    Maria's mother Lena was in the kitchen preparing plates for her boyfriend, Salvador, and his friends. From the other room Salvador yelled for her to hurry up. Maria sat on the floor in between the rooms playing with a paper mache doll. "¡Apúrate Magdalena! Tenemos hambre!" Lena's grip tightened around the knife she was using. She hated the name Magdalena. It was her mother's, or so she was told. Her mother had left her as a young child and ended up in prison for unspeakable crimes. She no more wished to be associated with her than Mexico wished to be associated with the cartels, but in both cases it seemed there was no escape. Lena had escaped a fate similar to her mother's by working for the cartel as a lookout, distraction, or mula. She had no choice. As she got older, she caught the eye of a much older Salvador. He took her as his property and as long as she kept him happy, she was safe. Maria was his daughter but he had little interest in her. He would routinely say Maria must be someone else's child because she was so ugly. Another man walked into the kitchen to get a bottle of tequila, "María. Dile a tu mamá que vaya más rápido o recibirá una paliza." Maria left her doll on the floor and ran terrified to her mother. "Mama! Por favor ándale! No quiero que te den una paliza!" Lena could hear the men laughing in the other room. Her grip tightened even more. She looked at the knife and for a moment thought about using violence to free herself from Salvador's tyranny, but one look at her daughter made her realize the foolishness of the thought. Compared to most women in the area, Lena and her daughter had it good. Instead, she quickly plated the food and grabbed two plates and urged Maria to grab a plate as well. She hurried to the other room and quickly set the plates in front of Salvador and the man next to him. Salvador's plate touched the table a moment after the other man's plate, but Lena did not notice and had already returned to the kitchen for the other dishes. She returned a moment later with two more plates but when she neared the men Salvador threw the plate at her head. She dropped both plates on to one of the nearby men who stood and pushed her to the ground. Salvador approached her, "¿Cómo te atreves a servir a otro hombre antes que a mí? Tú eres *mi* mujer." A rage had overtaken Salvador and he allowed himself to lose control. The more she begged for forgiveness the harder he hit her. Maria stood near her mother screaming in terror. She cried and begged for him to stop but he just backhanded her to the floor. She watched helplessly as pieces of her mother's flesh littered the floor around her. One of the men told Salvador that he should have avoided her face. The man laughed and said Salvador would be better off to have a goat as a girlfriend rather than a hideously scarred woman. Salvador stopped his assault and looked at Lena shaking in pain on the floor. He was disgusted at what he saw. With no hesitation he took the gun from his waistband and fired two shots into the defenseless woman, but this only fueled his anger and he fired again and again and again. Maria was speechless at first. Terror stole her voice and cemented her body to the floor. After multiple shots, Maria had lost the ability to count, her voice seemed to find its way into her throat and she let out a blood curdling scream. It drew the attention of Salvador and he turned the gun on Maria. He pulled the trigger and was met with a "click". He pulled again and again, "click" "click" with a frustrated yell he threw the gun at her hitting her in the head. Maria passed out cold. Salvador walked over to the six year old and picked up his foot to stomp on her head, but paused. For a moment he had a flash of remorse. As much as he refused to admit it, he knew this was his daughter. There would be no repercussion for disposing of his woman, but some might look down on him killing his own child. The pause was enough to bring him clarity. He spit on the girl and mumbled a comment that she wasn't worth the effort. He told one of his men to dump them both in the plaza del pueblo. A few hours later Maria regained consciousness. She blinked open her eyes and was met by the lifeless eyes of her mother. It took her a moment to register what she was seeing as her mother's eyes had almost completely swollen shut before her execution. She scurried back as far as she could and sat up finding herself covered in her mother's blood. She screamed but her voice was raspy and it only came out as a squeak. The plaza was full of people but everyone knew not to acknowledge a cartel dump. No one would help her. She slowly made her way back to her mother's side and desperately tried to wake her, but even in her innocent mind, she knew she was gone.

A loud bang brought Maria back to the present. She quickly looked in on Ray but he was still fast asleep. The pain of the memory was still fresh and she felt tears running down her face. She hadn't allowed herself to think about that moment for many years. She wasn't sure why thinking about the stray kitten brought it back up. She returned to the kitchen for some water. She glanced out the window and the kitten was still there, curled up under the table. Maria heard the distinctive sound of dogs fighting. This was closer than the earlier barking. Apparently the kitten heard it too because it had awoken and was cramming itself under the three prongs of the table support. Maria was overcome. She was no longer the strong ardent woman but the scared and devastated girl with no one to turn to.

      Maria's eyes were swollen and painful from crying. Her skin burnt from sitting in the hot Mexican sun. She had sat by her mother's corpse for a day and half until police came to remove it. They wouldn't touch the girl. No one on the police force wanted to go against a high ranking member of the cartel. They felt compassion for the child but were too afraid to act on it. Maria's throat was dry and she was weak. She had tried to approach a few people, but they all brushed her off as quickly as they could manage. She was alone. At nightfall a man from a shop near the plaza approached her. He cautiously looked around and then dropped a bottle of water and a sandwich. Maria didn't move. She just sat staring blanking ahead. The man pushed the food and water closer to her with his foot and started to walk away. A few feet from her he turned to look back. Maria still sat with no expression. The man cursed and muttered "Dios mio" and walked back to her. He picked up the water bottle and poured some water into her mouth. Maria spat it up and started crying. The man tried to shush her but only managed to muffle the sound. Terrified that someone might notice he scooped the girl up in his arms and returned to his shop. His wife was waiting and after yelling at him and hitting him with her shoe for putting them in danger, she looked at the little girl and started to cry. She hugged Maria and looked at her husband. It might mean death, but there was no turning back now, they had to help.

    Maria saw herself in the terrified little cat under her patio table. She didn't have the money to take on another mouth to feed, but she couldn't turn a blind eye. She could hear the dogs approaching. With no time to consider an alternative she rushed outside and scooped the little cat up in her arms. The action took the cat by surprise and it made a startled "haaaa haaaa" sound. Maria ran back inside and rested her back on the closed door. Not a moment later three big pitbulls ran up to the table. They were sniffing furiously but Maria couldn't decide if they were searching for the kitten or the piece of pollo she threw earlier. The kitten sat silently in her arms and seemed to be wondering the same thing. Maria found a big box and dumped the contents on the floor. She covered the bottom with old newspaper and put a small bowl of water down. She took out some leftovers from the fridge and put that in the box along with the kitten. She would figure out what to do with it after work tomorrow but for now she needed to sleep. A task she would find easier knowing that the kitten was safe.

***

Four years passed and the kitten had become an important part of Maria and Ray's life. Any problems they faced outside of their home, was always mediated by the unconditional love of their furry family member. They had named him Durito because even though he was tiny he was tough. Also, it was the name of Ray's favorite snack. Every time Ray would come home with cuts and bruises from being bullied, Durito would lick him and distract him with his crazy antics. Ray even nicknamed him Durito Loco when they played. Durito even managed to make a name for himself in the neighborhood. When Ray was seven years old, he was playing with some toy trucks in a dirt patch near the apartment. Durito was sunning himself on the patio table nearby. Without warning, the neighbor's dog burst through the screen on the window and made a beeline for Ray. The dog was about fifty pounds and had his hackles raised and teeth bared. Ray stood and tried to run to his home but the dog latched onto Ray's shoe and knocked him back down to the ground. The dog released his bite and lunged towards Ray's face, but before it could make contact Durito flung himself at the dog. Claws and fur were flying everywhere. Ray was able to make it up and run into his mother's arms, who had been drawn out of the house by the commotion. Durito kept attacking the very confused dog until it ran back to its house with its tail between its legs. After that the neighborhood started referring to Durito as Chingón. The older neighborhood kids that used to hassle Ray stopped bothering him after the incident and the neighbor's dog never returned. Durito acted like an older brother. Anytime Ray and his mom would argue, Durito was always there to swat at the aggressor or meow loudly until they calmed down. Whenever Maria had to work late, Durito was there to keep Ray company. When Maria and Ray left for work and school, they would let Durito out. He would roam the neighborhood but would always be waiting at the door when Ray got home. This day was no different. Ray and Maria left the apartment with Durito following at their heels. He followed them to the bus stop where Maria and Ray parted. Durito sat in a shady spot watching them both until they were out of sight. He then made his way back to the apartment buildings. He wasn't fond of being out in the Los Angeles heat, or having to constantly be on guard for cars or dogs, but he liked the freedom. He was a warrior and had lived lives running the jungles surrounding Aztec cities, sailing the ocean on Spanish Galleons, and hunting plague rats in Norwich. He knew the dangers of being an indoor/outdoor cat, but the danger was what excited him most. He also relished every opportunity to assassinate messengers of Kur. He had been given warnings to stop. The rules of the peace treaty demanded that aggression towards birds was to only be used as a last resort to protect a Ni or to sustain life. An indoor cat would never be able to convincingly claim they needed to eat a bird to survive, but as an indoor/outdoor cat he could periodically claim that his assassinations were necessary for his continued survival. Durito knew it was pawing the line, but he was never able to drop his grudge after the war of the Kahu. Luckily, this particular Girru gave him the opportunity to fight back against both the Avian and Canine Kahu. He suspected that his canine counterparts were using the same excuse for their violence against him. Durito left his shady spot and searched the surrounding houses for a parked car, preferably one in the shade. He finally found one in a carport. He peered through the window into the house. He saw the woman who usually drove the car passed out on her couch. Confident she wasn't going anywhere anytime soon, he made his way to the roof of the car, which happened to be a nice reflective silver, even if it was missing chunks of paint in places. Durito stared at the top of the car until his reflection was replaced by the image of a tortoiseshell cat. The cat had eyes the color of a blood orange. Her face had black that resembled the shape of an anchor over her nose and muzzle mixed with patches of black, tan, and brown. The rest of her body was an even mix of the same trio of colors. She had a tail, but it was only a nub, which made her back half appear almost rabbit-like. "Hello Iksuda. Right on time, as always. How are things in sunny SoCal? Are you regretting your long-term assignment yet?" Her voice was deep and smooth and it was comforting to hear. "Hello to you too Lumma. How could I get tired of the concrete jungle?" Durito answered with a hint of a smile in his voice. "I suppose that was more of a rhetorical question as I know you are having a good time based on the number of complaints we are getting from Lord Birdu of Kur. He not so kindly requests you, and I quote, 'Keep your filthy paws off his messengers'. He also made mention of forcefully neutering you with chicken wire, but I am a lady and will not repeat the words he used." Lumma said, trying to conceal her amusement. Durito however had no qualms about displaying his pleasure. "What can I say, it's the earth plane food chain. A cat's gotta do what a cat's gotta do." Durito turned and gave the evil eye to a few pigeons that had landed in the nearby street. Lumma jumped on the scrying mirror to get his attention, "Do you have anything to report or are you just going to gloat about terrorizing the avian community?" Durito chuckled but continued his report, "Nothing substantial to report. There is a lot of darkness around here, but I have successfully established a perimeter around the home and have, for the most part, kept both my humans free of any dark entanglements. There has been a weird atmosphere about. I can't quite explain it, but it seems as though the Darkness has actually calmed recently. Even though there are ample hosts in the area, I haven't noticed any significant activity, which worries me. It feels like a calm before a storm. I can't explain it, but it is nothing like anything I have ever felt before." Lumma tilted her head slightly, "I'm not sure I understand what you are saying, but I can check with Ninlil to see if the destiny of your Ni has shifted in any way." Durito exhaled forcefully, "Thanks Lumma. He is still young but is growing up fast. These circumstances can be rough on anyone, but especially so for teenage boys. I just hope that our bond is strong enough that I will be able to help strengthen him in more trying times ahead. I really care about him and his mother. I wish there was something more we could do to help them out of poverty and get them to a better place." Lumma nodded in agreement, "I know what you mean, but the Ni agree to certain circumstances before they are even incarnated. We can't break the contracts that they made, only help protect them along the path. Have a little faith in your humans." All Durito could do was nod and discretely roll his eyes. Luckily, Lumma didn't notice and continued, "Keep doing what you are doing. We will touch base next check in and I will let you know if Ninlil has seen any change in your Ni's path." With a curt nod, she was gone. Durito stretched and quickly hopped off the car in the direction of the pigeons, who quickly scattered with angry coos. He looked up at the sky. His boy would be home around three, which gave him time to do his patrols of the neighborhood, disperse any forming darkness, and still have time to harass some cronies of Kur.

CHAPTER TEN
Lil Rascals

The school bell was ringing in the distance but Ray had no intention of going today. His friend Flea was going to see the new movie 'Salpicadura de Sangre' and even though Ray didn't particularly like scary movies, he didn't want to look like a wimp. Flea told Ray that his friend's cousin could get them into the 'R' rated film. Flea convinced Ray to skip school. Ray couldn't wait to go on the weekend, because his mom would ask too many questions. She always knew when he was lying and there was no way she would let him see something called 'Blood Splatter'. Besides, she didn't like Flea and had forbidden Ray from hanging out with him. Ray didn't understand why his mom was so strict. She didn't understand the racial divide at his elementary school. In his school you could only hang with your own people. He didn't quite understand the reason, but he knew that no one tried to make friends outside their own race. There was even a divide within the racial groups. The rule was that you stuck to your hood. He lived on 103rd street near Success. So people from that area were his people or "gente" and it wasn't acceptable to make friends with anyone else. He only lived there because his mom had learned what the English word 'Success' meant and liked the idea of living near Success. It was really cheesy and he hated every time his mom told him that "Even though things look bleak, we are always close to Success." His mom didn't speak English well. She had lived in the USA since she was 16 but she had never really had the opportunity to learn the language. She always relied on Ray to be her voice. She always said "Mijo, di mis palabras en inglés. Por favor." Which translated to "Darling, say my words in English. Please." He hated the embarrassment of always being forced to run boring errands with his mom and help her. The other boys made fun of him for being a "niñito de mamá" usually including some additional choice words that if Ray ever repeated his mom would smack him with la chancla. Ray didn't mind being a mama's boy. He was the man of the house, so it was his responsibility to care for his mom. He just wished she would treat him more like a man. He was growing up. He was already ten and next year he would be in middle school. Some kids his age had already dropped out of school and were working for the bangers. His mom wouldn't let him anywhere near those guys and absolutely flipped out when he mentioned it. Flea was still in school but his older sister ran with one of the members of Las Calles or The Streets. Ray didn't really care for the bangers either. Though he could see the appeal. They always had money and no one ever bullied them. They were tough. Even the police knew not to hassle Las Calles. Above all they had each others' backs. Ray envied that. No one looked out for him. He had always been smaller than the other boys, so he had to learn to be tougher than most kids. He would have loved to have an older brother or a father to stand up for him and protect him from the beatings. At the park he would get jumped by kids from other hoods just because he lived in Las Calles' Barrio. Ray's mom was a guerrera and didn't seem to be afraid of anything, but she never stood up for him. She would only ban him from going anywhere dangerous. Not that it really mattered. She was always gone. She worked so much that Ray was usually left to his own devices. She probably wouldn't even know he skipped school. So why shouldn't he enjoy that freedom a bit.

When Ray got to the theater, Flea was already there with another kid. Ray knew him from school a few years back but he was a couple grades ahead of them and was the cousin of the local leader of Las Calles. His name was Lil Naco. Lil Naco had recently been made the leader of Los Callejones which roughly translates to The Little Streets. If you grew up in the hood and wanted to join Las Calles when you were older, the first step was runnin with Los Callejones. It made Ray uncomfortable that Lil Naco was there. He would get in a lot of trouble for ditching school and going to the movies, but if his mom found out that he was hanging out with bangers she would go completely out of her mind. Besides, he didn't want to get involved with Las Calles. They were one-hundred percent blood in, blood out. Once you were a Las Calles you were a Las Calles until you died. Ray wanted to play football. He was small, but he was fast and could catch any ball thrown at him. His mom didn't have enough money to get him into club sports, but one of the clubs had a scholarship for talented middle school athletes from low income households as long as they had good grades and had a clean record. Next year Ray would finally be old enough to try for the scholarship but he had to keep his grades up and stay away from kids like Lil Naco. Unfortunately, Flea had already seen Ray and was waving at him. If Ray left now Lil Naco would see that as a form of disrespect. Respect was very important to the gangs. If someone felt disrespected, they had to retaliate. Despite doing a lot of things that society deemed wrong, they had their own strict moral code. Strength got you respect and disrespect got you dead. Disrespect could be anything. Even something as small as not speaking the right slang or with the right accent might give a banger the idea that you think you're better than him and he will have to retaliate. Ray had learned to mimic the fashion and lingo to protect himself. He was also good at not using that lingo in front of his mom. His hood was a dangerous place and survival required that he learn to be a chameleon. Ray automatically slipped into his hood walk and greeted his "fam" with the appropriate handshake. He wasn't entirely sure why, but Lil Naco didn't seem to like Ray. He always gave him a hard time, so Ray knew he had to be extra careful. "Hey homie. How you finna keep us waitn'?" Lil Naco barked the moment Ray got close. "Bro my kicks be ancient, you na wha I mean? My moms ain't got me new ones yet. My feet kill." Ray answered, trying to shift focus. Luckily Flea interjected. "Bro you would na believe. Lil Naco finna hook us up fam. His cuz finna get us in fasho." As if on cue Don Ladrón ambled over. "Que pasa lil brothers? Cómo está mi gente?" Ray was officially terrified. Don Ladrón got his nickname because he was the boss of the neighborhood. One word from him and the entire force of Las Calles would jump to attention. He had been in and out of prison since he was twelve years old. Behind bars he gained power and alliances that he never would have reached on the outside. He was not someone you wanted as your enemy. As much fear as Ray felt, he also felt a touch of envy. What young boy wouldn't want to emulate someone with power and respect. Don Ladrón could have anything he wanted. It certainly was a tantalizing fantasy for a boy who was growing up with nothing. "Hey hombritos, I got my girl Juana working the movies today and she's gonna take care of you. Anything you want. You can get yo fix at the snack counter and watch whatever movies y'all want, but I need you to do me a favor right quick, ya feel me?" Don Ladrón smiled revealing multiple gold teeth. Before Ray could even think Flea answered for them. "Si. Whatever you need jefe. My homie and I can step up." Don Ladrón's gaze was serpent like as he hissed "Aight chico that's what I like to hear. Look, my boys and I need to get to business but la tira is staking out our joint. All you gotta do is slip by the policia and get our product. Once you bring it back here you can have the whole theater to yourselves. When you're done I'll even drive you home myself." Ray was afraid to mess around with the police, but the idea of living like kings for the afternoon was too enticing to turn down. Plus getting a ride home from Don Ladrón would be like having an invincibility shield protecting him from the bullies in his hood. He would be untouchable for at least a month. Either way it wasn't like he had much of a choice. No one says no to Las Calles.

Some guys dropped the three boys off around the corner from the taco shop where they were supposed to go pick up the packages. The cartel would stuff the baggies of product inside chilies and ship them to the taco shop. The strong smell of the peppers helped to cover the scent from search dogs. Ray was so nervous that he was shaking, but tried hard to hide it from the other boys. Lil Naco noticed before Flea and smacked Ray on the head. "Cálmate miedica! You finna get us nailed!" Flea was quick to come to his aid, "Yo it his first time but he be coo tho. We just gettin tacos Ray, ok?" Ray didn't like looking so weak. He shrugged his backpack higher on his back and forced himself to look hard. "I'm chill. I'm not scared. I'm just hyped." Ray walked off first to try and back up his lie. The other boys followed. The cops saw the boys, but they were not about to expose themselves to bust some kids on truancy. The boys were able to slip in without raising any suspicion. When they walked in, one of the O.G.s of Las Calles was waiting for them. He took their bags and gave them food. While the boys ate, the older man took their backpacks to the kitchen and when he returned they no longer had school supplies but were full of Don Ladrón's merchandise. The man gave the boys cups of horchata to take with them and they exited happily sipping away on their drinks. Nothing seemed out of the ordinary, just a few kids skipping school for tacos. They returned to the same spot they were dropped off at and a car quickly pulled up for them. Their mission was a success and they felt on top of the world.

The boys spent the afternoon and evening gorging themselves on sweets, popcorn, and movie nachos while watching every horror and action movie showing at the theater. When they were done Don Ladrón rolled up stacking. He used his left hand to make an 'L' using his pointer finger and thumb and his right hand to make a backwards 'C' which he placed directly under the thumb of his left hand. This made 'LC' for Las Calles but also looked like a 'S' for Streets, the translation of Calles. Then he moved his thumb to touch three of his other fingers making an '0' with the pointer finger sticking up and changed his right hand to have all four fingers sticking up with the middle and ring finger crossed making a '3'. This represented '103' the street that was home base for Las Calles. Lil Naco flashed the same signs back plus an additional hand sign of the right hand holding up four fingers and the left hand with all four fingers sticking up with the middle and ring finger crossed making a 'E' and crossing his wrists making a '4E' meaning forever. Both Flea and Ray knew what these signs meant but didn't dare attempt them as only initiated members of Las Calles or Los Callejones were allowed to use them. Don Ladrón reached into his pocket and pulled out a huge wad of rolled hundreds. Ray's eyes opened wide in shock. He had never seen that much money in real life. Don Ladrón pulled off three one hundred dollar bills and gave one to each boy. "Here you go little homies. Bring in the dough, get the bread. Las Calles takes care of its people." Ray caught himself staring at the bill in his hands. He couldn't believe it was his. He realized what he was doing and quickly shoved the hundred in his pocket, but kept his hand in his pocket. He didn't want to chance breaking contact with such a mythical thing and having it disappear. The group walked to Don Ladrón's car. One of his lieutenants was in the front seat but got out to open the door for the boys. Ray had never felt so important and he could tell by the way his friend Flea was beaming that he felt the same. Don Ladrón's car was a metallic blue 1985 Cutlass Supreme that he had personally modified. It was a low-rider with blue floor lights, the best aftermarket audio system with thirty-six speakers including a beast of a subwoofer, and a top of the line hydraulic system so he could hop. He did most of the work himself at one of the gang chop shops. If Don Ladrón ever gave up banging it would be for his car. A few years prior a rival gang had tagged his car and shot out one side. Within hours he had assembled the entire Las Calles army and completely obliterated the rival gang. There was no mercy. Now no one dared put as much as a fingerprint on his ride. The mix of fear and excitement that Ray felt getting to ride in such a prized item was euphoric. As they rolled down the street, Don Ladrón bounced the car to the Chicano rap blasting over the speakers. Ray was glad the music was so loud because he was sure he was giggling like a little girl. When they pulled up to his apartments, Ray saw the most petrifying sight he could have ever imagined. Standing on the narrow patio of their apartment, in clear view of the very conspicuous car with her hand firmly planted on her hip and eyes as wide and flaming as fire pois, was his mother. He couldn't show his new friends his fear and he couldn't look like he was having a good time. If his mom said anything disrespectful, that would be the end of him and he knew his mother would have to say something. She always talked about how much she hated the gangs and how the US was supposed to be different from the cartel violence in Mexico. Ray tried to get out of the car and thank Don Ladrón as quickly as possible but to Ray's utter horror, Don Ladrón parked the car and got out. A high pitched screeching rang out like an alarm "Ray Arturo Fransisco Solíz. ¿Tú crees que esto es un hotel o qué? Ve adentro! Apúrate!" His mother had shouted his full name and said 'Do you think that this is a hotel or what?' Meaning that she did not allow him to come and go as he pleased and solidifying that he was in life changing trouble. Ray's eyes bounced back and forth from his mom to Don Ladrón. This was it, the end. If Don Ladrón didn't kill him and his mom for disrespecting him, then his mom was definitely going to kill him. Don Ladrón didn't react. He just sauntered up to Maria and flicked his nose with his thumb. "Damn mamasita. I'm calling the popos for a 211 cause you just boosted my heart." Maria just glared at him trying not to let the confusion show on her face. "RayRay, you holdin' out on me. Why you not tell me your moms was fine as hell?" Ray made a disgusted face, which only confused his mom more. Don Ladrón circled Maria, "I ain't looking for a baby mama but slip me your digits and I might make an exception." Maria's stomach was folding in on itself but she lifted her chin in defiance and said "No entiendo lo que estás diciendo. Por favor, vete." Instead of getting angry Don Ladrón laughed. "No Ingles? Mami, esta es America. Tienes que hablar el idioma. Speak English. I'll give you night classes. Puedo darte clases nocturnas." He stroked her hair and she backed away. Without warning a large brown, feral looking cat jumped from the roof onto Don Ladrón's back and into Maria's arms. Don Ladrón swung around, his hands in fists, only to find no one there. He turned back to see the cat and Maria doing her best to suppress a smile. Rage lit up his face. Ray stepped forward, ready to defend his mother, but as quickly as Don Ladrón's fury had risen, it subsided. "That's one ballin gato. I'd cap a G too if he got close to my girl. Hermosa, no necesitarás un gato guardián si estás conmigo. RayRay, you should get rid of your mama's guard cat and find her a papi." Ray had no words so he just dumbly nodded and went to his mom's side. Maria shared Ray's dumbfounded stare. She was ready to fight for her son and thought she was ready to handle any threat the banger had to throw at her, but half-witted flirting was the last thing she expected. She wanted to rant at him and tell him exactly what she thought of him, his lifestyle, and his stupid come-ons but her brain had forgotten every word, in every language. The only comeback that she could imagine was sticking her tongue out and blowing the biggest raspberry her spit would allow, but she managed to keep that in her head. Instead she grabbed the back of Ray's neck with the hand not holding Durito and said "Vámonos" while not so gently urging him toward their apartment. Don Ladrón laughed "I'll hit you up later BG. Keep it chill." Flea and Lil Naco joined Don Ladrón in his laughter and they all headed back to his car. Ray could hear them talking about his mom but his mom's grip on his neck directed his thoughts elsewhere.

  They entered the apartment and Durito jumped out of Maria's arms and headed into the kitchen, holding his tail high and slowly wagging it from side to side. Durito was confident that he put that banger in his place. Ray, on the other hand, braced for the verbal lashing and not so verbal lashing of la chancla, but neither came. He turned around to see his mother latching all the locks and moving a chair from the kitchen to wedge under the door knob. After wiggling the chair around to make sure it was secure she just turned around to let her whole body slump against the door and slowly sink to the floor. Durito returned to the room dragging a chewed up flip-flop. He made his way over to Maria and dropped the flip-flop at her side and crawled into her lap. Even in Maria's lap Durito never took his eyes off Ray, flipping his tail as hard as he could manage without smacking Maria. If he was allowed to speak to humans, he would have given Ray a piece of his mind. Instead he was limited to a hard stare accompanied by ear and tail movement to convey his displeasure. Ray looked at his mom. He was preparing a list of excuses to counter her inquisition, but she said nothing. She wasn't even looking at him. The faraway look of fear in his mom's eyes was something he had never seen before. She was the strongest person he knew. He even believed she would take on all of Las Calles with her flip-flop and tales of La Lechuzza. Seeing her looking so frail and vulnerable was scarier than any punishment she could have given him.

CHAPTER ELEVEN
Felino Remorse

It took Maria a few days to calm down enough to talk to Ray. Maria had to work over the weekend, but when she came home Sunday night they had talked. Ray told her about skipping school and going to get tacos and see movies, but left out the bit about helping Don Ladrón. Maria stressed how dangerous people like Lil Naco and Don Ladrón were. They talked about Ray's dream of playing football and how that would be gone if he got mixed up with gangs. But Maria was exhausted and was having a hard time staying awake. Ray hated that his mom had to work so much just so they could keep a roof over their heads and food in their mouths. His hand unconsciously went to his pocket to touch the hundred dollar bill that Don Ladrón had given him. He was listening to everything his mother had been saying, but as he watched her nodding off on the couch, he thought about how his life would be different if he did work for Don Ladrón. If he could make a lot of money, his mom could quit one of her jobs. She would have more time to sleep and more time to spend with him. That night after they had gone to bed, he dreamed about being rich like the bangers in Las Calles. He dreamed about buying his mom nice things and getting her a lawyer to help her get her green card. He saw them living in a nice house with a picket fence just like the shows he saw on television. When he woke up his eyes focused on a giant brown stain on the roof above their bed. He felt angry. His dream was so different from his reality that it physically hurt him. His fist clenched and he silently vowed to do everything in his power to make his dream a reality, even if it meant disobeying his mom.

After school, Flea and Ray went to look for Lil Naco, but to their surprise, he was outside the school waiting for them. "Sup. My cuz said you did aight. He liked how we handled biness. Now I ain't sayin' you finna be accepted, but Don Ladrón said yous can intern, ya feel me? If you don't f up, then maybe, *maybe* we might let you be Los Callejones." Ray had decided he wanted this. So why did every muscle in his body tense like his soul was trying to escape? He forced himself to answer, "I feel you bro. You ain't gotta worry. I finna step up, na what I mean?" Flea was so excited, he looked like he was going to burst. He excitedly affirmed, "Yes Bro! That's wha I'm talkin' bout! We finna be real Gs! Ain't nobody finna mess with us Los Callejones homies!" Lil Naco glared at them, "Chill homie, you ain't Los Callejones yet. And you ain't finna be Los Callejones until you get approved by Las Cabezas and get jumped in. Then you get a strap and the privilege to stack. Until then I finna get you checked into the hood. Today we finna meet up with La Mano and he finna give you some work." The weight of what was happening started to really sink in and Ray's resolve wavered. He heard his mom's words echoing in his brain. However, her screaming was silenced by a cold voice, "You should do it for her. It's not wrong if you do it for family." Ray chose to listen to that voice and he repeated the thought over and over. He was doing it for his mom. She would change her mind about Las Calles when she didn't have to work anymore. She would forgive him for doing bad things if he could give her the things that she so desperately wanted. He wasn't bad, he was just doing bad things for good reasons. As he followed Flea and Lil Naco the guiding voice of his mother was completely silenced by the pounding of his heart in his ears.

***

Months passed and Ray continued to get more and more entrenched in the gang. Don Ladrón had personally taken him under his wing and Ray was drunk on the attention. He suddenly had a family, tons of older brothers protecting him and giving him things. He even had Don Ladrón who was almost like a dad. He played football with Ray, bought him new shoes, picked him up after school and took him for food. Ray was in heaven, but it was getting harder and harder to hide the change from his mom. One evening after Don Ladrón had dropped him off, Ray hid his new shoes under a pile of clothes. He was relaxing on the couch watching television with Durito when he saw his mom going around the apartment with the laundry basket. Panic hit him. He jumped up and ran to the bedroom before his mom could get there. When she knocked on the door, he lied and said he was changing into his pajamas so she could wash his clothes. He quickly moved his new shoes into his school bag and hid it behind the bed and changed his clothes faster than the first day in the school locker room. He unlocked the door and a suspicious Maria and Durito entered the bedroom. Maria eyed Ray dubiously, "Mijo, estas bien?" Ray smiled as naturally as he could, "Por supuesto mamá. Estoy bien. Todo está bien." Durito was not convinced and prowled the room sniffing. When he started to sniff near the backpack's hiding place, Ray scooped him up with a nervous chuckle, "Vamos Durito. Our show is back on." Ray handed his mom his clothes and kissed her on the cheek, "Gracias mamá.". Maria glanced around the room but didn't notice anything out of the ordinary so she shook her head and continued with her task. Durito wasn't as easily swayed, but Ray's nervous grip on him wasn't loosening anytime soon. Durito noted the behavior and vowed to follow up on his investigation later.

    The next day Durito left with Maria and Ray, but instead of occupying the day with his patrols, he followed Ray. Ray went to school as usual, but Durito was convinced something was up. He found a water fountain in the park by the school that had a semi reflective side. No one was around, so he focused on his reflection. Lumma answered quickly. She was never one to leave him waiting. She seemed in a particularly good mood. "Iksuda! Wassup... or How's it hangin'.. or Oh, what was the set phrase for greetings in SoCal? Cowabunga? Aw Kur, Sumerian was much easier. I'd even prefer ancient Egyptian to Southern California millennial slang." Durito laughed, "You are a few decades behind the times, Lumma. Perhaps you are due for a new Girru. Any news from Ninlil?" Lumma's demeanor changed and she was now all business. "Nothing surprising, which is good news. Your Ni's path is still swirling with darkness, but not more than it has been. Ninlil says that he is still in danger, but your presence there is successfully mitigating the danger to his Ni. She is confident that as long as nothing unforeseen occurs, the Ni will overcome the Darkness around him and become a bright, guiding light." Lumma seemed so pleased with her news, Durito didn't want to spoil the mood by voicing his concerns. He was happy that Ninlil confirmed that everything was going according to plan and Ray's destiny was safe, but his kitty senses were tingling. He didn't have to mention it now, but he wasn't about to let his guard down. "Thanks Lumma. I always have good luck when you've got my back." Lumma's scarlet eyes beamed even brighter, "Take care of yourself Iksuda. Peace out dude." Lumma laughed at her attempt at slang and her image faded back into Durito's reflection. Durito felt better after having heard Ninlil's prediction, but he preferred to err on the side of caution. He stalked birds in the park until he heard the school bell ring. He made his way to the school so he could clearly see the kids leaving but not be noticed. When he saw Ray his heart sank. He was walking towards Don Ladrón. Durito watched Ray get into Don Ladrón's car and disappear. Durito knew something was off. He would have to think of a way to get that creep out of Ray's life, and he would have to think quickly.

Don Ladrón took Ray to get some food and when it started to get dark, they met up with a couple of his guys and headed a few neighborhoods over. They were not in his souped up Cutlass but a dark colored, generic sedan. Ray started to feel nervous as he knew this was the territory of the Main Street Players. Back in the day Las Calles and other hispanic gangs were in a full-out race war with gangs like the Players. Being from Las Calles territory, Ray knew never to venture into neighborhoods controlled by other gangs. Even when he wasn't associated with Las Calles, he could not go to this neighborhood without risking death or at the very least a good beating. This time he was with Don Ladrón and his guys, but he wasn't sure if that made him more or less scared. He was happy that if anyone hassled them that he had the big guys as protection, but he also knew that being with them significantly increased his chances of being shot. Bullets don't care if you are a banger or not, they kill indiscriminately. Ray desperately wanted to ask what they were doing, but he knew it wasn't his place to ask questions, only follow orders. As if he could read his mind, Don Ladrón turned around from the front seat to talk to Ray. "Aight BG, we got some biness to take care of here. You gonna be our look out. If you see any Players roll up, you whistle and we gonna take care of it." Ray could only silently nod. He was so scared he was afraid he might pee his pants. The time seemed to crawl by. The bangers left him alone on the corner and he tried not to look nervous, but it was taking all his energy to keep his teeth from chattering. Every noise made him jump out of his skin. He looked down the street and saw the thing he was dreading the most. A group of Main Street Players were headed his way. He tried to whistle but his mouth was so dry no sound came out. He furiously licked his lips in an attempt to fix the problem, but the Players were approaching faster than his body could respond. The Players saw him and started yelling things at him. He tried to act like he didn't notice them. As they got closer Ray deviated from the plan and gave up on whistling. Choosing instead to yell "Oye!" The Players rushed him and started pummeling him. He put his arms over his head and tried to protect himself the best he could but one of the Players pulled out a knife and started slashing at him in between the contact of his buddies' fists. A few of the slashes made contact and Ray's life flashed before his eyes. He was going to die and his mom would be alone. He wanted to cry but his adrenaline wouldn't let him. It just kept him fighting to stay alive. A loud pop rang through the neighborhood quickly followed by more, pop, pop, poppoppoppop. The Players crouched and then fled for cover but not before a couple of them slumped to the ground. Two of the group fell almost immediately. Two more were able to flee a few feet before catching multiple bullets and falling to the pavement. The last Player took off running down the street. Don Ladrón rushed up and grabbed Ray by his shirt, dragging him along as they chased the final guy down. The Player quickly ran into a house on the next street but the Las Calles guys followed right behind him spraying bullets chaotically into the house. Don Ladrón told Ray to stay on the front porch and followed his guys into the house. Ray heard lots of shots and yelling followed by blood curdling screams. When the shots stopped Ray cautiously looked into the home. What he saw made him vomit. In the living room there were two kids, one around his age and a toddler, both with numerous gunshot wounds to their body and head from where the bullets passed through the window. Around the corner was an older woman desperately trying to put pressure on a wound on her neck, but with the amount of blood seeping through her fingers, Ray knew she wasn't going to make it. The Las Calles bangers came running out from a back room carrying a pillowcase filled with something, but Ray didn't know what. Two of their guys had been shot, but it didn't look too serious as they were still moving on their own. They all fled back to the car and took off. In the car Don Ladrón was shouting commands but what chilled Ray the most is none of them were scared or afraid. They all seemed exhilarated and happy. They were laughing and joking about killing everyone on the street and in the house. They even made a comment about rooting out future Players before they could sprout which Ray knew was referring to the murdered kids. Ray was in shock. He didn't know what to do or say but he knew he wanted to be as far away from the scene and Las Calles as he could get. Don Ladrón turned around from the front seat and dumped out the contents of the pillow case laughing. It was full of money, packets of white powder, and baggies of pills. Don Ladrón looked at Ray and the guys in the back seat and said "Looks like those fools paid us for their extermination." The other guys broke out in laughter and hoots.

Don Ladrón continued, "You know the drill, give me your straps. Don't want to go down for 187." They all emptied the bullets from their guns and put them in the pillowcase. Then Don Ladrón looked directly at Ray, "You gonna hide these with you til things cool down, aight? I will send someone to get them later. You gonna put them in the back of your toilet, in the tank. You get what I'm saying?" He spoke slowly and calmly but Ray could not believe what he was being told and just stared at Don Ladrón like a deer in headlights. "Entiendes?!" Don Ladrón's raised voice brought Ray back to reality and he fervently nodded and took the pillowcase. Ray knew his mom wasn't going to be home until the next day because of her overnight cleaning job for a local business complex. The bangers quickly dropped Ray off at his house and sped off. Ray mindlessly walked through the door. The weight of what had happened still hadn't fully sunk in. He dropped the pillowcase on the floor and just stared blankly ahead like a zombie. Durito followed him through the open door. He could smell death. He sniffed the bag and made a 'stinky' face leaving his mouth open and crinkling his nose. It was definitely the bag. The bag smelled like death. Durito kept sniffing. No, it wasn't just the bag. Ray had the smell of death on him too. Durito looked at Ray and saw that his right eye was swollen and discolored, and he had numerous abrasions and bruises forming on his arms and legs. His cheek was cut and bleeding and he had two fairly deep cuts on his right forearm, both of which were dripping blood onto the floor. Durito meowed at Ray and jumped up, placing his front paws on the boy's hip. Ray didn't respond so Durito tapped him a few times on the hand, which was hanging limply next to his body. No response. Durito weaved through Ray's legs meowing, but a good fifteen minutes passed and Ray didn't acknowledge him or even move. A knock on the door startled them both. "RayRay, it's us. You ok homie?" Flea's voice was an octave higher than usual but Ray couldn't tell if it was from fear or excitement. Ray slowly turned to face him and Lil Naco, who seemed irritated. "I'm so jealous. I've been begging Don Ladrón to take me when he goes to pop those wannabes. I don't know why he let you go. Did you get any of them? Looks like they got you good. Did you give it back to them?" Ray wasn't registering what Lil Naco was saying. The room was spinning and it was like he was looking down at his body. Lil Naco rambled on "Yo are these the straps?" He opened the bag and took out a gun and pretended to fire it. "It must have been so lit, pop pop pop take that you dirty f'n

Playas." Lil Naco continued firing in his personal banger fantasy and Flea joined him. They were acting like Ray had just gotten a new toy and were excitedly playing with it. Ray screamed in his head, but his body did not respond until Flea slapped him on the shoulder and his entire body shuddered in pain. Ray winched and Flea noticed, "They got you good. You gotta clean that up before your mom sees you. Ray went to the bathroom to look in the mirror. What he saw shocked him. He was bruised, bloody, and swollen. There was no way that he was going to be able to keep this from his mom, so he had better start thinking of a good story. Ray went back to the living room and closed the door, picked up the pillowcase and grabbed the gun from Flea. When he went to take the gun from Lil Naco, Lil Naco swung around and pointed the gun at Ray, shoving the barrel in his face. "How your pants be? I bet you dropped a load in 'em." Lil Naco laughed and Ray grabbed the gun. "The guns aren't even loaded anymore. I gotta hide 'em for Don Ladrón, not play with 'em." Ray snapped, then took the package to the bathroom and hid them in the tank of the toilet like he was told. When he returned Lil Naco was glaring at him, "Don't forget your place perro. You ain't even Los Callejones yet. Don't start thinkin you all that cause Don Ladrón got a thing fo yo moms." Ray's shock turned to a fiery anger and all his rage and fear was directed at Lil Naco, "Don't talk about my mom. Don Ladrón likes me. He sees that I am tough and can help him. It has nothing to do with my mom." Lil Naco burst out laughing hysterically, "You ain't nothin'." Ray made a fist and stepped towards Lil Naco who responded by grabbing his shirt and flinging him to the ground. Before Ray could react Lil Naco was on top of him with his fist inches from his face. "You ain't nothin' perro. If Don Ladrón wasn't protecting you, you'd be dead already." Durito had had enough. He ran to the position at the top of Ray's head and swiped three times with claws out, landing the first blow and raking his claws across Lil Naco's cheek. Lil Naco fell backwards and grabbed his face. Ray sat up and Durito moved to put himself between Ray and Lil Naco. Lil Naco moved to hit Durito but Durito swatted again, clawing Lil Naco's hand and arm. Durito hissed and spat, then settled into a low growl with Lil Naco frozen in front of him. Another spitting hiss and Lil Naco flinched and then scooted back enough to get up and run towards the door. Before he could exit, Maria opened the door. Her eyes quickly surveyed the scene. She dropped her bag and grabbed Lil Naco by the ear, dragging him out, all while screaming at him in Spanish. Her rant earned her a couple angry commands for silence from her neighbors. Flea didn't need any extra encouragement and he ran out after Lil Naco. When Maria returned she frantically cleaned up Ray's wounds and grilled him for answers. There was no way he could tell her the truth, so he made up a story about getting jumped at the park by gang members. He said that Lil Naco and Flea had helped scare the bangers off and helped him home. Maria was leery but seemed to accept his story. After all, they lived in a dangerous place and getting jumped by a rival gang or mugged on the street was not out of the ordinary. Ray tried to change the subject by asking why she was home early but Maria wouldn't allow the distraction. She questioned him until she was done treating his wounds and then only let him go to bed because he played the sympathy card, complaining about how much he hurt. He knew it wasn't the end of the conversation, but it gave him a temporary reprieve.

Lil Naco met Don Ladrón at the taco shop. His dad used to run it with his uncle until his uncle was killed. His dad used to be a high ranking member of Las Calles but after barely surviving a drive-by shooting, he had moved to semi-retirement in the taco shop. Don Ladrón was in the back counting the money from his earlier escapade. He acknowledged Lil Naco when he entered, but didn't say anything about the scratches on his face and arms. Lil Naco waited for a comment, but after a few minutes grew impatient and brought up the topic he wanted to speak to his cousin about. "I don't like Ray. He ain't got what it takes to run with my crew. And his moms is cray cray. She's-". Don Ladrón slammed his fist on the table, "Did I ask for your opinion primo? You run Los Callejones cause I allow you to. RayRay been stepping it up and his mom look better than a big slab of carne asada. I like my women loca. The feistier the better. That woman be a challenge but I always get what I want. To be honest witchu the more she turns me down, the better the hunt. So you keep her name outcho mouth til I be done with her." Lil Naco looked down. Don Ladrón looked him over again, "Those from her gato diablo?" Lil Naco just nodded. "That cat sure is gangsta, but no one, human or animal gets to draw blood on Las Calles without my permission. I think it time we get el minino out of the way." Lil Naco looked up, pleased but perplexed. "But how you gonna get with Ray's moms if you green light her cat?" Don Ladrón laughed, "You got a lot to learn little homie. You know what las mujeres love?" He paused for a moment to enjoy the confusion on his cousin's face. "Las mujeres love a knight in shining armor. If something happen to her gatito and she think her son is in danger, and I can offer them my protection, she will be eating out of my hands. I'll have to peel her off me like skin off a plátano." Lil Naco could tell by the half smile that Don Ladrón had on his face that he had a plan. Don Ladrón stopped what he was doing and went to sit with Lil Naco, "I think it is about time to initiate RayRay into Los Callejones."

    Maria let Ray stay home from school to rest up and heal. She threatened him on pain of death if he left the apartment. Durito stayed curled up on his legs as he rested. Ray felt Durito purring. It surprised him as Durito usually only purred for his mom and not that often. As Ray started to drift back to sleep, Durito slowly began to get up. He needed to check in with Lumma. There had to be something he could do to rip Ray from the grasp of these criminals. He didn't understand. Ray was a good kid. He was brave and compassionate. What could he possibly see in these creeps that kept him in their orbit? Before Durito could hop off the bed, there was a pounding on the door. Durito puffed up and hoped Ray would stay in bed, but he got up and answered the pounding. It was Flea. Ray opened the door and Lil Naco pushed in. Durito put himself in between the two boys and Ray. Something was very wrong. Durito could see the Darkness swirling around Lil Naco. The fog of darkness was so thick, he could hardly even see the boy. Durito swatted at the sparks of darkness flying off Lil Naco towards Ray, but Ray picked him up and put him in the bedroom. When he returned Lil Naco spoke before Ray could say anything. "I got news from Don Ladrón. Las Cabezas voted and they want you in Los Callejones. You just have to pass the test." Ray had mixed feelings. He wanted so badly to be accepted and gain the brotherhood that came with being part of the gang, but he didn't like what they did. He liked the money he got from helping, but he didn't want anything to do with drugs or any of the other criminal enterprises they ran. He wanted protection but he had never felt less safe. Lil Naco was expecting Ray to be grateful and his slow response angered him, but he had to follow Don Ladrón's plan. A devious smile crept across Lil Naco's face. He was looking forward to the initiation and he was determined to make it happen regardless of Ray's answer. Ray knew he had to answer, "I-I don't think I-" before he could say he had changed his mind, Lil Naco pulled a gun from his waistband. "Like my new toy? Don Ladrón gave it to me. It ain't like the one last night. This one got bullets." Lil Naco cocked the gun and the boys could hear the click of a bullet sliding into the chamber. Lil Naco looked directly at Ray. "You ain't ignant homie. You know you are either with Las Calles or against us. Don Ladrón has offered you a gift. It be rude as hell not to take it." Ray had no choice. He screamed in his head, "What have I gotten myself into? I don't want to be here! I want to go back to before!" Rays expression enraged Lil Naco even further, but he kept his cool. Ray, not having much of a choice, just nodded and said "Thank you." Flea was excited enough for both of them. He was practically jumping up and down, "What he gotta do? Is he finna get jumped in? Did the beating last night count?" Lil Naco let the smile return to his face. This is what he was waiting for. "Nah bro. He gotta prove he loyal to the crew above all else." Lil Naco pulled out a thick pillowcase. "Ray, get yo cat."

CHAPTER TWELVE
Purrder and Found

Ama-gi took her feet off the altar and quickly backed away from it. She hacked like she was passing a fur ball. She had to stop the Kanunuru. She couldn't watch anymore. She didn't even live it but she could feel all the pain and anguish that distressed Iksuda in his final moments. The overwhelming sense of betrayal she felt on his behalf almost consumed her. She was panting and weak from the egregiousness of the acts she witnessed. Iksuda had loved that boy and to be so utterly abused was beyond words. With every wound, with every puncture, she had seen the Darkness spilling into Iksuda. She was amazed he had held up as well as he did. Even with the tsunami of hate and darkness that had entered his body and soul, he was able to retain his light, be it severely dimmed. What chance did they have against that all encompassing evil? The Kahu had faced millennia of darkness and even Chaos herself, but humans brought a wickedness to the equation that Ama-gi just couldn't fathom. Humans are spectacular in their capacity for good, but also for evil. With this level of depravity, Ama-gi was not sure the protection of the Kahu would be able to keep the balance. Ama-gi made her way to É. Simtum the Temple of Fate to meet with Ninlil, the Lady of Destiny. Her name actually meant Lady of the Breeze or Lady of the Air, but Ninlil's talent was reading destinies, which, over time, made its way into her title. Ama-gi entered É. Simtum which was more commonly called the Temple of Destiny. The walls, assuming the most nebulous idea of the word, were a translucent white mist in roughly the shape of a donut. Through this mist, Ama-gi could appreciate the polychromous nebulae outside the walls. She watched the vibrant blues, pinks, purples, and oranges slowly swirling like a prismatic lava lamp. The sanctum was lit by a large and bright beam of white light running vertically through the center that cast a soft white glow throughout the cloud-like palace. The interior was mostly bare. The ground was neither solid nor gaseous but rather a version of squidgy not unlike just-baked angel food cake. É. Simtum looked quite empty. Unlike the other Kahu, the beings here did not require scrying mirrors or any such tools to see destinies. These beings could tap directly into universal threads of fate. They were responsible for identifying and monitoring the souls with the strongest energy that would undoubtedly be targeted by the Gaudium Cleptes. When a human was incarnated with powerful energy, Ninlil, and those like her, would mark them as Ni or someone with a strong potential to convey light to the world or, in the case where they were infected by darkness, bring pain and suffering. The Readers of Destiny would also determine if the Ni was at risk of contamination or infection of darkness. If the reader felt that a Ni would experience a trying time, then a Kahu would be assigned to a Girru to act as that soul's guardian during their time of need. These assignments could be short term or long-term. If successful, the Ni would retain their profound light and use it in a unique way to benefit humanity and strengthen the bonds holding Chaos captive. If the assignment was unsuccessful, the Ni would be reclassified as either a Halqu or a Dalkhu. A Halqu was a lost soul. This was a Ni that had been affected enough by darkness to lose their light but not hurt others. These souls neither helped nor harmed. Dalkhu on the other hand were souls that had succumbed to the Darkness inside them. They could only go on by creating more darkness around them. They received their sustenance by feeding off the pain of others like a parasite. Since a Ni is a soul with substantial power, one that became a Dalkhu brought that power to the side of darkness. Therefore, failing to protect a Ni to the point they became a Dalkhu was not just a loss, but a catastrophe of epic proportions. Thankfully, the Kahus' efforts, even when unsuccessful, rarely resulted in a Ni's transformation to Dalkhu. Over the centuries even the most heinous attacks by the Gaudium Cleptes seldom did more than create a Halqu. There were some exceptions of course. A certain German boy was labelled a Halqu in 1900 after the failure of a Feline Kahu and eventually became a Dalkhu after other failures by Canine Kahu in the 1920's. Though to the Canine Kahu's credit they never stopped trying to redeem the fascist dictator. It was generally accepted that once a soul became a Dalkhu, there was no bringing them back to the light. Readers of Destiny could see the cloud of darkness on a Ni's path, but they rarely saw specific details. Ninlil had explained this to Ama-gi when she first became Kahu. She said "The earth plane offers its inhabitants free will. Nothing is ever set in stone. Humans might agree to a particular path, but how they walk that path is their own choice. We can see the places on their path where they are likely to stumble, but this can change with every step. Therefore we must continuously monitor destinies to ensure that Kahu are always there when a Ni's stride might falter." However, when a shadow on the path had been successfully overcome, occasionally the reader was able to see a vision of their projected future. Once a Ni connected with their light, it was like they were vaccinated against the Darkness. No one ever reached full immunity, but their connection with their light gave them a fortified constitution against further infection.

Ama-gi looked around the Temple. She saw the rear of a brownish grey cat stuck high in the air. Its behind was swaying rhythmically. Its tail erect and waving in a hypnotic manner like a snake dancing to the flute of the snake charmer. She stood still, somewhat mesmerized by the fluid movement until she caught the movement of someone approaching her. A soft voice said, "Shai has a certain panache to his reading." Ama-gi turned to see a beautiful Siamese cat. She was a light, almost white, grey with a dark grey face and ears. The coloring on her tail and legs were slightly darker than her body. However, her most distinguishing feature was her eyes. They were a stunning shade of azure blue and so intensely crossed that her pupils appeared to touch the bridge of her nose, leaving slender crescents of white along the outer edges. Ama-gi bowed her head in reverence and greeted her elder, "Silim Ninlil. Shai is certainly focused." Ninlil joined Ama-gi in watching Shai, "Did you know that in the Hellenistic period a human seer had a vision of Shai reading destinies and because of his peculiar dance the seer thought he was a serpent and associated his greek name Agathodaemon with snakes. This led to him occasionally being depicted in Egypt as a serpent-headed pig. We still tease him about it." Ninlil chuckled, but Ama-gi was in no mood for anecdotes. She turned to Ninlil, "I am afraid we will have to change the designation for the Ni from Iksuda's last Girru. I completed the Kanunuru and believe the Ni should be reclassified as Dalkhu." Ama-gi hung her head in shame. Ninlil paused and closed her eyes for a moment. "No. I disagree. The young Solíz has been exposed to the darkness and emerged victorious." Ama-gi tucked her chin to her neck and rolled her ears back, "With all due respect Ninlil, I saw the opposite. What he did to poor Iksuda qualified him as the earthly personification of evil." Ninlil shook her head. "I see no evil in his soul. His light is shining brighter than ever before." Ama-gi was shocked. Surely they were not speaking of the same person. "But Ninlil, I saw what they did! They shoved Iksuda, who they called Durito, into a thick sack, hung it from a tree, and beat it with rebar. Then, when he was broken and bruised, they threw the bag to the ground and took turns stabbing it with a screwdriver. If that wasn't enough, they finished him off by covering him in lighter fluid and striking a match. Anyone capable of such horrors is not redeemable!" Ninlil paused to give Ama-gi a moment to catch her breath. "Is that all you saw?" Ama-gi looked at her horrified and cried "Was that not enough?" Ninlil took a moment to compose her thoughts and explained "A soul is judged not only by their actions, but their intentions. Ray was given a choice between the life of his feline friend or the life of his mother. Had he not gone along with this evil plot, he would have had to watch his mother go through the same, followed by the forfeiture of his own life. I do not deny that evil was conjured, but it was not in the heart of the Ni. Iksuda's mission was successful, even if he is feeling betrayed. Who among us would not gladly give up their life protecting their human?" Ama-gi had no response to contradict her. All Kahu, herself included, were not afraid to suffer and die to protect the soul of their human, but she couldn't see how a human could commit such a violent action and come out with their soul unscathed. Ninlil could read the confusion on Ama-gi's face. "The Ni could have given in to the temptation of money and power, but instead he held onto the love he had for his mother. Making the choice to sacrifice his friend was not easy, but that sacrifice, Iksuda's sacrifice, emphasized what was important to Ray. From that moment he made the decision to fight against that evil and protect rather than harm others." Ama-gi just shook her head. "I just don't see-" Ninlil interrupted. "I will see for you." Ninlil's eyes changed from their sparkling blue to a solid bright white. They were glowing so brightly that Ama-gi had to look down to shield her own eyes from the radiance. Ninlil touched her forehead to Ama-gi's forehead.

    Maria turned down the walkway towards her home. As she approached she noticed something sitting outside her front door. The door itself was tagged with gang graffiti that she had never seen in this neighborhood before. As she got closer she tried to make out what the blackened object was. The closer she got the more details emerged. She was perplexed until she noticed what looked like patches of singed fur. The realization of what she was looking at hit her like a bolt of lightning. It couldn't be. No one was that cruel. Not here. Not in America. She collapsed when she reached the step. She reached for the broken and mangled body of her poor cat but couldn't bring herself to touch it. She squeezed her eyes closed as the sting of tears burned through her closed lids. She prayed that she would open her eyes and nothing would be there, "No, Dios. Por favor, *no*!" She squeaked in a rough whisper. She opened her eyes and was assaulted again by the nightmare taking over her reality. The gravity hit her like a ton of bricks. "Ray!" Where was her son? She looked up at the gang tags on her door and burst inside in a panic. Where was her son?! So many horrific possibilities flooded her mind. How could she have left him alone? They had already attacked him once. Self hate pumped through her entire body with each rapid thump of her heart. She ran through the apartment screaming her son's name. Unable to locate him she burst from the house and frantically screamed his name while running through the apartment complex. People began peering out their doors watching Maria hysterically run from place to place. When she reached the parking lot, her heart fell to her stomach. Ray was standing next to Don Ladrón, surrounded by a group of bangers not so discreetly showing off the weapons in their waistbands. She burst through the group grabbing her son and hugging him, all why trying to check him for injuries. She spoke so quickly and frantically through sobs that Ray could barely understand her. He knew she wanted to know if he was ok. He hugged her, fighting back tears. "Estoy bien mama." He could barely speak but Don Ladrón was ready to fill the void. "Tranquilla mamasita. RayRay está bien. Algunos West-side idiotas intentaron hacerle daño, pero yo protejo a mi gente." Ray's mind was blank. He felt empty inside, a shriveled up shell that was undeserving of his mother's concern. He heard Don Ladrón speaking but it was like it was in a different language. He knew that Don Ladrón was telling his mom some lie about rival gang members attacking him and how Las Calles saved the day, but even the thought of listening to those lies made him nauseous. He was a devil and if his mom ever found out what he did, she would never forgive him. Ray continued to stew in his own self-loathing while Don Ladrón droned on, hating himself a bit more with each word, but his mom's angry outburst tugged him back to the moment. She began laying into Don Ladrón. She called him names that no one even dared to think about the leader of Las Calles. She got in his face screaming that it was his fault that her son was exposed to violence. She blamed him and all the scum like him for turning her land of opportunities into a weak reflection of the hellhole she escaped in Mexico. She cursed him and his kind, invoking the names of saints that Ray had never heard of before. Finally, she threatened that if any of his people came anywhere near her or her son again she would unleash the fury of hell on them until nothing was left except scorched earth. Before anyone could react she grabbed Ray by the arm and dragged him back to the apartment. Ray could not believe that they were not mowed down by a tsunami of bullets as they walked away. After a few steps he heard Don Ladrón laughing and commenting about how spicy Latina women are. For a moment Ray's heart swelled with pride in his mom, but then they turned the corner and he saw Durito's corpse. He vomited. Again. Maria wiped his mouth with her shirt, covered his eyes with her hands, and led him inside. She sat him down on the bed and got her favorite towel. She went back to the doorway and gently scooped up the body with the towel, loving folding it around what was left of Durito like a final hug. She had nowhere to bury him and she couldn't afford cremation. She was left with only one option, so she was going to make it as respectful as possible. She grabbed a beer from the fridge, cradled the funeral package in one arm, and grabbed Ray's hand. The cold beer can pressed against Ray's hand and the sensation helped him to feel less numb, at least on his hand. Maria dragged Ray to the dumpster at the back of their apartment complex. Maria set the beer on the ground and looked into the large bin. It was too deep to reach over and gently place the makeshift coffin down, so she climbed in and found the least sticky place to lay the precious remains to rest. She climbed back out and said a prayer asking Saint Maria to guide Durito's soul to heaven and entreating Saint Peter to welcome him through the pearly gates like the hero she knew him to be. Ray watched his mother as she cried and pleaded with the Saints and felt that the guilt was going to overwhelm him. Maria picked up the beer and opened it, pouring the contents into the dumpster. Every moment of the funeral was agony for Ray. He silently screamed apologies to Durito's soul and cursed himself. Nothing Las Calles could offer him could make up for what he had to do to join them. He wished for nothing else but to go back in time and avoid getting sucked in. He would have gladly taken daily beatings if he could reverse the horrible thing he had done. His mom grabbing his hand and dragging him back to the apartment did little to bring him out of his stupor. When they got inside, Maria kneeled in front of Ray and apologized, "Lo siento mijo. Lo siento mucho." He looked up and saw the devastation etched in her face and couldn't contain his emotions anymore. He bawled and started hitting his fists on his stomach and legs. Each blow on his already bruised body shot bolts of pain through him and he knew he deserved every one. Maria tried to grab his hands to stop him but he couldn't stop. She tried to tell him it was ok, that he was safe, but it made it worse. Not being able to stand the remorse he felt, it broke through, cracking his voice as he confessed everything. Once the dam burst, there was no going back. He recounted every detail from the moment he met Don Ladrón at the movie theater to witnessing Las Calles kill the rival gang members to what Ray himself had done to Durito. He tried to explain that he had no choice, but it felt like an empty excuse. Maria just stared at him, mouth agape, eyes glistening. Ray wanted to die. He loved his mom more than anything and he had wounded her deeper than any gang banger ever could. The silence was unbearable. Ray opened his mouth to attempt an apology when Maria scooped him up in her arms and squeezed him tighter than ever before. He couldn't breathe and his entire body screamed out in pain but the feeling was euphoric. They held each other and cried for what seemed like hours. When they were finally able to speak again, Maria desperately apologized to Ray. She lamented not being there for him enough, for letting him fall prey to people like Don Ladrón and Lil Naco. She told him that she forgave him for everything. She stressed to him that he was not a bad person, he just did a bad thing. Ray showed Maria where he had hidden the guns from the gang murders. Maria grabbed the phone to call the police, but then put it down. She was undocumented. If they went to the police, she would probably get deported. After all she had been through to give her son a better life, this could throw it all away. They would risk ending up in a situation far worse than they were facing now. Maria looked at her son. His soul was wounded. She would not sit by and watch Las Calles steal the love from her little boy. She asked Ray what he wanted to do and assured him that no matter what he chose, she would stay by his side. Ray thought about what might happen. He was scared of the police and he didn't want his mom to be sent back to Mexico because of him. He thought about seeing the bodies of the two kids at the drug house and Durito. Durito wasn't afraid of anything. He took on dogs four times his size to protect the people he loved. His heart ached for his furry friend and fresh tears stained his cheeks. He looked up at his mom and told her he wanted to do the right thing. Maria retrieved the bag of guns and concealed them in a larger bag and they left for the police station.

Ama-gi blinked open her eyes. Ninlil spoke softly, "Now do you see?" Ama-gi reluctantly nodded her head. Ninlil continued, "Maria and Ray went to the police and told them everything. Ray has agreed to testify against Las Calles and with his knowledge of the inner workings of the gang, he can help put all of them in prison for a long time. The Solíz family are being placed in witness protection and Maria will be given citizenship with her new identity. They will finally be able to live a normal life away from the gang violence and poverty that has defined their life up to this point. Ray is going to bravely stand up against the evil that tried to draw him in and his testimony will effectively cripple Las Calles. Ray's light is so bright I was given a glimpse of his future. As it is now, he grows up to be a strong and caring man. After playing football throughout college, he decides to become a police officer. He eventually makes his way onto the gang unit and, with his experiences from his childhood, he is a valuable addition to the squad. He earns the respect of his peers and local council members and uses his influence to establish a community center that helps support at-risk youth and gives them an alternative to gangs. Iksuda may have sacrificed his life, but the act helped Ray find his path and in turn will save many lives. Don't be so quick to write off a soul. Everyone reacts differently to trauma. The boiling water that hardens the egg can soften the potato." Ama-gi regretted her rashness. "I suppose I was a bit too hasty in my condemnation. I just hope the fire that refined Ray doesn't destroy Iksuda." Ninlil sat back on her haunches and rubbed her front paw over her face. "Give Iksuda time to heal. Kahu, like humans, are more resilient than you give them credit for. That will all be resolved in its own time. For now we should discuss the vacancy in Iksuda's next Girru." Ama-gi was ready to leave the Solíz saga behind and move forward. "That's already taken care of. I'm handling it myself." Ninlil stood back up. Keeping her front paws forward and leaning her butt back, she pushed her chest to the floor in a stretch. "I'm glad to hear that. I will check on the Ni's destiny and convey the details to Ninimma. She will prepare for your departure." The felines bowed their heads to each other and Ninlil sauntered off to find a comfy spot in the Temple.

***

Ama-gi did one last round to make sure things in Barag were sorted during her absence. Dingir had informed her that Ki-Ang was responding well to his Ti therapy and would be returning around the same time Ama-gi was scheduled to complete her Girru. With all of her experienced Kahu currently in Girru or Ti, there was not much to be done in way of a counteroffensive against the most recent attacks by the Darkness. Things had calmed down again and it was decided that all Kahu in Girru would use that time on earth to gain intelligence while fulfilling their duties to their assigned Ni. There was most certainly another attack in the works, so the more they knew about this new evolution of the Gaudium Cleptes the better. The newest recruits were left in charge of Barag, with the gentle guidance of Dingir. Everything would be fine, but just in case she would cross all her toe beans for luck. Ninimma trotted up to Ama-gi and Ama-gi could tell she had something on her mind. "For the love of Dingir Ninimma, no more bad news please." Ninimma jerked her head up to meet Ama-gi's eyes. "No bad news I swear, only a request. Just a itty bitty, teeny tiny, minuscule really-" Ama-gi rolled her eyes "Nini!" Ninimma snapped her mouth shut and nodded, "Right. There is a new request for assignment from the readers. They caught the disturbance early so it is a meager level one assignment-" Ama-gi interrupted, "Give it to Maahes. He was due an assignment before everything went topsy turvy." Ninimma didn't seem satisfied , "Right well, here's the thing, I want to do it. I want the assignment." Ama-gi wasn't expecting such a request. Some Kahu specialized in field work and others excelled in a more supportive role. Ninimma was definitely the latter. Her vast knowledge and keen insight was a valuable resource and she always seemed to enjoy her role. In fact, she often complained loudly when asked to visit the earth plane. "What is the assignment? Why do you want to go?" Ama-gi asked. Ninimma brightened at the prospect that she might get her way. "The Ni is a little girl named Callie. She has such a sweet and beautiful light. She recently lost her mother and has been living with her father full time. Her parents were divorced you see. It was quite nasty a business. Her father is quite similar to a tomcat, always howling in a new yard if you get my meaning. He-" Ama-gi sighed loudly, "Nini, the assignment?" Ninimma cleared her throat nervously, "Right sorry. As I was saying, Callie is now living with her father and his girlfriend. This woman is quite a piece of work, very shallow and vapid. She has been harassing Callie quite harshly because well, because Callie is a bit… by current human beauty standards Callie would be considered Rubenesque." Ama-gi blinked, expecting an explanation so Ninimma elaborated. "Sir Peter Paul Rubens was a Flemish artist considered to be the most influential artist of the Flemish Baroque tradition in the 1600's. He was quite fond of painting full-figured females and had quite a talent for capturing the beauty of more shapely ladies. His style should have stayed in fashion. If it's not Baroque, don't fix it. That's my philosophy." Ninimma giggled at her cleverness, but seeing Ama-gi's patience waning, she got back to the point. "Anyway, Callie is beautiful, but she is being bullied into hating her body. I think I am particularly equipped to handle such a problem." Ninimma exaggeratedly shook her curvy behind. Ama-gi couldn't refute her logic. "Alright Ninimma, if you want it, take it. Just try to be back by the time Nuska, Ki-Ang, and I return. I will need your help moving forward." Ninimma closed her paw and pulled it towards her chest in victory. "One more thing Ama-gi. I would like to request Lumma's assistance. Callie has already lost her mom. I don't want to position myself as her pet since the Girru will be so short. She doesn't need to lose another member of her family." Ama-gi nodded her approval, "Granted". Ninimma was so excited she was prancing. "I have readied your brief at this scrying station. Once you have gone over it, you are cleared to proceed to Babu. Since this is a short Girru, you will enter the Girru as an adult stray cat and you will have to make your way to your Ni. Just be careful. You know how ferals can be when a strange cat appears in their territory. Be sure to keep your guard up." Ama-gi nodded, "Thanks Ninimma. Good luck to you as well."

    Ama-gi completed her preparation and made her way to Babu. She approached a huge stone archway. The grayish tan stone arch was guarded by two statues. The statue on the right was a large stone bull with eagle wings and a human's head. The statue on the left was a large stone lion with matching eagle wings and human head. Ama-gi passed through the arch to a lake. The water was not deep, nor was it wet for those worthy to pass upon it. She walked on the water to the center of the lake. Above her were billions of stars. The stars twinkled and were reflected by the surface of the water making the entire area seem to sparkle. At the center of the lake was a large whirlpool-like hole. Water poured over the sides into the hole in numerous waterfalls. Pale, seemingly colorless vegetation protruded from the sides of the deep hole. This was Babu, the gateway to the earth plane. All Kahu had to pass through this place to enter earth. The gatekeeper was in charge of sending the traveler to the correct time and place, be it Girru or Ti. No one had ever seen the gatekeeper and Ama-gi's curiosity to know their identity had long since dissipated. It was time for her to go. In a loud voice she called "Ati Me Peta Babka" which meant 'Gatekeeper, Open Your Gate for Me'. A soft light began emanating from deep within the hole. The vegetation that before was pale and lifeless began to take on a vibrant green color and sprout blooms of different colors. With a deep breath Ama-gi leapt.

CHAPTER THIRTEEN
CAT - Classic Autism Therapy

Leo sat in the oversized chair next to his mom. He was holding a Hoberman sphere and quietly expanding and collapsing it repeatedly. Chandra sat silently next to her son. Her eyes fell on the engraved name plate sitting on the desk in front of them. "Dr. Emmett Lewin". Chandra had been to many doctors with Leo. Everyone had a theory as to why he behaved like he did, but no two had the same theory. Leo was different. He was four years old but had yet to speak except for the odd single word demand, which was sometimes more of an insistent sound than a word. He did not interact with other children. He had already been banned from three daycare centers because of his 'unruly behavior" but Leo wasn't a bad kid, he was just particular. He had his quirks and if she let him do his thing, there was never any problem, but if she tried to get him to behave like other kids or how she thought a four year old should behave, he would throw epic tantrums. She had learned that when he was getting upset, he would flap his fingers, hitting the heel of his hands. She couldn't get him to stop for anything. One doctor had said he had ADHD because of his fidgeting and severe lack of attention, but Chandra didn't feel like that was the correct diagnosis. She wanted a suitable explanation. She wanted a solution that didn't involve drugging her son into a vegetative state. The doctor was taking forever. This was their follow up visit and Chandra was desperate for an answer. Chandra jumped at a quiet knock at the door. Dr. Lewin entered, greeted Chandra, and attempted to greet Leo, but Leo was completely focused on his toy and didn't even acknowledge that there were other people in the room. "So Mrs. Durant. How have things been with Leo?" Chandra did not care for the pleasantries. She wanted answers and waiting even a moment longer was torture, but decorum called for the exchange of dialogue before demanding results, so she went along with it. "Leo has been pretty much the same. He doesn't talk. He just watches his shows and will only eat macaroni or exactly four and a half dinosaur nuggets. My boyfriend tried to get him to play ball with him, but Leo just took the ball and stared at it for a long time. When Enzo raised his voice to try and get Leo's attention, Leo jumped up and ran to his rocking horse and just rocked on it for the next hour. I'm really worried. Leo is supposed to start kindergarten next year and the way he is now, I can't even keep him in daycare." Dr. Lewin nodded his understanding. "I do believe I have the answer to Leo's behavior. It is my professional opinion that Leo has Autistic Disorder." Chandra stared blankly at the doctor. He handed her a stack of stapled papers labeled 'What is Autistic Disorder?' The papers listed the DSM-IV criteria for Autistic Disorder and then broke each line down in layman's terms. He gave her a moment to read it over. The more she read the more the lines popped out at her;

>'impairment in the use of nonverbal behaviors such as eye-to-eye gaze - doesn't make eye contact.'

>'failure to develop peer relationships - doesn't make friends.'

>'lack of spontaneous seeking to share enjoyment, interests or achievements with other people - doesn't reach out to share joys.'

>'lack of social or emotional reciprocity - doesn't respond to others socially or emotionally.'

>'delay in, or total lack of, the development of spoken language - doesn't talk or limited speech.'

>'lack of varied, spontaneous, make-believe play or social imitative play - doesn't engage in play that mimics life like playing house.'

>'encompassing preoccupation with one or more stereotyped and restricted patterns of interest that is abnormal either in intensity or focus - shows hyper intense focus'

>'apparently inflexible adherence to specific nonfunctional routines or rituals - needs strict routine.'

>'stereotyped and repetitive motor mannerisms - finger flapping, rocking back and forth, twisting, etc.'

Chandra was shocked how many of the descriptions matched Leo exactly. When Dr. Lewin noticed she had stopped reading, he continued. "Leo exhibits numerous behaviors consistent with these criteria. So much so that I would even go as far as to describe him as 'textbook'. The good news is that with this new understanding of his behavior, we can better help him to interact with the world on his terms. The not so good news is that Leo will never be what one might consider a 'normal' child. We can help him to adjust the best he can, but some everyday activities, especially those involving socialization and deviation from routine will be extremely difficult for him." Chandra felt sick. How could this man sit in his pompous chair behind his fancy desk and tell her that her son won't be normal. What was her son's future going to look like? She wanted to scream at him and tell him he was wrong, but after reading the information he gave her, a part of her knew he might be right. She looked over at Leo. He was still focused on expanding his ball. She tried to stroke his hair but he pulled away, not once losing focus on his toy. Chandra could feel the tears gathering in her eyes and tried her best to hold them back. Dr. Lewin noticed Chandra struggling and broke the silence. "It is a very good thing that we caught this before he started school. There are special education schools that can create an individualized education program to help Leo with his development, both social and educational. We can find him specialists that will combine speech and language pathologist, special education, and occupational therapy to best meet all of Leo's developmental needs. Personally, I prefer a therapy called Applied Behavior Analysis. ABA is a behavioral modification approach that teaches the use of desirable behaviors and extinguishes problematic responses." Chandra felt a bit more relieved after listening to the doctor. He was actually presenting a plan for helping Leo that did not involve over-reliance on mediation. Her hope was extinguished by a creeping worry. All these treatments and experts sounded very expensive. She knew she was going to have a hard time convincing her boyfriend Enzo to invest in such fancy treatments. Enzo was a 'pull yourself up by your own bootstraps" kind of man. He thought force was enough to make Leo behave properly and he was constantly accusing her of coddling him too much. His favorite line was that his father beat the stupid out of him so a good whooping could do the same for Leo. Chandra would never allow Enzo to put a hand on Leo, but she knew he was getting frustrated. The last thing she wanted was a frustrated Enzo upset by outlandishly expensive 'woowoo' therapies. Chandra forced her attention back to Dr. Lewin. Before she confronted Enzo, she would be sure to absorb as much knowledge from the good doctor as she could.

**

Ama-gi sat curled up under a park bench. It had rained non-stop the day before and her fur was emanating the most horrendous odor. She looked down at her reflection in the puddle of water in front of the bench. Her eyes were large and bright yellow. She was lean and her face was slender. Her fur was short and the darkest hue of black she had ever seen. Ama-gi absolutely hated that she had been incarnated as a black cat. Humans had such stupid superstitions about black cats that it made the mission ten times more difficult than it needed to be. She would have to be on guard to avoid capture. Some disgusting humans thought it was righteous to torture and kill black cats in the name of their religion. Their misconstrued idealism disgusted her. Yes, darkness was bad, Darkness the entity not the color. Ama-gi grunted, she knew that to equate evil to something based solely on its outer color was asinine. However, this was the form that Ninimma chose, so it must serve a purpose. Still, Ama-gi found herself in a very foul mood. It had been ages since she was on Earth and she had forgotten how uncomfortable it was. She felt pain, she was hungry, she was cold, and everything just felt heavy. A human with a small dog approached the bench. The small dog looked at Ama-gi, sniffed, and then began to growl. Ama-gi had had just about enough of Earth and she had only been here for three days. She lost her temper and attacked the small dog, sending it, and its owner running. She hid further under the bench and continued growling out of spite. Ninimma had put in her report that this park was frequented by the Ni but with the rain, the park had been a ghost town. Ama-gi knew she wouldn't be able to wait much longer. She needed to find food but the idea of stalking a bird through the mud and consuming something raw just didn't appeal to her. "Why is the Earth plane so savage and unclean?" She thought to herself. A noise on the other side of the park caught her attention. A small child with dark brown hair and chubby cheeks was fussing and fighting his mother. The woman was tall and had defined upper body muscles, probably from trying to control a difficult child. The woman's hair was short and just a tad lighter than the boy's. The boy was trying to take a bag out of his mom's very large purse and she was trying to stop him. "Leo, we are not going to eat lunch in the park today. It is wet and dirty. We can eat at home." Leo was not happy with this deviation from their normal routine and was irritated and violent. He was making grunting sounds and hitting himself and his mother. In the struggle, Leo ripped open the bag and Ama-gi could smell the delicious aroma of food. Her nose began to sniff the air and with a mind of its own it dragged her towards the scene. When she got close, Leo noticed her and stopped in his tracks. They just stared at each other for a moment. When Chandra noticed the wild cat she reacted by grabbing Leo and lifting him up. Dropping her bag in the process. Leo did not take kindly to being man-handled and started flailing his arms and legs. Chandra had no choice but to put him back down. Even at four he was too big for her to control anymore. The moment his feet touched the ground, he ran directly toward Ama-gi. Chandra was frozen with shock. Leo had never shown any interest in another human being, yet he was looking directly at this stray cat and showing interest in interacting with it. Before she could react, Leo reached the cat and grabbed at it. Ama-gi was not pleased with the grabby hands, and swatted him, but did not employ her claws. Leo fell onto his butt and stared at the cat in shock, but the most amazing thing to Chandra was that he was making eye contact with this cat. Chandra tried to take Leo's hand and pull him towards home but he resumed his earlier fit. Knowing that she didn't have the strength or willpower to fight with him for three more blocks, she gave in to his demands. She took a throw blanket out of her bag and placed it on the driest patch of sidewalk she could find. Leo promptly and pleasantly fell back into their routine. He got up and calmly went to his usual spot on the blanket. He waited for his mom to get his food out and place it in its usual place in front of him. Ama-gi discreetly followed and situated herself nearby. Chandra opened a small bowl of macaroni and cheese and a Tupperware container with five dinosaur shaped chicken nuggets. When Leo saw the five he became upset and pushed the container away. Chandra tried to push it back towards him but that only caused him to become more upset. "I'm sorry Leo, I didn't have time to cut it this morning before our appointment with Dr. Lewin. Can't you just eat five today?" Leo was ramping up to a full meltdown. This was the third time today that they had deviated from their normal routine and the change was too much for him. Chandra knew that she was fighting a losing battle so she quickly grabbed one of the nuggets and broke it in half and placed it back in the container. Leo immediately picked up the unwanted half and threw it as far as he could. Ama-gi did not waste the opportunity. She raced after the discarded piece of chicken and gobbled it down greedily. Leo watched her with such extreme focus that his mom was worried he was scared and headed towards another meltdown, but Leo did the last thing she would have ever expected. Leo's eyes grew wide and he burst out in uncontrollable laughter. Laughter. She had never heard him laugh. He had displayed the occasional amused mumblings when watching his cartoons, but never full blown laughter. Leo grabbed the other half of the chicken nugget and threw that at the cat before Chandra could stop him. Again, Ama-gi gobbled it up resulting in a roar of laughter from Leo. Chandra couldn't help herself. She began crying. As hard as she had been trying, nothing she did was able to break through her son's impenetrable walls. Yet here was a small, scroungy cat that, within five minutes, was able to form a connection with her son that she had only dreamed of. Leo had thrown two more of his nuggets to the cat before he decided to eat one himself. He then took two bites of the final nugget and threw the rest to the cat. He calmly finished the rest of his meal and his juice box never taking his focus off the cat. Time seemed to stand still as Leo stared at and silently interacted with his new friend. He even managed to scoot closer to the cat, who was content lying near them. After about an hour a loud rumble in the sky let Chandra know it was time to go home. "Leo, we have to go home baby. It's going to rain." She packed the food containers back into the bag and pulled Leo up so she could put away the blanket. Leo was content staring at the cat until Chandra tried to pull him towards home. He grunted his disapproval and tried to pull away but Chandra held firm. She braced herself for the tantrum and struggle she knew was coming, but to her amazement, the cat, who Leo was still fixated on, got up and approached them, passing by and turning around expectantly. Leo turned and calmly followed the cat. Chandra started walking home and the cat eagerly walked beside them. Leo mumbled happily, like he was speaking to the cat. He even gestured occasionally. Chandra was stupefied. When they arrived home, the cat waited at the door with them and, not needing an invitation, walked in with Leo. Chandra looked at the weathered animal and said "Well Leo, I guess we have a cat now."

***

Chandra had managed to bathe the cat and get it to the vet. They scanned it for a chip and with nothing coming back determined that she was a stray. It wasn't a hard decision to keep the cat. Leo absolutely adored her and even started using a word to refer to her. He called her "Tat" in his attempt to say 'cat' and it stuck. Chandra knew she should have asked her boyfriend for permission before deciding to keep the cat, but he was a truck driver and was gone for days at a time. She hoped that when he saw how much progress Leo was making that he would be as happy as she was.

Ama-gi was settling into her assignment. She really liked the boy. His neurodivergence made him unique and entirely his own individual self. It was like he was unspoiled by social influence. She even liked the name Tat. Leo's innocence made Tat feel extremely protective of him but with a desire to instruct him as well. Leo often tried to open the door and go outside by himself, but Tat was now a dedicated babysitter. Any time Leo would head towards the door, Tat would block his way and smack at him until he gave up. She knew never to use claws with the boy, everyone else was fair game. Her overprotective nature and disdain for anyone other than her two humans earned Tat the reputation of being 'spicy'. However, Chandra saw the softer side of Tat. Tat always slept with Leo and would cuddle with him when he needed calming. Her presence alone seemed to keep him centered. He was less nervous whenever Tat was around. Chandra even got Tat a harness and leash so they could all go to the park together. At first the attention from the other kids made Leo nervous and he acted out, but after a few trips and under the firm guiding paw of Tat, Leo grew accustomed to the presence of the other children. He still would not attempt to play with them or even acknowledge them but he was comfortable with them approaching him and Tat. It was almost like he was making friends. One day a little girl that they had seen at the park multiple times brought Leo a cookie. Chandra tried to explain that he is a very picky eater and doesn't usually accept strangers, but was stopped mid sentence as Leo took the cookie and reached back in an attempt to pat the girl on the shoulder. He refused to look at her but made an effort to interact. Chandra burst into tears and hugged the girl's mom. "I have no words. This is the first time he has ever interacted with another child. Thank you. Thank you for such a wonderful gift. I think she may be Leo's first friend." Both mom's were emotional and spent the afternoon chatting while the children played with Tat. On their walk home Chandra silently marveled at Tat's behavior. She was perplexed that a cat that was so antisocial with most adults could be so incredibly gentle with children, especially a child like Leo with special needs. That night Chandra spent extra time cleaning the house and making Leo presentable with a fresh haircut and a new outfit for tomorrow. Enzo was scheduled to get home and she wanted everything to be perfect. She had told him about Tat over the phone and he had not seemed pleased, but she had explained how much it was helping Leo and he seemed to accept the idea. He only made the demand that when he was home that the cat wasn't allowed in the bedroom. Chandra was pleased. Tat always slept with Leo, so the demand was easy to follow.

The next morning Chandra was buzzing with nervous energy. She made breakfast for Leo and then prepared a large breakfast for two. She kept looking at the clock and fussing with Leo's hair. Tat watched Chandra with Leo. She was a bit perplexed about this assignment. She had yet to see any signs of darkness. Chandra obviously loved her son and Leo was unique, but Tat didn't see anything wrong with him. She knew that he faced challenges thanks to the rigid demands of society that rarely made concessions for those with a different approach to life. Before the thoughts could further progress in her mind a chill fell upon her. The hair down her spine stood on end. She needed no reminder as to what this sensation meant. It had been almost a century since she faced the darkness in the flesh, but that had not dulled her senses in the least. She began making a low grumbling sound and moved herself in between Leo and the door. Leo sensed the change in Tat and started to get nervous and fuss. Tat calmed herself for his sake but stayed alert. She heard keys in the door and prepared herself to attack the intruder, but Chandra ran to the door and swung it open. She hugged the man standing on the step, but he only half-heartedly hugged her back before removing her arms and pushing through the door. He threw his duffel bag on the sofa and headed to the table. Tat watched every step. She could see darkness flowing off him like stench lines in a comic book. Now she understood the mission. To Tat's surprise, it seemed like Leo could see, or at the very least sense, it too. From the moment the man entered, Leo was agitated. The man gracelessly sat at the table and began eating before Chandra could join him. "Hey Leo. No hello for me buddy?" Leo began flapping his fingers and saying "Tat" on repeat. Tat ran to the side of the table and meowed until Chandra helped Leo down. He just sat on the floor with Tat as she cuddled with him and rubbed her forehead on his. "So this is the cat?" Chandra was excited to share all the breakthroughs that she felt Leo had made since Tat entered their life, but Enzo's lack of excitement diminished her spirit. She didn't want to annoy him with something he had no interest in. "Yes, that's right. She has really been a Godsend with Leo." Enzo was more impressed with his breakfast. "Where is the jam for my toast? You always forget the jam." Chandra went to the fridge and brought back the rhubarb jam. Enzo looked up at her and then to Leo, "The boy still ain't talkin' though." Chandra was disappointed. Enzo never really listened to her and she was getting very tired of his cutdowns towards Leo. She knew that if he would just spend more time with him, that he would understand him a lot more. Chandra picked up his toast to add the jam, "Remember I told you that the doctor said he has Autistic Disorder? He probably won't improve much verbally until he sees the specialists I told you about. But he has been doing a lot better with his tantrums and he even started gesturing. Maybe you could go with us to the park today. I know you will be impressed by-" Enzo cut her off. "Damn it Chandra you know I like the toast buttered before the jam goes on. Just give it to me if you're not going to do it right." He grabbed the toast and knife from her. "I'm not going to the park with you. I just got home, can't you give me even one damn day to relax before you start in on your nagging and demands?!" Tat watched as darkness gathered together in a rough form and launched itself towards Chandra. She stepped back like she could feel the impact, but Tat knew that Leo's mom was completely oblivious to the form being hurled at her. Leo on the other hand was very agitated. Tat was fascinated that Leo seemed to react to the Darkness like he was aware of it. It was thought that only the Kahu could see the Darkness. There had been some cases of human bodhisattvas who were able to sense the Darkness, but other humans had long since lost the ability to see such things. Tat kept her eyes on the Darkness and made sure she was in a good position to protect Leo. Just as she had expected, the Darkness lurking around Enzo formed itself into a pointed shaft and shot towards Leo. Tat crouched til the last second then pounced on the evil form, clawing it to the ground and breaking up the energy. The movement caught Chandra's eye but didn't seem to faze Enzo. She rushed to her son, "You're right, I'm sorry. We are just excited to have you back is all. Please don't raise your voice around Leo, it will just upset him." Enzo grabbed his plate and aggressively pushed back from the table, storming off into the master bedroom mumbling about how he couldn't even enjoy his breakfast in peace. Chandra sighed. Enzo used to be so loving. When Leo was a baby, Enzo doted on him and treated her like a princess. She was convinced that he was her knight in shining armor, but as time passed he began to change. He developed such a terrible temper. Chandra tried to be understanding. Enzo had grown up with a very abusive father and a paranoid mother. No one had ever protected him and she knew his temper was just a response to him feeling unsafe. If she could just be a bit stronger or a bit more supportive, then she knew he would go back to being the sweet, caring man she fell in love with. It had to be work. Being on the road for those long hours, not being able to relax or have the support of his family had to be stressing him out. Chandra chided herself for adding more pressure and vowed to be more understanding. Enzo was having a hard time and being the strong woman that she was, she should support him through it. After all, she wouldn't dream of giving up on Leo because of a meltdown, so why should she feel any different with Enzo? Tat watched as Enzo left, leaving a haze of shadow behind him. Tat quickly traced his steps swatting at the leftover darkness, chasing it around like a laser pointer. Leo laughed at her antics. If she didn't know any better, she would have believed that Leo was aware of what she was doing. The boy really did fascinate her. Chandra also took notice and released her nervousness through laughter, albeit quietly so Enzo wouldn't hear and think she was laughing at him.

***

  Things got progressively worse over the week. As hard as Chandra tried to keep the peace, everything she was doing seemed to be triggering Enzo. She did her best to confine their arguments to their bedroom, away from Leo, but the house seemed to be getting smaller and smaller. Chandra put Leo to bed and went to relax in bed with Enzo, who was watching some sort of sitcom. She tried to put her head on his chest but he pushed her away "Babe can you not. It is hot." She settled on her side of the bed but was moving around too much and Enzo slammed his fist on the bed. "Chandra! Would you stop moving!" She froze up. She tried to not even breathe but as her luck would have it her back started cramping. She did every distraction technique she could think of to ignore the pain and stay still, but the pain got to be too much and she tried slowly lifting her hips to adjust without disturbing Enzo. "Damn it Chandra! I am trying to watch this show. If you can't stop fidgeting would you mind kindly getting the hell out of here? Your restlessness is getting on my nerves. You know what? I just need you to go away and leave me alone." Chandra felt dejected, but to avoid an argument she decided to go to the kitchen for some tea. She had bought a book on Autistic Disorder and she could use the time to read. She sat down with her chamomile tea and opened her book. Not even one page in, Enzo came into the living room. "You couldn't even be bothered to offer me some tea?" Chandra was caught off guard, she put a bookmark to hold her place and responded "Sorry, what?" Enzo's face started to turn red. "Don't play dumb. You came out here and made yourself some tea and didn't even bother to offer to make me some." Chandra was shocked, "But you told me to leave you alone. I didn't want to bother you. Would you like me to make you some?" She started to get up but Enzo's yell scared her back down. "You are so selfish! Are you trying to piss me off? I really think you like upsetting me. What is it? Do you enjoy fighting with me? Do you get some weird kick out of making me mad?" Chandra was fighting back tears. "No. No, I'm sorry. You're right. It was selfish of me not to ask. Don't be mad." She got up and grabbed her tea. "Here you can have this one." As she tried to hand him the mug, he knocked the mug back at her, spilling hot tea all over her arm and onto her leg. Chandra screamed out in pain and Enzo stormed out, slamming the bedroom door behind him. Chandra rushed to the bathroom and ran cool water over her arm and leg. She sat on the ground in the shower and cried. She was tired. She wanted to be strong and supportive, but this was too much. She wanted things to be different. She wanted the man she had fallen in love with. She didn't want to be alone again and Leo needed a father figure. Leo wasn't good with change and Enzo was the only father he had ever known. She should be strong for Leo's sake, or at least that is what she told herself. Perhaps she was just too afraid of the unknown. Things were bad, but it was a bad she was familiar with. Chandra was terrified that if she left things could be way worse. Things here had to get better, they couldn't get any worse.

CHAPTER FOURTEEN
Haute Kottur

Callie sat in her room chewing on her candy bar. She felt empty inside and even the comfort of her favorite chocolate bar couldn't penetrate the vast cloud of sadness rapidly expanding within her. She was mindlessly staring at a framed photo of her and her mother on the nightstand. She took another big bite of chocolate in an attempt to block the pain bubbling up. The sadness and chocolate seemed to collide in her throat and create a lump that she could neither release nor swallow. From the other room she heard her dad and her grandma arguing about what to do with her mother's things. Her dad wanted to sell everything but her grandmother wanted to keep everything in storage until Callie was older and could decide what she wanted to do with everything. Callie's mother Demmi had suffered a sudden cardiac death. Callie's parents were divorced and Callie had lived full time with her mom. She has not seen her dad for a few years as he lived in a different state. They talked on the phone on special occasions like Christmas or Callie's birthday, but to Callie he was more of a distant acquaintance than a father. Callie's grandma had offered to take custody of Callie, but her father insisted that she should live with him. The changes were all happening too fast and Callie was feeling scared and overwhelmed on top of her grief. Demmi did not have a will, so the laws of the state dictated that the whole of her estate should go to her daughter. Since Callie was only eleven and her father was taking custody of her, the decisions about what to do with the house and all Demmi's assets fell to him as Callie's guardian. He had already decided to sell the house and put all liquid assets into a trust for Callie, but his girlfriend, Cashlin, was pressuring him to sell everything because she said they would need the money to cover the expenses of taking care of a child. Callie's grandma didn't want to let go of the only mementos she had of her daughter. As the arguing grew louder and more heated, Callie escaped into her mom's bedroom. All her mom's clothes were piled on the bed in different stacks. Callie pushed them all together and crawled onto the pile like a nest. She pulled a large coat, her mother's favorite, over the top of her clothing roost and closed her eyes. She could smell the faint scent of her mother. She pulled the clothes closer around herself and imagined that she was in her mother's warm embrace. The realization that this was as close to her mother's touch as she would ever be, crushed her. She couldn't breath but at the same time desperately needed to immerse herself even deeper in the memories. Someone entered the room and Callie heard the sound of plastic rustling. A woman's voice yelled, "Braant, I'm just going to separate her clothes for the yard sale and donation." Callie heard drawers being opened and felt more clothes being thrown on the bed. The woman continued talking to herself. "Oh my god. These are so hideous. There is no way we are going to get any kind of money for any of this garbage. I'm not sure the thrift shop would even want this. How did she manage to leave the house in this? Was she allergic to fashion? What is this? A mumu? Gross. How many X's can you fit on a size tag?" The woman was amusing herself with her thoughtless chatter while Callie fought to control the rage bubbling up inside her. Suddenly, a hand ripped away the coat concealing Callie in her den. Callie grabbed the edge of the coat and pulled it back towards her. The resistance scared the woman and she screamed. "For fu- I mean for Pete's sake Callie. You scared me half to death! Oh shoot. Sorry. I didn't mean to say death. I'm not trying to remind you of your dead mom. Damn it. I mean darn it. You startled me is all." The woman composed herself and her demeanor changed as Callie's father entered the room. The woman tried to soften her voice and appear as sweet as honey. "Everything is ok Braant. This little girl just scared the bejesus out of me. She was hiding in here, quiet as a mouse." Callie didn't speak, she only ripped the coat from the woman's hands and wrapped it tightly around herself. A flash of shock and anger danced across the woman's face but she quickly controlled herself and leaned towards Callie. "Now sweetheart, I'm trying to organize your mama's things so we can donate them, so I need you to stop knocking over the piles. Ok hun?" She paused and quickly looked at Braant to gauge his reaction. Unsatisfied with his expression she turned back to the girl. "You can help me if you want to. Why don't we work on it together?" Callie grabbed a few more of the items of clothing laying near her. "I don't want to donate mom's clothes. I want to keep them. I want to keep her mug collection too. And her gnomes. She loved her things and wouldn't want them to get dumped at a stupid thrift shop." Braant sat on the bed next to his daughter. "Callie, I know this is hard for you. I know you want to keep as much of your mother around as you can, but we talked about this. Our house is not big enough for all our things, your things, and your mother's things. I thought we agreed to donate them so they could go to people who really need them." Callie began to tear up, "I really need them! Can't grandma keep the stuff for me?" Braant sighed. He was way out of his depth. He cared about his daughter, but he had no clue how to deal with a child, especially one in desperate need of comfort. "Callie, Cashlin had a really good idea. She wanted to do a yard sale with all the stuff you don't need anymore, then when we get back to Connecticut, Cashlin can take you on a shopping spree. She is a fashionista and you two can make it a girl's day with a spa trip and everything that girls do." Cashlin eagerly nodded. "That's right, we can update your entire wardrobe. We'll take you from Southern Chic to Haute Couture." Callie didn't care about any of that. She wanted her mother back. She didn't want to move to a new place and change her style. She wanted the life she had, but all that was gone now and everything she was used to, everything she loved, was being ripped away from her so she could better fit into her dad's life. Callie's grandma looked in and saw the pain on Callie's face and the bewilderment on Braant's face. Without hesitation she pushed past Cashlin and Braant and grabbed Callie in a tight hug. She cooed to Callie in her sweet southern drawl "This is hard for me too baby girl. How 'bout this? I have four big boxes in my car. Why don't you pick out your favorite things from you mama's stuff and whatever you can fit in those boxes I will keep at my house for you. The rest of the stuff you can sell. I know your mama would want you to have the money so you can get nice things for yourself and not just hold on to her old junk. She liked her stuff but she loved you." Callie nodded while tears poured down her cheeks and she relaxed into her grandma's hug. Braant was not amused that Demmi's mom used the opportunity to undermine him, but he acquiesced for Callie's sake.

***

A year had passed and Callie was beginning to realize that adults were liars. Everyone told her that loss gets easier with time. Callie was discovering that this was in no way true. Time did not make things easier, it only increased the emptiness growing inside her. Her dad kept telling her that she would get settled and feel better, but all she felt was isolated and resented. Her dad tried to hide it, but Callie could tell he was having a hard time adjusting to her full-time presence in his life. Her dad and Cashlin used to take romantic weekend trips to Nantucket or Martha's Vineyard a few times a month, but now he either had to take her along or find a sitter and Cashlin definitely preferred the latter. Cashlin did try to connect with Callie at first. She tried to get Callie to do facials, go shopping, or get manicures but Callie just wasn't interested in those sorts of things. Callie missed cooking with her mom or going out to a movie and ice cream. Cashlin was always following the newest diet fad. She wouldn't allow 'cheat' foods in the house and since Braant couldn't go anywhere without Cashlin, and Cashlin refused to do anything that might derail her diet, Callie never got to do the things she liked to do. After a particularly embarrassing incident, Cashlin stopped asking Callie to go shopping with her altogether. The final time Cashlin tried to connect with Callie, she took her to some fancy department store and had picked out a few outfits for Callie to try on. Callie tried to tell her that the items were too small, but Cashlin was convinced they would look great if Callie just 'sucked it in". Callie did what she was told but when she exited the dressing room to show Cashlin the look, the seam next to the zipper ripped and compressed sections of Callie's side burst forth like a popped can of biscuits. The changing room attendant gasped, Cashlin looked horrified, and Callie ran back into the dressing room in tears. From that point on, Cashlin made a point to say that real fashion only came in certain sizes. Callie didn't fit those sizes so she was excluded. The more isolated Callie became, the more she turned to food to fill the void. Comfort food reminded her of her mom and every time she snuck to eat junk food it was like she was getting a little piece of her old life back. However, her coping strategy was turning into a destructive cycle. The more she felt alone, the more she ate. The more she ate, the more she gained weight. The more weight she gained, the more isolated she became from her family and peers causing her to feel alone. Callie had always been, as her grandma called it, big-boned, but since she moved in with her dad she had gone past big-boned to, as Cashlin called it, porky. Her dad had tried to get her into sports, but Callie just didn't feel like being active. It was not that she was lazy. She wanted to be active, but she felt heavy. A heaviness that had nothing to do with her physical weight. Callie's weight problems were really driving a wedge between her and her father. Braant was worried that Callie's weight was affecting her health. Demmi had suffered from type two diabetes, so much so that it ultimately led to her untimely death. Braant did not want to see the same thing happen to Callie. He constantly pushed her to exercise, join gymnastics, try swimming, anything he could think of that might get her to be more active. He tried to force her to eat healthy, but didn't have the heart to deny her the one form of comfort she relied on. He meant well, but his constant focus on her weight did more to warp Callie's view of her body than to motivate a healthier routine. Cashlin was not as solicitous in her interactions with Callie about her body. She hated being seen with Callie. She was constantly worried that people would think she was a bad mom for having an overweight child and made sure to point out that Callie was not her daughter. Callie's physical appearance was the epitome of Cashlin's fears for herself. Therefore, Callie became an affront to Cashlin's ego. Cashlin would never say anything in front of Braant and any time Callie tried to complain to her dad about Cashlin's remarks, Cashlin would play it off like a concern for Callie rather than what it was, blatant bullying. It started out small with little comments like "A moment on the lips, a lifetime on the hips." Or "You'd be so pretty if you were thinner." But progressed to flat out insults and constant criticism. The unrelenting digs were slowly chipping away at Callie and she began to believe what Cashlin said about her. Callie wanted Cashlin to like her. No one would ever replace her mom, but Cashlin was the closest thing she had to a female role model. Callie probably wouldn't have been so impacted if it was just Cashlin saying mean things, but it wasn't just Cashlin saying critical things. Everywhere she went she heard snide comments about her weight. "Oh, how unfortunate to be so heavy." Or "Her parents really should do something to help her instead of enabling such destructive behavior." "Poor thing. Food addiction is unforgiving." Callie couldn't even enjoy a meal in public anymore without choking on the judgement of others. School was worse. She was bullied mercilessly. Kids would draw pictures of pigs or cows and tape them to her locker. Her nickname around school was 'Cowie" usually accompanied by mooing sounds. After suffering so much abuse, Callie was at the end of her rope. She made the decision to fit in at any cost. Food, the thing that had always been a comfort, had become her enemy. Callie began skipping meals. She would avoid the cafeteria at lunch time and avoid dinner altogether if her dad was gone. Cashlin didn't seem to notice whether or not Callie skipped meals. She only noticed if she saw Callie eating. On the occasions that Callie was forced to eat with her dad, she would eat as little as possible then force herself to throw up afterwards. Between the starvation and purging, Callie was losing a little bit of weight, but not enough to satisfy her bullies. To make matters worse, the negative change in her eating habits had started wreaking havoc on her body's systems. Her hormones were way out of balance resulting in severe acne. The times she couldn't avoid eating and forced herself to purge was causing problems with her salivary glands and was causing severely bad breath. The lack of desired results despite her extreme methods made her feel worthless and ashamed. These feelings began to lead Callie to self-harming behavior. It started small. She started wearing girdles in an attempt to conceal her fat rolls, then she turned to wide belts and would tighten them until they cut into her skin. She would hold ice packs on her larger areas in an attempt to freeze the fat off her body. None of these actions made any difference in her weight, but the pain helped her mediate the feelings of shame and gave her a sense of control. The unhealthy behaviors went on, gradually increasing, for almost two months. Callie's school performance was suffering so much that her teacher called Braant to request a parent-teacher conference.

  Callie was forced to wait in the classroom after the bell. She sat at her desk at the back of the room and picked at a scab on her knuckle. Cashlin walked through the door. She had on a pair of oversized sunglasses with diamonds on the outer rims. Her outfit was a white low-rise pleated mini skirt, white tube top with a light blue collarless leather jacket, and matching light blue Jimmy Choo pumps. Her look was completed with a Louis Vuitton Centenaire Chelsea Bag. Callie was far from a girly girl, but she did admire the opulence of her makeshift stepmother. She was petite and thin and everyone thought she was pretty. Cashlin looked at the clock, not bothering to hide her annoyance. Braant walked in the door with a self-assured stride. He was handsome, no doubt about that. Her mom had told her that she had always thought Braant was good-looking, even when he had a bit more chubbiness to him. When Callie asked her mother why they weren't married anymore, Demmi told her that they had grown apart. The truth was that as Braant got older he had become obsessed with his appearance and dedicated all his free time to working out and changing his style. After he had achieved his goals, he felt that Demmi wasn't on his level physically and decided he was no longer attracted to her. Braant had been ok with setting off for bachelor life and found his match in Cashlin. The teacher finally walked in to begin the meeting. "Hello Mr. And Mrs. Mitchell-' Cashlin interrupted the teacher. "Oh no no, we are not married… yet. I'm just Miss

Foley for now." The teacher was a bit annoyed at the unnecessary interruption but continued. "Okay, my mistake. Thank you for coming to meet with me Mr. Mitchell and Miss Foley. I'll get right to the point. I am worried about Callie. Her school performance has deteriorated rapidly over the past month. She doesn't pay attention in class and her ability to concentrate seems to be suffering. Some of the teachers, myself included, have noticed some physical changes in Callie that have us concerned. Has she been having any medical concerns that we should be aware of?" Braant looked over his shoulder at Callie. "No. No medical issues that I am aware of. We have been trying to better regulate her diet. Her mother, god rest her soul, was a bit too indulgent with her and it has been a struggle to get her to give up those bad food habits. But other than that, she is healthy, as far as I know." The teacher continued cautiously. "Has Callie ever been checked out by a doctor for possible learning disabilities or challenges? A learning disability can sometimes cause severe stress and affect a child's physical health." Braant started to get a bit defensive. "Are you trying to say my daughter is dumb?" Cashlin chimed in, "Babe she is a bit slow to respond sometimes. I'm sure her teacher is just trying to help." The teacher tried to get ahead of the rising tension. "Forgive me Mr. Mitchell, it was not my intention to imply that Callie lacks intelligence. She is a very smart girl and until recently has been a very dedicated student. Hence my concern that she may have some sort of health or minor developmental challenge that has been giving her a difficult time. I would like for all of us to have a conversation with Callie and try to discover what might be causing the focus issues in class." Braant nodded, "Callie, come here and have a talk with me and Mrs. Lehrer." Callie stood to head towards the front of the classroom but before she could take her first step the room began to spin and then everything went dark.

    A rhythmic beeping lulled Callie into a sense of peace as she blinked open her eyes. She looked around in dazed confusion as her surroundings began to materialize. She was no longer in her classroom, but a hospital room with saffron walls and wall stickers of dump trucks and hot air balloons. Her dad was sitting in a chair near her bed and sat forward when he noticed that she was awake. "Hey kiddo. Welcome back. You really scared me there. How are you feeling?" Callie just shrugged. Braant didn't really know what to do. The nurse passed by and noticed that

Callie was awake, "Oh, it's good to see your beautiful eyes! I'll let the doctor know you are awake. You want any water or anything darlin'?" Callie didn't speak, she only shook her head. Callie and Braant sat in uncomfortable silence waiting for the doctor. The silence made the machine noises and hospital soundtrack sound as loud as a rock concert. After what seemed like a lifetime, they heard a commotion outside the door. Cashlin burst through the door, followed closely by the doctor. She ran to Callie and draped herself over the girl in a very showy hug. Not using her indoor voice, Cashlin moaned, "Oh my poor Callie! I was soooooo worried about you!" Callie looked at her father, obviously confused. Perhaps she had woken up in a parallel universe where Cashlin actually cared about her, but one glance at the young and very good-looking male doctor helped Callie understand the performance. The doctor stood by awkwardly as Cashlin superficially fawned over Callie until Braant intervened. "Cashlin, would you just come here and sit down so the doctor can do his job? Please?" Cashlin made sure to pass closely by the doctor and grip his arm, "Thank you so much doctor, for taking care of our sweet little girl." The doctor could smell a faint hint of alcohol on her breath, but didn't think it was out of the ordinary for a worried parent to have a drink to calm their nerves. The doctor turned his attention to Callie. "Hi Callie. My name is Dr. Galen. Can I ask you a few questions?" Callie didn't speak, only nodded her consent. "Great. When was the last time you had anything to eat or drink?" Callie thought for a moment and shrugged. The doctor pressed a bit harder. "I need you to think real hard for me, ok? Did you eat breakfast today?" Callie thought about lying so she didn't get in trouble, but the kindness in the doctor's eyes urged her towards honesty. She shook her head no. Braant tried to make an excuse, "We have been really busy, she probably was just running late for school and forgot." The doctor briefly nodded to Braant but kept his attention on Callie. "Do you skip breakfast a lot?" Callie nodded and the doctor's calm response motivated her to elaborate. "I don't like eating breakfast. It gives me a stomach ache." The doctor kept his voice calm. "It does, that's too bad. I love breakfast. How about lunch? Do you eat lunch at school? What do you normally eat at lunch?" Callie paused. She didn't really want to admit that she had been skipping lunch too but she was finding it hard to think of a lie that would fool the doctor. "I dunno. Maybe like uh, maybe a apple or like granola or something like that." The doctor made a 'hmmm' sound and made a couple of notes on his clipboard. "Do you like snacks? I used to like string cheese for snacks, but my mom always gave us oatmeal cookies. Do you usually eat any snacks during the day?" Callie got pulled into the conversation and let her guard down. "My mom and me used to make Cowboy cookies every Sunday or sometimes we'd make pinwheel cookies or snickerdoodles or pies and she'd let me snack on those after school, but I don't have those anymore. I'm too fat for that sugary stuff." The doctor tried to make light of the admission. "What? You are just right, kids are supposed to have cookies occasionally. It helps you grow tall. I know cause I'm a doctor." Callie laughed but shook her head. "You're silly. I know that stuff isn't good." The doctor didn't push. "Ok. Well apart from skipping the sweets, when was the last time you ate a full meal?" Callie looked up and off to the side while she thought. Braant interrupted, "We all ate dinner together the night before last." Callie nodded. The doctor looked directly into Callie's eyes. "That's good. How did your stomach feel after that dinner? Did you keep everything down or did it come back up?" Callie looked away embarrassed. "I think I ate too much and it made me sick." The doctor looked at her with compassionate understanding. "Mmhmm, Does that happen a lot? Getting sick after you eat?" Callie looked at her dad and Cashlin and back at the doctor and sheepishly nodded. Braant was finally catching on. He sighed and clenched his jaw. Cashlin was still cluelessly ogling the doctor. Dr. Galen made a few additional notes on the chart and documented some of the numbers from the machine next to the bed. "Okay Callie. Thank you for talking with me. I'm going to step out and chat with your dad for a second. If you need anything you can press this button right here. Dad will be back in really soon. Okay?" Callie nodded. Braant and Cashlin followed Dr. Galen into the hall. Braant practically jumped on the doctor with his question. "So what is this? Some kind of stomach bug or digestive problem that is keeping her from eating?" The doctor cocked his head slightly. "Mr. Mitchell. After looking at Callie's blood work, ecg, and talking to her, I believe your daughter has a very severe eating disorder. I'm not an expert on eating disorders, but just based on what I have seen I would say that Callie is showing aspects of Anorexia Nervosa and Bulimia Nervosa. She admitted that she rarely eats and when she does, she throws up. I can see signs on her hands and in her mouth that suggest that the throwing up after meals is purposeful purging and not a stomach issue. Callie has abnormal electrolyte levels, hypotension, low thyroid levels, and bradycardia. These are all signs present in individuals with eating disorders. Also, I don't think this is a recent development. Based on her blood work levels, acne, hair thinning, halitosis, etc. I would say this has been going on for over a month if not several months. It probably has been building up for a long time." Cashlin finally decided to chime in, "But doctor, I don't understand. How can Callie have anorexia? She's chubby. Anorexia is like a problem for really skinny models. If anything Callie eats too much. I mean look at her, there is no way she is starving herself." Dr. Galen was beginning to suspect where Callie's issue might be coming from but answered as respectfully as he could. "I have looked at her. Eating disorders affect people of all shapes and sizes. Anorexia is a disorder where someone restricts their food intake in an unhealthy manner. She doesn't have to be a skeleton for her body to react to starvation." Braant grabbed Cashlin's wrist. "Cashlin, can you just shut your mouth. Why don't you go home and let me deal with this." Cashlin scoffed, looked back and forth from Braant to Dr. Galen who pretended to check his notes. Not getting the sympathy she was expecting, she made a frustrated face and threw her hands up, stomping out of the ward. Braant forcefully exhaled, "Sorry about that. She gets a bit too wrapped up in her own world sometimes." The doctor waved off his apology. "My only concern is for Callie. Notwithstanding the obvious concerns about an eating disorder, we also noticed signs consistent with self-harm, such as some cuts on her waist and abrasions to the skin. It is not uncommon for children and adolescents with eating disorders to have comorbidities like nonsuicidal self-injury disorder." Braant was horrified. He had no idea anything was wrong. He knew Callie had been depressed, but he thought that was normal after losing a mother. After a lengthy talk with Dr. Galen, Braant began to understand the predicament facing his daughter. Dr. Galen recommended an inpatient treatment facility that specializes in adolescent mental health disorders. He referred them to a Dr. Sandra Avery, a child psychiatrist who worked solely with adolescent eating disorders. The doctor's recommendation was that Callie be admitted to the hospital until they could stabilize her and be sure she was out of immediate physical danger and then transfer her to the inpatient program. Braant agreed.

***

Dr. Sandra Avery sat in her office reading a recent study on eating disorders in adolescent females with and without diabetes. She brushed her long hair out of her face and tucked it behind her ear. Her dark locks boasted a scattering of grey that announced her generous life experience. She unconsciously brushed the deep crows lines near her eye and on her forehead. Sandra was not ashamed of her wrinkles. To her it was a badge of honor for a life well lived. She liked how they made her look distinguished and wise. A buzz on her intercom let her know that her next appointment had arrived and she requested they be sent in. A young woman entered, rolling a bag on wheels behind her. The young woman walked with the confidence of a much older person. Her quiet confidence made Sandra feel a bit like she did when she interviewed for her first internship, but today Sandra was the one doing the interviewing. Sandra stood and extended her hand. The woman slightly pulled back and paused for a moment, her nostrils flaring.

Lumma approached the human woman who stood and shoved her hand at her. Lumma was unprepared for this. She had seen humans do this with one another, but she had never paid close enough attention to repeat the action herself. Was it still done the same as in Babylon? How long was the connection supposed to be? Is she supposed to grab the hand, lightly touch, or hover her hand next to the other one? What was she supposed to do with her claws? Humans can't retract their claws, wouldn't the other woman find the exposed claws offensive? Being in human form was hard. A small voice popped in her head, "Lumma, she is waiting for you to shake her hand. If you would kindly reach your right hand forward and gently grip her extended hand then slowly move it up and down one time." Calm returned to Lumma and she did as she was told. She always panicked on the Earth plane when she had to visit in human form. This form had so much anxiety tied to its genetic makeup. Dr. Avery released the nervous energy that had built up during the odd pause with a chuckle. "You must be Ayaan Mubarak. I hope I pronounced that correctly. I am Dr. Sandra Avery, but the kids all call me Dr. Sandra. We try to keep things as relaxed as possible here while still retaining structure and healthy boundaries." Ayaan smiled and replied. "It's nice to meet you Dr. Sandra. You said my name correctly. Please call me Ayaan" Dr. Avery noticed that Ayaan had a slight accent, but she couldn't quite place the origin. She thought it must be African or

Middle Eastern from the way some of the letters took on a rounded sound, but she wasn't familiar enough with the nuances of different languages to guess the country. Ayaan was very pretty. Dr. Avery admired her style of baggy tan cargo pants, fitted grey long sleeve shirt, and black vest left undone. Her hair was styled back in Fulani braids with a natural hair puff bun. She looked like she walked right out of a catalogue shoot for H&M. She could already imagine the comments from the girls about how cool the new staff member was. Dr. Avery made her way back into her chair and gestured toward the seat across from her, "Please. Now let's talk about how you and your partner might fit into our program. I have been considering implementing an element of animal assisted therapy into our program here since I read an article by Barker and Dawson in '98 about the positive effect it had on anxiety ratings in hospital patients. I am excited to finally be able to test it out in this setting. Tell me a little bit about yourself and your animal, its training, and how you got into this line of work." Ayaan looked at Dr. Avery, slightly overwhelmed. "Well, okay. Cowabunga. Sorry. I am still not entirely sure how to appropriately use that slang, but I really do like how it rolls off the tongue." Ninimma meowed from her carrier on the floor. Ayaan had almost forgotten she was there. "Not to be too forward, but would it be ok if I brought her out with us. She is as much a part of this as I am." Dr. Avery smiled and nodded. "Of course. I'd be delighted to meet her as well." Ayaan opened the carrier and pulled Ninimma onto her lap. The doctor's eyes widened slightly at the sight. Ninimma's appearance was exactly the same as it was in Barag. She had short legs, a round body, and not a single strand of hair. Dr. Avery couldn't contain her surprise. "What a, um, unique looking animal. I'm curious as to the reaction she usually gets, especially with children. Are kids ever scared or put off by her look?" Ninimma was highly insulted and felt her hackles lifting, even if she didn't have any fur to raise. Ayaan jumped in without hesitation. "To be honest, children hardly ever have an adverse reaction to her appearance. They will most definitely comment on the unusualness of it, but once they get over the newness, they love it. We feel that, especially in a therapy setting, the unconventional nature of her appearance acts as a comfort or even an eidolon. They can see an example of someone who is unorthodox in their appearance or someone who greatly deviates from the traditional idea of beauty-" Ninimma shot Ayaan a look that convinced her to move on. "-or rather someone who is beautiful in their own unique way and still is loved and accepted. We feel it provides a template for them to learn how to be unapologetically themselves without the pressure of normal therapies. Our goal is to help others accept themselves by first showing them what that looks like, then offering them that unconditional acceptance that can only be conveyed by an enlightened being such as a cat, horse, dolphin, or even a do- well mostly cats." Dr. Avery nodded her approval. "Sounds great. What's her name and how long have you been her handler?" Ayaan looked at Ninimma and smiled. "Her name is Bella and we have been working together for ages. She has taught me so much, sometimes more than I wanted to know." Bella flicked her tail and it smacked Ayaan on the nose. Dr. Avery continued the interview. "Now I sent you over a summary of our program here and the typical goals we have with the patients. How do you see Bella and yourself fitting into that program?" Ayaan thought this process was a little bit silly. Ninimma had set everything up before they entered the Girru so there was no question whether or not they would get the position. She felt a little silly answering so many questions for something that she knew was a sure thing. "Bella and I don't really do the traditional therapy model. We would basically float. We would be around for free time if the children wanted to interact with her. She could be incorporated into group therapy or individual sessions depending on the need of the child and your preference. Bella can be a very calming influence for emotional sessions. I usually follow Bella's lead as she can sense when someone is in need of her presence. We can also change to a more structured protocol if you feel that would suit your needs better, but it is usually best not to force therapy with Bella or any animal unless the patient is willing." Dr. Avery had heard what she needed to hear. "Sounds perfect. I understand that you are willing to secure your own lodging nearby? I would like to try a probationary period to see how the animal assisted therapy is received and then if things go well, we can negotiate a longer contract." Ayaan smiled and nodded. She had no intention of staying here in this cumbersome form for longer than necessary to protect the Ni, but she was sure that Ninimma had a plan to substitute an actual human and therapy animal upon their departure. Now that the formalities were out of the way, they could get down to business.

CHAPTER FIFTEEN
Domesticated Violence

Chandra had just finished folding the last of the laundry. Enzo had his feet on the coffee table while watching college football. He was on the phone with someone talking about point spreads, alternate lines, and money line so Chandra figured he wasn't just watching but betting as well. She didn't like gambling. She was too practical to enjoy the risk when money was tight enough on a day to day basis, but Enzo enjoyed it. He made decent money as a truck driver so if a little sports betting made him happy, then she didn't really mind. After he hung up the phone she approached to ask him a question. "Do you want me to put your clean clothes into your duffel bag?" Enzo didn't take his eyes off the television. "No. Put them in the dresser. You can put my duffel bag away." Chandra was confused. He was supposed to be leaving for another shift at work. As a long-haul trucker, Enzo was usually gone for two or more weeks, then would spend a few days to a week home before heading out again. It had already been five days since he got home, so she expected him to need his duffel bag very soon. "You want me to put it away? Don't you have to go back to work?" Enzo didn't say anything. She repeated her question, "Enzo, don't you need your duffel bag when you go back to work?" Enzo reached for a bowl of chips on the table. "Nope. I'm not going back to work." Chandra waited for more of an explanation, none came. "You're not going back to work?" Enzo finally looked at her with his brows furrowed. "Are you deaf or stupid?" Chandra was annoyed and struggled to keep her anger in check. "Don't call me names. What do you mean you aren't going back to work? What happened?" Enzo turned back to watch the game and shoved a handful of chips in his mouth before answering, "Got into an argument with the guy workin' the loading dock and had to knock some sense into him. Dispatch cow said she heard the whole thing over the CB and I was a jerk so I told her to shove her opinion where the sun don't shine. Turns out she's the boss's sister-in-law. So they sacked me." Chandra was speechless. She couldn't believe that he would keep something so important from her. "What are you planning to do? Are you going to try to find a spot with another company?" Enzo turned the volume up on the tv. "Would you stop grillin' me and let me enjoy the game? If you are so worried about it, why don't you get a job instead of lazing around the house all day?" Chandra threw the basket of

Enzo's clean clothes on the floor in front of him. "If that's how you feel then maybe you can take care of your own laundry and cooking from now on, since I'm so lazy." Enzo flew out of his seat in a rage, grabbed the basket and threw it at her. The handle of the basket smacked her in the eye. Before she could put her hand on the painful spot Enzo grabbed her arm with one hand and backhanded her with the other. Tat could hear the scuffle from Leo's room. He was still asleep with his music drowning out the sound. Tat was pressing her face under the door trying to see what was going on. When she saw Enzo hit Chandra she tried sticking her arm out and clawing at the carpet and the door, trying to break out of the bedroom. The shadows being catapulted from Enzo during the beating were seeping through the cracks around the door and Tat was forced to turn her attention to the apparitions before they could make their way to Leo. Tat heard Enzo yell, "Don't you ever run your mouth at me again. Your nasty attitude is why no one loves you, you want to drive me away too?" Tat looked under the door to see Enzo push Chandra into the wall then storm out of the house. Tat meowed loudly and stuck her paw under the door towards Chandra in hopes of getting her attention. Tat loved Leo, but right now she knew it was Chandra who needed her support.

    Chandra had gotten Leo up from his nap and was soothed by the normalcy of their routine. Despite the twenty minutes of frozen peas on her face, Chandra was still graced with a baseball-sized lump and the forming bruise on her right cheek. This wasn't the first time Enzo had put his hands on her, but it was the first time he had ever properly hit her. Usually it was just him grabbing or pushing her. She was feeling the full gamut of emotions from anger and fear to empathy and loss. She was furious that he put his hands on her and wanted to tell him how angry she was, but she was afraid to express her feelings because it would just make Enzo angrier. She thought about leaving him. She thought about leaving him all the time, but she was caught between being afraid and being brave. The part of her that was afraid, worried about how she would make ends meet and take care of Leo on her own. Even though it had been a while since she saw the loving side of Enzo, she worried about losing the opportunity to recover the man she loved. She kept telling herself that she wasn't in love with a monster. The Enzo she loved was his true self, this mean side of him was just a symptom of his PTSD and stress. She believed that with love and empathy, she could help him to get back to his true self. She couldn't abandon him in his time of need. However, the other part of her, the part that was feeling angry, told her that she was worth more. It screamed that no one, regardless of their mental or physical health excuses, had the right to demean her or hurt her. Her internal conflict was making her dizzy. For every complaint she had against Enzo she found herself making an excuse. This made her angry with herself more than she was with Enzo. Ultimately her arguments boiled down to concern for Leo. She needed to be financially secure to be able to care for him, something she didn't think she could do as a single parent. She wanted Leo to have a father figure in his life, but she worried that a negative influence was worse than none at all. She worried that such a major change would irrevocably harm Leo. Her one consolation is that even in his worst fits of rage, Enzo had never harmed Leo. Chandra was lost deep in her thoughts while preparing dinner and did not hear Enzo enter. She jumped when he hugged her from behind at the stove. "Chandra, I'm so sorry for how I acted earlier. I was a jerk and I had no right to lay hands on you. Baby, I'm so sorry. What can I do so that you will forgive me?" Chandra turned to face him. He grabbed a bouquet of flowers and a large toy dinosaur from off the table. "These are for you and the Dino is for Leo. I hope we didn't scare him too much this morning." He also picked up a pack of cat toys from his pile on the table. "I got some cat toys so Leo could play with his cat. You are right about how much he likes that thing. I'm really glad it is helping him." Chandra was still angry, but this sort of consideration was reminiscent of the Enzo she loved. Maybe he was still in there somewhere. Enzo looked at the bruise forming on her face. "Oh god babe. I'm so sorry. You should hate me. I hate that I get so triggered by you sometimes. I shouldn't have reacted the way I did, I'm just so stressed about losing my job. I want to be able to provide for you and Leo and it made me mad when you questioned my ability to do that. I lost my cool, but I promise it won't happen again. I love you and I need you in my life." Chandra was tearing up. She was so angry with him and she desperately wanted to express her feelings, but he had apologized and now if she said anything about how she felt it would only start another fight. On the other hand, this is what she wanted. She didn't want to leave him, she wanted him to go back to the man he used to be. Was it really worth it to tell him how she felt when she was just starting to get a little piece of that good man back? She looked at his face and convinced herself that she saw true contrition. She took the flowers and smelled them as she gathered her thoughts. Risking further conflict wasn't worth her getting to vent so she chose to forgive him, wrapping her arms around his shoulders for a comforting embrace. Although she wasn't sure if the comfort was for him or for her.

  The next day had them back to their normal routine. Enzo had gone to see a trucker friend of his in hopes of getting a lead on a job. Chandra, Leo, and Tat were headed to the park for some play time and lunch before Leo's nap time. At the park they ran into the cookie girl and her mother. The girl ran up to Tat and Leo to tell them about her new dress. Tat listened and let the girl pet her while Leo absently stared off at the sun coming through the trees. Tat was sure he was paying attention with some part of his mind, but outward appearance would suggest otherwise. The girl's mom gasped when Chandra removed her sunglasses to reveal the large shiner bleeding into her orbital socket. The woman went off on a barrage of questions about the injury. Chandra stopped her "Wendie, thank you for your concern but it really is nothing. Enzo and I had an argument about him losing his job and in the heat of the moment he… I mean I, uh tripped. It was my fault. I put too much pressure on him when he was already feeling stressed and it triggered him. I should have let him be and not pestered him and we wouldn't have fought. He has already apologized and it won't happen again." Wendie looked at Chandra with a mixture of shock and skepticism. "Honey, that is what all abusers say. It never gets better. It is only going to get worse. How long has this been going on for?" Chandra was uncomfortable with the questions. Her private life was her business. Besides, she wasn't an abused woman. She was strong. In fact, she was so strong that she could support Enzo through this hard time instead of leaving him when he needed her the most. "I know how it looks, but I'm not being abused. It was a misunderstanding. Oh god, please don't look at me like that. We all have bad days. We are supposed to love in sickness and in health. Enzo just happens to be going through a 'sickness'. This isn't the real him. I really appreciate you worrying about me though. It means a lot to me to have you as a friend. Leo too. He has his own world, but I know he likes Dakota. Look how he lets her play with Tat. He won't even let me play with Tat sometimes." The prestidigitation had worked as Chandra intended. The two women began chatting about their kids which is where Chandra preferred the attention. Before the women parted for home, Wendie hugged Chandra. "I want you to know that I am here for you no matter what. If you need help with anything, or even if you just need to talk, you can call me." Chandra hugged her again a bit tighter to avoid her seeing her tears. "Thank you Wendie. I am so happy to have you and Dakota in our lives."

When they returned home, Chandra was shocked to find Enzo and three of his friends drinking and watching tv in the living room. Leo was not ok with the intrusion of the loud strangers and started to flap his fingers and moved closer to Tat, almost stepping on her. Tat jumped out of the way in time then jumped up with her front paws on Leo's waist, gently knocking him down. Once he was seated on the floor she crawled into his lap, head butting him on the cheeks and forehead so his attention would be on her. This seemed to calm him down, but the noise was still hard for him. Chandra quickly snapped the leash off Tat so she didn't get tangled on Leo. Chandra was upset. Enzo knew that Leo didn't do well with strangers and they had agreed to limit visitors. He didn't even bother to give her a heads up so she could do her best to make Leo ready. Having the loud group of men in her living room felt very invasive. She knew better than to embarrass Enzo in front of his friends, so she picked up Leo and Tat and took them to Leo's room. She put on his Wiggles show but the men were so rambunctious that they could still be heard over the loud theme song. She left Leo safe in the bedroom and went out to discreetly ask Enzo to quiet them down. From the moment she exited the bedroom, Enzo was all over her. He wasn't normally a touchy-feely person. The only time he became overly touchy was in front of other men. It made Chandra uncomfortable like she was being claimed as his territory. She didn't feel like it had anything to do with affection at all. She allowed it because she knew he wasn't very confident and if an occasional smack on the bum in front of his buddies made him feel more masculine she could put aside her own discomfort. Today was worse than normal. He reeked of beer and his touch was rougher than usual. She hugged him and whispered in his ear "Can we talk for a second?" Then discreetly gestured towards their bedroom. Enzo made a big show to his friends "Be back in a minute. The ball and chain wants to see me in the bedroom." He attempted to lean forward and give a dramatic wink, but he lost his balance and stumbled, forcing Chandra to catch him. He stood quickly and smacked her hands away. "Get off of me. Show a little restraint until we get in the bedroom." Chandra was so embarrassed, but did as he said until they were alone. "Enzo, we agreed no parties. Leo can't handle the noise. Can you and your friends go to the pool hall or something? I wasn't prepared to have guests." Enzo swayed while staring at her. "You're such a prude Chandra. A little noise won't hurt the kid. It's good for him to have some guys around. You're turnin' him into a lil' sissy. And I can haf my friendsss over if I wanna. You're not *my* mom." Enzo was slurring his words. Chandra knew there was no reasoning with him like this. "You are right Enzo, you can have your friends over, but could you please ask them to be a bit more quiet so Leo isn't so stressed?" Enzo just stared at her and she couldn't read what he was thinking. Without warning he pushed past her, knocking her onto the bed and returned to the living room. Chandra followed him. "Okay you mutha truckers, Chandra says that we are scaring the kid, so I think we should bring him out and show him how real men are." Before Chandra realized what he was planning, Enzo burst into Leo's room and dragged him out by his arm. Leo was scared and screaming. Chandra flew across the room and peeled Enzo's hand off Leo's arm. Enzo reached around to smack her but before he could, Tat came bolting out of Leo's room and flew at him like a furry missile with claws. He stumbled back into the wall. His friends had gone dead silent. Enzo steadied himself on the wall and stepped forward like he was going to go after Chandra, but one of his friends intervened. "Woah Enzo, it's a bit crowded at your place. Why don't we go to Brewster's? They've got the game on and I think Thursday's are twenty-five cent wing night." The other guys chimed in supportively so Enzo agreed. They all left in a whirlwind, leaving Chandra feeling raw and dissociated. She mindlessly tended to Leo and started cleaning up the mess in the living room.

    Chandra was asleep when Enzo returned home. The door slamming startled her awake. She listened as Enzo stomped through the living room and threw his keys on the table. She thought she heard him mumbling to himself, but she was still half asleep, so she assumed she was imagining it. She started to drift back to sleep when she heard Leo scream. She jumped out of bed and ran to Leo, hitting her shin on the dresser, banging her shoulder into the door frame and almost falling over a toy in the hall. She heard Tat hissing and growling and Enzo yelling. She flipped on the light in Leo's room and was frozen in terror. Enzo had removed his belt and had Leo pinned on his stomach and was whipping him with the folded belt. Tat was attacking his arm that was holding Leo down and Leo was screaming and flailing the best he could under the grip of the large man pinning him to his bed. In less than a millisecond, Chandra has crossed the distance between the door and the bed and used all her strength to push Enzo off of Leo. She tried to pick him up to flee but Leo was still screaming and flailing. Tat was still frantic and running around Leo trying to decide if Chandra was hurting him or not. Tat had also been sound asleep when Enzo entered the room, but the cold chill from the approaching darkness woke her with a start. Chandra thought the cat was panicked, but each pounce, swat, and bite that she was doing around Leo had a purpose. Enzo regained his footing and started screaming at Chandra. He was so drunk that she couldn't make out what he was saying but it seemed to have something to do with her making him look bad to his friends. The neighbor's light turned on, but nothing fazed Enzo. He continued to scream and when he managed to get around the side of the bed he turned the belt on Chandra. This time he was not using the folded leather side but had gripped that part and was hitting her with the loose end and buckle. She threw herself over Leo. He was panicking so his thrashing arms and legs were connecting with Chandra's stomach and chest while Enzo was slashing the metal of the belt across her back and head. The prong on the buckle caught her night shirt and was ripping chucks out of the shirt and Chandra's back. She didn't realize it but she must have been screaming at the top of her lungs because after a while there was a loud banging on the front door. An authoritative voice yelled "Police! Open up!" Enzo kicked Chandra then made his way to the front door with the belt in his hand. When he pulled open the door he quickly stepped out and took a swing at the cops with the belt. They easily dodged it and took him down to the ground. A few moments later an officer entered the bedroom and saw Chandra screaming and bloody, laying over Leo. He helped her up, asking if she was ok and if she could hear him. She tried to get up but everything felt woozy and she almost fell. The police officer caught her and helped her onto the bed. Leo was still upset but had stopped thrashing around and calmed to where he was only rocking and flapping his fingers. Tat was draped over his legs, but even that was not enough to offset the trauma of the evening. Before long the whole house was crawling with cops. Enzo had been handcuffed and placed in the back of a cruiser and an ambulance was on its way to take Chandra and Leo to the hospital. The only thought running through Chandra's mind was "Wendie was right." The realization that she was in an abusive relationship stung worse than the cuts on her back or the bruises on her ribs. She did this. She put herself and Leo in this situation by not ending this sooner and the guilt was eating her alive. She wanted to hold Leo but he wouldn't let her touch him and she couldn't blame him. A female officer escorted Chandra and Leo to the hospital. As they headed to the ambulance, Chandra could hear Enzo screaming about how he was going to kill her and the officers for this. The officer stayed with Chandra as she received care. She questioned Chandra about what happened. The officers had already done their best to obtain Enzo's side of the story and since he had initially tried to attack them and did end up landing a couple blows while they tried to put him in handcuffs, the officer explained that he would be arrested. She also explained that since a child was involved and their injuries were severe enough to warrant medical attention, that the case would be assigned to a detective and Enzo would be held for twenty-four hours while the case was investigated further. "Based on the evidence it is likely that he will eventually be charged with aggravated domestic violence, a class five felony, and aggravated child abuse, a class two felony. I would recommend that you use the next twenty-four hours to see a judge and get an order of protection against him for you and your child." Chandra was feeling overwhelmed. She couldn't believe how fast everything was coming undone. She didn't argue though. She knew the officer was right and there was no way she was forgiving something so heinous. The officer continued, "If the detective finds evidence of these felonies, Enzo will be formally charged and held in jail until he can see a judge for arraignment. This will most likely be Monday morning. If the judge allows him bail and he can post it or have it posted for him, he will be released until his scheduled court date. If you get an order of protection, he will not legally be allowed to return to the house. That being said, not being legally allowed to return doesn't always mean they don't. I don't want to tell you what to do with your life, but I can tell you that from what I have seen, these situations rarely get better. Do you have somewhere safe you can go?" Chandra didn't know what to say. Her parents lived a few states away and she had lost touch with a lot of her friends because her life revolved around Leo. Wendie's voice popped in her head, "You can call me if you need anything." Chandra nodded to the officer.

    The next day Chandra called Wendie. It was difficult for her to open up and even more difficult to admit that Wendie had been right. Wendie was kind but Chandra felt like an obstinate child. Chandra asked Wendie if she would go to the court with her, both for emotional support and to help with Leo. The process of getting a temporary protection order was very simple. All she had to do was file the paperwork and see the judge. Since Enzo was currently in jail for battery on a law enforcement officer, the police could serve him easily. No charges had been filed for the assaults as of yet, but all the judge needed to see was the police report and her injuries to be more than willing to grant the order. Wendie stayed with Chandra for the afternoon, preparing food and helping with Leo, but mainly she stayed to comfort Chandra. Surprisingly, Leo seemed relatively unfazed by the previous night's events. However, at home it was obvious, at least to Chandra, that he was traumatized. He wouldn't go anywhere near his room and he was more hyperactive than usual. Not even Tat could get his focus for too long. Both women were extra careful to keep their voices down as any loud sound made Leo jump and get agitated. When Chandra finally seemed to settle, Wendie asked what her plans were. For a long time Chandra just stared into her mug of tea. "I think I am going to go home. My parents live in Northern California. I originally came here for work, but after I had Leo, I never felt like it was right to go back. Really the only thing keeping me here was Enzo. I am worried that I won't be able to find a doctor there that understands Leo the way his doctor here does. I don't know. I guess Leo isn't the only one who doesn't like change." They sat in companionable silence for a bit before Wendie spoke up. "What can I help you do? Dakota is staying with her auntie for the day so I can help you start packing some things up. I can come by again tomorrow if you don't mind me bringing Dakota." Chandra smiled. She was so grateful for the friendly support. She really did not know how she would be coping without it. "I still have to call my parents, but the officer that sat with me gave me a lot of good information. I guess in situations like this, you are allowed to break your lease, so I just have to call up my landlord and let them know. I am so embarrassed, but I can't stay here, especially if he makes bail." Wendie didn't say anything, only placed her hand on top of Chandra's. Chandra couldn't contain her emotions any longer. Her emotions broke through like doors opening on black Friday. She sobbed into Wendie's beige cardigan for what seemed like an eternity. When she felt like her eyes had become the Saharan desert and no longer had even a single drop to spare, she sat back and took Wendie's hands. "I don't know how to thank you." Wendie started to dismiss her gratitude, but Chandra wouldn't relent. "No. I mean it. You don't know me well and you could have easily ignored my situation, but you didn't. You reached out. At a time when I was drowning and didn't even know it myself, you reached out so I knew I wasn't alone. I could not be doing this alone. I think about women like me in similar situations, but without anyone to turn to and my heart aches." Her eyes had found fresh tears and they were freely falling. Wendie turned to Chandra with such pain and seriousness on her face, Chandra thought she may have said something wrong. "Honey, this sort of thing happens way more than you know. When I was younger, way before I met Dakota's dad, I was with this guy I thought I was in love with. We started dating in High School and my naive young heart thought that he could do no wrong, but he could and he did. After we finished school we were eager to run away together. We both had jobs and got a little apartment in a dumpy neighborhood and thought we were the masters of our own destiny. That was until money started to get tight. We began to realize that our little paradise was only a mirage. We started fighting about everything. He thought the man should rule the house, and when I started questioning him, he started hitting me. I justified it for so long." Wendie paused to compose herself and swallow back tears. "One night we had a particularly bad fight. He grabbed a bottle, the ones that the fancy orange juice used to come in, busted the end and attacked me. He stabbed me five times. I woke up in the hospital. They told me that after stabbing me, he turned the bottle on himself and slashed his own throat. Sometimes I tell myself that he felt bad for what he did and that was why he killed himself, but in reality it was probably just the final expression of a violent soul." Chandra was crying again and Wendie let herself join in. Chandra felt such a strong bond and she hated that they shared such grisly experiences. Wendie wiped her eyes, "I wish someone had been there to help me escape that hell or even just be there for me to reach out to, so I am so incredibly grateful that I could be there for you." The women finished their tea in silence. Neither had the energy for anymore conversation. When Wendie left, she hugged Chandra tightly.

Chandra wasn't sure if the hug was more for her or for Wendie, but she was glad to have the support. Wendie reminded Chandra again that she was there for anything she needed and promised to be by, first thing, with boxes. When they were alone, Chandra put Leo to bed in her bed. He still wouldn't go anywhere near his room. Tat laid with Leo until he was asleep, then out of routine, came to sit with Chandra on the couch. Chandra absentmindedly stroked the cat. With a forceful sigh, she picked up the phone and called her parents.

***

The weekend was over too quickly. The two women had gotten a lot packed and Sunday, Wendie's husband joined them, but there was still so much to do. Chandra's landlord was disappointed, but understanding. He came by and helped her change the locks to be safe. Chandra had reserved a rental car for the weekend. She wanted to leave sooner, but some convention had made finding an available vehicle almost impossible. Monday evening Chandra got the call she was dreading. The detective called to inform her of the charges they were filing and to let her know that Enzo had posted bail. There was no way Chandra was going to be able to sleep knowing that Enzo had been released that afternoon. The temporary order of protection paperwork was sitting on her nightstand and she couldn't take her eyes off of it. She pretended that it was a magical force field that could protect her from a raging troll, but she knew that even though paper covered rock, paper was no shield against blockheads. The next night was better. She almost had everything packed and Wendie was going to help her sell the furniture and send her the funds. As tired as she was, Chandra still couldn't sleep. She found herself having nightmares and when she woke, she couldn't stop thinking about women who had no one to turn to. She suffered from such bad survivor's guilt. How was it fair that she had help to escape her bad situation when so many others did not. She thought about what she could be facing if she didn't have Wendie or her parents to help her. What if she didn't have Leo to protect? Would she have been strong enough or lucid enough to realize the bad situation or might she have continued to excuse it away? She had always judged women in abusive relationships. Nothing too harsh, more condescendingly pitying them for having such low self-esteem. The reality of the situation was very different. She didn't feel like she was lacking self-esteem. She questioned her judgement. The years of gaslighting had made her question if it really was her who was the problem, but she didn't feel weak. She was strong. She was strong enough for both of them. Even now, with the cuts and bruises still fresh, she longed for the man she fell in love with. Those feelings would never go away. Luckily, she had the kind guiding voices of her friend and parents as well as the maternal instinct demanding that she keep Leo safe at all costs. One thing was for sure, she no longer looked down on women in abusive relationships. Love is a beautiful emotion, but sometimes it can cloud judgement. Her love for Enzo was like a powerful painkiller. She felt great under its influence, but it deadened her senses to the warning signs of danger. Chandra frustratedly turned to look at the clock. 3:23 in the morning. Chandra groaned. She really was going to have to get some sleep before their roadtrip to California.

    On Saturday morning, after five days of Enzo being released and no contact, Chandra had a false sense of security. They were finally going to be on their way to her parents house. The road was long but she might finally feel safe after putting the 1,800 miles in between them. Wendie had left Dakota with her father so she could pick up Chandra and Leo and take them to get the rental car. As the women loaded the boxes into the rental SUV, Leo sat at the kitchen table coloring while Tat batted around a few of his unused crayons. Chandra left Wendie at the SUV to organize the boxes as she went back to the house to get the next load. When she walked in the door her blood ran cold. Enzo was standing at the table opposite Leo. Tat was crouched on the table in front of Leo hissing and swatting at the uninvited guest. Enzo took a small step back away from the aggressive feline. He quickly turned his attention to Chandra. "Chandra, babe please. We need to talk. What is all of this? Are you leaving?" Chandra wanted to scream but her mouth was too dry. "You can't be here Enzo. You have to leave. Please. Leave now and I won't call the police." Enzo turned around and slammed his fist into the freezer door. Leo started screaming. "Damn it Chandra! I just want to talk to you. How can you be like this? I thought you loved me." Chandra didn't know what to say. Enzo was too close to Leo but she couldn't call Leo to her and she didn't want to make any sudden moves and send Enzo into a rage. She slowly started to walk towards Leo. "I do love you, but we need to give each other some space for a little bit." Enzo ran his hand through his hair and she noticed he had his hunting knife in its sheath on his belt. He groaned and huffed like he was crying, but there were no tears. She had chosen the wrong words and he was getting more upset. "I'm sorry Enzo. You are right. We should talk. Let's go outside and talk so we don't upset Leo more." Enzo nodded and she was grateful for the opportunity to get him away from Leo. Tat didn't take her eyes off of Enzo as he rounded the table and headed towards Chandra. Unexpectedly, Leo got out of his chair and ran over to his mom. The happiness that Chandra felt about Leo choosing to come and hug her was buried by her terror that he was now directly in harm's way. Chandra tried to direct Leo back to the table but the lack of attention on him, upset Enzo. "Would you let the kid be and focus on our problems?! I can never have your full attention because of him. This is important. We are important. Can't you just be with me for one damn minute!" Chandra grabbed Leo and stepped back. Wendie came into the house yelling for Chandra "Hey Hun, did you get lost?" She stopped dead in her tracks when she saw Enzo. She tried not to let her fear show. Chandra looked over at her and pleaded for help with her eyes and then looked at Leo. Wendie understood the silent plea. "So sorry. I didn't realize you had company. Why don't I get Leo out of your hair so y'all can have a little chat." Wendie quickly walked to pick up Leo, but he did not go quietly. Wendie managed to drag him outside to the SUV and immediately got on her cell phone to call the police. She wanted to run in to help Chandra but couldn't leave Leo alone. Back inside Chandra was still trying to calm Enzo down. He had started pacing and forcefully running his fingers through his hair over and over again. "I don't understand why you are doing this to me. You didn't even give me a chance to apologize before you sent me that stupid order to stay away. Do you have any idea how that made me feel?!" Chandra didn't know what to do, but she was used to talking Enzo down and as long as he was in here with her, Leo was safe. "You're right. I reacted too quickly. I only did that because the police told me to." Chandra was willing to say anything to de-escalate the situation. "How could you listen to the cops without even talking to me!" Enzo left the kitchen and crossed the living room towards Chandra. She reactively took a step back. The action set him off and he raised his hand to punch her. Chandra brought up her arms in an attempt to protect her face, but before she could get her arms all the way up a black streak flew across the room. Tat had run in from the kitchen and attacked Enzo, clawing his face and biting his hands. Enzo frantically swung at the cat trying to simultaneously detach the cat from his chest and protect his eyes from the furious swipes. Every time he managed to grab a part of the cat she would contort and free herself from his grip then resume her onslaught. Blood dripped from his hands, arms, and face by the time he was able to toss Tat to the ground. Tat crouched to launch herself at his face again, but Enzo pulled back and kicked as hard as he could. The full blow made contact with Tat's chest and abdomen as she jumped, sending her flying into the opposite wall. She fell limp to the ground. The attack had stunned Chandra at first and she stared dumbly at the scene before her. When Tat fell to the ground before being kicked Chandra was able to come to her senses and make a run for the door. She saw Tat get kicked out of her peripheral but couldn't turn back. Chandra closed the door behind her and then ran to Wendie at the SUV. Before she could make it all the was there two police cars sped up and came to a screeching halt. Wendie pointed them towards the house and Chandra shouted a warning about the knife on his belt as she ran to Leo in the backseat of the SUV. A few moments later another two squad cars pulled up. Chandra recounted the story to the officer that stayed with her and told him about the cat. She begged him to help her get Tat to an emergency vet if she was still alive. As soon as the other officers had Enzo in handcuffs and out of the house, Chandra and the officer went in to check on Tat. Her broken body was laying near the wall she was kicked into. Chandra started bawling as the officer gently checked Tat for signs of life. When his hand made contact, Tat started slamming her tail on the carpet and growling. She tried to get up but instantly fell back down. Chandra looked around and saw Leo's travel blanket sitting near the table. She ran and grabbed it then returned to gently pick up the injured Tat. The police officer put Chandra and Tat in the back of his car and with a quick word to one of his fellow officers, they headed off to the closest emergency vet.

    The emergency vet took over Tat's care and Chandra had to return to the scene to complete the report and check on Leo. When she finally got to hold him he was repeating 'Tat' over and over. "Tat is seeing her doctor right now." Chandra didn't know what to say to her son. She didn't even know if Tat was still alive. She knew the vet was doing their best to save her, but she didn't know how to explain it all to Leo. When the police had cleared out, Wendie stayed with Leo and Chandra returned to the vet. Tat was still alive. They had given her IV fluids, pain killers, wrapped her abdomen, and were keeping her in an oxygen chamber. The vet let Chandra come to the back to sit with Tat while they talked. "Tat is doing ok for now, but I suspect that she has a pulmonary contusion, along with some broken ribs and a broken leg. The good news is that her chances of survival are good. We will need to keep her here for a while for treatment though." Chandra was devastated and broke down crying. The vet had said 'good news' but Chandra didn't know what she was going to do. They had to leave. She couldn't stay any longer, especially after what had happened today. She couldn't leave with Tat in this condition and she couldn't take her with them. She told the vet the whole story of how Tat saved her life and how her and her son had to escape the abusive situation. A woman that was sitting with a cat nearby approached Chandra as the vet excused himself for a moment. "I am so sorry to interrupt, but I couldn't help but overhear your story and it broke my heart. I run a cat rescue here in Dallas and I would like to offer my help. This brave little hero deserves to be saved. I know you are in a difficult position. Here's what I can offer. I can accept this baby into the rescue. We will pay for all her vet bills and stay with her while she heals. Then when she is better and you are settled, you can choose to adopt her back, if you are in a place to do that. If not, we can find her a loving home worthy of the furry little savior." Chandra was speechless. She was undeserving of the overwhelming kindness of this stranger. The woman shifted her weight to her other foot while waiting for an answer. "Why don't I give you some time to think about it." The woman turned to leave but Chandra gently stopped her. "I don't need to think about it. You are heaven sent. I will sign whatever you need me to. I hope that when we are settled in California I can come back and get her, but I would even be ok if you said there was no chance of me getting her back, as long as you save her life. I can't bear the idea that she might die because of my mess." Chandra started crying again and the woman softly patted her on the back. "I'll let the vet know of our arrangement. I have the surrender forms in my car. I'll be back with one in a jiffy." Chandra turned to Tat. "I'm sorry Tat. This is my fault and it kills me to see you like this. Leo misses you like crazy. He's not going to understand this. I can't take you with us. I want to. I do. I wish more than anything that today never happened and we were on our way to Redding. But the vet said you can get better. You have to get better." Chandra put her hand on the plastic window of the oxygen chamber. "You saved my life today. You saved Leo's life. From the moment he saw you, he has been different. You brought out something in him that had been buried so deeply. We love you so much. I'm sorry I couldn't protect you, but I will do what I can to protect you now. You've inspired me. I want to be as brave as you. I'm going to make you a promise. If you get better, I promise I will dedicate my life to helping others in this type of situation. I want to help women leave bad situations before anyone gets hurt. I want to help them leave safely with their children and their pets. No one should ever have to be in this position." The rescue lady cleared her throat to announce her return. She handed her the paperwork to fill out. "Do you really mean what you said just now about helping other women in abusive homes?" Chandra nodded. She had never felt so strong about anything. The woman smiled, "If you are serious about that, I will put you in contact with some people I know in California. Their rescue offers temporary foster homes for the pets of displaced people." Chandra knew this was a sign. She had found her purpose. Maybe things happen for a reason.

***

Leo was strapped into his carseat in the backseat of the SUV. Chandra had spent longer in her goodbye to Wendie than she should have. Before they left for Redding, Chandra and Leo stopped by the vet hospital to say their goodbyes to Tat. Leo didn't really respond much in the office. As Chandra turned onto the road from the vet hospital, Leo started flapping his fingers. Chandra braced herself for the oncoming tantrum, but instead of screams, Leo said "Bye Tat." then again "Bye Tat. Bye Tat. Bye Tat. Bye Tat." Chandra had no more tears so all she could do was smile.

Tat sat in the cold metal kennel at the vet's office. The techs had placed clean towels down, but Tat had to move them so she could clearly see the light reflecting off the floor of the kennel. When the tech finally left the room, Tat focused on her reflection which gradually changed into that of a large orange cat with folded ears and a smushed face. "Nuska. Good to see you made it back. Any trouble with the mission?" The large cat threw his head back, "Shut yer gub! Dinnae teach yer Granny tae suck eggs! Alls daein fine, whit aboot yersel?" As much as she hurt Tat was smiling on the inside. She had missed this big lug. "I'll live, but that is the problem. What is the word from Ninlil? Is my Girru complete? Can I return to Barag?" Nuska paused and looked at her with such a solemn expression that her heart sank. "Aye, all's barry. Bring ye bahookie home." Tat exhaled, "Nuska, don't do that to me! I thought something was wrong. If the Ni is safe, then all that is left is to get out of this hospital and journey home."

***

  Chandra hung up the phone and put her head in her hands. An older woman put her arm around her. "What's wrong sweetheart?" "Tat is gone. They don't know what happened. She was better. She was scheduled to be placed with a foster, but when they went in to get her she had escaped. They still haven't found her after two weeks of searching." Chandra's mom rested her cheek on the top of Chandra's head. "I'm sorry. I was really looking forward to meeting her." Chandra smiled. "I guess she wanted to be wild again. Honestly, I don't know why she chose us in the first place. I hope wherever she is, she is happy." Chandra looked at Leo sitting with his grandfather in the backyard. The only thought in her mind was "Bye Tat.".

CHAPTER SIXTEEN
Body Pawsitivity

A nurse had helped Callie get settled into her room at the treatment facility. Her dad and her had met Dr. Avery. She spoke privately with Callie for a little bit and then passed them off to the nurse for a tour. Callie was only allowed to wear soft material pants without a drawstring and soft material shirts without buttons, ties, or zippers. Her dad had bought her a few new pairs of t-shirts and sweatpants for her stay. Cashlin made disgusted faces when Braant was showing the new clothes to Callie. At first Callie was embarrassed to wear the things that must have been hideous according to fashion standards, but she noticed on the tour that everyone was wearing similarly ugly and unmatching outfits. Callie didn't particularly want to be here. Even if she could learn how to like her body like the doctor said, it wasn't going to stop how people looked at her. It wouldn't stop the bullying. On the bright side, it would give her a few weeks away from school. If nothing else, Callie looked forward to the break from that environment. Callie sat on the bed in her room. The only thing she was allowed to bring was a squishy stuffed animal, one with no hard parts for eyes or the nose, and a picture of her and her mom that had been removed from the frame and placed in a plexiglass holder on the wall. Bored with staring at her picture, Callie made her way to the common room. There were some paperback books, a tv playing some silly cartoon, and a couple kids playing 'go fish'. She wandered over to the books and, not being too discerning, grabbed one. She got comfortable on one of the couches and flipped through the book until she felt a soft tap on her leg. When she looked to the source of the tap she gasped and almost fell over the side of the couch. Staring at her was the ugliest giant rat that she had ever seen. After regaining her composure she took a better look. It wasn't a rat, it was a cat, but a cat with no hair and lots of gross wrinkly fat folds. The cat had pale blue eyes that stared at her with a tinge of sadness that made Callie ashamed for reacting the way she did. The cat had its two short front legs on the sofa and tapped at the cushion. Callie giggled at the way the cat's chubby little leg wiggled with each tap. "Do you want to sit with me?" Callie patted the cushion and the cat returned its paws to the ground, crouched, wiggled its ample behind a few times, then awkwardly launched itself onto the sofa next to Callie. "You can jump pretty high for something so fat." The cat looked at her and Callie almost felt bad for calling her fat, but it wasn't like the cat could understand her. A long moment passed and the cat was still staring at her. Cautiously Callie stuck her hand out, palm down, towards her tubby little companion. This was what the cat was waiting for and it eagerly pushed its head into her hand and then maneuvered its body so Callie's hand slid all the way down its back and off its tail. It eagerly turned to be stroked again. At first Callie cringed at the feel of the cat's bare skin, but it didn't take long for her to get used to it. A woman approached them. She was wearing scrubs, but even in such simple clothing, the woman was still gorgeous. "Hello. My name is Ayaan. I see you have already met Bella." Callie looked at the cat. "Is this your cat?" Ayaan smiled and sat down on the opposite end of the sofa. "She is my friend. We are here to help support everyone here as you learn about yourself." Callie wanted to ask about Bella, but didn't want to make Ayaan mad. Her curiosity ended up getting the better of her, "What's wrong with Bella?" Bella looked up at Callie and Ayaan had to work hard to suppress a laugh. "How do you mean?" Callie felt like she said the wrong thing but was already invested. "Well, like, is she sick? Why is she so short and fat? And why doesn't she have any hair? And why is she so wrinkly?". This time Ayaan couldn't help but laugh. "Bella is not sick. She is a Sphinx Munchkin cat. They are all bald, short, and wrinkly. Bella is round because that is just how her body was made." Callie pet Bella for a bit, working up the courage to ask another question. "Do you think Bella ever gets embarrassed about how she looks?" Ayaan marveled at Ninima's foresight. She had chosen the perfect form for this Girru. Not even ten minutes into meeting Bella, Callie was already relating to her looks. Ayaan scratched Bella above the tail, "I think Bella is very happy to be the beautiful queen that she is. A rounder body means more space for scritches." Callie smiled. "My mom used to say that. She said a bigger belly meant there was more of her to love." Callie fell silent and the three sat together without saying another word until a voice over the loudspeaker said it was time for dinner.

***

Weeks passed and Callie was really benefiting from the program. She never got to grieve for her mother. No one ever wanted to talk about it. Whenever she was sad or missed her mom, her dad would try to make her feel better. He would say

"Don't cry." Or "You're mom wouldn't want you to be sad." So eventually she just pushed the feelings away, but they were always still there. Talking with Dr. Sandra and the other therapists helped her to feel comfortable sharing her feelings. They told her that it was okay to be sad and cry, so she did. When she felt all cried out it was like the rocks in her stomach had been removed. She was still sad, but they said that was okay too. Dr. Sandra said that her grief would never go away, but if she wanted it to, her heart could grow around her grief so that it didn't feel quite so big or quite so heavy. Callie thought that made more sense than 'it won't hurt forever'. Losing her mom would always hurt and she didn't like the idea that one day she wouldn't miss her mom. Callie was still struggling with her relationship with food and her own body. She tried to accept herself the way she was, but she couldn't shake the feeling of disgust when she looked at her fat. She thought she was a good person, but how could anyone ever love someone so repulsive? Callie was feeling better about eating healthy foods. She met with a dietician twice a week and they were teaching her about healthy diets and how eating good food is better than not eating at all, even for weight loss. Dr. Sandra was encouraging Callie to feel confident eating 'bad food', in moderation of course. She told Callie that food was not good or bad, it was a tool to sustain life. Dr. Sandra wanted her to reconnect with her love of food but to also realize it wasn't the food she loved, but the companionship and connection she felt to her mom through their shared love. Callie still wasn't ready to eat sweets again, but she was making progress. She made her way from her one-on-one session to arts and crafts in the common room. When she walked in, she ran to the table where Bella and Ayaan were. Bella was the star of St. Borromeo Center for Adolescent Wellbeing. She was loved by patients, staff, and visitors. Bella always knew who needed a helping paw and would always be there for a little extra support. Ayaan was quite popular too but for different reasons. She was friendly, but also a little weird. Ayaan wasn't bothered by her weirdness, instead she embraced it. Whenever she did something odd, she never got embarrassed. As Callie walked past the nurses station, she remembered one afternoon in particular. The charge nurse had received a basket that had some potpourri in it. During movie time, Ayaan picked some up and ate it. She quickly spit it out and told the nurse that her trail mix had gone bad. Everyone laughed and the nurse explained that it was potpourri and was meant to make the room smell nice.

Ayaan nodded, then started rubbing the potpourri on her face and clothes. Callie had been there for the spectacle and felt sad that everyone was laughing at Ayaan. To Callie's surprise, Ayaan didn't care that she was being laughed at. She kept doing it and Callie noticed that two of the patients and even one of the nurses stopped and discreetly rubbed a bit of potpourri on their shirts and neck. Callie had to be quick to sit with Bella and Ayaan. Everyone would want to sit with them, so Callie was glad she got there first. Bella spent time with everyone, but for some reason Callie always felt special around her. It was like Bella was friends with everyone but Callie was her best friend. When it was just Callie, Ayaan, and Bella, Bella would always choose Callie's lap over Ayaan's. That made Callie feel important. Callie greeted Ayaan and hugged Bella. As she sat down Dr. Sandra came over to the table. "Hello Callie. Ready for some macaroni art?" Callie nodded as Bella batted round a piece of macaroni. Dr. Sandra turned to Ayaan. "Can I ask you a quick question? We are having a class on respect for ethnic and gender identities. Would you be willing to participate?" Ayaan looked a bit confused, "I'm not sure how I might help, but if you want me to take part I will." Dr. Sandra smiled and clapped her hands together in a clasp near her chest, still holding her small notepad. "Wonderful. Do you prefer the term African American or Black?" Ayaan tilted her head slightly and shifted her eyes to glance at Callie for a moment. "Neither of those describe where I am from nor do they describe my appearance. If you must describe me based on skin color then I would say I am 'foxfire brown' but if you are going to refer to me, right now I answer to Ayaan." Dr. Sandra looked a bit sheepish. "Yes of course. Ayaan. I hope I didn't offend you. It was not my intention to make you uncomfortable. I want to create an inclusive environment where everyone can feel open to asking questions but also learn how to do so in a respectful manner." Ayaan waived off her apology. "No offense taken." Dr. Sandra flipped the page of her notepad. "How about gender identity? Is it ok to refer to you as her or she? Or do you have a different preference?" Ayaan was perplexed again. Humans had such odd categories of division. "She is fine. Those like me are usually always genetically female as opposed to gingers who are usually male." Her answer confused the doctor, but everyone had learned not to question Ayaan's quirkiness.

Callie placed her macaroni Eiffel Tower on the far table to dry, then made her way to claim the giant beanbag chair for free time. Bella waddled after her and meowed her demand to be placed on the bean bag. Ayaan made her way to sit on the chair near the table with the Newton's cradle. Callie found it amusing that Ayaan was so fascinated by a bunch of swinging kinetic balls. No matter how much she played with them, she never seemed to get bored. Callie scratched Bella's ears and belly. Ayaan felt the tension in the air grow. She knew Callie had something to say. Ayaan looked at the little girl 'Okay. Cal. Out with it." Callie looked at her surprised that she could read her mind. "Why did you pick Bella? Didn't you want a cat that is… prettier?" Ayaan chose her words carefully. "I could have picked a cat that people thought was better looking, but are looks really that important? Bella is my friend and I love her because she loves me and we can be there for each other. She makes me laugh, she comforts me, I like that she is smart and confident." Callie didn't know how she expected Ayaan to answer. She looked at Bella and longed to understand why everyone could love such a funny looking cat but be so mean to a funny looking human. "I guess it isn't important for cats to be pretty. Girls are supposed to be pretty and thin." Ayaan didn't see the appeal of skinny. She always preferred to have a plentiful primordial pouch and felt quite exposed without the extra fluff. She knew she had to answer Callie. "It's true that a lot of people feel that way, but why? Can only pretty people give hugs? Do you have to be thin to listen to a friend? Are pretty people better at having fun or telling jokes? Sure a beautifully made bed is pretty, but do you care what a bed looks like when you crawl in and snuggle under the blankets? No. It only matters that the bed is warm, supportive, and comfortable. I think people are the same. Yes, it is nice to look at pretty people, but what I think is most important is if that person is warm, supportive, and comfortable to be around. What do you think?" Callie looked down. "I think that most people would rather be around someone who is pretty and mean than someone who is fat and ugly." Ayaan nodded, "That is true." Callie was not expecting that answer and looked at Ayaan confused and a bit hurt. Ayaan elaborated. "A lot of people judge others by what they look like. You know what I think? I think that it is because they are afraid. I think they are afraid that other people will judge them, so they try to judge others before they can be judged themselves. I imagine it makes them feel safer. It is easier to point out the flaws of others and take any attention off of themselves, than it is to face their own flaws." Callie contemplated Ayaan's answer. Could that really be true? Did the kids at school make fun of her because they were afraid people might make fun of them? That didn't seem very logical to her. She had been working with Dr. Sandra on her feelings about being bullied. Dr. Sandra told her that it was ok to be sad that the other kids were being mean, but she should try hard not to take what they say personally. That the only person that was allowed to make judgements about Callie's body was Callie. At first, Callie's judgments about her body were a harsh echo of the judgements of others. However, after working very hard during her stay at the center, she had come to better accept her shape. The rule she wasn't allowed to break was that she had to treat her body with the love and respect that she would give to a best friend. One day, Dr. Sandra employed Bella to help Callie understand the principle.

Dr. Sandra picked Bella up and placed her on the couch in between them. "Callie, I would like you to help me write an introduction for Bella. Let's work on respectfully describing her. How would you describe our sweet little Bella? Let's use the starter, 'Bella is …' sound good?" Callie nodded. She thought for a moment. "Bella is … playful. Bella is nice. Bella is funny. Bella is … um… my friend." Dr. Sandra smiled, "Very good Callie. I want you to think about all those important things you just said about Bella. Did any of those things have to do with the way Bella looks?" Callie thought about it and shook her head. "I really want you to think about that Callie. Out of all the things you thought were important about Bella, none of those things had to do with her appearance. Would you say that you left out appearance because when it comes to the important things, looks really aren't that important?" Callie was surprised. When Dr. Sandra told her to describe Bella, she never once thought about describing how she looked, because how she acted seemed more like the real Bella than how she looked. "I didn't think about that before." Bella started to make biscuits on the sofa by pressing down with her right paw and then her left, then falling into a rhythmic alternation of the two. "Now Callie, next let's try something a little bit different. Let's pretend you were trying to describe Bella so someone could recognize her. How would you describe her looks?" Callie had to think very hard. "Bella has short legs. Bella has no hair. Bella has pink skin. Bella …." Callie thought about how she could describe Bella's weight. She didn't think fat was the right word. Bella was round, but fat was an ugly word and Bella wasn't ugly. She liked that Bella was fluffy. "Bella is beautifully round." Dr. Sandra let out an approving 'hmm'. "I like that. Now why did you choose 'beautifully round' instead of 'fat' or 'chunky'?" Callie furrowed her brows and crinkled her nose. "Those words sound mean. Bella is cute and if I call her fat, people might not know that she is cute." Dr. Sandra smiled and pet Bella. "You are right, Bella is cute. She can be cute and big. I want you to notice that when you were talking about who Bella is, you didn't use words that described her looks, you used words to describe her personality. Would it be fair to say that just like Bella, how we look on the outside is not who we are?" Callie nodded. "Now if you can talk about Bella's body and use such kind words to describe her, why do you use such mean words when I ask you to describe yourself?" Callie just shrugged. "I dunno. Maybe cause I like Bella more than I like myself." Dr. Sandra turned to a blank page in her notebook and wrote something at the top of the page. "Let's do some homework. Before I see you on Thursday, I want you to write ten things that describe how you look, but you are only allowed to write things about yourself like how you described Bella. You like Bella so you used nice words to describe her. I want you to do the same for yourself. One more rule. From now until our next meeting, you are not allowed to say or think anything about yourself that you wouldn't say to Bella. Okay?" Callie made a face but agreed.

***

Ayaan sat in the dark on her bed. The apartment wasn't much, but it was only temporary. Ayaan was struggling trying to eat ramen noodles with a fork. She heard a voice in her head. "Why are you eating that stuff? I told you to stick to sushi and rotisserie chicken." Ayaan spoke out loud, "That scary nurse gave it to me and I know she is going to ask me how I liked it when she sees us next. Besides, I would rather eat this so we can talk about noodles rather than listen to her go off about her Pomeranians for hours. If I see one more picture of those little fluffy yappers I am going to lose my lunch." The voice in her head became condescending, "Lumma, dogs are not all that bad. They have actually been quite helpful since the truce." Ayaan rolled her eyes, "Leave it be Ninimma! I know we are allies now, but I still don't fully trust them. I mean what kind of twisted psycho wags their tail when they are happy? It's not right." Bella hopped up on the bed. Being in a physical cat form, Ninimma could not speak, but could communicate with Lumma via telepathy. Unfortunately for Lumma, human form did not come equipped with such an ability. Ayaan was forced to speak out loud to Bella if she wished to communicate, which had earned her a bit of a reputation. As progressive as humans had become, having a conversation with a cat was still considered moderately unhinged. Bella looked up at Ayaan with wide eyes, "Lumma, I know you are focused on your noodles there, but would you mind opening one of those pate cans for me? I would also like dinner. The lack of telekinesis on this plane is very inconvenient." Ayaan shoved a forkful of noodles in her mouth. "Listen, having thumbs is not any better." When both Bella and Ayaan were fed and content, they turned their thoughts to the mission. "Ninimma, how much longer do you suppose it will take to complete this Girru? Callie is such a strong light and she seems brighter every day. I think she is great and I want to stay until she is secure in her light, but this is exhausting. Darkness is rampant around these poor kittens. Every little one that comes into this place is fighting off shadows. I'm doing my best to disperse them, but I am finding it hard to effectively do that while being discrete. You know, I am expected to teach an Urban dance class next week because Dr. Sandra caught me trying to scatter that dark form. Why did you tell me to lie and say I was practicing Uprock? I don't even know what Uprock is!" Bella contorted in an attempt to reach her back foot up to scratch her ear. "Uprocking is a style of dance created in the 1970's in the Bushwick area of Brooklyn. It was originally conceptualized by a character named Rubber Band who-" Ayaan collapsed back on the bed with a loud sigh. "Right, it's not important. Lumma you are doing a wonderful job as a guardian, especially in human form. I myself am continually mystified how these poor little souls can find the strength to keep the Darkness at bay. I mean, they are constantly under-siege by those nasty vampiric shadows but they are putting up a fight that would rival even the strongest of Kahu. The humans refer to it as 'mental illness' but these are some of the strongest souls I have ever been around. They are faced with unrelenting daily attacks and still find the will to keep fighting. I'm not sure I could be that brave." Ayaan touched her fingers to her tongue then rubbed a spot of ramen broth off her cheek. "I agree Nini. You and I can see the Gaudium Cleptes, but these humans are fighting an enemy that none of them can see. I would be so frustrated.". The guardians sat in silence and marveled at the strength and endurance of those they were sent to protect. Finally, Ninimma broke the silent contemplation, "It makes me quite sad that this will all be over in a week. Callie has connected with her light and by the time she graduates the program, the main shadow shall be out of her life and we can return to Barag." A creeping feeling of melancholy fell over Ayaan. The thing she disliked most about being Kahu was that every victory went hand in hand with a goodbye.

***

Callie put on her nicest set of treatment center approved clothes. Every first Saturday of the month was Parents' Day. On this day parents got to join the activities, including a family counseling session and group therapy class. Callie was excited to share what she was learning with her dad. The therapy had been going very well for her. She hadn't lost weight, but she was eating healthy and starting to appreciate her body. She even started enjoying different dances and was considering asking her dad to sign her up at a real dance studio after she completed her treatment. Before she would have been too self-conscious about her body to even consider dance, but she was beginning to realize that she could enjoy the dance even if no one else in the world enjoyed watching her dance. Callie was even excited to see Cashlin. Tomi, Callie's roommate, was really into makeup and had been teaching Callie about highlighting and shadowing. Callie still had no idea what she was doing, but she was starting to be more interested. It made Callie happy to think she might finally have something in common with Cashlin. Something that they could enjoy together. When the parents were let into the common room, Callie jumped up and down to try and spot her family. When she saw her dad and Cashlin she waved energetically. Her arm flab jiggled back and forth but it was bothering her less and less and she was so excited that her normal negative thoughts were easily dispersed by her happy anticipation. Callie ran to her dad who picked her up in a big hug. Cashlin patted Callie on the back and slowly removed her sunglasses. "Wow. You look… comfortable." Braant shot her a disappointed look but let a huge smile grace his face when he turned back to his daughter. "You look happy! Have you been having fun? Learning a lot?" Callie enthusiastically told them about all the activities she had been doing. Every other sentence she mentioned Bella. Braant tried his best to follow, but was a little lost. "So is this Bella girl your roommate?" Callie laughed, "No. Tomi is my roommate. Bella and Ayaan are my friends that help us with therapy." Callie dragged Braant and a less than exuberant Cashlin around for a tour. They got through their private family session and the group session with not a lot of sharing. Callie was open and Braant did his best to meet her halfway, but was still uncomfortable openly sharing feelings. He was trying to be a good dad, but he was just raised differently. He felt slightly emasculated by what he felt was forced oversharing, but did his best all the same. Cashlin, on the other hand, had no problem talking about herself in a private or public setting. She was so eager to share every small detail about herself that the facilitator in the group session had to politely thank her for her 'generous contributions' and direct the group's attention elsewhere so Cashlin could not monopolize the full hour. Before dinner, Callie led her guest back to the activity room and looked around for Ayaan. When she spotted her she practically ripped Bryant's arm out of the socket trying to pull him to meet her friends. Cashlin followed a step behind holding onto Bryant's other arm. She looked around. Under her breath she sneered "There are so many fat, sad kids here, it's depressing." Braant shot her a warning look. His patience was waning, but he didn't say anything. "Dad, this is my friend Ayaan. She is funny and smart and pretty and likes potpourri." The last part Callie said with a giggle. Ayaan turned to pick up Bella and put her on the table. "Dad, dad, dad, this is Bella. Isn't she cool?" Braant suppressed a grimace and patted Bella on the head. Cashlin, who had been staring blankly out the window turned towards Bella and let out a high-pitched shriek, stopping all other conversation in the room. "Oh for the love of god! What the hell is that?" Braant turned bright red, "Cashlin, easy with the language. There are kids here." Cashlin was flustered and didn't appreciate the reprimand. "I'm sorry Braant, but that thing is hideous. It is making me sick to my stomach." Bella was wagging her tail and sending the sharpest thought daggers she could at Cashlin. Ayaan opened her mouth to say something, but before she could get out a sound Callie spoke up. "Cashlin! You are being very mean! This is a safe space and you can only say things that are positive and uplifting. Those are the rules. Bella is unique and beautiful. She is my friend and everyone here loves her. It's ok if you feel scared or upset about something, but trying to distract yourself and others from your flaws by pointing out the flaws you think Bella has is not very mature." As soon as Braant was able to pick his jaw up off the floor, he had to bite his lip so as not to burst out laughing. It was obvious that Callie was absorbing the advice from her treatment team. "My goodness. I might have to start calling you Dr. Callie." Cashlin, on the other hand, was not as amused. When she worked past her shock. Her anger was cold, but burned a hole in her chest nonetheless. "Braant, this is not funny. You shouldn't let her talk to me like that." Cashlin's voice raised slightly louder and higher pitched with each syllable. Braant tried to diffuse the situation. "Oh Cashlin, don't be so stiff. You did insult her not so furry friend." Cashlin started huffing and puffing and was turning red from hyperventilation. "Braant! Why do you always take her side?! I can't help it if that thing scares me! How can they even have something like that here? It probably terrifies the kids. I didn't even want to come to this stupid thing. You made me and now you're being a jerk!" Dr. Sandra approached to de-escalate the situation. "Hello. Perhaps I can help? Callie lets try to practice respect for opinions we don't agree with. Ms. Foley, I understand where you are coming from, non-traditional veneer can be unnerving to some people. However, Bella is a lovely animal and the children adore her. You don't have to interact with our therapy animal if she makes you uncomfortable. How about we step into the hall so you can catch your breath and we can talk about how we might help you to feel more comfortable?" Braant was rubbing his temples. Cashlin glared at him. "You know what? Leaving sounds like a great idea. I think Mr. Mitchell and I need a bit of space. Braant, I hope you enjoy the rest of this, since it is so much more important to you." Cashlin turned and stomped into the hallway. A moment later she passed by the archway again. A few minutes later she passed a third time. Everyone heard her shout from the hall "How the hell do I get out of here?!" Dr. Sandra signaled to one of the nurses who rushed out to help the irate woman find her way out. There was a painful silence as the others in the room slowly resumed their conversations. Callie's lip trembled. Dr. Sandra waited to see how Braant might handle the situation, but he just stood there looking around the room. "So. Callie, Mr. Mitchell, let's take this opportunity to practice being more open about our feelings. That was a tense experience. How are you feeling Callie?" Callie's nose and upper lip twitched as she forced back tears so she could speak". "I am mad." Dr. Sandra stopped her. "Let's rephrase that a bit. Remember what we learned about 'I am' statements? Emotions are temporary. They are not who you are. Let's reflect that in our language. Try 'I feel" instead." Callie nodded. "I feel mad. I don't think it was nice for Cashlin to be so mean to Bella. It made me feel sad, like when I get bullied." Dr. Sandra put her hand on Callie's shoulder and gave a gentle squeeze. "Good job. Mr. Mitchell, how about you? How are you feeling?" Braant had to fight the urge to roll his eyes. He was already irritated with Cashlin's behavior and talking about his feelings or singing Kumbaya wasn't going to help. He looked at Callie. He could see the pain on her face and it was like a punch in the gut. At that moment, Braant knew he was done with Cashlin. He swallowed his pride with a physical gulp. "I feel embarrassed." He hoped that would be enough, but both Dr. Sandra and Callie kept looking at him so he knew more was expected. "I feel disappointed that Cashlin wasn't more supportive. I feel upset that Callie had to put up with something negative on a day that was supposed to be fun." Braant turned to Callie. "I'm sorry Callie. Cashlin is not really an animal person and I apologize if she hurt your feelings. I think Bella is really nice." Dr. Sandra was pleased. She could tell that emoting was not easy for Callie's dad but it was heartening to see a father willing to try anything for his daughter's sake. "That was a really good start. We can talk about this more later if you want, but for now, why don't you two enjoy your time with Bella and Ayaan before we have dinner?" Bella meowed in agreement.

***

Ayaan and Bella were waiting for Callie and Dr. Sandra near the exit. It was Callie's graduation from the treatment center. She would still be visiting for additional therapy sessions, but she was moving from inpatient treatment to outpatient. Callie was feeling much better about her body since she had started processing her grief from losing her mom, but healing an eating disorder was a long process and was not going to happen over a few months of intensive therapy, but even baby steps are victories. Callie had asked that Ayaan and Bella join her for her final task. Dr. Sandra had a ritual for those leaving the inpatient program to help them build real world confidence. She had every one visit a cafe on their last day and eat something they had considered a 'bad food' before. The goal was to help them face their own judgmental thoughts about the food and their fear of societal judgment of their food choices. Eating at a public cafe helped Dr. Sandra evaluate the patients progress by observing their reactions in an uncontrolled setting. When the group was fully assembled, they headed to a cafe in the hotel across the street. Bella and Dr. Sandra sat at a patio table and Ayaan and Callie went in to order. The line was quite long and Callie was feeling a bit exposed being out in public after being so protected in the center for so long. Ayaan felt her tension and broke the ice with some silly dance moves and they laughed and talked about Callie's plans to join a dance troupe. Ayaan was a bit uneasy herself. The man in front of them scared her. He was saturated in darkness. The real reason for Ayaan's impromptu dance moves were the projectiles of shadow and hate flying off him in all directions. Ayaan kept Callie at a distance and always placed herself in between them, but blocking the spores of gloom was exhausting. Ayaan would have to find a nice patch of sunshine to recharge in when this excursion was over.

***

Ray stood in line with his mother Maria. They had settled into their new life in Connecticut. The U.S. Marshals let him choose his new name. He chose Andre after one of his favorite NFL receivers. Maria chose the name Oriana. The Marshals had gotten her a job as a housekeeper at a nice hotel in New Haven. She was taking English classes and had made a lot of progress. Ray, Andre now, often visited her on her lunch break and they would visit the hotel cafe. This week in her English class, she was learning about shopping vocabulary. Oriana was very excited to practice in real life at the cafe, but was nervous at the same time. While they waited in line she quietly practiced saying her order in English. "Quisiera una cafe con leche por favor. I …. Would like a coffee con… with… ehhh milk please. Puedo comer un sándwich de jamón y queso? En Ingles… ehh May I….eat. No. Mijo, como se dice la primera parte?" Andre was proud of his mom for practicing in public. She was shy when it came to language and she hated looking unintelligent. He was happy she was stepping out of her comfort zone and trying to speak English. "It's 'May I have'." Oriana snapped her fingers. It had been on the tip of her tongue. "Graci- uh Thank you. May I have a sandwich… ehh a ham and cheese sandwich." When they finally reached the front of the line, Oriana panicked and froze up for a moment. The cashier politely asked for their order. Oriana attempted to say her order in English but was slightly struggling under the pressure of observation. The man behind them was making frustrated sounds, but Andre ignored him and encouraged his mom to keep trying. After only another minute the man lost his temper. "This is ridiculous. There is a line! If you can't speak properly go back to your own country. We don't want you inbred, moochers dirtying up our city." The young cashier was speechless. Andre could feel his anger boiling up. Oriana was close to tears and kept apologizing, which just infuriated Andre more. Before he could speak, a girl behind the man spoke up. "Hey! You can't talk to them like that. You are being mean! If you don't want to wait, you are the one who should go." The man whipped around to face the girl. Callie stood there with her hands on her hips. She was not going to allow bullying. She had had her fill of bullying in her lifetime and wasn't going to be quiet and take it for even a moment longer. The man glared at her. "Look girl, you should mind your own business. Maybe if you ran your legs as much as your mouth you wouldn't be so fat." Callie was shocked and her first instinct was to cry, but Ayaan's words echoed in her brain, "People who are scared try to point out the flaws in others so others won't see the flaws in them." Ayaan was ready to claw this man's face off but as she started to say something in Callie's defense, Callie put her hand on her arm to silence her. "Sir, I am sorry you hate yourself so much that you feel you have to bully others, but it is not ok to say those types of things to people. I may be curvy, but I am healthy and beautiful and I like how I am, no matter what you say." Callie said it more as a mantra for herself rather than a lesson to the evil man, but it had an effect. The man turned to complain to the employee, but the young girl had recovered her composure. "Sir. I'm going to have to ask you to leave. Please go now or I will have to call the police." The man scoffed and flipped the cashier the middle finger and stormed out. As he left, Callie deflated and tears started to run down her cheeks. Oriana walked up to her and gave her a big hug. "Thank you". Andre also approached Callie. "That was really cool. Don't be sad about what he said. You aren't fat, he was just dumb." The two kids chatted while Oriana attempted her English order a second time.

    Outside the cafe Bella felt her skin begin to crawl. Now on high alert, she frantically looked around to locate the source of her unease. The jerk from the line plowed through the door and stomped past the table that Bella was perched on. Bella had never seen something so terrifying on the earth plane. The man was shadowed by a large human-like figure that was three times his size. The apparition was attached to the man by multiple tube-like cords. The darkness was not black but a void. Flashing inside the void were harsh colors of red, brown, and orange. The darkness of the form seemed to be melting like candle wax. Bella hissed as the man walked by. Bella was silenced mid growl. She knew that man. "It couldn't be." She thought. Dr. Sandra tried her best to soothe Bella, not understanding why the cat was so upset. Not long after, Ayaan and Callie returned accompanied by Andre and Oriana. Callie and Andre waved their goodbyes and Callie sat down with her pumpkin cream cheese muffin. Callie and Ayaan recounted their line experience and Dr. Sandra was excited to hear that the thing Callie was focusing on most was not the behavior of the nasty patron, but her new friendship with Andre. Ayaan noticed the fear written in Bella's face and stance. Her questioning look was answered by a voice in her mind. "I know that man. He used to be a Ni under our protection. His name is Gideon and if I hadn't seen it with my own eyes, I would not have believed it. He has become Dalkhu. I am glad that Callie has finally found the connection with her light, because we need to return to Barag. Now."

CHAPTER SEVENTEEN
Hisstory Repeats Itself

Ki-Ang sat silently in front of the large rainbow obsidian piece of glass. He had finally gotten through his Kanunuru of his lives with Gideon. The pain was still fresh but tempered by the strength he received in his rehabilitation Ti. His reflection stared back at him from the huge slab. As he blankly stared at the stone, two more faces materialized beside his reflection. Ama-gi and Ninimma gave Ki-Ang time to process the Kanunuru of his lives with Gideon. The sting of his failure still hurt and he had trouble meeting the gaze of his fellow Kahu. After spending time with his little girl, Asha, he remembered the reason he became Kahu. He loved humans. When safe from the influence of the Gaudium Cleptes, humans were loving, passionate, funny, brave, generous, creative, resourceful, stubborn but magnanimous. He loved everything about them. It was why he fought so hard to protect them from the perversion of the Darkness. His failure with Gideon had been a result of his own impatience and ego. He had let himself become complacent, which was his first mistake. He then overcorrected and derailed things further. His stomach felt as if he had eaten barbed wire, but he could not go back to change anything, he could only learn from the experiences and do better moving forward. He closed his eyes so he could hold tighter to the memory of his time with his girl. If he could just keep the feeling of that love strong in his heart, he would have the strength to continue his calling. First things first, he had to smooth things out with Ama-gi. "Ama, I'm sorry. You were right. I should have backed off and trusted you when you cancelled the second Girru. My pride was hurt and I let my emotions get in the way of my logic. I'm ready to get back to work, if you'll have me." Ki-Ang bowed his head in contrition. Before Ama-gi could answer, a loud sob diverted their attention. Ninimma's bottom lip was trembling and her eyes were as big as saucers. "Oh, I'm sorry. I just love happy reunions and I am so happy to have you back!" She ran and pounced on Ki-Ang, head butting him and rubbing her face on his. Ki-Ang accepted the affection but freed himself as soon as he could. Ama-gi tried not to show her amusement. Inside, she felt the same as Ninimma. She would never admit it though, at least out loud. Ama-gi avoided eye contact so as not to give away any hint of her feelings. "Your insubordination is forgiven. Don't let it happen again. Now let's get to work." Ninimma made a little 'ahem' sound. "Shouldn't we tell him about, you know, the um, development?" Ama-gi glared at Ninimma and gave a small but vigorous shake of head. The action did not go unnoticed. Ki-Ang watched as Ninimma turned pink and Ama-gi tried to change the subject. "We should head to Ziana Giš. The others are waiting for us." Ki-Ang's curiosity was killing him, but as a cat, he tried not to let it get the best of him. He refrained from asking more questions and followed Ama-gi and Ninimma to the Tree of Life.

The trio entered an area that looked like it was raining light. A humongous Banyan tree stood in the center of the clearing. It was so large and had so many prop roots that it looked like a forest in and of itself. Above there was a bright warm light that spilled over the impressive tree. Its canopy was all encompassing, but was dispersed enough to allow scattered rays of light to pour through the branches, like the appearance of rainfall in the distance. The main base of the tree did not appear to be a solid trunk but looked like a plethora of skinnier trees huddled together. The massively thick branched jutted out parallel to the ground in multiple levels. At the center of the tree, there was a flat open area like a natural tree house. This spot was called the heart of Ziana Giš. No branches covered this circle and the light flooded the spot like a spotlight on a stage. The tree had hundreds, if not thousands, of branches. The higher branches had sprouted smaller offshoots with leaves. The lower branches were smooth and growing moss in places. Some of the Kahu like to nap on these mossy pillows and recharge in the beams of light. This area was a refuge for the Kahu. It was a place to regain their strength or contemplate their past Girrus. Most of the Kahu used the tree of life as a meeting place, as the energy of the tree was supportive and aided in clear thinking. The tree itself was alive with its own spirit. The spirit of the tree was nurturing and some of the Kahu referred to her as Grandmother. Grandmother was permissive of the Kahu's feline behaviors and allowed them to sharpen their claws on her trunk or chase each other through her branches. Ninimma, Ama-gi, and Ki-Ang were met in the heart of the tree by a group of senior Kahu. Ki-Ang recognized Lumma, Ninlil, Shai, and Nuska, as well as some senior Kahu from other quadrants but he couldn't remember their names. The situation must be more dire than he had imagined if so many experienced Kahu had paused their Girru to meet. Dingir was absent as well as Iksuda. Ki-Ang noted the absence to ask Ama-gi about it later. Maahes noticed the three approaching and ran to meet them. He stayed sheepishly quiet, but took a place by their side. When Ama-gi made her way to the center of the group, a hush fell over the congregation. "Silim. We all know why we are here, so I will get to the point. The Gaudium Cleptes has changed. For the first time in recorded history, it would appear that the Darkness has accomplished a coordinated attack on not only Ni but Kahu as well. This would suggest a level of sentience that we have yet to attribute to this mindless force. I have reached out to the other quadrants and there is a theory developing that may help us to better understand what is happening. Kaibyō is Eridu Kahu and has a theory that might help us in our effort to understand and neutralize this new threat." A cat that was slightly larger than a normal house cat made his way to the center of the group. His legs were longer and he was thinner than the average cat. He was tan but covered in black spots of various sizes except along his back which sported three rows of elongated spots. His long tail was also spotted with faded rings near a black tipped end. His chest and short muzzle were white and narrow. Two distinct black stripes ran up the sides of his nose touching the insides of his orbital sockets and extending up past his long, rounded ears. He spoke in Japanese, but the group heard him in their preferred language. Since a large part of the Sanu Erdiu quadrant spoke English as the main language, most of the Sanu Eridu Kahu preferred to use English. Some of the more experienced Kahu, such as Ninlil, who began their journey in the Eridu quadrant, still preferred Sumerian. Ama-gi strongly encouraged all the Kahu in her quadrant to use modern languages to keep them fresh in their minds for their Girru. Kaibyō spoke in a soft but authoritative voice. "As luck would have it, my most recent Girru was with a Japanese virologist. My Ni, Hitoshi, has dedicated much of his career to studying the evolution of different viruses. Virus evolution or mutation is a process that happens over time. Please forgive my short science lecture, but I think it may help us understand what is happening. A virus, has two different phases. There is the Lytic phase or active phase and the Lysogenic phase or dormant phase. In the lytic phase, a virus uses the host cell to replicate rapidly, this can overwhelm or even kill the cell. In the lysogenic phase, the virus lies dormant, only replicating when the host cell replicates. In this latter phase, the virus can survive, slowly replicating, until conditions are appropriate for an outbreak or rather, for the virus to switch back to the lytic phase. Recently, colleagues of my Ni at the Weizmann Institute discovered that viruses can release molecular messages into their environment that other viruses can read and use to decide on the best infection strategy. For example, a virus that over replicated and killed the host cells too quickly might leave messages so that other viruses or even its own replications could know that the lysogenic phase or dormant phase is a better strategy. Viruses can use this secreted information to actually coordinate their attacks. I believe this is what we are seeing with the Darkness. Think of us, the Kahu, as immune cells and the Darkness as a virus. The Darkness uses a host, the Ni, to replicate and infect other Ni. Our job is to stop them from infecting our Ni therefore preventing their replication and further infection. However, if a virus is dormant, the immune cells can not destroy it. Viruses use this coordinated dormancy to reduce the presence of immune cells. When the immune cells are sufficiently absent, the virus can switch from the lysogenic phase to the lytic phase and create a tsunami of replication. I believe that was what we experienced with the Darkness. Over the centuries, the Darkness has been mostly dormant, replicating passively along with human replication. We would see the occasional outbreak of darkness, but rarely anything on a global scale. This lulled us into complacency which the Gaudium Cleptes used to achieve their synchronized replication. Viruses have been known to exhibit rudimentary forms of hive mentality, so perhaps that is what we are seeing here. Thankfully, just as viruses cannot replicate without the use of the host and they cannot create their own energy, we only have to refocus our efforts to cut them off from the hosts in order to stop them. If we redouble our effort to ignite the light of the Halqu and continue to protect the Ni, we should be able to effectively cut off the Gaudium Cleptes from further replication." When Kaibyō went silent, a loud snoring sound was heard from the surrounding cats. Ki-Ang looked to his right and saw the source of the sound. Nuska had rolled onto his back to absorb the bright light from their place in the heart of Ziana Giš and had fallen asleep. Ki-Ang looked away while quickly and discreetly kicking Nuska with his back foot. Nuska flipped onto his feet and shouted, "Ma hovercraft's breemin' ower wi eels!" He quickly looked around as he got his bearings. Embarrassed he said "Och! Sorry. Gi'es a do 'ver. I was actin' a numpty." Ama-gi took control of the symposium once again. "I agree with Kaibyō's assessment. We will be divvying out new Girru. We will need to mobilize many more Kahu to add protection to vulnerable Ni and you, more experienced Kahu, will be assigned to those that have succumbed to the Halqu stage. Ninlil and Shai will divine the best timing for your interventions. I have spoken with the leaders of the Canine Kahu. They will be recruiting a new wave of Kahu and I feel we should do the same. From now on we will be working more closely with the Canine Kahu." A unanimous groan came from the gathering. An arched back from Ama-gi quickly quieted them down. "We *will* put our differences aside in order to best assist the humans. We are in dire times. Another urgent matter we need to discuss is the confirmed sighting of a Dalhku." A collective gasp brought an eerie silence over the gathering. Ninimma stepped forward. "I can confirm that while on Earth for my Girru, both Lumma and I had a seemingly chance encounter with a fully formed Dalkhu of the soul of the former Ni, Gideon Chance. It was suspected after his murder of his Kahu that he had transitioned, but it had not been confirmed until now. Furthermore, the Dalkhu is targeting Ni. The seers and I have been looking into its behavior and have noticed a pattern of contact with Ni. It is unknown if these interactions are intentional or a result of the Dalkhu being drawn to the strong energy emitted by Ni. Either way, this puts all Ni in severe danger, especially those that have not fully connected with their light. If even a small seed of the Dalkhu's darkness enters an unprotected Ni, they could be instantaneously transformed into a Halqu. Worst case, we might see the reproduction of more Dalkhu. The host needs to be stopped immediately before its Dalkhu energy can spread." Ki-Ang was devastated. His heart still could not give up on Gideon and a small part of him continued to hold out hope that Gideon might be redeemed. He did not like the implication of Ninimma's words. If Gideon could not be redeemed, he had to be stopped, yet the only option available to stop the Dalkhu was to kill the host. Ki-Ang was desperate to believe that his friend was still in there somewhere. He did not want to condemn his soul in an attempt to rid the Earth of the Dalkhu. He didn't know what to do. Ama-gi took the floor again. "As Kahu, we took an oath to protect Ni. Now we are faced with a situation that demands that we harm one we once vowed to protect in an effort to save others. I believe that the needs of the many outweigh the needs of the one." Ama-gi looked directly at Ki-Ang. "I know others might have a difference of opinion, but the longer we procrastinate, the stronger the Dalkhu will get and the greater the threat of harm becomes. This sort of formidable blitz by the darkness has never been seen before-" A voice rang out from the base of the tree. The sound caused a commotion among the gathered Kahu. Everyone turned their attention to the approaching feline.

The elder Kahu seemed to recognize the voice, but Maahes being relatively new to the Kahu was at a loss. He strained to see over the crowd. Approaching in a smooth saunter was the most beautiful calico he had ever seen. The cat looked like someone had taken an orange tabby and a brown tabby and smushed them together, all while peppering in splotches of black and white. Her long hair flowed like silk. Her body was faintly tiger striped, alternating stripes of orange and brown. On her sides were patches of white, orange and black. Her front paws looked like she was wearing dainty white gloves. The top of her head displayed a distinct 'M', half being orange and the other half being brown. Her eyes were shadowed with a perfect Egyptian eye liner pattern with orange under shading. A perfect pink nose stood out on a backdrop of white. When the graceful feline breached the center of the circle of cats, Ama-gi gasped and ran to her. Ama-gi gently head-butted the calico and rubbed her face on hers affectionately. "Inanna! You're back!" Others approached Inanna to greet her, but she leaned back on her haunches and put both her front paws up in the air to get everyone's attention. "I am afraid I must correct Ama-gi. This type of event has happened before." A few of the more experienced Kahu hung their heads in shame. The majority of the group looked around confused. Inanna continued. "Centuries ago, in my final Girru before deciding to dedicate myself to enlightenment, I was witness to a similar situation. Those of us in leadership positions, not only among us Feline Kahu but Avian and Canine Kahu as well, made the decision to keep the events quiet. We made the decision to attempt to quell the Darkness by allowing the removal en masse of those infected by darkness. Those of us that had a paw in the decision are ashamed of what we did, but like you, we believed that the good of the many outweighed the good of the few. We had believed that our strategy was successful, but as we are yet again facing this predicament, we see that the cost far outweighed the benefit." Ama-gi was befuddled. As the current leader of the Sanu Eridu Kahu, she thought she knew the full history of the Kahu. It hurt that her mentor could have kept something so important from her. She tried to hide the feeling of betrayal from her voice. "I don't understand what you are talking about." Inanna looked at

Ninlil. With a nod, a large bubble appeared over the gathering. Ninlil, Shai, and two other seers formed four corners around the bubble and Inanna made her way to the center, directly below the large effervescence. "It is too difficult to explain so we will show you." The four seers' eyes turned bright white and shot beams of light into the sphere above Inanna. As their light lit the bubble a single beam broke through and connected to Inanna and an image began to appear in the bubble. The group watched with rapt attention. As the image came into focus they all felt drawn into it and with a final burst of energy, they were all pulled in.

CHAPTER EIGHTEEN
Bite The Hand

Tammo sat on the earth floor of his family's hut. They didn't have much in the way of luxury, but he was warm and his belly was full so he was happy. He was hard at work stripping a large stick of its branches to turn it into a training sword. Tammo was born to farmers, so he had no hope of ever becoming a knight, but that didn't stop his daydreams. He pretended that their large watch dog was a valiant steed and he was a heroic knight defending the realm from evil invaders. The dog's name was Count after Maurice I the Count of Oldenburg. Tammo's father hated the Count and it pleased him to insult the nobleman by naming his dog after the title that meant so much to the nobles. The pigs were called Maurice, also named after the Count, along with any animal bound for slaughter. This particular evening, his father and some of the other influential men of the community were discussing important matters. They were Stedinger, peasant farmers that inhabited the land of Stedingen, a region between the lower Hunte and Weser river, opposite the city of Bremen. Tammo was happily focused on his work until fists slamming on the table drew his attention to the men. "The tyrant is demanding to be paid a portion of the dowry or he will exercise his right of jus primae noctis!" The man yelling was named Otbald. He was not a tall man, but he was muscular thanks to his toils in the fields. Otbald's daughter was to be wed in the spring. Maurice I the Count of Oldenburg had increasingly been demanding more and more taxes from the Stedinger people. Stedinger were farmers with freehold of their land, meaning that other than certain taxes and tithes, the fruit of their labors and gifts of the land belonged to the farmers. Most Stedinger were subjects of the Prince-Archbishop of Bremen, but their land bordered the Duchy of Oldenburg to the northwest and some of the farmers were subjects of the Count of Oldenberg. The Stedinger men were angry because the Count of Oldenburg and Hartwig Von Stade, the Archbishop of Bremen, were encroaching on their rights as freemen. Stedingen had been a free community for almost as long as the Duchy of Oldenburg had existed. The Oldenburg Duchy had only been established in 1091 by the Archbishop of Bremen Adalbert I. The archbishop had created the Duchy to help the ascension of his niece Richenza and her husband Eglimar I. Most of the other farmers in the surrounding areas were serfs, leasing the land from either the noblemen of the area or the representative of the Holy Roman Empire, such as the Prince-Archbishop of Bremen. The Stedinger were different though. In 1106, Archbishop of Bremen Fredrick I gave the Stedinger freehold of the land, made them exempt from most taxes, and gave them autonomy over their community. This bill of rights was called the Ius Hollandicum or Hollandic Right as most of the Stedinger people had migrated from Holland to escape Viking raids. For ninety-eight years, the Stedinger people had worked hard to cultivate the unwanted marsh land given to them by Archbishop Fredrick I. They had developed a well-defined community and were living in peace and a degree of prosperity. Unfortunately, political unrest and a number of crusades had put financial pressure on the Archbishop and noblemen of the area. Their hardship was pushing them to get evermore creative in their attempt to fund their pursuits. These men of the upper class began to see the Stedinger people not as an independent community under common law, but as an untapped resource within their domain. Demands for tithes had increased. Taxes that had been waived were now imposed. This latest threat to enforce the right of the first night was just another ploy to levy yet another tax on the people. Otbald paced the small area. "I will not allow that disgusting beast to lie with my daughter on her wedding night. If he even thinks to touch her I will have his hand or any other part he lays on her! And I will be a pig fart before I pay him even one heller to leave my daughter to her husband!" Another man placed his hand on Otbald's shoulder to calm him. "I agree that the upper class has been overstepping much of late and it will only get worse if we stand by and do nothing. However, yelling about it will not change anything. I have had my ear to the ground and many of us feel the same as you. Perhaps it is time we stop complaining and act like the free men we are." The older man retreated to a bench and lowered his more rotund body to the seat in order to better see the reaction of the others. Tammo's father Clays broke the silent contemplation. "Renerus, it is best if you speak your thoughts clearly. If you are suggesting a course of action, you may feel safe to share. None here suffer from loose lips or tender spots in our hearts for the Count." Renerus smiled. "While watching my flocks, I have had my share of encounters with greedy wolves who wished to take what did not belong to them. It has been my experience that the only way to deal with wolves is a show of force." Otbald's anger was beginning to reemerge. "Donnerwetter Renerus! Just tell us your plan!" Renerus stood and crossed back to the table, using leftover food items to create a makeshift war table. "Bremen and Oldenburg are short on men, thanks to Emperor Frederick's conflict with Henry the Lion and Pope Innocent's great crusade on the Holy Land. We can easily gather men to mount an attack against Maurice. We have allowed the Count to encroach on our territory and build two castles within. I suggest we destroy these affronts to our independence. This would make him think twice about revoking our rights or over-reaching into our lands again." Tammo listened with rapt attention. His fantasies of becoming a knight and fighting a war quickly morphed into Sir Tammo fighting his way through the tyrannical regime of Count Maurice I and setting fire to his castles. His dog Count left his spot by the fire to lay his head in the boy's lap. Tammo scratched Count behind the ears. "When I am a brave knight protecting the free realm of Stedingen, you won't have to be my horse anymore. You can be by my side."

***

Weeks went by and Renerus, Clays, and Otbald were able to recruit most of the men they spoke to for their campaign against the Count of Oldenburg. Almost all the volunteers lacked any kind of formal military training, but they were strong, resourceful, and determined. The prospect of handing over their hard earned wealth in illegal taxes to a distant overlord did not sit well with them. They would pay what was agreed upon in the Hollandic Right. No more, no less. As all the men gathered to launch their assault, Tammo rushed to his home to grab his wooden sword. His mother grabbed him by the tunic as he tried to rush out. "Mutti! I have to go. We are storming the Schloss!" His mother took his bag and sword. "You have a few more years yet before you can stage a revolt." Tammo tried to grab his bundle back from his mother and escape, but it was futile. "That is not fair! Count gets to go!" His mother was proud of her son's bravery, but tried not to encourage him. "Tammo, Count will help keep your father and the others safe on their journey and if your father needs to send a message, he can send a note with Count. You need to focus on growing. I am sure there will be many opportunities for you to help protect our people in the future." Tammo was not satisfied by her answer and twisted to break free of her grip. He ran as fast as his short legs could carry him. When he reached the men, his mom caught up with him and tried to drag him back to their home. Clays, hearing the scuffle made his way over to assist. "Rosafiere, let the boy go." Tammo ran to his dad, thinking he had won and would be allowed to join the group, but his dad kneeled down next to him. "Tammo, you will respect your mutter. You are getting too big to make her fight you." Tammo crinkled his brows "She would not give me my sword so I can go with you to fight." Clays laughed. "You are my boy. You will get your chance, but for now I need you to stay here and protect your mutter and the other women and children." Tammo didn't like being left behind, but the idea of being left with such an important job pleased him. "Ok vater, I will protect mutti, but next time make Renerus stay. He is old and likes women more than I do." Clays's hearty laugh brought a lightness to the otherwise dark morning. The men said their goodbyes and headed off.

    A half a day's walk into their journey, the men stopped to rest and revisit their strategy. They would split into two groups and under the guise of delivering payment, they would enter the castles, overpower the garrisons, drive them from the land, and destroy the castles. As the men divided themselves for this overly simple plan, Count ran around frantically sniffing the ground to clear the area of any possible threats. Satisfied that the men were safe, he made his way from the clearing to a small wooded area. He relieved himself on several trees and sniffed the air in an attempt to locate water. A few feet away he found what he was searching for. A pool of water had formed in a decaying tree stump. Count peered into the water at his reflection. He had a fat but long head with scruffy fur. He was a mutt, probably with a predominance of Alaunt and some mix of Terrier. He was stocky and strong but had the quickness of a greyhound. As he stared into the water it began to ripple and an image appeared. A different dog stared at him. They had one blue eye and one gold eye but both seemed to pierce straight through his soul. They were large, larger than even he was, and their muzzle was long and defined. The fur on their face was pure white. It was smooth around their eyes but flared out as it went down their neck. They were much more wolf-like than any of the dogs he knew. The wolf-dog spoke with a calm tone. "Dazhbog- Apologies, what do they call you this Girru?" The dog staring into the water wagged his tail at his old name. "They call me Count here, Uchitel." The gorgeous colors of his companion's eyes sparkled when he called them teacher. It wasn't often that he was able to use Slavic dialects. Uchitel continued. "Ah yes, Count. Many of the Ni in your pack's care are rapidly approaching their confrontation with darkness. What is your status?" "The men are en-route to defend their freedoms. As predicted, they will remain free by either fighting to regain their autonomy or dying as free men. My pack and I will accompany them and do what we can to preserve their lives." The white wolf-dog shook their head. "Do what you can, but the protection of their light supersedes the protection of their lives. Remember that a human life is short, but the loss of their light would doom them to a continual Ti cycle while they fight their internal shadows. Do your best to keep up their morale and courage. As long as it is only their physical form that perishes, their light will remain strong and be reborn." A loud whistle alerted Count to the group's movement. "My pack and I will keep our Ni strong and stay by their sides. Worry not." With little more he took a quick drink of the water and was off.

***

Tammo sat by the door staring off to the north. His father had been gone for weeks. The women and few men that stayed behind had kept things in the settlement operating as usual, but the more time passed, the more they worried about the fate of their loved ones. Tammo did not share his mother's concern. There was no doubt in his mind that his father and fellow Stedinger would return triumphant. As dusk began to fall into night, Tammo begrudgingly pushed himself off his log perch and turned to go inside. A distant barking tickled his ears and he turned to locate the sound. To the northern horizon, slightly lit by the westerly setting sun was the faint shape of a scruffy hound. Tammo called to his mom and the nearby villagers milling around outside their homes. As fast as his feet could carry him he ran towards the dog. Count closed the distance between them faster than the boy could and jumped up with his massive paws on the boy's shoulders knocking him to the ground. Count jumped over him multiple times, licking his face between each jump. Tammo laughed and hugged Count all while trying to look past him in the direction he had come from. A moment of panic settled over Tammo when he didn't see anyone, but then he heard a loud whistle. Count perked up his ears and took off in the direction of the whistle. A few moments later a group of men breached the horizon, slowly making their way towards the village. Many of the villagers had begun to gather in the square and shouts of welcome were building on each other like thunder rolling in over the mountains. Tammo heard the high pitch squeal of his mother as she rushed into the homecoming crowd. He followed her as she made her way through the men not unlike a snake slithering through a rodent hole. Bringing up the rear of the group was Clays supporting a singed Otbald. Rosafiere shouted commands to some of the idle women and they went to fetch healing herbs. Clays helped Otbald into the arms of his daughter just in time to catch Rosafiere as she flung herself into his arms. "You took your time." She cried as small hiccups of laughter escaped her lips. Tammo followed suit, hugging his father and mother so hard they almost all toppled into a pile. Count, not wanting to be left out, let out a series of barking howls. "Looks like Count is taking control of announcing our victory." Clays said as he affectionately ruffled up the hair on his son's head. By the time the group made it to the village square, most of the villagers had come out to meet them. Renerus shouted to get everyone's attention. "We, the *free men* of Stedingen have introduced the Count of Oldenburg to the fires of hell at not one but *two* of his mighty castles. All that is left are ashes and soot!" A cheer rang up from the crowd. Tammo noticed that his mother did not appear as jovial as the others. Clays lifted her chin. "What's wrong, my fiery rose? We are victorious. We have warned the Count that we are not the underfoot serfs he is used to trampling on. We accomplished our goal." Rosafiere smiled weakly and placed her hand on his cheek. "I know. I am so proud of you. I just fear that we have poked a beast we may regret having awakened." Clays nodded his understanding. In the background Renerus began recounting their hero's journey. Clays tried to reassure his wife, "Oldenburg left us no choice. We had to show both the Count and Archbishop that we are not to be trifled with. You need not worry so much. Our land is blessed with many natural fortifications. It took us much effort to move our large group out of these lands. It would be close to impossible for heavy laden knights to mount an offense. Besides, with the crusades, neither the Count nor the Archbishop have armies to spare. The castles we decimated had only a handful of men protecting them. The resistance we were met with mounted to little more than the prick of a thorn. Poor Count received the largest share of injury while attacking their archers." Her husband's reassurance raised Rosafiere's spirits but something deep in her stomach would not let the nagging feeling of doom be discarded completely.

***

Eight years passed. Count was lying on a pile of hay near the dirt path to his home. The years were beginning to catch up with him and his new favorite pass-time was falling asleep in the path of the sunshine. His ears began to twitch as they picked up the faint sound of someone approaching at high speeds. Count rolled to his side and plopped a paw over his face. His nose sniffed the air and he gave a lazy "boorf" without expending much effort. Rosafiere exited the house to place some freshly cut herbs on the drying rack. She shaded her eyes to the sun and looked towards the approaching noise. Before she could make out the figures. Tammo flew by, leaping over the fence. Following closely at his heels were four young pups. Rosafiere couldn't decide if the pups were more excited to be chasing after Tammo or the old wooden sword he was carrying, an item that had become one of their favorite chew toys. Tammo leapt over the sleeping Count and rounded the back of the home. The pups were less coordinated and didn't pay much heed to the sleeping dog, trampling right over him. The offense earned them nips on the butt from a very angry grandpa. After the revolt in 1204, the Stedinger people continued to defy illegal demands of the Count of Oldenburg and the Archbishop. Luckily for Stedinger, Archbishop Hartwig had fallen too ill to spend energy worrying about a small patch of land and its uncooperative peasants. After his death in 1207, Burchard Count of Stumpenhausen became Archbishop, but he was only interested in Hamburg, while Vlademar of Denmark took up the title of Archbishop in Bremen. Burchard was part of the Oldenburg line, but the political rivalry between him and Vlademar had kept them both far too busy to think about Stedingen. More good tidings came to the Stedinger people in 1209 when they heard news that Maurice I, Count of Oldenburg had died. Many had hoped that this would mean an end to the greed of the House of Oldenburg, but such happy endings are only for daydreams. In 1210, Gerhard I von Oldenburg-Wildeshausen became Archbishop of Bremen. Gerhard I was the late Count Maurice's cousin. Maurice I had been succeeded by both his sons Otto I and Christian II who ruled jointly as Counts of Oldenburg. Stedinger found themselves surrounded by the house of Oldenburg and around 1211 the imposition of illegal taxes began to be pushed on the Stedingen community once again. Just as the offices of the noblemen had been renewed with fresh blood ready to make their mark, so too had the Stedinger people. Tammo was fourteen and eager to prove he was as much a man as his father. He had worked hard every day and spent every free moment he had training his body and his mind. He knew the land of Stedingen like the back of his hand and could run the trails blindfolded. He knew every rock and tree and hill better than anyone in the Holy Roman Empire. More and more often, messengers from the Archbishop's ministeriales, groveling serfs given the rank of knight, ventured north of Hunte to press for what they felt the Archbishop was owed. Now, in the spring of 1212, Stedinger were losing their patience once again. Tammo finished his run at the southeast border of the village. His pups caught up with him, followed by a perturbed Count, who was still growling his displeasure at the young brood. Count unexpectedly redirected his growling from the pups to four strange men at the door of the nearby farmhouse. Tammo recognized their attire as that of the Archbishop's men. They had come on foot, as large groups of horses had a difficult time negotiating the marshy land. They didn't have much in the way of weapons. One had a crossbow, but it was not loaded and appeared to be tied to his belt. Two had swords, but one was so rotund that Tammo doubted he had the dexterity to even unsheathe the weapon. The fourth had no weapon and looked mousey and far too high strung. Tammo would have wagered that a loud fart would send the weakling to an early grave. Not wanting to give into his hotheaded predilections, Tammo brought his dogs to heel and watched from the cover of the trees. A girl around Tammo's age answered the knock of the men. Tammo knew the girl, but they were not especially close as he didn't have time for idle socialization. Her name was Amelina. He couldn't hear what was being said, but by the look on Amelia's face, he deduced it wasn't a friendly visit. He heard her shout for the men to leave, but they didn't listen. The large man tried to push his way into the house, but Amelina stepped back and kicked him in the nether region with all her might. The man hunched over in pain and out of rage grabbed Amelina by the hair, dragging her out of the doorway. When the brute threw her to the ground and kicked her, Tammo knew it was time to act. With one whistle, Tammo and his dogs were flying towards the fight. He yelled "Angriff!" And all four pups led by Count lunged in attack. As Tammo expected, the mousey man, seeing the onslaught of bared teeth, fainted. The dogs went after the large man beating the girl. As the man with the crossbow struggled to free it from his belt, Tammo charged the man drawing his sword. The only defense Tammo had was his wooden play sword and his wits. He swung his practice sword at the man's sword hand, hitting him with such force that he heard three of the fingers break. When his opponent swung with his opposite hand, Tammo slid under the blow, scooping up a handful of sandy dirt in the process. In a fluid motion he threw the sand in his opponents eyes, who doubled over, desperately trying to clear the debris and regain his sight. Using the opportunity, Tammo unsheathed the man's sword and turned his attention to the one with the crossbow. He could hear the struggle of the dogs with the large man, but he couldn't be distracted. He trusted his hounds and knew that even though Count was old, he was a warrior. What Count lacked in energy would be made up by the youthful vigor of his grandpups. Based on the screams he was hearing, Tammo gathered that his dogs were in control. Crossbow man finally freed his weapon but not in time to load it before Tammo was forcing him into defensive actions. He tried to use the crossbow as a shield to block Tammo's overhead swings of his newly acquired sword. The sword was heavier than Tammo had expected and his arms were shaking with the effort. The subtle shortcomings of their young opponent were lost on the tax collectors. Tammo lifted his sword and brought it down in a mighty stroke. The force was so strong that when it hit the crossbow, it split the tiller across the bolt groove. The man dropped the useless piece of wood and put his hands up in defense. Tammo did not strike but held the sword at the man's chest. A subtle shift in the unarmed man's gaze made Tammo turn around. The original owner of the sword had recovered his sight and was standing over Tammo with a dagger. The young man had not noticed the dagger earlier and he cursed himself for his lack of observance. Tammo tried to whirl the sword around, but before he could defend himself, the man slumped to his knees, revealing a panting Amelina holding a large rock covered in blood. She yelled a warning and Tammo turned to find the crossbow man lunging at him with another hidden dagger. This time Tammo was able to position the sword in time and the charging man lunged into the tip of the blade and sank to the hilt. Tammo stood in stunned silence. The tearing of material drew his attention. The pups were latched onto the large man on the ground. Count was latched onto the man's shoulder close to his neck. Two pups were tugging on the man's right arm. His left arm was pinned under the weight of his own body. A pup was tearing at the leg of his trousers. A fourth pup was lying listless near the bleeding but alive man. A smaller man would have probably succumbed to the injuries, but the ample layer of fat had protected the man enough to preserve his life. Tammo's first reaction at seeing his lifeless dog was to grab the dagger from the man on his sword and drag it across the man's throat. As he slashed, a strong hand grabbed his hand holding the knife. Over his shoulder Tammo saw his father and a group of men. "We should question him. He might be able to tell us about the plans of the Archbishop." The other men grabbed the two men left alive and Clays commanded "Mildern!". Count released his hold on the fat man. The pups were harder to convince, but a few barks by Count encouraged them to let go. Tammo turned to the fourth pup. Amelina had scooped up the body and was holding it in her lap. "He is not dead. He just has a nasty bump on his head. I will take him to my mutter. She has a talent for healing." Tammo helped Amelina up and she walked off carrying her precious cargo.

***

The Stedinger men gathered to discuss the Archbishop's insult. "The gaul of the ministeriales of the Archbishop! To think that they could send men into our land and attack us, a young girl at that! He should pay." Otbald was red in the face with outrage. "We had hoped that by showing force but continuing to fulfill our obligations of the Hollandic Right, that the Archbishop would honor the promise his predecessor made to our people. This is not the case." Clays was beginning to show his age. He would do anything to protect the interests of his people, but he was getting a bit old for burning down castles. A young voice spoke up. "The noblemen of Bremen and Oldenburg have broken the agreement for a second time. If they will not honor their word, what binds us to ours? This is our land. We cultivated these marshes when no one else cared to muddy their tunics. The nobility gives us nothing yet dare to demand that which we have earned. We owe nothing to those greedy leeches. Our previous message was heard by Count Maurice I but has been lost on his sons. Perhaps we should remind them of the might of Stedinger." Tammo was ready to contribute to his people. All of the young boys who had idolized the men for going against Oldenburg years ago were now men ready to take up their fathers' mantle. Many of the more combat knowledgeable men in the village had been training the boys in the rare case that the nobles did seek to escalate the conflict. As a result the young men were now eager to put their skills to use. Renerus spoke up. "The lad is right. Attacking the Count worked last time, there is no reason why it should not work again. In the interim, why should we pay anything at all to brutes that would assail us on our own land?" Remarks in agreement rippled through the gathering. Clays was reluctant to renege on their side of the agreement. The wrongdoings of one party did not seem like a valid reason for the other party to commit the same evil. Stedinger were honorable people. Dishonorable acts by the noblemen should not be cause for Stedinger to lose their honor as well, but he could tell by the enthusiasm of the crowd that his objection would not be looked upon favorably. The men started devising a strategy to cause the most destruction to the Counts of Oldenburg and the Archbishop with the least amount of risk to themselves. Chief among the planners was Tammo.

***

The Stedinger people ceased paying all taxes and tithes and ejected all of the Archbishop's men from their land. Over the next three years they launched attacks on Archbishop Gerhard I's castles, successfully driving off his ministeriales from Hunte. To the Stedingers' surprise, no action was taken against them by the Archbishop. In 1219, they got word that Gerhard I von Oldenburg-Wildeshausen, Archbishop of Bremen had died and was being succeeded by Gerhard II Sur Lippe as the Archbishop of Bremen and Hamburg.

***

Gerhard II slowly walked through his castle, surveying his new domain. As the fifth son of his father Bernard II, Lord of Lippe, he had little chance of inheriting his father's title or lands. To further decrease his chances of becoming Lord of Lippe, his brother already had three healthy sons. Gerhard II never had much interest in religion, but the Prince-Archbishopric was an elected secular title. One need not be an actual bishop to rule in this position. Gerhard II had spent his entire life craving the kind of power that his father's title might bestow and now as Archbishop he ruled even more land than his older brother and certainly wielded more power. No more would he be looked down upon as the least of the sons of the Lord of Lippe. As he walked, he was being informed of the current state of Bremen by one of the ministeriales. When told of the cease in taxes and tithes from Stedingen, Gerhard stopped and gave his full attention. "Why did my predecessor allow such dissent in his lands? First you inform me of unrest from the citizens of Bremen and now you tell me that a group of rural peasants have been allowed to cease their required payments to their betters?" The ministerial was unsure how to answer. "My lord, the Stedinger people were given special dispensation by Archbishop Frederick I. They own their land and had been given autonomy. They feel that the extra taxes by previous Archbishops and the House of Oldenburg were unjust." Gerhard II lowered his head and glared at the ministerial. "I care not for their thoughts or feelings. I am now the ruler of these lands and they will abide by my word as law. Regardless of any previous understanding, these pissants have ceased any payment. This nullifies any agreement they may have had. Take note. You will inform them that their freehold will now be converted to a lease. They belong to me. Any farmers working land on my territory are no longer free to move around. They are bound to the land and may only travel or move with my blessing. Their daughters may not be married off to anyone outside my land without my permission and payment to offset the lost labor. They will resume payment of the demanded taxes and tithes and they will pay double until the missed payments are made with an additional percentage to be paid to compensate the patience of their Archbishop. If anyone objects they will not only forfeit their lives, but also the lives of their family and the whole of their property to the Archbishop. I will restore my authority over this ungrateful pack of beasts within my domain!" The Archbishop stormed off and the ministerial was left to disseminate the orders.

***

The Stedinger found themselves fighting for weeks. They argued over who was to blame for the Archbishop's new hardline stance. Their bickering, though heated, led to a unanimous conclusion. They were no longer facing unjust taxation, but forced servitude. This new decree left them worse off than all other lowly serfs. They had no choice. They would continue to live free or they would die fighting to hold on to that freedom. Their destiny had been set. The Stedinger people spent the next ten years defying the Archbishop and forcefully ejecting any who entered Stedingen unbidden. They learned what they could of battle and added additional fortifications and traps to their already protected land. In 1229, before Christmas, the Archbishop officially excommunicated the Stedinger people for their continued failure to pay taxes and tithes. In secret he had gathered an army of knights led by his brother Herman II, Lord of Lippe. The army positioned themselves to invade Stedingen.

***

Amelina left the church after receiving the Eucharist. She had her one year old on her hip and her other three children trailing behind her. Her two oldest boys were battling each other with sticks they had picked up on the path home. Her daughter was happily shouting encouragement to the boys and pretending to be the maiden they were battling over. The boys hit each other with their stick swords. Amelina allowed it because their heavy winter tunics protected them from any harm the blows might cause. Tammo, who was now her husband, had been elected magistrate and chose to stay home to meet with other community leaders. As Amelina and her children returned home, she noticed a white rose blooming on the rose bush by her door. Inside she was surprised to find the meeting still in progress and with many more men than she had expected. Amelina situated the children in a separate room and greeted the assembly. Tammo took her aside and asked if she could prepare a meal for them. "Engilram just returned from his journey to Bremen. He has learned that the Lord of Lippe is leading a host to Stedingen on behalf of the Archbishop. They plan to attack us while we are off our guard during the Christmas festivities." Amelina tried to hide the fear she felt. "I knew war must be close as there is a white rose blooming outside." Tammo was not one for old superstitions or negative omens. "Do not fear. We are ready for them. We will finally get the chance to show our enemy the true strength of our people!" Tammo was as excited as Amelina was afraid. He had been waiting his whole life for this moment and he had been more worried that he would be an old man before he was given an opportunity for battle. At thirty-two years, he was still virile enough to best an opponent in combat. A large scruffy dog approached Tammo. He was so large that he could place his head on the table without jumping up or stretching. Clays had been encouraging breeding in the larger dogs. The larger the dog, the better they were in their jobs as protectors. Since the conflict in

1204, Clays had been teaching the dogs to attack on command and he preferred the larger dogs as they instilled more fear in his enemies. Tammo rubbed the dog's head. "Good news Knight. You are going to get your chance to take a bite out of nobility and make your great, great granddoggy proud." Knight barked in response which started a chain of barking from his littermates resting outside. The dog watched his humans and paid close attention to their preparations. When the meeting adjourned, Knight went to his fellow Kahu and brought them up to speed on the upcoming hostilities. As Canine Kahu, they believed that loyalty was the best strategy to protect the light of the Ni. The pack would follow their Ni through hell and back before they tried to manipulate them in any way. It was their creed that to help a Ni step into their power, the Kahu must relinquish control and hand over the dominion to the human in a sort of sink or swim mentality. This usually worked for them because sink or swim the Canine Kahu never abandoned their charge. The pack assigned to protect the light of the Stedinger people had cycled through multiple physical forms, but they remained loyally by their side and would continue to stay strong through the upcoming battles.

***

Herman II, Lord of Lippe led his band of knights through the marsh lands. Their numbers were smaller than he was used to commanding, but conflict over the German throne had diminished his numbers. Herman II was not an aggressive or belligerent man, much unlike his father. He preferred to act as an intermediary before resorting to conflict, but the horrors that his brother Gerhard II had described warranted action against the Stedinger barbarians. His brother had lamented about the violence enacted upon those he sent as peaceful representatives. He referred to the people of Stedingen as beasties and told tales of their communion with other beasts of the earth that they would control as only other beasts could. Some of his knights had expressed concern at facing such a strong and supernatural foe, which had not helped recruitment for the campaign. On the positive side, their smaller force was better suited to invade the difficult terrain. Herman II's host made camp a safe distance from a Stedingen village. Their plan was to attack this first village on Christmas Day and continue through the land, defeating the bulk of Stedinger by the end of Christmastide.

Herman II was confident that there would be little resistance from the peasant farmers. He anticipated that most would flee before his invading force. The next morning he discovered how wrong he was. At dawn, Herman II was roused from sleep by barking and shouts. As the invading army slept, the Stediger force had surrounded them. With the rising sun, they charged the sleeping enemy and took them by surprise. The chaos of the battle worked in the farmer's favor. Many of the knights were unable to don their armor, which put them on equal footing with the plainly clothed peasants. The fighting went on until Herman II's force could regroup. Herman II was determined and rallied his forces. The battle continued through the day. Herman II and some of his knights were able to get their armor on and were cutting through the Stedinger force. Tammo and his dogs were fighting beside Tammo's friend Ditmar and his father Clays. Tammo had encouraged Clays to stay in the village, but Clays would not succumb to his age and insisted on being with the force defending their land. To Tammo's surprise his father was holding his own against the much younger knights and footmen. As Tammo pursued an opponent, he watched as his dog Knight took off to where he had been previously standing with his father. He turned to see Herman II and another soldier descend upon Clays. Tammo left the man he was chasing and tried to rush to his father's aid, but he was too late. The knight engaged his father from the front and Herman II ran him through from behind. Ditmar returned at the same time as Tammo. He battled the knight as Tammo faced the Lord of Lippe. Herman II was covered head to toe in impenetrable armor. His sword was much better quality than the sword that aided Tammo, but Tammo had something that the Lord did not. He had a desperate rage that demanded his father's killer be held accountable. An eye for an eye and a life for a life. The two fought for what seemed an eternity. Both were fatigued, but both continued. Herman II had the advantage of weaponry, armor, and training. He blocked blow after blow from Tammo's steel and then used his body as a weapon ramming his plated chest into Tammo's, who fell to the ground. Herman II raised his sword to dispatch his foe but Knight bounded up and leapt from the ground, landing all four feet in the center of Herman II's chest. The force and weight of his armor catapulted him backwards into a tree, knocking his helmet off and causing the chain mail hood to slip over his face. Tammo raced to the downed Lord and ripped the mail hood from his head. Aiming his sword down, he pierced Herman II below the left collar bone and sank his sword deep into his heart. As Tammo stood, his chest heaving from the effort, Ditmar rushed to his side and seeing the defeated Lord let out a victory scream. "The Lord of Lippe is dead! Victory to Stedingen!" The news travelled across the battlefield and what remained of Herman II's force sounded a retreat. Stedinger declared victory on Christmas Day. Tammo left his sword in its new sheath and ran to his father's side. They had claimed victory, but the cost was high.

CHAPTER NINETEEN
CATholic

Elizabeth carried her son in and placed him in a basket near the spindle. She could have asked the nursemaid to care for her one year old son Hermann, but he was in a good mood and she liked spending time with him while she worked. As Landgravine of Thuringia, she did not have to work at all. Landgrave was a noble title slightly below a Duke but above a Count. Elizabeth came from a long line of European nobility going all the way back to Vladimir the Great. She was the daughter of King Andrew II of Hungary and as such she had been promised from a young age to Hermann II, the eldest son of Hermann I, Landgrave of Thuringia. She had been raised from the age of four in Thuringia. When Elizabeth was nine, her betrothed died and her engagement was transferred to the Landgrave's second son and heir, Louis IV. Louis IV ascended to the Thuringian throne in 1217 at the age of sixteen and married Elizabeth three years later. Even though she was only fourteen when she was married and Louis IV was twenty, they were truly in love. She had always admired him when they were children and when she was given the news about her betrothed, the sadness she felt was somewhat mitigated by the news that Louis IV would one day be her husband. A year after they were married, they welcomed their first child. Elizabeth looked at her son and smiled, which was returned to her with a bit of babble and spit bubble. She could fawn over her son all day, but she had a task that needed completing. From a young age Elizabeth had a passion for helping those less fortunate than herself. It pained her to see others in need and she dedicated as much of her time as could be spared to helping the poor. Today she had planned to spin wool into thread for the poor. She sat on the stool in front of the spinning wheel and reached for a fistful of wool. In doing so she disturbed a large mouse, who ran towards her son's basket. She screamed and quickly scooped up her son and stood on the stool. Her scream brought in guardsmen. Being informed of the small invader they searched the area. Elizabeth waited in the courtyard for the all clear. A commotion caught her attention. A group of Franciscan Friars had arrived at Wartburg castle. Elizabeth was a devout Catholic and relished every opportunity to listen to sermons and immerse herself deeper in her faith. Forgetting about her task, Elizabeth handed her son to the nursemaid and welcomed the Friars Minor. She was like an inquisitive sponge, soaking up every word she was told. They taught her about the ideals of Francis of Assisi. They preached service to the poor and demeaned. They venerated the worth of every unique individual. They praised and revered the beauty and perfection of all creation. Most importantly they stressed faith in a personal and sagacious God. Elizabeth was completely enamored. When the guards interrupted to tell her that the mouse was nowhere to be found the Friars were at a loss. "Forgive me milady, but why are your men searching for a mouse?" Elizabeth felt guilty expressing her fear and disgust after the Friars had just emphasized that nature was a mirror for God, but the Friar was waiting for an answer. "It is I who should beg for forgiveness Brother Rodeger. I am embarrassed, but earlier I was attempting to spin wool for the poor and I was startled by a mouse. With all due respect to the creations of our Lord, mice have become such a problem when it comes to keeping wool and grain for the needy." The Friar laughed and took Elizabeth's hand. "My sister, while I appreciate your reverence for the creatures of God, they were created each for their own purpose. God gave us animals to provide wool for clothing and those to provide meat for sustenance. Our Lord does not consider the removal of pests a sin." He whispered something to one of his fellow friars who hurried off. "However, if you are reluctant to harm one of the creations of our Lord yourself, I may have a solution for you." The other friar returned carrying something in his robes. He handed the bundle to Brother Rodeger, who extended his hands to Elizabeth. As he opened them, his hands revealed a small ball of gray fur. The small package turned and opened two overly large blue eyes that seemed to claim most of its fluffy face. Elizabeth was instantly smitten. As the kitten stretched, it unveiled its tiny white paws that looked like boots. Its body was the same light grey as its head but with faded dark grey stripes. Above its eyes there was a defined dark grey 'M'. Brother Rodeger gently dumped the kitten into Elizabeth's arms. "We found her on the road during our travels. I felt guided by the hand of the Lord to take her with us. This noble Katze was blessed by the Divine mother as evident by the 'M' on her forehead. It is told that in the nativity, Mary, mother of our savior Jesus, had a similar problem to you. A large rat was upsetting baby Jesus and he was turning restlessly in the manger. A cat, sensing the distress of the son of God, pounced on the rodent, killing it and removing the carcass from sight. When it returned the Blessed Mother kissed it on its head, leaving the mark you see on this creature. An 'M' for Mary." Elizabeth had tears running down her face. As she leaned forward a piece of her headdress fell forward. The kitten reached up with its paw to smack the rogue piece of fabric but ended up gently brushing a tear from Elizabeth's cheek. "Brother Rodeger. This is truly a blessing from the Lord. I can feel the love of the Blessed Mother from this beautiful little angel." Elizabeth and the Friar shared a prayer and the Friar excused himself to attend to other business. Elizabeth turned to her lady-in-waiting, "This little one needs a name. What say you Guda?" The woman was caught off guard. "Your Grace?" Elizabeth smiled. "Yes. I do think that fits." Elizabeth looked at the kitten and stroked its fur. "What do you think, Lady Grace?" The kitten purred and rubbed its head into Elizabeth's hand. "Very well. Lady Grace it is."

***

Lady Grace daintily pranced down the main hall of Wartburg. As she passed, the maids and guards alike would bow their heads to her and greet her just as they would Lady Elizabeth. Everyone in the castle loved her. She was cleaned and cared for just as any member of the Landgrave's family. Her fur had become soft and supple and was a length in between long and short. Her coat had lightened in places but was mainly a light, smokey grey with dark grey strips. She had white on her muzzle which travelled down her neck onto her chest and belly. All four of her paws sported pure white boots, which she was meticulous about keeping clean. Her presence was enough to discourage the rodent population. She did not even need to debase herself in their chase or capture. On occasion, Elizabeth would allow Lady Grace to accompany her on her charitable errands. Lady Grace brought much comfort to the sick and elderly. Louis IV was kept busy with his duty as Landgrave, but he supported his wife's altruistic endeavors. They both believed that distribution of their wealth to the poor would bring them rewards in Heaven and Louis IV saw that it brought Elizabeth great joy to help others. Her happiness brought him happiness. Lady Grace was not particularly close with Louis IV, but they shared a bond in their mutual love for Elizabeth. Today, Elizabeth had snuck out of the castle to deliver bread to the poor and Louis IV was out with his brother Henry and a hunting party. This left Grace with the castle to herself, apart from the occasional servant. She made her way to the Rittersaal or

Knight's Hall of the palace. This was the room where most of the castle business was attended to. On display here was Louis IV's armor including his heater shield. This shield's shape was an upside down Reuleaux triangle. It was wooden with a thin, decorated metal plating. The base kept the silver metal sheen but was decorated with a rearing lion with its tongue out. The base metal had just enough of a polished sheen to be reflective, which made it perfect for Lady Grace's needs. She calmed her mind and stared into the reflection until her image changed to a grey, spotted cat whose tail swayed behind him like a serpent.
"Greetings Shai. I have little to report. My Ni continues to connect with her light. The more she helps the less fortunate, the brighter she shines. I do feel the presence of a dark force, but I have yet to identify the source. I feel it grow closer by the day. As I attempt to locate the disturbance, I will do my best to stay by my Ni's side every moment. The only source of darkness I have been able to spot is the Landgrave's brother Henry. However, he does not concern me much as his darkness is that of normal human lust for power. He greatly desires his brother's position and has entertained dark thought forms, but seems to be effectively blocking such thoughts from consuming him. I see no indications that the threat to the Ni originates with him." Shai agreed. "My most recent visions show the Darkness descending upon the Ni like a storm cloud. I agree that the threat has yet to show itself, but the strength of that cloud is increasing so be on your guard. Be wary of any new additions to the Ni's circle." Grace's ear twitched and she quickly began to clean herself. Sitting on her haunches and lifting a back leg straight in the air, she began to lick herself. The maid passed and consciously chose not to look at Lady Grace in such an undignified position. When the maid was out of sight, Grace resumed her conversation. "Please forgive my indecent position. I have found that such actions embarrass the humans of this period and they will hastily leave me to my own devices. It is quite effective in ensuring privacy." Shai was understanding. "There is one final development you should be aware of. The Ni is with child." Grace barely heard the news as her fur had stood on end and she was distracted by the feeling of doom approaching her. "I feel that something wicked this way comes. I must investigate. Farewell." With haste, she jumped from her perch and made her way towards the source of the feeling. As the feeling got stronger she saw one of the guardsmen leading a man towards the chapel. She discreetly made her way closer so she could overhear the

conversation. "Magister Konrad, my Lord and Lady are currently occupied with their duties, but I will send word to them of your arrival. Please feel free to make use of the chapel while you wait. Shall I have someone bring you a meal?" The man dismissed the offer with a wave of his hand. "I will occupy myself with prayer until the Landgrave may grant me an audience." He kneeled at the altar and the guardsmen accepted this as his dismissal and left. Grace appraised the stranger from the doorway. He wore what looked to be a cloak over his shoulders, but upon closer inspection, Grace realized that it was not a cloak at all but a mantle of darkness. Her pupils widened as she watched the dark form flow around him. She had no idea what he was praying about but whatever the subject, it was causing the Darkness around him to crackle and pop like a strand of hair too close to a flame. She had no doubt that this man was the cloud of darkness that she had been anticipating.

Elizabeth returned to the castle tired but happy. She had left early that morning and had not had time to visit the chapel for her daily devotionals. As soon as she was able to change out of her traveling cloak, she headed to the chapel. Lady Grace met her on her way there. Her behavior was odd. She was being very vocal and weaving her way in front of Elizabeth's every step. Elizabeth didn't know what to make of the behavior. Usually Lady Grace loved visiting the chapel with Elizabeth. She would take a place on the ledge of the triple window behind the altar. However, today Grace seemed to be trying to herd her away from the chapel. Elizabeth assumed that Grace was just hungry and handed the cat to a maid and instructed her to get Grace some goat's milk. With the furry speed bump out of the way, Elizabeth hurried to the chapel so she might complete her prayers before her husband returned home. Brother Rodeger had stayed in the village to help the sick, so she would be on her own, but Elizabeth came from a long line of pious Catholics and was comfortable leading her own prayers.

Konrad sat quietly at the altar. He did not allow himself to be distracted by the sound of the door. When his prayer was complete he stood to investigate the interruption. A beautiful young woman had taken a position near the first row of chairs from the altar. She was deep in her prayer by the time Konrad turned his attention to her. He was pleased at the reverence she showed by not disturbing him at the altar by getting too close.

He took the opportunity to observe her while her eyes were closed. Her face was small and her skin was pure white and smooth as cream. Her head was covered, but he could see some strands of unruly reddish blonde hair escaping from under her veil. Konrad was a man of God and considered himself liberated from such base temptation of sin such as lust, but he found himself inexplicably drawn to this woman. Something about her compelled a need deep within him to possess her, body and soul. He thought about rousing the woman from her prayers and chastising her for entering the Landgrave's Chapel without an escort, but the idea of getting closer to her brought on a slew of improper yearnings. He pushed the unwanted impulses from his mind and returned to prayer, but before he could completely rid himself of the sinful thoughts, the chapel doors opened and a host of men entered. Based on his attire and entourage, Konrad deduced that this must be the Landgrave of Thuringia. Louis IV did not think twice about interrupting the priest's prayers. He was a busy man and had other duties to attend to after welcoming the inquisitor. "Magister Konrad of Marburg. Welcome to Thuringia. The Archbishop of Mainz has written to inform me of your commission. We are pleased to host you in our lands." Elizabeth had finished her prayers and stood by waiting to be summoned. Louis IV extended his hand to her. "May I introduce my wife, Lady Elizabeth, Landgravine of Thuringia." Elizabeth greeted the priest and welcomed him to Thuringia but stood in silence for the remainder of the conversation. Konrad had been commissioned to seek out heretics in the lands of Thuringia and Hesse. Being a magister and priest, Louis IV offered to allow Konrad to stay at Wartburg when his travels allowed it. Konrad accepted the hospitality on behalf of the church.

***

Over the next two years both Louis IV and Elizabeth came to greatly admire Konrad. He was strict and devoted to his faith and all the letters they were getting from the Archbishop of Mainz were singing his praises. Despite their twenty-seven year age difference, Konrad and Elizabeth developed a close friendship. Elizabeth looked to him as a mentor who could satisfy her cravings for religious instruction. Konrad was enamored by her piousness and struggled daily to conquer his darker longings. When the Franciscan Rodeger was recalled to his order, Elizabeth found herself in need of a new spiritual advisor. Konrad, like the Franciscans, spoke of love of God before anything else, rejection of the comforts of the material world, and service to others in the name of the Lord. These were ideals that spoke directly to Elizabeth's heart. She even refused to wear her crown as she said that if the King of kings wore only a crown of thorns that no crown of gold would grace her head. She routinely gave away her wealth to help the needy. These like-minded beliefs and Konrad's ever growing admiration of Elizabeth's virtues led him to suggest, in one of his letters to the Archbishop of Mainz, that he would be willing to fulfill the role of confessor to the Landgravine. The Archbishop in turn made the suggestion to Louis IV who was thrilled with the idea. Lady Grace on the other hand was not. She had been doing everything within her power to keep Elizabeth away from Konrad, but every time he visited, he sought her out like a mouse seeks out cheese. Every time his dark countenance was around Elizabeth, Lady Grace had to fight to keep his darkness from completely enveloping Elizabeth. The shadow of his desire was becoming more and more deliberate. Thankfully, this was not Grace's first Girru. She was powerful in her own right. Just her focused presence in Elizabeth's lap prevented the dark forms from encroaching on Elizabeth's aura. Then there was Elizabeth's family. The strong love and support from her husband and children kept her firmly rooted in the light. Still, there had been developments that had Grace troubled.

**

Grace heard news that Konrad had departed Mainz for Goslar to advise upon a replacement for the Provost. The previous year Konrad had led an inquisition into Heinrich Minnike, the previous Provost. The investigation had lasted two years and finally resulted in Heinrich being found guilty of heresy and being burnt at the stake. Confident that Konrad would not return to Wartburg for at least a few days, Grace felt comfortable to leave Elizabeth long enough to check in with Barag. She was comforted by the familiar face of Shai. "I am afraid I must skip the pleasantries, Shai. I am distressed and need your insight. The Darkness threatening my Ni is manifesting in ways I have never seen and cannot explain. At the end of last year, I began to notice the Darkness forming into what looked like human hands with disgustingly long and sharp nails. These shadow hands would reach towards the Ni as if beckoning her. Other times they would desperately grasp at her like a child trying to capture fog. I was always able to prevent this shadow from touching the Ni, but this last meeting between them has me frightened. The shadow, which usually appears as a cloak around the vessel's shoulders, began to shift and squirm. Out of the Darkness appeared disembodied faces. Faces with terrifyingly tortured expressions. They appeared to scream and push through the barrier of darkness as if they were trying to escape. In their umbra I felt such intense devastation and suffering. I have heard tales of such feelings from Halqu returning from the horrors of battle, but I have never heard of such a thing in an ordinary human. Furthermore, this man is reputedly a Christian, and an educated one at that. I do not understand the reason for such immense darkness." Shai did not react with the surprise or horror that she had expected. "Inanna, your opponent is much more terrible than you realize. I asked the Keeper of Zikru to monitor the vessel's activity outside of your interactions. This human is known as a heretic hunter. When not with the Ni, he travels the land searching for those who he believes act contrary to the orthodoxy of the church. Wherever he goes, he incites mobs against those accused. Over the past two years he has become evermore incredulous in the possibility of innocence in those accused. He relies heavily on torture to extract confessions. His brutality correlates to his rendezvous with the Ni. The more time he spends with her, the worse his torture in subsequent interrogations. I do not think I can explain it with enough austerity. I must show you." His eyes turn white and that light reflected in Grace's own eyes.

> Konrad and his Dominican assistant set up their torture table. The man tied to the chair watched as they brought in object after object and placed it on the table. There were certain rules of torture that Konrad was obligated to follow; no bloodshed, no mutilation, and no torture unto death. However, the accused did not know that and Konrad did not feel obligated to tell them. Furthermore, the pope was far away and had little knowledge of the day to day goings on of his inquisitors, nor did the pope care to know the details. If more extreme methods of torture were called for, Konrad was bound by the rules, but those in his service or those he recruited from the villages were not. Konrad instructed

that cold water be thrown on the victim to ensure his attention. "Gisilfrid von Paderborn, you have been accused of heresy by two witnesses. List those who bear mortal hatred of you." A procedural rule Konrad was forced to follow was to allow the accused to list those who he believes hate him. If the accusers are listed as mortal enemies by the accused, Konrad was supposed to release the accused. Konrad believed that heretics were crafty and could be warned by the devil, so even if they were able to name their accusers as enemies, Konrad would not accept this as proof of innocence. Nevertheless, he was required to suffer through the performance for the sake of procedure. As Gisilfrid named those he thought might hold a grudge against him, Konrad absentmindedly brushed his hands over his instruments of torture. He examined a hand-held, pitchfork-like device called a cat's paw. The four prongs of the fork were curved and sharpened to a violent point. When raked across the skin, the points were sharp enough to rip through flesh. Another device was the breast ripper. This was a set of tongs with two sharp prongs on each arm for a total of four. This iron device could be heated in the fire and used on women or men to rip off certain parts of flesh. As Konrad imagined the device in use his thoughts strayed. The image of Elizabeth crept into his thoughts and he found himself imagining the shape and feel of her breasts. He caught himself and rebuked his mind for such vile thoughts. He was a man of God and above such temptations of the flesh. Thinking of flesh brought his mind back to the image of Elizabeth's soft, perfect skin. He imagined brushing the back of his hand softly across her cheek, down her neck, and onto her chest. Enraged by his own weakness he yelled, "Enough!" Gisilfrid stopped speaking instantly. Konrad's attention was brought back to his prisoner. He honestly had not been listening so he had no idea if the accusers had been named, but that was of little importance to him. He needed the distraction of torture to help purify his wicked thoughts. He ordered the prisoner's hands be tied behind his back. The wrists were then attached to a rope slung over a sturdy beam. When Gisilfrid was secured, the rope was quickly pulled and he was hoisted four feet off the ground by his wrist behind his back. He screamed in agony as his shoulders contorted under his own weight. Konrad yelled at him to confess, but Gisilfrid continued to beg for mercy and proclaim his innocence. "Please Magister, I am no heretic! I follow the church. I may not be a learned man, but I do as I am instructed by our priest. I know not any teachings of the goodmen or any others, only that of the holy father. Please have mercy!" Konrad was far from convinced. He ordered the prisoner to be hiked up further, until he was six feet off the ground. With a drop of his hand, Konrad signaled that the rope holding the prisoner should be released and caught. Gisilfrid dropped quickly and then was jerked back up moments before hitting the ground. A horrible cracking sound could be heard and Gisilfrid screamed and cried. Konrad felt like he had been hit with a warm breeze and inhaled deeply. The Darkness engulfing him sucked in the screams and grew larger. In that moment, Konrad was free from his thoughts of Elizabeth and only felt the buzz of adrenaline. This was repeated multiple times. Weights were even added to the prisoner's feet to increase the strain on his shoulders. Still he did not confess. Konrad ordered the man to be placed back in the chair. He grabbed a rectangular device from the table. It had three vertical bars spaced at a distance and fixed to a flat horizontal bar. A second movable horizontal bar was attached to the vertical bars, held in place by a screw. This was called a thumbscrew. The Dominican took the thumbscrew from Konrad and went to attach it to a finger of the accused but Konrad stopped him. "That will not do. Look at his hands. He has lost feeling in them. Attach it to his toes." The Dominican nodded and did as he was told as Gisilfrid screamed and pleaded. Konrad had to suppress a smile. He told himself that this work excited him because it was God's work. After all, by torturing the mortal body, he was saving their immortal soul. However, even if he refused to admit it, he knew that something in him craved the sounds and visuals of the torment.

Finally after two years, Konrad was able to secure a conviction of heresy for Heinrich Minnike. Konrad was extremely frustrated by the snail's pace of the proceedings. It was ridiculous that something so obvious should require such superfluous procedure and proof. The church was being threatened and by wasting so much time, the threat was increasing. It was better to kill fifty innocents if it meant destroying even one heretic, than it was to allow one heretic to pervert others. Today, Konrad finally got to bask in the fruits of his labor. Minnike had been handed over to the secular arm of the government for punishment for his crime of heresy. Since the church and the rulers were entwined, heresy against the church was considered treason against the emperor. The punishment for this crime was death. As a priest, Konrad could not take a life, but the secular rulers could. Minnike was scheduled to be burnt at the stake. A huge crowd had gathered to watch the punishment. Konrad, who thought he would be contented, found himself ill at ease. He wished that Elizabeth was by his side. He wanted to share this victory with her. He wished to hold her in his arms and console her against the violence of the punishment with the reassurance that the flames would cleanse Minnike's soul. He disparaged his thoughts and was angry with himself for allowing them to stray. He cannot think about Elizabeth. It is a sin to covet another man's wife. More than that, he was a priest and had taken a vow of celibacy. Base things such as carnal pleasure were beneath him, yet he could not control his own desires. He knew it must be the devil trying to lead his soul astray, but his daily mortifications were becoming less effective. He wore hairshirts, denied himself food, and used a discipline for self-flagellation but his thoughts always returned to the young Landgravine. If not for her pious zeal for the Lord, he may have suspected her of witchcraft, but he could never accuse her of such evil. She was too pure. Konrad felt as if the weight of creation was on his shoulders. The daily torment was becoming unbearable. He was forced to leave his thoughts for the start of the immolation. He thought that the righteousness he felt for protecting the church from the heretic being set ablaze would provide enough glory to drown out his needs of the flesh, but as he watched the flames rise, he noticed that the color of the flame was a reflection of the color of Elizabeth's hair. No sooner did the thought enter his mind than he began to see her form in the flames. The form in the flames was not the pious young mother that he knew, but a seductive demoness tempting him to join her in the flames. He reached into his robes and pulled on the chain cilice wrapped around his thigh. The pain almost made him cry out, but it was better to suffer the physical pain than risk damnation of his soul. Still he found himself evermore tempted to hurl himself into the flames to be with this shadow mistress with Elizabeth's countenance. Then the flames reached the body of Minnike. His fiery temptress turned her attention to the heretic and as the flames consumed Minnike, Konrad was free of her. No more thoughts of desire raced through his mind. He was free. He understood now. Elizabeth was the messenger of God. She was a saint sent to keep him dedicated to his true purpose, to seek out and destroy heretics. He had been complacent. His pursuit of the papal deniers had not been ardent enough. Elizabeth was sent to him to remind him of the urgency of his quest. As long as he sacrificed the heretics to the flames, he would be safe from the sins of his flesh. The thought fled from his mind to the cloak of darkness that weighed down his shoulders. The evil intent transformed the Darkness from a humble cloak to an eccentric papal mantum or cappa magna. There were no more sparks of red or brown but a complete lack of any color. The deepest pitch of black possible. The Darkness fell over his shoulders, down the front and back of his body into a liquid mass around his feet. A large spike circle formed behind his head like a halo of darkness and shot out continuous spikes of shadow. In response to the invisible force, the Dominican standing next to Konrad shivered and unconsciously shifted away. The Darkness created an invisible vortex that sucked any shadow in the area towards itself and shot it out again through the spikes of the halo.

Lady Grace shook her head vigorously to rid herself of the terrifying image. "This cannot be true. I have never before seen a human wield such darkness. This human was never identified as a Ni. His energy without the Darkness is unremarkable. Why would the Darkness be drawn to him? I thought that the Darkness only fed off the strong negative energy in humans, but this appears like the Darkness is using this man to create more darkness and feeding off of it. Is that even possible?" Shai showed no emotion. "I know not. I have asked for a gathering of the Kahu to consult with Lord Utu and Lady Ereshkigal." Grace made a hissing sound and swatted at the shield. "We need not involve those two. We can handle this on our own. The Lady of Birds and the Lord of Hounds will only complicate things, as always." Shai only shrugged. "It is too late. They have already been summoned. Ninlil will speak on your behalf." Grace stared at the shield furiously wagging her tail. "Very well, but I will not be chastised or commanded within my own domain. We will hear their thoughts but we will make our own decisions." Shai nodded and they parted ways. Grace had a million worries running through her mind, but worry was only a negative prayer and did little to help the outcome. She would stay rooted in her present and focus on protecting her Ni at all costs.

***

Konrad returned to Wartburg to accept the position as Elizabeth's confessor and spiritual advisor. Though he would continue to take frequent trips to hunt heretics. Konrad urged Elizabeth to practice asceticism. This was strict self-denial of all forms of indulgence. He insisted that the only way she could be close to God was through rigorous abstention from hedonism or any form of physical comfort. Elizabeth willingly followed his advice, giving up anything that might be considered a luxury. The influence of her husband was a mitigating one. He insisted that she eat well and honor the traditions of her station. Believing that fealty to her husband was as important as denial of the flesh, she followed her husband's requests. Konrad did not like being overruled by Louis IV. His jealousy grew with every moment spent in the presence of the happy couple. Both Konrad and Louis IV encouraged Elizabeth's charitableness. Occasionally, when he wasn't busy with his duties and Landgrave, Louis IV would accompany Elizabeth on her humanitarian tasks. This infuriated Konrad. He could not stand the knowledge that a man, other than himself, was the object of Elizabeth's affection. He believed her to be too good for any mortal man. A woman as beautiful, selfless, and pure as Elizabeth should only belong to God. Konrad began to plot. A Landgrave as loved as Louis IV was beyond the reach of his heresy investigations, but there had to be a way to remove him from Elizabeth's life. He would get his chance. Louis IV was summoned to Cremona by Emperor Fredrick II. At the Emperor's request, he took up the cross to join the sixth crusade to the Holy Land. Despite the dangers, Louis IV was excited to be serving both God and the Emperor in such an important task. Elizabeth was less enthusiastic. She had a sinking feeling that her husband might never return, but she could not ask him to turn his back on his oath. Konrad paid close attention to the Landgrave's plans. As the day of his departure approached, Konrad was on one of his heretic hunts. During his investigation, he heard rumor that plague was rampant through some of the small villages near Swabia. A dark idea entered his mind and he ceased his hunt to return to Wartburg.

Konrad requested an audience with the Landgrave. He claimed to bless the journey and offer confession and sacrament to the departing host. Konrad, seeing that Louis IV planned to travel to Brindisi by way of Bavaria and the Tyrolian Alps, asked the Landgrave for a favor. "I do not wish to impose, but I was wondering if perhaps, during your journey, you might deliver a letter for me to the Archbishop of Augsburg. I am deeply concerned with what I believe is corruption by heretics within his church and I need to inform him of the dangers. I cannot be sure how far the corruption reaches, so I am afraid I cannot trust a messenger in this task. If you travel to the crusades by way of Swabia, you could deliver the letter for me without much trouble. May I count on you for this important task?" Louis IV was slightly insulted that a priest would ask someone of his standing to be his errand boy, but he admired the priest for his wife's sake. "Of course. I will deliver the letter to the hand of the Archbishop of Augsburg myself." Konrad allowed a wicked smile to grace his face. "I am forever in your debt. Just one more thing. This must stay between you and I. You must tell no one of what we have discussed, nor can you tell anyone the reason for the shift in your journey." Louis accepted the terms and Konrad took his leave to write the fictional letter.

***

The day of Louis IV's departure arrived too quickly for Elizabeth. The knights gathered to say their farewells to their loved ones. A pregnant Elizabeth made her way to her husband's side. She did not sleep the night before. Her dreams were plagued with nightmares.

> *She saw a golden knight on a white horse. The knight waved goodbye and set off towards a white cross but was stopped by a menacing figure cloaked in darkness. The knight transformed into a golden lion and the cloaked figure transformed into a black arrow. The lion ran towards the cross but the arrow flew straight and pierced the lion through the heart. In a flash she took the place of the lion, the arrow piercing her heart. Before she died, the cloaked figure returned and chopped off three of her limbs, throwing them far from her reach. Her remaining limb takes on a life of its own and starts to slap her face as her surroundings fade into the darkness.*

When Elizabeth reached Louis IV's side, her two children in tow, she threw her arms around his shoulders and buried her face in his neck. "My love, do not promise me that you will return. Promise me that whatever happens, we will meet again in the house of our Lord." Her tears stained his tunic. "Why do you cry so? I go to fight for the Holy Land. God will protect me. His will be done." She refused to release her grip. "I have had a terrible vision that we shall not meet again." Louis IV hugged her tight. He understood her fear, but his path was set. When Elizabeth finally released him, he kissed his daughter Sophie on the head and scooped up his son Hermann II. His farewell to his children was short, as his strength to leave with his head high was beginning to wane. As he rode off, he forced himself to look forward. He knew if he looked back he might never be able to leave.

***

Lady Grace sat in Elizabeth's lap as she mended clothes to give to the poor. She reached for a new spool of thread but her basket was empty. She attempted to stand but her large belly and the sleeping cat refused to move. Elizabeth called to her ladies-in-waiting. No one answered. She called again. Still no answer. Without moving Lady Grace began to growl and glare at the door. For a moment Elizabeth felt the chill of fear, but to her relief, Konrad walked through the door. "Oh Father, you startled me. Might I trouble you to send in one of my ladies, Guda or Isentrud? I am in need of new thread." Konrad stared coldly at Elizabeth for a moment. "I am afraid I cannot do that as I have dismissed your ladies-in-waiting." Elizabeth was confused. "Forgive me. Perhaps I misheard you. Did you say you dismissed my ladies?" Konrad gave a single nod. Elizabeth was perplexed. "May I ask why?" Konrad walked up to where Elizabeth sat. Grace continued her low growl, never taking her eyes off the priest. "Dear Elizabeth. You have become much too reliant on your entourage. The Lord tells us to be humble and hard working. I worry that you are becoming over-reliant on the help of others, when you should be toiling yourself." Elizabeth hung her head in shame. "Forgive my insolence. I suppose that, with the baby so close to arriving, I have given in to the sin of sloth. I have sinned. May the Lord forgive me." Konrad walked over and placed his hand on her head "My dear Elizabeth, you have confessed to me a humble person who has not power to forgive sins, which belongs to God alone; however through His divinely spoken word which came to the Apostles, saying, Whosesoever sins you forgive are forgiven, and whosesoever sins you retain are retained, I am emboldened to say that God forgives you in this world and in that which is to come. In the name of the Father, and of the Son, and of the Holy Spirit." Making the sign of the cross above her bowed head, he placed his hand on her shoulder and slid it down her arm, gently rubbing up and down. Grace had had enough and being mindful not to make contact with Elizabeth's arm, she swatted the unwanted hand away. No blood was drawn, but the attack startled Konrad to an acceptable distance. "Oh father, forgive her. She has learned to be protective of me." Though not amused, Konrad was not about to admit anger at a beast. He again made the sign of the cross, but this time over the cat, from a safe distance of course. "All is forgiven." Konrad beckoned towards the door and two old women with horribly sour expressions entered. "This is Hildegund and Wigburg. They will be replacing your ladies-in-waiting. Both are well educated on the tenets of asceticism. They will help keep you on the straight path so that you do not stray again." A cold feeling swept over Elizabeth, but she trusted Konrad. If he believed that this was best, then she should follow his edict.

**

Elizabeth sat on the cold stone floor playing with Hermann II, Sophie, and Lady Grace. Without warning the guardsmen burst through the door, escorting a messenger. She stood and crossed to him and he handed her a letter, then curtly bowed and took his leave. Elizabeth opened the letter and began to read. At her scream the guards quickly returned. "Milady! What is wrong?" Through her sobs she recited the letter "This day the eleventh of September in the year of our Lord 1227, Louis IV, Landgrave of Thuringia has died. He fell ill of plague on his journey to the sixth crusade and succumbed to his sickness in Otranto-" She could not continue reading as the reality of the letter set in. "He is dead. He is dead! It is to me as if the whole world died today!" Sophie, seeing her mother upset, also began to cry. Elizabeth dropped the letter and grabbed her stomach. It was as if the weight of the world had collapsed upon her and a crushing pressure brought her to her knees. "Fetch the midwife. The baby is coming!"

CHAPTER TWENTY
The CATechism

    Elizabeth looked out her window in the residential tower of Castle Pottenstein to the village below. Lady Grace slept on the hem of her dress purring loudly. Easter was approaching and Elizabeth was strictly observing Lent. She restricted herself to only bread and water at the urging of Konrad. Elizabeth had left Wartburg after her brother-in-law Henry Raspe took over the regency of Thuringia on behalf of her son Hermann II. Since the time that Henry moved into Wartburg castle with his wife, many accidents had been befalling Hermann II. Elizabeth's maternal instincts had kicked in and she suspected that Henry was trying to harm her son so he could claim the throne. To save her son, she sought the protection of her uncle, Bishop Ekbert of Bamberg. In the beginning things were well and Elizabeth was able to continue her philanthropic activities, but her uncle was not as keen on her giving away his food supplies as Louis IV had been. His frustration with her charity and her behavior unbecoming of a Princess of Hungary led to many clashes. Her uncle, with the support of her family, decided it was best that Elizabeth get remarried and they insisted that she submit to marrying Emperor Fredrick II whose wife Yolande of Brienne had died just three years prior. Her family saw the marriage as an opportunity to increase their power and cared little for Elizabeth's feelings. Elizabeth sighed and shifted her weight, waking Grace who jumped into her lap and made herself comfortable again. Elizabeth spoke out loud, not really to the cat or anyone in particular, just to the void. "They do not understand. My heart has always and will always belong to Louis. My heart will be entombed at the abbey of Reinhardsbrunn with my love. How can I vow to love and honor another when I will no longer have my heart? I cannot lie to God and make an empty vow before a priest just to satisfy the ambitions of my family. And even if I were to marry, how could I marry Emperor Fredrick II, the man who was responsible for my husband joining the sixth Crusade. I hold no ill will, but he would be a daily reminder of what I had and all that I have lost." Grace meowed and rubbed her head against Elizabeth's arm to demand pets. Elizabeth mindlessly scratched her head. A soft rap on the door was followed by a growl from Grace. Moments later Konrad was admitted. Grace evaluated the threat. Today, Konrad's darkness had taken the form of thorny branches that seemed to reach for

Elizabeth at every opportunity. Elizabeth's light had been dimmed by grief, but with the help of Grace's energy, it was still strong enough to dissipate any tendril that got too close. Whenever Grace was with Elizabeth, Konrad always kept a healthy distance. "You seem troubled child." Elizabeth nodded. "My family wishes me to marry the Emperor. I do not wish this. I wish to devote myself to helping the poor. Louis always encouraged me and now when I serve those in need, I can feel him with me. I do not wish to give that up. I know not what to do. Henry will not return my dowry and without it I am at the mercy of my uncle. I have told them that I would rather cut off my own nose than be forced to marry. If I were hideous and no one wished to marry me, then perhaps my uncle would leave me to my Divine calling." Konrad tapped the tips of his finger tips together in rapid succession as he appeared to consider the predicament. "Perhaps you could find someone to marry who would encourage your altruism. Someone who would protect and care for you. Someone you could trust." Elizabeth shook her head. "I know no one like that.". Konrad continued, "I am like that. I boast many years compared to you, but in marriage I could keep you safe." Elizabeth was surprised at such an offer. She smiled and gently took his hand. "Father Konrad. Your charity knows no bounds. I am touched by your devotion to me and my family. However, I would not, in a million years, ever dream of asking you to break your oath to God for my sake. I would rather die than be the cause of your laicization, but I am eternally grateful for your kindness, even if it is in jest." Konrad's anger burned inside him. How dare she turn him down. He offered to turn his back on everything he had dedicated his life to for all his forty-eight years for her and she tossed his offer aside without thought. Grace watched as Konrad's darkness spit and flared with shockwaves of red and deep orange. The thorny tendrils that had previously reached for Elizabeth now plunged themselves deep within Konrad's chest and abdomen. Grace could see the flashes of crimson hate in Konrad's eyes but Elizabeth was blissfully unaware. Konrad tried his best to soothe his anger. If Elizabeth would not marry him, then he would ensure that she would never belong to anyone else. If he could not have her love, then no one else should have it either. His first hurdle was her family. An idea came to Konrad and Grace shivered under the shadow of his evil smile. "Then if you truly do not wish to marry, you must devote yourself fully to God. You must join the Order of Penance of Francis and vow to me and God that you will live in obedience, humility, poverty, and in chastity from now until you are called to the Lord." Elizabeth's eyes lit up. Could it be that simple? She placed Grace on the floor and knelt before Konrad. She repeated the vows after him and he blessed her with the sign of the cross. "Now you may *never* break these vows or you will put in peril your immortal soul." Elizabeth nodded and Konrad helped her up. "Now I will see your uncle and inform him of your vows."

Elizabeth was pleased with her decision until her uncle burst through her door in a rage. "How dare you make such a decision without consulting me first! You have no idea what you have done! You have risked the legacy of your husband and the future of your children with such a rash and selfish decision!" Elizabeth fought back tears. She did not think that a vow she made dedicating her life to God would negatively affect her children. Konrad followed the Bishop of Bamberg into Elizabeth's room as the Bishop continued his tirade. "How do you suppose you will manage to bring up your children in a manner befitting a future as a noble while living in poverty and submission? How will Hermann II learn to be a strong Landgrave if you keep him locked away in some shabby convent for the next ten or so years?!" Elizabeth had no answer. Konrad stepped in. "Perhaps I might have a solution. There is no reason for the vows Elizabeth took to alter the future of her children. You are correct that the children should be reared in the manner of nobles. They would be done a disservice to be dragged along on the holy mission of their mother. I think it would be best if the children stay here under your wise tutelage until they are old enough to assume their roles in society." Elizabeth screamed. "No! No, I do not wish to abandon my children. I am their mother. They need me." Konrad shot her a sharp and disapproving look. "My dear child, not moments ago, you swore an oath of obedience to me and to God. Are you so eager to break those vows?" Elizabeth's eyes went wide. She did vow to be obedient, but never did she imagine that obedience would call for her to leave her children while they are yet so young. She was bound to her oath, as she would not break a promise made before God. "Forgive me Father. You are right. I will do as you advise." Grace jumped up next to Elizabeth. She could feel her Ni's light getting dimmer. As the men, satisfied with the solution, left the room, Grace purred and rubbed her head against Elizabeth who scooped the cat into her arms and began to cry. "I know I must be strong. I do not know what purpose God has in all of this, but I must trust his guidance in my life. I will say goodbye to my children and sustain myself on the love of my God and your sweet love Lady Grace."

***

Konrad had left Elizabeth to meet with Pope Gregory IX to update him on his work seeking out heresy and to ask for his intervention on behalf of Elizabeth in regards to her dowry. The dowry which her brother-in-law was still reluctant to part with. While Konrad of Marburg awaited his audience with Pope Gregory IX, he noticed a man staring at him. The man had to be a bishop or archbishop as he wore a pallium on his head, denoting his status. A few moments later a young servant boy ran up to Konrad. "Excuse me sir, but are you Konrad von Marburg, esteemed heretic hunter of Thuringia and Hesse?" "I am. Who asks?" "Mi'Lord Gerhard II, the Archbishop of Bremen and Hamburg of the House of Lippe. Mi'Lord wishes to speak to you, if that be agreeable." Konrad followed the boy to the man in the pallium. "Mi'Lord, may I present Konrad von Marburg." The boy scurried off to let the men speak. Konrad bobbed his head in a curt bow. "Your Excellency. It is an honor to meet you." "The honor is mine. I have heard word of your great service to our Lord and His church. The Archbishop of Mainz holds you in high regard, as does Pope Gregory IX. I believe our meeting has been Divinely guided. There is a matter I would much like to hear your thoughts on. For many years now, my predecessors and I have had contention with a group of farmers who fancy themselves free men. They have ceased in their payment of taxes and tithes, rejected the appointment of clergy, and recently have enacted violence on both my ministeriales and traveling men of the cloth, Dominican and Franciscan alike. I am attempting to enlist my brother in a campaign against them, but many fear their ungodly strength and wit. You must have come across many vassals of Satan during your travels. How might one go about proving such possession on a large scale? How might I be sure that their actions are at the behest of the devil. Or rather how might I prove to His Excellency the evil of these people?" A man motioned to Konrad beckoning him to his audience with the pope. "My apologies, but His Excellency awaits. If it pleases you, we can revisit this discussion at a later time. I would be glad to offer my services as an inquisitor." Gerhard II gestured his release. "I look forward to it. I will send my servant to fetch you when you are finished." Konrad hurried off. The archbishop was elated. If he could get the great Heretic Hunter on his side, the Stedinger revolt was as good as quashed.

***

Thanks to his visit with Pope Gregory IX, Konrad was appointed as the official Defender of Elizabeth's case for her dowry as well as given the position as her guardian. With this authority, Konrad was able to secure the two-thousand marks of her dowry. During this time, Louis IV's body was delivered to Elizabeth by his faithful followers. Konrad was pleased that the body had finally been transported back from Otranto. Konrad had allowed Elizabeth to stay with her uncle and children until she buried her husband. Once she entombed Louis IV in his family's church at Reinhardsbrunn Abbey, then Konrad had commanded that she leave her children and family and travel with him to Marburg in Hesse to officially take her vows and join the Third Order of St. Francis of Assisi. Elizabeth had been following the tenets of the Franciscan Order since she was introduced to them by her previous spiritual director Brother Rodeger the Franciscan. Francis of Assisi had died two years earlier, but in his meeting with the pope, Konrad had learned that the pope planned to announce Francis's canonization later that year in July. Konrad knew that it would please Elizabeth to become a tertiary of St. Francis of Assisi given the respect she had for Francis of Assisi and his preachings. He could tell that Elizabeth was struggling with the idea of leaving her children and hoped that the chance to join an order of Franciscan lay people would help her cope with the separation.

***

Elizabeth stood in the Abbey, allowing herself a final goodbye to her love and her previous life. The following day, she was scheduled to leave for Marburg with Konrad. She did not wish to leave her children, but she herself was separated from her mother and father at age four and sent to be raised among the family of her betrothed. This was just how things were done. As she stood staring at her late husband's effigy, a woman approached her and placed her hand on Elizabeth's shoulder. The woman was finely dressed and had a long oval face. She wasn't particularly pretty, but she was pleasantly plain. Elizabeth recognized her, but couldn't recall her name. She remembered that the woman had attended her marriage. She remembered that she was the daughter of Jutta, Louis IV's aunt. She thought hard to recall her name. She remembered the woman was married to a Count, a Count named Henry like her brother-in-law. He was Count of an area to the east. Sayn. Count Henry III of Sayn and his wife was Mechthild of Sayn! The woman silently consoled her cousin Elizabeth, then the two women walked through the Abbey grounds talking and catching up. When Mechthild discovered that Elizabeth was relocating to Marburg and planned to use her dowry to build a hospital, she was elated. "My dear Elizabeth! Marburg is only a day or two ride from my home at Sayn Castle. We will be living close enough to visit each other!" Mechthild was happy at the prospect of having another noblewoman in the area. Especially a noblewoman so kind and devout as Elizabeth. For Elizabeth, the idea of having some family close was reassuring. She was excited to finally be able to dedicate herself to God and his work, but it was a major transition and having the extra support was comforting.

***

After her husband had been buried and mourned, Elizabeth and Konrad, along with Hildegund, Wigburg, and Lady Grace, set out for Konrad's home town of Marburg in Hesse. Konrad would continue to act as Elizabeth's confessor and guardian, but he had plans to use more of his time to hunt heretics. He had thought that the release he felt after the burning of Minnike would last forever, but after a while his desire for Elizabeth had crept back into his mind. The only thing he could use to free himself from his own passions was the burning of heretics. His journeys to search out heretics would take him months, but he did not mind because he knew that Elizabeth would be waiting for him upon his return. Konrad had never been so happy in his entire life. Though he desired more than what their current relationships offered, it was a consolation to have her near him in any capacity. Knowing that he would be the only man allowed to get close to Elizabeth was good enough for him. Secure with the financial support of her generous dowry, Elizabeth decided to give away five-hundred marks and used the rest to build a hospital in Marburg. She was happiest when she was helping those in need. She stayed at the Franciscan hospital she had built. The two women appointed by Konrad stayed with Elizabeth all the time. Elizabeth soon found out that their jobs were not to assist her in her work with the sick, but to keep her on a strict asceticism path. Konrad had instructed the women that whenever Elizabeth should stray from the tenets of denial of all earthly comfort they were to discipline Elizabeth by slapping her across her face or beating her with a rod. When Elizabeth would kneel to pray, she was not allowed to kneel on a cushion, only the hard stone floor. Her bed was not to be cushioned nor were her clothes to be made out of soft material. Between fasting, she was not allowed to eat anything that was not approved of by Konrad himself. Over the next two years, his allowances for her dietary choices were getting increasingly limited. Elizabeth was taken aback by her guardian's cruel tendencies. She had always known him to be a zealous devotee, but she had never before seen his sadism. She had heard in whisperings at Wartburg that her mentor was too severe and harsh in his hunts for heretics, but she dismissed much of what she heard as embellished stories to deter heresy. However, she now knew that the stories were more than just rumors. She did try to stand up to him, but her questioning was treated as disobedience. Since she had vowed to obey, that disobedience was punished as betrayal of her promise to God and resulted in severe beatings or forced fasting, sometimes for up to seven days. This extreme penal action contributed to Elizabeth's ever declining health, but her own weakness did little to cool her fervor for helping those struck with the worst diseases. She did not shy away from any patient and could be found joyfully completing any task from cleaning soiled beds to washing those with leprosy. Her devotion to the sick was one of her saving graces. The others were her visits from her cousin, Mechthild of Sayn and the companionship of Lady Grace. As often as she could, Mechthild would join Elizabeth at her hospital and aid in whatever way she could, often bringing alms for those Elizabeth cared for. The women quickly became closer than sisters. Seeing her declining health, Mechthild began to worry about Elizabeth, but Elizabeth would always dismiss her concerns. She assured her that it was her desire to live in poverty and humility. Mechthild accepted this excuse until she witnessed Hildegung hit Elizabeth with a rod five times for the sin of gluttony because she did not take the smallest piece of bread during a meal. Grace was also worried about Elizabeth. The cat had gotten quite good at sneaking into the kitchen to steal bread, cheese, and fish to put them on

Elizabeth's bed. Elizabeth thought it was Konrad's way of helping her and allowed herself to eat the gifts. Even though Grace was worried about Elizabeth's health, she was pleased to see that despite her harsh treatment and grief from the loss of her family, Elizabeth still retained her connection to her light. In fact, being allowed to finally live a life of service to others had actually made her light shine brighter. Her light shone brighter than the light of five other Ni combined. Grace noticed that the more Elizabeth suffered the more her compassion for those she cared for grew. Grace was trying to keep in contact with Barag, but since Elizabeth had decided to live a life of poverty, they were no longer around many items with reflective surfaces and Grace loathed using water as a reflective medium as she always ended up getting some on her fur. Luckily, Elizabeth kept one trunk that she used for her few possessions and that trunk had metal clasps that, when the light was right, gave off a blurry reflection. However, today was not the day for reporting in. Konrad had returned from his latest hunt and Grace was not about to leave Elizabeth's side. Mechthild met Elizabeth at the hospital's entrance. Their first duty was to serve food to break the night's fast. The guests who were well enough were able to collect their own food from the nuns. Those that were unable to get up were brought their meal by Elizabeth or one of the ladies who worked with her, who were named Irmgard and Elizabeth. After Elizabeth and Mechthild finished serving breakfast, Elizabeth lost her balance and almost fell into Mechthild. Seeing her so weak, Mechthild got Elizabeth a tankard and bread. Elizabeth tried to refuse because the pious only ate two meals a day and it was seen as more holy to forgo the first meal of the day. However, Mechthild insisted and Elizabeth obeyed. As she lifted the tankard to her lips, Konrad entered the room. Disappointed that Elizabeth would give in to the temptations of the flesh, he slapped the tankard out of her hand. Both the ladies were startled, but Grace was furious. She jumped from her perch to stand with her back arched between Elizabeth and Konrad. He reached to grab the bread from Elizabeth's hand, so Grace attacked. One clean swat with her nails out made contact with the priest's arm. The swipe tore the sleeve of his cassock and slightly tore the skin beneath. Konrad was familiar with torn flesh. His daily mortifications often included self-flagellation, but receiving such treatment from an animal was a shock to him. As horrified as Elizabeth was, Mechthild found herself equally amused. She had grown to dislike Magister Konrad due to his treatment of Elizabeth. Her husband disliked him because he was constantly receiving complaints from peasants, as Sayn bordered Hesse and Konrad the heretic hunter often allowed his hunt to cross into Sayn. Henry III was also aware of his wife's loathing and the treatment of his cousin. Even though Elizabeth was only his cousin through marriage, both hers and his, he had grown fond of her through his wife. They had often pleaded with Elizabeth to return to her life as a noblewoman for her own sake, but she refused every time. Elizabeth scooped Grace up in her arms to soothe her and then quickly handed her to Mechthild so she could attend to Konrad's injury. Her touch on his bare skin was almost too much for him to bear. All the fury he felt at the cat instantly evaporated and all he could think of was her hand on his arm. The fire that was blazing in his stomach seemed to transfer to her touch. The slightest touch of her fingertips on his skin felt like fire. The closer she got to him the more he felt like he needed to pull away. Grace watched intently. As Elizabeth got close to Konrad, her light pierced through his darkness. It pushed it back to the point that it was being ripped from his body, but the darkness was fighting to regain control over its host. Mechthild held Grace close, ignorant of the battle she was watching. Grace was amazed how Konrad's body had been turned into the rope in this spiritual game of tug of war. Grace willed every bit of her energy to Elizabeth in hopes that her light might prevail, but Konrad's darkness was too strong. It shot out arrows of shadow which pierced through Konrad's body, expanding like an anchor as it burst through the front. Konrad pulled back his hand and stepped back, out of Elizabeth's reach. He mumbled some excuse and quickly left. Grace jumped out of Mechthild's arms and rubbed against Elizabeth's legs. "Lady Grace, you really should not have done that. I am sorry he scared you, but Father Konrad is a devoted man of God who deserves our respect and obedience. My flesh is weak and I should not have given into the temptation to break my fast so early." Mechthild could not believe how enthralled Elizabeth had become. Mechthild saw Magister Konrad as a cruel, power-hungry zealot of the faith but Elizabeth, despite his beatings, saw him as a holy messenger of God. It saddened Mechthild, but she knew she would never convince Elizabeth to leave his care.

Konrad could not stay in Marburg. His physical cravings for Elizabeth had grown too strong. His only remedy was to find and punish enough heretics to make up for the weakness of his flesh. A letter from the Archbishop of Bremen was the escape he needed. Gerhard II, Archbishop of Bremen and Hamburg had invited Konrad to visit and advise on the Stedinger situation. Konrad sent a messenger ahead of him informing the Archbishop he was en route. Konrad was sure that the journey to Bremen would give him plenty of opportunities for interrogation along the way.

***

Gerhard II paced back and forth in his chambers. Before, he had been fueled by his greed, but now after the murder of his brother during the battle on Christmas 1229, he was fueled by vengeance. Before he had wanted the Stedinger people as serfs to work the land and increase his wealth, but now he wanted to wipe the Stedinger people from the face of the earth. A knock on the door stopped the Archbishop's seething thoughts. A young servant informed the Archbishop of the arrival of Magister Konrad of Marburg. Gerhard II calmed himself. If anyone could help him devise a plan to eliminate Stedinger, it was the feared heretic hunter with the ear of Pope Gregory IX. Gerhard II met Konrad in the cloister. "Magister Konrad, thank you for coming. I wish we were meeting again under better circumstances. As you no doubt have heard, the vile heretics of the land of Stedingen have killed my brother the Lord of Lippe. I did as you suggested and had the Stedinger people excommunicated. I spoke with Pope Gregory IX myself to ask him to confirm the excommunication, but the Stedinger people care little about the punishment. They have lost what little support they had from the surrounding communities, but not much else has changed for them. They continue in their refusal to pay their taxes and tithes. The land is already naturally fortified, but they work to increase that natural fortification. The pope in his unending mercy has assigned the Provost of Münster Cathedral to validate the charges for excommunication. You deal with godless animals and heretics often. What is your opinion on the redemption of such beasts? Not to question His Excellency, but I personally do not feel that these animals can be brought back to communion." Konrad evaluated the Archbishop. He considered the possibility that this was a trap to get him to speak against the pope, but dismissed the idea. He could feel the hatred from the Archbishop when he spoke of the Stedinger people. It was not unlike his own loathing for heretics who betray the church. This kinship, forged in hatred, urged Konrad to do what he could to assist the Archbishop of Bremen. The sides of his tight little mouth began to curl as an idea came to him. He had been frustrated of late at the slow pace and procedural hurdles to his inquisitions. The church had far too many rules that kept him from efficiently seeking out evil-doers. Minnike's trial had lasted two years and Konrad was not interested in such delays in the future. Konrad chose his words carefully. "I do not think you are wrong Archbishop. I, myself have lamented at the delays and restrictions in the punishment of those who go against God. I feel that heretics and those who betray our Lord by going against His church need to be made an example of for those who may be in danger of straying from the path of righteousness. Your beasties, along with the heretics I identify will not repent on their own, they must be made to pay for their sins. Every moment wasted on undeserved offers of mercy allows for another moment of temptation to those who have yet to stray. Your problem with Stedinger will continue to grow and spread like a plague. The same with the spreading problem of heresy. I see the two as one in the same. You have heard of Willibrand, Bishop of Utrecht? He is the nephew of your predecessor, Gerhard I." The Archbishop nodded his familiarity "I am very familiar. His predecessor was my brother Otto II. My brother Herman II, God rest his soul, and I both sent knights to the Battle of Anne where my brother Otto II lost his life." Konrad nodded solemnly and continued. "Just like your brother Otto II, Willibrand is facing a problem, not unlike your own, with the inhabitants of Drenthe. He has been granted a crusade by Pope Gregory IX, which is currently being preached across the country. Willibrand was able to argue that the killing of Otto II, the Bishop of Utrecht, made the people of Drenthe guilty of heresy. The pope agreed. Should you be able to gather enough evidence against the inhabitants of Stedingen, you too could ask the pope to declare a crusade against them." Now it was Gerhard II's turn to be suspicious. "You offer wise advice, but I wonder what benefit you might seek in offering such helpful counsel." "I am tormented daily by the thought of the unchecked scourge that is heresy. This sickness spreads like wildfire throughout the land. Every heretic I identify and bring to punishment, three more scurry into darkness. I wish to increase my reach. I wish to have the authority to cut off the head of the snake before it has a chance to regrow. As my authority is now, I am bound by too many restricting laws put in place by those who are too far removed from the problem. Should we be able to prove that this problem is more widespread than originally believed, I may entreat the pope for more freedom in resolving the problem. I seek only what you seek, the destruction of the vessels of Satan who dare to question the servants of God on earth." The men had a deeper understanding than the words that were spoken. Gerhard II knew that just like himself, Konrad's motivations were not as he claimed. Both men were driven by their own selfish desires. Gerhard II assumed that Konrad, like most other men, desired power and would use any excuse he could to get it. That was fine with him. They were made allies in their hostility. The Archbishop had only one problem. "I agree with your proposed course of action, but unlike the people of Drenthe, Stedinger have not murdered their Bishop." A cold expression settled over Konrad's features. "It matters not what they have done, only what we claim. You mentioned that the people of Stedingen have killed your emissaries?" "Yes, but those were not clergymen. They were insignificant men of little standing." Konrad held up a hand to silence him. "Forgive me Your Excellency, but if the men were sent on your behalf, I would argue that they were acting on your behalf making any violence enacted against them a violent act against your very person and therefore an act against the church. From what I have heard these peasants are guilty of murdering priests, superstitious practices as all peasants are, burning churches and monasteries as they burnt down the castles of the Counts of Oldenburg, which most certainly housed a chapel or monastery, and desecrating the eucharist. Any guilty soul who participates in the eucharist is desecrating it. I am sure that between the two of us, we can find enough evidence to satisfy Pope Gregory IX. All you need do is travel to Rome to argue the case. His Grace will undoubtedly order an investigation and we will be able to gather our proof. I would expect that as the investigation moves forward, my expertise will be solicited at some point. It is at that time when I might aid you in your request for a crusade. I will inquire about the probable heresies of the Stedinger people and write to you with what I discover. If all goes well, we may solve both our problems."

***

When Konrad returned to Marburg, he was upset to find not only Mechthild of Sayn visiting Elizabeth, but her husband Henry III of Sayn as well. He did not like the idea of any man being near his Elizabeth, especially a man who was more than fifteen years younger than him. There was no doubt in Konrad's mind that the Count of Sayn desired Elizabeth. How could he not? If Konrad himself, a devoted servant of the Lord, could be tempted by Elizabeth, then what chance did a secular and sinful man stand against her natural charms? Konrad vowed to do whatever he must in order to keep Henry III and his meddlesome wife away from Elizabeth. That evening Konrad confronted Elizabeth about the distraction he believed Mechthild and her husband were causing Elizabeth. He accused her of giving more of herself to them than she did to God and chastised her for breaking her vows. Konrad instructed Hildegund and Wigburg to discipline her and made her promise to send her cousins away for good. She begged for forgiveness and promised to not lose herself during their visits if Konrad would just allow them from time to time, but Konrad had no interest in sharing Elizabeth with anyone else and used the excuse of devotion to justify his command. Fighting off tears, Elizabeth sent her cousins away and further dedicated herself to her work. Mechthild honored Elizabeth's wishes to be left to her work for over a year, but come fall, she began to feel overwhelmed by her loneliness and wanted nothing more than to see Elizabeth again. Henry III and Mechthild decided to visit Elizabeth for the feast day of Saint Martin of Tours.

   Elizabeth and Grace were in the hospital tending to an elderly woman suffering from dysentery. Irmgard entered to inform her of her cousins' arrival. Elizabeth was elated and devastated at the same time. She was so happy to see her family, but feared Father Konrad's reaction. She was intent on staying focused on her duties so as not to lose sight of her vows. She asked Irmgard to inform her cousins that she would be free in the evening, but not before. Elizabeth was confident that if she did not stray from her responsibilities, that Father Konrad would not take offense to a short visit. That evening, Elizabeth accompanied Mechthild and Henry III for the lighting of the bonfires on Martinmas Eve. Hand in hand they watched the Laternelaufen, a parade of children with their homemade lanterns, singing songs. Methchild and Henry III enjoyed the pretzels being handed out, but Elizabeth did not partake in such luxury. They asked her to join them for the feasts the following day, but Elizabeth held fast that she must first attend to her duties but agreed to join them after, but would not partake in the feasting. Konrad had not returned from his latest hunt and the rebellious side of Elizabeth hoped that he would stay away for a bit longer so she could enjoy her cousin's visit without reprimand. She hoped that they would leave before Father Konrad's return and he might stay ignorant of the visit. However, Elizabeth was anything but lucky. Konrad returned on the night of feasting. He was in a foul mood. He did not approve of the gluttony on display and felt that many of the traditions were of pagan origin. He feared that the church's acceptance of such heathen practices was an open invitation for the devil to corrupt. He looked forward to a quiet night of prayer with his pupil. This anticipation was turned to rage when he returned to find Elizabeth at the feast. He did not care that she was not eating. It was bad enough for her to even be present. His anger burned so hot he dared not confront her, but before he could escape the revelries, he was approached by Henry III. "Magister Konrad, welcome back from your travels. May I speak with you for a moment?" Konrad wished for nothing more than to push the Count of Sayn into one of the bonfires, but was forced into a diplomatic reply. "But of course Count. How may I be of service?" Konrad offered an insincere smile. "It is about Lady Elizabeth." Konrad tried hard not to audibly grind his teeth as Henry III continued. "My wife the Countess of Sayn is concerned for her well being. It has been some time since we have last seen Lady Elizabeth and in that time she has lost a considerable amount of weight. She appears to us as death in humble robes. Perhaps you can encourage her to eat more as is befitting a lady of her stature?" Konrad could take no more. He was not about to be told how to care for Elizabeth by some pompous secular prick. "I assure you, Count, that Elizabeth eats what she must to survive. It is not befitting for one who lives by the tenets of St. Francis to consume more than is minimally necessary. To do so would go against her beliefs in the sanctity of her poverty vows. I fully support her in her choice to observe long fasts and forgo the sin of gluttony." Henry III was feeling dismissed, a feeling he was not used to as a Count. "I must insist that you take action. Lady Elizabeth is young and eager to prove her devotion. Would not she be a better servant of God as a healthy and strong woman as opposed to starving and weak?" Konrad was finished with this lecture from a man without devotion. "Elizabeth is sustained by her Love of God and we do not need the advice of a secular Count on the teachings of our Lord. You should take care to watch what you say. A stranger might misunderstand your concern and think you were speaking against the teaching of the church." Henry III was not one to be bullied, but Konrad was hinting at heresy and Henry III was wise enough not to push boundaries with a heretic hunter. So he did his best to keep his anger in check and curtly dismissed himself. Konrad was not so quick to dismiss his anger. He called to Hildegund and commanded her to retrieve Elizabeth and Wigburg and meet him in the church.

Lady Grace could feel that something was wrong, but she had been locked in Elizabeth's room. From the window she watched Konrad enter the church. His shadow sparked like the collapsing bonfires in the courtyard. Grace frantically looked for Elizabeth. She saw her being escorted to the church by the two termagants assigned to her by Konrad. Grace pounded on the window and meowed as loud as her lungs could, but Elizabeth did not see her. Grace jumped from the window and ran to the door. She scratched furiously on the wood. A passing nun heard the commotion and fearfully opened the door to investigate. Like a bolt of lightning, Grace bound through the door and headed to the church.

Elizabeth approached Konrad at the altar. She knew something was wrong. His usual calm demeanor was gone and replaced with a heavy silence. Something in the air made her afraid. She glanced back at the door. Something deep in her soul urged her to run but she suppressed the urge with logic. This was her advisor and mentor. He was strict but he was a servant of God. He was not some godless, evil criminal, but her gut suggested otherwise. Elizabeth spoke in the most normal voice that she could conjure. "Father Konrad, I am pleased that you have returned safely. Were your journeys-" "Silence you insolent child! Did I not forbid you from fraternizing with those people?" Elizabeth was confused. He did tell her not to see her cousins, but she thought it was because of her lack of focus. She had completed all her tasks and was honoring the tenets she swore to. "I have completed my work and my devotions. I did not invite my cousins, they came to surprise me for Martinmas. I was not aware that you wished for me to send them away so soon." Konrad turned towards her. The darkness in his eyes chilled her soul. "Yet again you have disobeyed my commands and broken your vows to God. You know I care for you, so I cannot allow your sinful acts to go unpunished. For sins of the flesh, you must pay with your flesh. Remove your garments." Elizabeth began to object. *"Remove your garments and kneel before Christ!"* Hildegund and Wigburg dragged Elizabeth to the altar. Elizabeth tried to follow the order but her hands shook in fear. The two women holding her helped strip her of her clothing and forced her before the crucifix. Konrad looked away in disgust. He picked up a wooden rod and as the women placed Elizabeth's hands on the cold, stone altar, Konrad swung the rod, hitting Elizabeth across her back. He repeated the punishment until the rod broke. He then nodded to the two women who picked up a piece each of the broken rod and continued to beat the kneeling woman. Lady Grace paced outside of the church looking for a way in. She could hear the repressed cries from Elizabeth. Every time Elizabeth cried out Konrad would add lashes. Grace was fuming. Her yowls could be heard throughout the courtyard. The desperate cries drew the attention of Mechthild and Henry III. Approaching the cat they heard the whimpers of a woman in distress. Henry III burst through the church doors and was horrified by the sight. Mechthild, peeking in over his shoulder gasped and ran to cover Elizabeth with her cloak. Henry III drew his sword when the two women protested the interruption. Mechthild called in some servants and they carried Elizabeth to her room. Konrad was livid for the interference and vowed at that moment that the three intruders, Henry III, Mechthild, and the cat would pay for their impertinence.

***

Mechthild and Lady Grace sat with a dying Elizabeth. Grace silently cursed herself for not being by her side, a sentiment shared by Mechthild. Elizabeth's body was bruised and swollen. No amount of compresses or herbal remedies were making any difference. The Count and Countess begged Elizabeth to return with them to Sayn, but Elizabeth refused. If she was going to die, she wanted to die surrounded by the people she cared for, in the hospital she built. Henry III tried to send Konrad away but Elizabeth refused that as well. She insisted that Konrad was just holding her to the same standard that he held himself. Still Henry III made sure he was present whenever the priest visited Elizabeth. The morning of November 17, 1231, Grace rested on Elizabeth's chest, trying her best to heal her with her purr, but she could feel Elizabeth's life slipping away. A rap on the widow caught her attention. On the widow seal perched a brightly colored starling. Its head was an iridescent purple that faded to a deep blue and green on its wings. Its chest was a bright yellow that faded into an orange. Grace acknowledged the intruder. "Ereshkigal. It is not often that you leave your domain. To what do I owe the pleasure?" Ereshkigal cocked her head to the side. "As Queen of Kur I see little need to ever leave my lands. However, I was curious to see the evil described by your Kahu Shai, so I volunteered to escort this Ni to the afterlife myself. Also, I bring you a warning. My agents in this land have overheard that the vessel of the darkness intends to kill you." Elizabeth blinked open her eyes, looked around the room, then settled her gaze on the starling. "Did you speak little sister?" Ereshkigal and Grace were shocked. "The human can hear me?!" Elizabeth's eyes widened. "What a miracle from God. He has blessed me with a feathery angel. But sweet messenger, did you say someone wishes to kill me?" Ereshkigal was still in shock but corrected Elizabeth. "Not you, you silly human, the feline! You are already on your path to the afterlife, now sleep and worry not." Grace purred and rubbed her head into Elizabeth's hand. Hearing Elizabeth speaking, Mechthild rushed in. "Are you ok dear? Do you need anything?" Elizabeth grabbed her cousin's hand. "I need you to promise me one thing" Mechthild did not like the severity in Elizabeth's voice, but nodded. "Anything my dear." "Promise me that when I am gone you will protect and care for Grace. This angel told me she was in danger." Mechthild looked around the room but saw nothing. "Of course. Of course I will care for her as my own child, but please don't talk like that. You will get better." Elizabeth weakly shook her head. "Please would you call Father Konrad? I need to make my last confession." Elizabeth fell into a coughing fit and spit blood all over the bed. Tears ran down Mechthild's face but she did as was requested.

Konrad entered Elizabeth's room. Grace was licking her hand but froze when she felt the evil enter the room. Ereshkigal on the window seal could not believe her eyes. The figure she had viewed through scrying had evolved to something terrifying. Gone was the eccentric robes of darkness and in its place was a fully formed human-esque figure. The shadow was four times larger than the man and instead of having smooth features it seemed to bubble and melt like boiling stew. Konrad kneeled by the bed and took Elizabeth's hand. The regret and grief he felt had taken on a life of its own. He hated himself for beating

Elizabeth out of anger. He knew he was responsible for her death, but refused to accept it. She confessed her sins for the final time and received absolution. No longer fearing the final adventure, Elizabeth took her last breath. Grace and Ereshkigal watched as Elizabeth's soul, still shining as bright as it had ever shone, sat up from her body. She stood and walked to the starling. Grace followed her to the window and was rewarded with a final pet. Elizabeth's soul said nothing but the love and gratitude in her eyes spoke for her. In an instant, her light shot out like a supernova and she was gone. Ereshkigal nodded to Grace and then flew off. Konrad began to realize that Elizabeth was gone. He squeezed her hand and brought it to his lips and let out a pained scream, which he quickly swallowed. His grief turned to rage and he knocked over a chair near the bed. He stood and kicked the chest at the end of her bed, then, looking up, made eye contact with Grace. Konrad transferred all the hate and rage he felt for himself to the furry surrogate. Grace arched her back and hissed at him. The dark form lunged at her before the man followed suit and Grace let out a screaming growl and dodged the attack. Hearing the commotion, Henry III and Mechthild entered. Seeing the priest chasing the cat confused them, but Mechthild quickly scooped up Lady Grace, fully intending to keep her promise to Elizabeth. Konrad approached Mechthild threateningly. Henry III placed himself between the irate priest and his wife. "Hand over the demon cat. We must kill it. That vessel of Satan is responsible for the death of Lady Elizabeth. It was sent by the devil to corrupt her and when it could not accomplish its mission it killed her with black magic. It was sent to drain the life blood from a saint of God! I saw it lapping the blood from her just now before her death!" Henry III placed his hand on the hilt of his sword. "Do not speak such lies. It was you who caused Lady Elizabeth's death! The mortification that you set upon her broke her body to the point of mortal wounding. Were you not a priest and were it not for Elizabeth's devotion to you and God, I would have you killed!" Konrad could listen to no more. He stormed out of the room and left Marburg.

CHAPTER TWENTY-ONE
CATerwauling, Fowl Play, & Mad Dogs

After Elizabeth died, Konrad found himself consumed by her memory. Visions of his staff hitting her naked body tormented him daily. The only solace he found was in his work. The first year after Elizabeth's death, he tirelessly searched for evidence of her reported miracles. Konrad put together a booklet of testimonies from people who knew her and began examinations of those who had been healed at her grave after her death, calling the booklet 'Libellus de dictis quatuor ancillarum s. Elizabeth confectus'. Konrad travelled to Rome himself to recommend Elizabeth for sainthood. Pope Gregory IX assigned others to continue the examinations of miracles so that Konrad could return to his work as an inquisitor. Due to the information provided by Konrad about a spike in heresy and the reports he was receiving from the Archbishop of Bremen and Hamburg, Pope Gregory IX granted Konrad special dispensation to ignore standard church procedure in his investigation of heresy, raising him to the newly created position of Papal Inquisitor. He also provided him help by assigning Conrad Dorso, a Dominican layperson, and a secular priest named John the One-Eyed. If Konrad was fervent in his inquisitions before, he was nothing short of obsessed now. He saw heretics everywhere. Everyone who was accused was guilty until proven innocent and very few were able to convincingly argue their innocence. Konrad had deified his memory of Elizabeth and held anyone claiming to be innocent to those impossible standards. Under the stress and grief, his mind began to break. He retold himself the story that a cat was responsible for Elizabeth's death and the memory of seeing Grace lick Elizabeth's hand morphed into a feline succubus drinking the life blood from a terrified Elizabeth as the devil inside it tried to steal her soul. If anyone accused of heresy had anything to do with a cat, they were automatically guilty. If a cat crossed the path of someone in Konrad's presence, that person would be suspected of heresy. Dorso and John were equally as bloodthirsty and zealous as Konrad. Free from the restraint of rules and oversight, they relished in torture for the sake of torture. Even if one confessed early, they would not be spared the torture. After a while, the inquisition was no longer appeased by just a confession. The accused would be forced to confess and name at least three other heretics. This method led to the decimation of entire villages under Konrad's order. Konrad would update the Archbishop of Bremen on his progress. Basic accusations of disobeying the church had not been enough to convince the pope to declare a crusade. The men decided they needed more. A story to scare the clergy and the nobles alike. Luckily, for the pair, Konrad's mind was slipping just enough to create the perfect nightmare.

***

Konrad, Dorso, and John the One-Eyed rode into a small village on the outskirts of Verden. A name continued to be mentioned by the villagers. A man named Snorri was accused of heresy. The villagers described him as odd and frightening. He lived alone outside of the village and spoke with an abnormal slur. Some said he used to be involved in the village until he suddenly withdrew and became a recluse. Children were afraid of him and women never traveled alone near his hut. Konrad did not need any more evidence of evil. He captured Snorri and subjected him to days of torture. Snorri was not a violent man. He had withdrawn from society and developed a slur after being kicked in the head by a horse. He had lost much of his brain function and lived a fairly peaceful life as a simpleton, but the villagers had to offer up someone to the heretic hunter and everyone agreed it was best to sacrifice Snorri. After the days of torture, Konrad began the interrogation. He didn't bother with his previous scare tactics as he was free to spill blood or mutilate his victims if he deemed it necessary and word of his sadism had already spread. Konrad entered the cell with John the One-Eyed. Snorri was shaking from fear and pain and the sight of Konrad caused him to release his bladder. Konrad was disgusted, but it was just further evidence that this was not a man but a beast. Konrad had taken a fancy to using mandrake to loosen an accused's lips. Coupled with the power of suggestion from a dominating figure, Konrad had elicited many fantastical tales from his victims. This was no different. Snorri had been given a small meal laced with mandrake leaves. "Confess your sins and you shall be released." Snorri nodded. "Ee cumfoss. Ee deed jit." Konrad needed more to relay to the Pope. "Tell us how Satan captured your soul." Snorri was confused but ready to say anything to stop the agony. "Ee wiz wukkin een dee furuss. Ee sur a tood. A beeg tood." Konrad did not wait for the man to finish his story. He knew where he wanted the story to go and led the gullible man down his fantasy. "Did the toad make you kiss him?" "Jess. Ee keeys beeg tood." "Did the toad's kiss make you sleep?" "Jess. Ee slip." Konrad looked over at John who was quickly writing to document the story. "What happened when you woke up? Did you see the devil's cat?" Snorri wavered in his chair. The suggestion of a devil cat playing itself out in his mind. "Jess. Scurry dubeel kit! Beeg stoon kit, but stoon kit nut stoon, jit aleev!" Conrad continued his leading questions until he was satisfied. Konrad had hoped to burn Snorri at the stake after making him name others, but the toxicity of the mandrake leaves proved too much for him and he died before Konrad could get his satisfaction. Though he did not get to feed his immolation cravings, he did get enough information to report to the pope that he had uncovered a satanic cult which worshiped the devil in the form of a demonic man and of a diabolical black cat. He shared the information with the Archbishop of Bremen, who also wrote to the pope about similar accusations in Bremen, which he attributed to the Stedinger people. From Verden, Konrad traveled to Bremen to finalize his scheme with Gerhard II.

***

The Archbishop of Bremen was elated with his choice of recruiting Konrad of Marburg. Since he started his carte blanche hunts, people had been falling over themselves to prove they were not heretics. What little support Stedinger retained after excommunication had completely evaporated as rumors spread about their involvement in the ever spreading satanic cult. When Konrad was announced, the Archbishop had to control himself so as not to seem too excited. "Magister Konrad! Our plan is progressing perfectly. My nephew, Count Adolphe of Schauenberg, travels to Ravenna for the Congress of Princes where he will entreat Emperor Frederick II to issue an imperial ban on the Stedinger people. My latest letter to His Excellency detailed the accusations of Stedingen holding orgies and worshiping devils. All that is lacking is your confirmation." Before Konrad could answer a messenger was ushered in with a letter. The Archbishop's smile grew as he read. "His Excellency, Pope Gregory IX has granted my request and declared a crusade against Stedinger. The crusade is to be preached in the dioceses of Bremen, Minden, Paderborn, Hildesheim, Verden, Münster, and Osnabrück. He has instituted indulgences of twenty days for those who attend a crusade sermon, three years for knights serving in another's pay, and indulgences of five years for serving at one's own expense. He even offered full remission to those who happen to die in the campaign. Any who contribute financially may also receive indulgences. Surely with this, I will quickly have an army of eager knights to destroy Stedinger. My brother will finally be avenged." Konrad tilted his head and bowed it to the Archbishop. He was glad that the pope was reacting as he had expected. Konrad, like the Archbishop, also had some scores to settle. Now he can finally set into motion his plot against the Count of Sayn.

***

Ereshkigal sat in her palace Ganzir before a large stone basin. She watched the water inside intently. When something caught her eye, she would reach into the basin and pull the image toward her. This would focus the vision in the center of the basin. The visions she was seeing did not please her and her anger was apparent. Namtar, Ereshkigal's trusted advisor, entered her court. "Queen of the Great Earth, I am afraid the onslaught continues in the land above. The humans continue to send souls to Kur unbidden. Combined with Lord Nergal's continuous wars, we are being overrun with wayward souls. Your Kahu are overburdened and your spies on Earth are being recruited to assist, weakening our intelligence on Earth." Ereshkigal splashed up an image of Konrad of Marburg. "The influx of unscheduled souls is due to this Dalkhu?" Namtar shuddered at the sight of such a fully formed shadow. "Yes my Queen." Ereshkigal slapped the image in the water with her hand, losing a feather that slowly floated down to rest on the rippling surface. "I will not have my authority undermined by a human, no matter what his connection to the Darkness may be! These souls are not being given ample time to sort out their karma on earth! How are my Kahu supposed to help souls through judgement when they were not given enough time to clear their debts! The gaul of this human offends me. I want him stopped." Namtar perked up his head. It had been ages since masters of Kur were allowed to drag a human soul to the underworld and how he missed it. Ereshkigal saw the enthusiasm on her sukkal's face. "No Namtar. The terms of the treaty forbid us from reaping souls before their time. Though I too miss the chase, we must abide by the terms of peace. We may not take the human's life or we shall face the wrath of the counsel. I will not be brought before them again. We must abide by the laws of

Kahu and only influence, not force, human activity. Send a flock to intercede on behalf of the Dalkhu's victims. We will use his superstition against him. Perhaps seeing our ravens might scare him into mercy. Order all our agents on earth to act with hostility towards the Dalkhu, but they must not take his life. Dispatch a Kahu to work with it in its dreams. The Kahu must do what she can to separate the human from the Darkness." Namtar bowed deeply. "Understood my Queen."

***

Amelina and Tammo sat around the fire lost in their tasks. The children were quietly playing, Amelina was mending their clothes, and Tammo was sharpening his sword. Knight and his brood lay comfortably inside away from the winter cold. Amelina had something on her mind, but had been trying her best to hold it back. The quiet of the moment got to her and she had to speak. "I do not see why you must leave again. Is capturing the fortress of the Archbishop not enough? The Archbishop has already called for a Holy War against our people. We are shunned by everyone outside of the community. Must you antagonize the Counts of Oldenburg as well?" Tammo paused his work. "The Counts antagonize us by building their Abbey on our land. We must strike while it is being built to avoid more bloodshed than is necessary. None of us want to attack an Abbey inhabited by monks or nuns." Amelina bit her lip. She supported her husband and her people in their fight for their freedom and she understood that there was no other choice, but she worried that she would lose the father of her children, the love of her life. "Cannot you wait until the weather lifts? It is so cold that I fear I might lose you to the harsh conditions." Tammo put down his sword and crossed to kneel before his wife. "My dear, the weather assures us an easy victory. Stedinger are used to this weather. Not many will be watching the Abbey and there will be fewer builders due to the cold and snow. We do not wish to spill innocent blood, we only wish to harm the Counts and Archbishop where they will feel it most, in their finances." Knight, seeing his master on the floor, accepted the invitation for cuddles. He unceremoniously plopped his head in Amelina's lap and lifted a large paw onto Tammo's shoulder. The silly pose broke the tension and the couple laughed. Drawn by the laughter, the children added to the dog pile until they were all rolling around and laughing. Satisfied that he had successfully brought them back into their light, Knight slipped outside to a frozen over trough of water. He used his nose to brush the snow from the surface so he could see his reflection in the ice. It did not take long for Knight to receive an answer. A massive face filled the entirety of the trough. The head and outer parts of the face were a tannish blonde while the mask around the eyes and muzzle were black. The skin of the face was plentiful and hung down in places like wrinkles, but nothing about this canine was frail or aged. Knight immediately bowed to the image. "Master Utu. I was not expecting you. I was only expecting to make a routine report." Utu licked the drool off his oversized chops. "I have become involved at the request of the feline Kahu. We are working together with Lady Ereshkigal and her winged Kahu to address the issue of what appears to be the emergence of a Dalkhu. However, the human this darkness has possessed was never identified as a Ni. We are investigating the claims, but I wished to inform you myself as it has direct implications for your mission." Knight nodded to indicate his focused attention. "This vessel of the Darkness has been actively infecting many humans, including the enemy of your Ni. I anticipate an escalation in the conflict as a result. Your humans will need your loyalty and love more than ever before if they are to stay true to their light. Now is not the time to hold back as your mission may well be approaching its completion. Stay strong for your humans' sake." Knight looked over his shoulder to listen to the laughter of his humans. "Yes master. My pack and I have felt an increase of shadow at our borders, but we have held our territory and our humans remain strong. My pack and our humans will hold fast to our creed and our light or we will perish in the attempt." Utu beamed with pride in his canines. "Very good. May Dog be with you." And with that he was gone.

***

As the heat of summer brought spring to a close, Konrad of Marburg traveled to Rome to meet with Pope Gregory IX. He had spent the winter spreading the lies that Luciferians had taken hold of the Holy Roman Empire. He had encouraged the spread of his rumors of a satanic cat cult and now had been summoned to give testimony on those rumors to the pope himself. All was going according to Konrad's plan. When brought before the pope, he wasted no time in relaying the testimony he had extracted from his victims. "Your Excellency, I have pieced together a general understanding of the ritual from my interrogations. An initiate is approached on a road by a specter, taking the visage of a large toad, dog, or a man of fearful pallor. When the initiate encounters this specter they are enticed to kiss it. When they do, the kiss sucks out all remnants of faith in the Catholic Church and they would lose consciousness. When they awaken, they are deep in the forest sharing a meal with other cult members around a giant statue of a black cat. At the end of the meal, the cat statue would be imbued with the spirit of the devil and come to life. The devil cat approaches each initiate walking backwards with its tail erect. All present would take turns kissing the devil cat's buttocks. The people, in turn, say to the cat 'Save us' and then those present respond three times and say, 'We know the master.' Then four times they say, 'and we ought to obey you.' With this task complete the lights are extinguished and the coven members would descend into obscene acts, sometimes consisting of men with men and women with women. They all participate in a wild orgy until the lights are relit. Finally, a figure of a man appears, which I believe to be Lucifer himself. The upper part of his body from the hips upward shines as brightly as the sun, but his skin is coarse and covered with fur like a cat. Each person present presents the man with a gift to which he replies 'You have often served me well and may you continue to serve me well. I commit to your care the one whom you have dedicated.' It is my belief that one might identify these sinful heretics by their behavior around cats or their desire to protect and worship felines." Pope Gregory IX stood in silent contemplation, shocked by the story relayed to him by his trusted Grand Inquisitor. "I am left speechless to the depravity of this cult. It is shocking the speed at which evil can spread through the dark corners of this kingdom of our Lord. I thank the Lord that he has gifted us such talented protectors, such as yourself, who can root out that which plagues the shadows. Hearing this fearful tale, I must insist that measures be taken to eradicate this evil." Konrad agreed. "Your Excellency, I have traced the cult to an area around Hesse near Bremen. I believe that that area may be the seat of the cult." The pope thought on this. "I have received many letters and visits from the Archbishop of Bremen and Hamburg with similar complaints. He believes the inhabitants of Stedingan to be the cause of this strife among believers." Konrad pretended to think on the pope's words, but his mind was already set. "Based on my investigations, I must agree with the Archbishop. It would make sense based on the pattern of heresy I have observed for the source to be in that area." As Pope Gregory IX turned away, lost in his thoughts, Konrad allowed himself a smile.

Konrad returned to Marburg and awaited the pope's decision. On June 10, 1233, Konrad received a letter from the pope titled 'O altitudo divitiarum', which included his letter of Vox in Rama. This letter instructed Konrad to begin preaching the Stedinger Crusade but elevating it to be on the same level as the crusades to the Holy Land. He was authorized to offer plenary indulgence or full remission not only to those who died in the crusade but to all who had taken up the cross and fought. Konrad was ordered to Mainz where he should begin a full scale inquisition to seek out and destroy any and all heretics connected to this cat cult. Konrad wasted no time in following these instructions and he knew just who to seek out and accuse first.

When Konrad and his assistants arrived in Mainz, the Archbishop had quarters ready for him. He had prepared cells and an interrogation room. Everything was ready for Konrad to begin his tribunal. His staff was increased as well. Along with Conrad Dorso and John the One-Eyed he was provided aid by a Franciscan friar named Gerhard Lutzelkolb and a papal official named Bernard, to add more authority to the proceedings. Konrad wasted no time in calling those accused to the tribunal for torture. He began his search by instructing his men to kill any cat they came across. Should anyone object, they were arrested under suspicion of heresy and brought to Konrad for torture. Though his previous companions were as ruthless as Konrad, some of the more civilized men of Mainz were finding Konrad's methods a bit hard to stomach. Konrad was relentless. He would torture the accused to the point where they almost lost consciousness, and then while they recovered he would threaten them with the stake, and for many this proved to be more than an idle threat. Konrad paced the interrogation room in a fit. He had been questioning a woman named Gisila for hours without cease. She was a baker's wife who had been brought in because she objected to the extermination of her two mouser cats near their grain store. She tried to explain that she was upset because they had paid a large amount for the talented little hunters and did not want to be out the money, nor did she want to deal with a mouse problem again, but Konrad would not hear her. Even after hanging by her wrist on the strappado, she still claimed to be innocent of anything more than mouthing off to his men. Her husband had tried to come to her aid, but when threatened with the suspicion of heresy, he abandoned his wife to her fate. Konrad screamed his questions at the woman. "Where is your master?! Where is the vessel statue of the cat?! Who else participates in this sacrilege?!" The woman could hardly answer through her wails. "Please mi'lord. You are mistaken. I know nothing of the evil you speak. I am a god-fearing woman. I make my confessions and pay my tithes. I took the Eucharist just a half moon ago." Konrad swept the torture device off the table in a rage. "How dare you desecrate the Eucharist with your filth!" Without bothering to pick up an instrument from the ground, Konrad grabbed a dagger from the guard stationed at the door and used the hilt to smash Gisila's pinky finger. She screamed. "Please have mercy!" Konrad matched her scream. "Confess and you will be shown mercy!" "I cannot confess to something I am not guilty of for fear of punishment from God for my lies. I can only repeat the truth and pray that the mercy of God finds me." Konrad spit on the woman. "The only mercy you will find, you obstinate heretic, is the mercy of the flames on the stake." Bernard watched horrified from the corner. He could not believe that this man was a papal Grand Inquisitor. He did not think it was right that this man with so much rage was acting as accuser, investigator, and judge with no oversight. Bernard had heard praise of how effective a heretic hunter Konrad of Marburg was, but now he began to wonder how many of Konrad's heretics were actually heretics and how many were innocent. As Konrad continued to smash Gisila's fingers, he shouted commands. "Who leads your sect of this detestable cult?! Is it a nobleman? Is that why you bite your tongue? Child, fear God above man. The heretics you name will surely be punished. You have nothing to fear from speaking the truth. Is it Lothar, Count of Wied? Heinrich II, Count of Solms? Henry III, Count of Sayn." Gisila said nothing, but another smashed finger made her call out. Konrad turned to his colleagues. "You are witness. The accused has named Henry III, Count of Sayn as a facilitator of these abominable ritualistic orgies. Summon the count to the tribunal for interrogation!" Bernard opened his mouth to object, but seeing Konrad looming over an innocent woman holding a knife, possessed with a psychotic look, Bernard thought it better to hold his tongue. The woman was condemned to death for her obstinate refusal to repent. When Bernard was alone with Dorso, he asked him about the interrogation. "Are the interrogations always like this?" Dorso smiled. "No. This was quite mild. He must have been quite confident in her guilt to spare her the pain of confessing." Bernard felt emboldened to probe more. "Do many of the accused refuse to admit their guilt?" Dorso looked at Bernard like a simpleton. "Of course. Not many would openly admit to heresy." "Do you not worry that the people you interrogate are actually innocent?" Dorso scoffed. "Why? It matters not. We would burn one hundred innocents if there were just one guilty man among them." Bernard was appalled, but he dare not let his colleagues catch on to his disapproval. He excused himself and quickly penned an official letter to Pope Gregory IX informing him of Konrad's radical behavior. Bernard, dismayed by the reproachful way in which Konrad arrived at the conclusion of Henry III's guilt, made the decision to warn the Count of Sayn.

***

Henry III's quiet evening was interrupted by an urgent request for an audience. Bernard was brought to the Count. He told the Count all he had witnessed and warned that if brought before the tribunal, there would be no trial, only judgement. Mechthild, listening outside the door, burst into the room. Lady Grace trailed behind her. Since Elizabeth's death, Grace had been living with the Count and Countess. She had originally planned to return to Barag, but her fear of the damage Konrad and his darkness could do kept her in her Girru. The more time she spent with Henry III and Mechthild, the more she began to notice the power of their auras increasing. Their light was nowhere near as bright as Elizabeth's, but perhaps the time they had spent with her had awakened their power and catapulted them to the level of Ni. Grace decided to stay and protect them while simultaneously monitoring the Konrad situation. Grace stopped in her tracks, her eyes fixated on Bernard. She did not need to hear his conversation with the Count to know this man had been in contact with Konrad of Marburg. Attached to his back like leeches were four blob-like shadow forms. Grace knew she must dispatch these immediately. She ran to the table near the man and jumped up with ease. Mechthild, out of respect for Elizabeth, allowed Grace to do as she pleased. Bernard was acutely aware of the novelty of an animal roaming freely, but said nothing in fear of offending the Count. Grace got within swatting distance, but sensing the man's unease, was careful to scale back her force when swatting the shadow forms off his back. Once she was able to detach one she would roll around on the table, kicking and biting her invisible foe. Bernard suppressed a giggle at the entertaining antics of the cat. The occupants of the room watched in amusement as Grace dispatched the four dark wraiths. Before they could continue their conversation a second messenger was shown in. "Henry III, Count of Sayn, you are hereby summoned to the tribunal at Mainz by the Grand Inquisitor of his Excellency Pope Gregory IX, Konrad of Marburg. Failure to appear in a timely manner will be seen as an admission of guilt and will result in harsh punishment. You must submit yourself no later than the 30th of July in the year of our Lord 1233." The messenger handed the summons to the Count and left. Henry III turned to Bernard. "I must entreat you to do a favor for me. Deliver my appeal to Siegfried III, Archbishop of Mainz. Entreat him to assemble a synod in Mainz so that I may plead my case directly to the bishops. Do this and I shall reward you in kind with whatever you shall ask of me." Bernard agreed and left in haste to deliver the Count's request. When they were alone, Mechthild rushed to her husband's side. "Promise me everything will be ok. I knew we would never be rid of that evil man. He tormented poor Elizabeth and now he seeks to torment us." Henry III brushed a loose strand of hair back into Mechthild's veil. "Be calm. I have faced craftier foes than Konrad of Marburg, and I have an idea as to his defeat. I need you to write to your cousin Conrad of Thuringia. If my memory serves me, he is closely acquainted with Hermann von Salza, the Grand Master of the Teutonic Knights. Hermann von Salza has an influential relationship with Pope Gregory IX. I will write my brother Eberhard, who is also a knight of the Teutonic Order. With the help of your cousin Conrad and the help of my brother, we might be able to recruit Hermann to our cause in ridding the civilized world of Konrad of Marburg."

***

What felt like ages passed for Henry III and Mechthild, but finally Bernard sent word that the synod had been approved and would hear his appeal on July 25th. Henry made arrangements to attend. He had sent letters to his brother and cousin to request their support and the support of the Teutonic Knights. Erberhard had agreed quickly. Conrad of Thuringia took longer to reply, but agreed to help however he could for Elizabeth's sake. None of the nobles of the Duchy of Thuringia were all that fond of Konrad of Marburg. When Henry III arrived at the assembly in Mainz, he brought with him multiple character witnesses and documentation of his tithes and donations to the church. Henry III felt more fear than he expected upon standing before the synod. Konrad was in attendance and Henry III could feel his piercing gaze upon him. After hearing all of Henry III's evidence, the assembly asked Konrad for his proof of Henry III's guilt. "I have the testimony of a fellow heretic." The Archbishop of Mainz spoke for the assembly. "Bring forth the accuser." Konrad lifted his head in defiance. "I cannot." The Archbishop's annoyance with Konrad rang through in his voice. "What reason could you possibly have to withhold the accuser from offering their testimony to this assembly?" "The heretic is dead. She was convicted of heresy and sentenced to be burnt at the stake. That sentence was carried out while this synod was being assembled. Is my word as a witness to the accusation not sufficient?" The bishops of the assembly quietly discussed. Henry III silently said a prayer. When the discussion was complete the Archbishop spoke. "Given the abundance of evidence provided by the accused and the inability of this assembly to question the accuser, I am afraid your word is not sufficient enough to condemn such an honorable man as the Count of Sayn. Without any direct evidence of heresy, we must acquit Henry III, Count of Sayn of these charges." Konrad slammed his fist on the table. He began to rant about the plague of heresy sweeping the land and loudly preached the Stedinger Crusade. Konrad insisted that because Henry III had not taken up the cross against the inhabitants of Stedingen that it was further proof that he condones satanic rituals. The assembly saw his tirade as further proof of the Count's innocence, but they let Konrad have his say until he was out of breath. With a disappointed rebuke, the Archbishop of Mainz sent Konrad away and apologized to Henry III. Thankful that the proceedings had gone his way, Henry III headed home to Sayn Castle.

***

Konrad was beyond livid that his plans for revenge had been thwarted. He no longer received any pleasure from torturing heretics. His mind was consumed with thoughts of revenge against the Count. Konrad decided the only thing that would quench his thirst for revenge was watching flames devour Henry III and everything he loved. Konrad exited the interrogation room with friar Gerhard. In the courtyard, they were met by a murder of crows. Konrad felt unnerved by the birds' caws. He felt that they were all staring at him with their beady little eyes. He picked up stones and cast them at the birds, much to the surprise of his companion. The birds scattered then reformed. Konrad screamed at them in frustration. Gerhard spoke in a whisper. "Are you unwell Inquisitor?" Konrad felt as if his body burned with rage. "Yes I am unwell. The condonation of such evil in these lands makes me sick. The Lord is punishing me for not dispensing His Holy justice upon the deceitful Count of Sayn. His entire household is corrupt. The countess attempted to corrupt the Lady Elizabeth, God rest her soul, while she served the Lord in Marburg. Now they encourage the spread of satanic rituals and they even shelter and worship a cat in their home. With no shame! I cannot standby and allow such evil in the Holy Roman Empire. God demands that I do something." The friar stood speechless. He knew he should try to calm the Grand Inquisitor, but he was afraid Konrad might turn his wrath upon him. "What would you have us do Inquisitor?" Konrad paused. What should he do? "If the assembly has been bewitched by this servant of the devil, then we must act on our own. We will travel to Sayn and under the cover of night, if needs be, see that Henry III and his wife Mechthild along with the cat that acts as a vessel of the devil are all touched by the cleansing fire of God until they no longer can facilitate evil in this world." Gerhard was confused. "You want us to kill them?" The idea spoken aloud was sweeter than honey. Konrad's inner fire blazed at the fantasy of watching his enemies burn. Finally the cat that stole Elizabeth's love, the love that should have been his, would suffer and die. The crows watched as parts of the dark figure looming behind Konrad began to fuse with the man. The arms of the creature no longer shadowed Konrad's arms but had become one with them. The legs flashed back and forth between fused and separate. Only Konrad's head and torso remained isolated from the darkness, but it was clear that should he accomplish his iniquitous purpose, that the fusion with the darkness would be complete. The crows sent the vision to Ereshkigal with urgency.

***

Ereshkigal screeched and set the stone basin on fire in her rage and Namtar cowered in the corner. "How dare he! How dare that lowly human think he can lay a hand on Inanna, the Queen of Heaven! That worm is not worthy to pluck a hair from her head, whether it be in her glory or this lowly temporal form. I will not allow such insolence! Not only did he disturb my peace and order by forcefully sending souls to Kur without my permission, now he threatens the budding Ni and a leader of the Kahu! I will have his head and feed the remains to my vultures!" Namtar slowly approached. "What would you have me do, Queen of the Great Earth?" Ereshkigal calmed herself and centered her thoughts. "He must be eliminated. His darkness threatens a pillar of the Kahu. We know not what the Darkness would do to Inanna if she is exposed in a weakened state. It is a risk that is not worth taking. Send a group of warriors. They must take human form so as not to draw attention. Many on the Earth plane hate this human, so death by the hand of a man would not be of any concern."

***

Konrad left Mainz by the north road. He told his colleagues he was returning to Marburg, but planned to only return for a day before heading to Sayn. Friar Gerhard agreed to accompany him on his dastardly pursuit. As they approached Hof Kapelle they found their road blocked by a large mischief of magpies. Konrad cared little for the fate of the birds and urged his horse into a gallup. They had to make good time on the road. The sooner he arrived in Marburg the sooner he could head to Sayn to exact his revenge. The magpies squawked their annoyance at the assault but flew away over the ridge. A mischief of five magpies touched down on the obscured side of the hill. When they landed they transformed into a human-like form. Their bodies were that of men, but their heads were shrouded in a black hood and mask. The mask had small round eye holes protected by glass that reflected the light, hiding the eye. The center of the leather mask sported a large beak-like protrusion that curved slightly. Their clothing resembled the full length black cassock of a priest. It covered every inch of their body, except hands and feet which were covered by thick black gloves and boots. Only moments after the bird men transformed, Konrad and Gerhard rode over the hill, rapidly approaching them. One of the mischief raised his hand and summoned a powerful gust of wind that scared the horses. The horses reared, throwing their riders to the ground. Leisurely, the bird men approached their quarry in a 'V' formation. Konrad was filled with fear. His arms and legs burned and ached, like they were trying to escape without him. The leader of this bird man group was Pazuzu. He watched as the dark figure attached to Konrad tried to free itself and escape. This was Pazuzu's favorite part of the hunt. He savored the fear his target felt upon his approach. Both the man and the darkness attached to him instinctively knew to fear this looming figure. Konrad tried to speak but his voice caught in his throat. He reached up to grasp his chest. He broke out into a cold sweat and intense pain spread to his shoulder, arm, back, neck, jaw, teeth, and even his upper belly. He felt dizzy and his breath came in short gasps. Pazuzu tilted his head in confusion. He was accustomed to the intense fear of his victims, but he expected more screaming and pleading. This reaction caught him by surprise and slightly disappointed him. Konrad's chest raised, arching his back and then he collapsed. The Darkness attached to the body shot high into the air and exploded into millions of tiny shadow droplets, quickly scattering in every direction. Pazuzu looked back to see one of his number with a hand lifted, palm up, in a tightly clenched fist. "Lamashtu! What have you done!" Lamashtu quickly released her hand to her side. "What?! All I did was explode his heart. You were taking too long. We came here to kill him, did we not?" Pazuzu brought a hand to his temple to massage away his frustration. "Yes we came to kill him. *As men*! We can't use powers to kill him. It is supposed to appear as if he was killed by *men*! You *fool*!" Lamashtu just shrugged. "Shed. Pazuzu, you are no fun." Pazuzu shook his shoulders and back in a shudder. "Don't curse at me. I am the leader here!" As the bird men argued, Gerhard, shaking in terror, managed to roll to his hands and knees and was attempting to crawl away. The bird man to Pazuzu's right tapped him on the shoulder and pointed at the fleeing friar. Pazuzu removed his glove, revealing a scaly bird's foot with five toes with long talons. Pazuzu extended his toes and the talons fused together and grew into a sword. He slowly followed the crawling friar and stabbed him between the shoulder blades with his talon sword. He turned to Lamashtu. "Fix your mess this instant!" Lamashtu sighed forcefully, removed her glove, and formed her own sword. She stabbed Konrad's body through the heart, removing it slowly to watch the blood drip off the blade. She then continued to stab him.

After six thrust, Pazuzu squawked at her loudly and she stopped. Pazuzu looked at the mess Lamashtu had made and shook his head. As he watched blood seep from a wound and run down Konrad's body, he saw the corner of a letter sticking out of his pocket. He retrieved it and his natural curiosity drove him to read it. We should deliver this to our Queen. She will want to share it with Lord Utu. It seems Lady Inanna was not the only one in danger.

***

Lady Grace rolled over to reposition herself in the center of the ray of sunshine in the interior courtyard. Unexpectedly, her sun was blocked by a large shadow. She blinked open her eyes to see a barn owl perched on the side of the well. It hooted and she jumped up to silence it. "Quiet nungarra! These humans believe that hearing three hoots of an owl is bad luck! They might get spooked just by seeing an owl in the daylight. What would possess you to choose this form?" The owl bent down and retrieved a blood stained letter from its talons with its beak and dropped it next to Grace. "Forgive me Lady Inanna, but I could not carry this letter in my usual form and my humanoid form would have garnered too much attention." Grace sniffed the letter. "You are forgiven, but what is this and why do you bring it to me?" The owl rotated its head around to look for humans. "I bring word of the death of the Dalkhu. The human was dispatched and its darkness eradicated." Grace was not pleased. "Who authorized such action? We do not know what happens to such powerful darkness if it is forcefully separated from its host. The consequences could be dire." The owl ruffled its feathers and smoothed them out again. "We had no choice. The Dalkhu was on his way here to kill you and the Ni you protect. The risk of such a powerful Kahu being tainted by darkness was more dangerous than the unknown risk of killing the Dalkhu, but I am afraid that we have more pressing concerns. One of the other human's contaminated by the Dalkhu has evil intentions towards a group of Ni protected by a pack of Canine Kahu led by Dazhbog. The community includes many Ni and this infected human seeks to destroy them all, leaving none alive. We have warned Dazhbog, but without help from external sources, his pack and their Ni are doomed." Grace nodded her understanding. "I will do what I can." Grace's ear twitched. She could hear someone approaching. "Stay put. When the human sees you, hoot twice. I will pounce at you before the third hoot. At which time you should silently fly away. Do not return in this form again." Mechthild rounded the corner. The owl did as it was told. Mechthild watched the scene unfold and rushed to Grace when the bird was out of sight. "Oh dear Lady Grace. How brave you are!" Grace pawed at the letter. Mechthild picked up the note and began to read. Fear flooded her eyes as she realized what she held. Forgetting about the cat at her feet, she rushed to find her husband.

***

Eberhard of Sayn sat in a chair near the fire as his brother Henry III paced in front of him. He silently read a blood stained letter, occasionally making small sounds of surprise. When he lowered the letter to his lap, he found himself at a loss. Henry III had no problem filling the silence. "You understand what this means, do you not? This implies that Konrad of Marburg fabricated the stories of heresy and satanic rituals in order to gain power and assist the Archbishop of Bremen and Hamburg in his vendetta against these people of… of Stedingen. This crusade he was preaching is just a farce designed to enrich this Gerhard II and the Counts of Oldenburg." Eberhard sighed. "What do you care about some schemes by nobility in Oldenburg and Bremen against peasants? What business is it of yours?" Henry III clenched his fist. "It concerns me because I was falsely accused of the same crimes! These people be they peasant, serf, or nobility are innocent and may pay for the lies of that despicable Konrad of Marburg with their very lives." Eberhard stood and placed his hands on his brother's shoulders. "Brother, your righteous anger is admirable, but you cannot be this ignorant. These things happen all the time. Do you really think all these crusades are motivated purely by devotion to God? Absolutely not. The crusades are to defend the church and part of defending the church is protecting its interests, both in religious matters and in financial matters. As we fight to expand God's Kingdom on earth we are simultaneously increasing the power and influence of the church. The crusades are equally as political as they are spiritual." Henry III brushed off his brother's hands and slumped into the chair. "These people are innocent and this action against them based on lies is wrong. I cannot stand to allow Konrad of Marburg another victory." Eberhard sat in the chair across from Henry III. "Konrad of Marburg is dead. Many rumors claim you hold responsibility." "I did not take his life, though I cannot say I am sorry he is dead. The justice of God finds its way to every man. It angers me that even in death, his ungodly schemes might still find their mark. There has to be something we can do to stop this unnecessary bloodshed. After all, if they are innocent it means that it will be Christian blood being shed. Surely as a knight of the Teutonic Order you are duty bound to protect the innocent." Eberhard knew his brother wasn't wrong and despite his aloof manner, he was deeply disturbed by the circumstances. "You are right. I must at least try to act. I will travel to Rome on behalf of my Order and request that Pope Gregory IX intercede on behalf of Stedinger. I cannot promise that my request will be heard, but for your sake and the sake of the innocent, I will do my best."

***

Gerhard II, the Archbishop of Bremen and Hamburg stood over his war table. Across from him stood Otto I, Count of Oldenburg. They were positioning pieces on the war table to represent the armies joining the crusade against Stedinger. Gerhard II placed a number of horses bearing flags with crests upon the table. "Leading the main charge will be Henry I, Duke of Brabant, Henry IV, Duke of Limburg, Louis, Count of Ravensberg, and myself. To the east, blocking the escape over the Weser, there will be Flores IV, Count of Holland, and Otto II, Count of Guelders. Circling in from the west will be your force with Henry III, Count of Wildeshausen and William IV, Count of Jülich, supported by the lords of Breda and Scholen, along with the barons from Flanders. We will reserve Dietrich V, Count of Cleves to attack the flank. I must say, your family has proven to be a valuable asset. Are you truly related to all these noblemen?" Otto I eyed Gerhard II from across the table. "Yes and we expect to be compensated befitting our contribution. These plans are suitable for now, but we should revisit them when the Duke of Brabant arrives. He is experienced in such dealings and will most assuredly lead us to victory. Last I heard, he should arrive on the morrow. The rest of the men are camped around Bremen and are ready to march when the order is given." Gerhard II could not restrain his grin. "We have been blessed with a mighty force. Surely this time we will defeat the heretics and claim what should have rightfully been ours from the beginning. It is a pity that Konrad of Marburg has perished before seeing our victory.

In his name we must not allow a single heretic to escape our bloody justice. Everything in Stedingen must burn, no exceptions." Otto I sighed. "It seems wasteful to destroy perfectly good villages and kill the villagers. I would prefer to retain them as labor, but if Pope Gregory IX insists upon their destruction, then we must obey." Two of the Archbishop's men entered the room, accompanied by a messenger. "Pardon the interruption Your Grace, but there is an urgent message from His Excellency Pope Gregory IX." Gerhard II turned to the Count of Oldenburg. "Shall we reconvene when the Duke of Brabant arrives?" Otto I nodded and excused himself so the Archbishop could turn his attention to the messenger. "What message do you have for me?" The young man was not large in stature. He was chosen as a messenger because what he lacked in size, he made up for in speed. The shorter man was able to ride faster and longer than heavier jockeys, which made him perfect to deliver time sensitive messages. The messenger handed a letter labeled 'Grandis et gravis' to the Archbishop. "His Excellency, Pope Gregory IX hereby orders a halt on the Stedinger crusade. He has dispatched his legate William of Modena to mediate the dispute between the Stedinger and the Archbishop of Bremen and Hamburg, Gerhard II of Lippe. No action shall be taken against Stedingen until further edict from His Excellency." Gerhard II's right eye began to twitch. He bit his tongue so hard it bled, but he said nothing. Controlling his choler, the Archbishop calmly responded to the waiting messenger. "I thank you for your timely remittance of this information. Might you rest a moment? You should eat and drink to regain your strength, and I will pen a response to His Excellency." The messenger bowed. "Thank you, Your Grace. I humbly accept your hospitality. I will await your letter." Gerhard II instructed one of the men to show the messenger to the dining hall and summoned the other to him. "No one must know that this message arrived here and that messenger must not be allowed to speak it to another soul. When night falls, I order you to take him outside the city and kill him. Dispose of his body on Stedinger land and speak of this to no one. I am too close to victory to have my plans foiled by a messenger. I must see this finished before the legate of the pope arrives."

***

Amelina approached the Stedinger encampment at Altenesch. She had left her children with her mother. This war was no longer being fought for their freedom but for their very souls and anyone who was able bodied had enlisted to fight. Amelina was not going to stand idly by waiting for her children's father to be slaughtered. She would aid in stopping the devils at the door. She found Tammo in the leadership tent with Ditmar and a man named Bolko from Bardenfleth. She marveled at the Stedinger army. For a bunch of peasants with pitchforks, they were holding their own against much stronger forces. Even with the numerous past conflicts, the Stedinger force still numbered in the thousands. Amelina brought food for the men hard at work strategizing their defense. A Stedinger scout entered behind her. "News of the crusaders. They march north on the east bank of the Weser, shadowed by ships of Bremen, Holland, and Brabant. They are followed by a throng of priests carrying church regalia. It really is a sight to behold. They carry banners and crucifixes and swing censers, filling the air with a thick smog of incense, giving the appearance of the presence of dragons. The knights are not alone. There is also a large army of peasants. We are outnumbered four to one." Bolko moved the crude pieces on their war table to reflect the new intelligence, adding more pieces to show the greater numbers. "The time of Judgement is upon us. If we return home, we return home as free men."

As the invading army approached, Stedinger readied themselves for battle. When the deafening sound of the enemy's march had ceased, all that was left was petrifying silence. The silent threat of the upcoming destruction. Not even the air dared to move. The tension was palpable until a lone yip, yip, howl rang out from the Stedinger frontline. Knight knew he had to rally his humans. Even though they faced certain death, he had to keep their spirits up. Fear and despair would not only threaten their lives, but also dissolve their light. The other dogs on the battlefield answered Knight's call. In the heat of the moment, Tammo joined the howl and began to stomp his feet and bang the hilt of his weapon on his crude heater shield. The energy spread through the crowd like a wildfire. Cries for freedom rang out from the fighters. Their ruckus only served to irritate the Count of Holland who answered with an order to charge. He thought he would easily cut through the Stedinger ranks, but his force was met with the solid wall of determined farmers. The groups clashed like a ram butting its head against the solid bark of a tree. The other Counts followed suit, with the Duke of Brabant leading them. The first of the Counts to fall in battle was Henry III of Wildeshausen. The fighting raged on until both the crusaders and the defenders of Stedingen were exhausted and could barely muster the strength to lift their arms. With the sound of a loud horn, the Duke of Brabant signaled for Dietrich V, Count of Cleves. This reserve force flanked the Stedinger force. The attack from the rear caught Stedinger off guard and scattered their defenses. Tammo saw the commotion from behind. He tried to shout commands to regroup, but the damage had been done and his fighters were scattering from the onslaught of the energetic reserves. Count Dietrich V's soldiers took no prisoners. As the farmers turned to defend from the rear invaders, the frontline force of the crusaders renewed their attack. Being besieged from both sides was too much for the peasant warriors and they were dropping like flies. Tammo's heart broke as he looked around the battlefield at his fallen countrymen. These men were his friends and relatives and they now lie dead or dying, anointing the earth with their blood. Desperate, Tammo looked around for his wife, Amelina. He needed to find her to tell her to retreat, fetch their children, and flee to a land beyond the Archbishop's reach. Despite the chaos of the conflict, he spotted Amelina. She was isolated by debris and doing her best to defend those around her with her crossbow. Tammo abandoned his position and dodged blows on his way to the only thing left in his life that mattered. Tammo whistled for his dogs, but none responded. He whistled again and from under a pile of corpses, Knight hobbled his way. Bleeding and limping Knight made his way to his master. Tammo pointed to his wife and commanded Knight to her side. With all the strength he had left, Knight bounded to the woman. When Tammo was within shouting distance he yelled to her to retreat. Hearing his voice, she dropped her guard for just a moment, but that moment proved fatal. Approaching archers loosed their arrows toward her position. Knight, who had reached her side, jumped up on her to knock her out of harm's way, but he was too late. Both Knight and Amelina were hit with a slew of arrows. Knight's body protected Amelia's gut and the right side of her chest, but arrows penetrated her left side, piercing her lung and heart. The weight of Knight's body fell on top of her. Tammo reached them in tears. He moved his loyal friend off Amelina and held his wife in his arms. He couldn't speak everything he wanted to say. He wanted to tell her how much he loved her, tell her how sorry he was that he couldn't protect her, and promise her that he would save their children, but nothing came out except for sobs. Amelina weakly reached up and wiped his tears. "Knight tried to save me. Such a good…" Her collapsing lung didn't afford her enough air to continue. With her final breath she spoke the only thing that was left to say. "I love you." As she bled out in his arms, Tammo let out a primitive scream. The sound of approaching knights dragged him to his feet. He scratched the ears of his loyal dog for the last time and turned his attention to the approaching enemy. He knew he should have run. He should have found his children and fled, but what point was it to save their lives and condemn them to a life of servitude and misery? He would make his final stand, fighting for his beliefs. He did his best to fend off the three knights attacking him, but his exhaustion and grief got the better of him. The knights were able to knock the sword from his hand and knock him to the ground. All three stabbed him simultaneously. One sword plunged straight down through his chest just below his breastbone, the second angled down from the right, entering near the top of his liver and exiting below his left kidney. The final sword entered through his left lung and stomach, exiting near his ascending colon. Tammo surveyed the battlefield with the eyes of a dying man. So much carnage caused for what? Greed? Power? Even now, knowing the outcome, Tammo did not regret the fight. He followed his heart. He defended that which he held dear. As his soul left his body he uttered a final prayer. "Let us be remembered as were. Let history look upon us as the brave men who stood up to tyranny. Let us be remembered as we lived and died, as free men." As he slowly closed his eyes, a gentle nudge of a cold wet nose urged him awake. Knight stood before him, not as the scruffy mutt that he knew, but as a different dog completely. This dog had a very long face, like someone had pulled down on its nose until it stretched. It looked to be as tall as a man, should it stand on two hind legs. His fur was long and silky with a slight curl from the neck down. Instead of the dark colors he was used to, Tammo saw that the fur color was a blondish red. Though he looked completely different, Tammo knew this was Knight. The eyes were the same. Knight nudged him again. "It's time to go, my friend." Tammo looked at his furry friend in shock. Did he really just speak? "Do not tarry here. You have fought valiantly, but now you must proceed to your next escapade. Do not fear. I will guide you. You are not alone." Knight looked over his shoulder and Tammo followed his gaze. A short distance away standing with a pack of hounds were Amelina, Ditmar, Otband, and many of his fellow Stedinger. Tammo stood and looked back down. Hunched lifeless with three swords still stuck in him like pins was his body. He took one last look at the land he had called home. He thought he would feel sorrow, but he realized that it was not the land that he loved, it was the people. He followed Knight to join the group and with one bright flash, they were gone.

***

When the battle was over, the crusaders had killed every last Stedinger on the battlefield. The Duke of Brabant met with the Counts and the Archbishop. "We are victorious. The land will be divided among the houses of the Lords who took up the cross according to their contribution." Gerhard II interrupted. "Our quest is not yet complete. We will not be victorious until every last Stedigner is dead. Send your men through Stedingen and annihilate every last living soul and burn the villages. I do not want anything left standing. Do not spare anyone. I don't care if it is man, woman, child, or beast. Kill them all. We must cleanse this land of their evil with their blood." Henry I was not fond of killing children, but the Archbishop spoke for the pope, so he was honor bound to follow his orders. The crusaders' forces swept through the land massacring everything in their path. Few survived. Those that did were forced to flee to the Frisian lands in the north, but even there they would not be safe from the vengeful arm of the Archbishop. The bodies were thrown into a mass grave or burned with little regard for the life they used to possess. When the pope discovered that his edict to stop the crusade was not followed, he questioned the Archbishop who denied any knowledge of a messenger. Gerhard II stressed the righteousness of his actions by embellishing the stories of their 'evil deeds'. Immediately after Stedinger's defeat Gerhard II established a day of remembrance to be observed annually before the feast of the ascension. This was to be a day of celebration, complete with the singing of joyful songs and included indulgences for twenty days for all those who gave to the poor. The celebration was called 'dies victorie habite contra Stedingos' or 'day of victory against the Stedinger'. The Archbishop continued to push the rumors of devil cats and cult rituals to justify his severity against the people of Stedingen.

With each retelling, the fear felt by the listener opened them up to the Darkness.

CHAPTER TWENTY-TWO
Repurrcussions

Inanna lowered her head as her eyes regained their original color. The seers plopped down in the light, exhausted from the exertion. No one dared speak, except for Maahes who was too inexperienced to control his curiosity. "Master, there is something I don't understand. When you spoke before, I understood that you were warning us not to kill the Dalkhu Gideon, but from your story it appears to me that killing the Dalkhu Konrad effectively destroyed its energy." Nuska approached the young feline and swatted the back of his head. Inanna shook her head and Nuska backed off. Inanna looked at Maahes and then around at the surrounding Kahu. "It did appear that way. For many more years we were confident in our victory, but that arrogance would come with a cost. For the next century, the small fragments of Konrad's immense darkness spread. Each fragment retained the enmity and hostility of its former self. Konrad's story associating cats with the devil had been validated by the pope. With such intense fear of the inquisition among the people, many succumbed to the fear and began exterminating cats to prove their devotion to the church. The fragments of the Dalkhu survived and sought out such fear, feeding off the energy and growing rapidly. The number of felines in the Eridu quadrant was culled significantly. As you might imagine, this made it very difficult for us Feline Kahu to enter Samsara and complete our Girru. We even attempted to complete Girru in human form, but outsiders were not accepted or trusted enough for us to do our work. With our Feline branch of Kahu effectively crippled, the Canine and Avian branches were being overwhelmed. Without adequate protection, Ni were being turned to Halqu in droves. The number of souls infected by the fragments of the Dalkhu grew exponentially. Every fragment that found a host grew in power and spread. Without strong Ni to bring balance, it was not long before the darkness had taken over. As with any virus, the darkness will continue to spread until it destroys every available host." Inanna continued to promulgate the series of events in Barag and on Earth at the end of Earth's 13th century and the beginning of its 14th century.

Inanna scaled the steps of the Ziggurat in her cat form. She found it was easier to negotiate the never-ending steps of the numerous staircases with four legs rather than two. The Ziggurat of Barag was a mirrored version of the ones built by the humans in Sumer. It was pyramid-esque in that it had slanted sides, but the Ziggurat had four sides rather than three and instead of coming to a point at the peak, it leveled off in three separate terraces. The front had a long main staircase at its center and two long staircases on either side of the main staircase all leading up to a small domed structure and another staircase. This next staircase led to the first terrace which was fifty feet high. The first terrace wrapped around the entire temple and was decorated with trees and shrubs. Almost connected to the second staircase was another steep staircase leading to the second terrace, which was slightly smaller than the first. The final staircase led to the third and top terrace. On this terrace sat an impressive temple with large, evenly spaced pillars that enclosed the structure. Inside the temple was a long hall enclosed by rooms on either side. At the far end was a raised podium and a set of stairs. In the center of the hall was a large square stone altar and a half circle, somewhat shorter, basin. Ereshkigal demanded that this basin be filled with water, which Inanna fervently objected to. Utu stayed neutral on the subject, as he did for most arguments between Inanna and Ereshkigal. When Inanna reached the temple, she transformed into her human form. In days of old, they were forced to use their human form when dealing with humans as the humans did not like to think that the beings they saw as gods and goddesses did not share their physical form. They preferred to believe that their species was the dominant one. In every civilization that Inanna had dealt with, her human form was considered the most beautiful. Her long, silky dark hair was the darkest shade of brown like dark chocolate or espresso. Her skin was perfectly sun kissed and as smooth as a rose petal. She had large oval eyes that were perfectly spaced and voluptuous naturally dark wine colored lips. Her nose was broad and commanded attention. Her oval face terminated in a strong pointed jaw. Waiting near the altar was Utu in his human form. He was strong and radiant and his skin seemed to glimmer, even in the darkness of the temple. His face was almost rectangular, or at least it seemed that way due to his long, full beard.

His round eyes seemed to curve more on the bottom than they did on the top and were separated by the tall bridge of his nose. His top lip was completely covered by his mustache making his bottom lip appear almost pouty. His muscular body had a robust aura that demanded more space than was physically necessary. The pair waited in companionable silence. Ereshkigal was always late. She did things on her own time and would not allow anyone to dictate even the smallest detail to her. Her temper was as fiery as her passion. Ereshkigal swooped in, in bird form, and transformed as she landed on the podium. Even in human form she retained much of her avian features. Though her face was round, her mouth and nose were small and pointed. Her eyes were oval but formed strong points at either end. Ereshkigal refused to give up her wings, even in human form and they draped over her shoulders like a cloak unless she needed them to smack an offending subordinate. With all three leaders of the Kahu present, they could begin their discussion on current affairs. Ereshkigal was not amused to be called from her palace. She hated leaving Kur and made sure that everyone was aware of her displeasure. "Let us make haste. I have many things to attend to. Unlike some here, I am still actively completing my duties." Inanna held her temper in check. The peace between them was frail at the best of times. She would be the better creature and rise above the petty baiting. "It is the obstacles to our mission that forced me to call this symposium. Since the murder of the Dalkhu, without the reversal of his lies, humans have been overrun by an illogical fear of cats and continue to eradicate them. Humans are reluctant to associate with a creature that one of their leaders connected to evil. Many of my Kahu have been killed prematurely in their Girru, many times resulting in the transformation of their Ni into Halqu." Ereshkigal interrupted. "You do not need to lecture us. It is our Kahu who have been forced to compensate for your absence. Do you know how difficult it is to help a Halqu on their journey to Judgement? We have lost so many. Too great a number are being reborn with no spiritual power, after spending lifetimes strengthening their light. It is a travesty." Inanna was quickly losing her patience. Ereshkigal's complaining was not helping them to find a solution. "I am aware of the difficulty, hence why I have reached out for assistance with the problem. However, if a certain someone would not have acted so hastily and killed the Dalkhu, we might have been able to figure out a way to decrease its power and separate it from the host rather than splintering the powerful darkness into millions of Dalkhu seeds." Ereshkigal's wings lifted with her rising anger. "I did it to protect you from infection. Things would be much worse if the darkness absorbed your power. And you are welcome by the way." Inanna exhaled through gritted teeth like a hiss. "Do you think me so weak as to not be able to handle myself? I, too, was there during the battle to subjugate Chaos. Have you so soon forgotten my aid in reversing your great transgression? Once again your impetuousness caused repercussions you did not care to foresee." Before Ereshkigal could retaliate, Utu intervened. "*Enough*!" A shock wave emanating from his body knocked Ereshkigal and Inanna to the ground. "Save your bickering for a time when the Earth is not threatened by darkness. Have either of you observed the state of light on Earth? Behold." From the shining basin an image of the Earth appeared. "This was the state of light before the Dalkhu." The image of Earth showed a multitude of bright beams of gold light from every land surface and some in the waters. "Now, after the seeds of the Dalkhu have spread." The image turned and changed. Many beams of light remained in some areas but in the lands of the Holy Roman Empire and its surroundings, most of the lights had disappeared. "I do not need to remind you of the significance of the beams of light. My Kahu have been cultivating the light of the people in Sanu Eridu, but despite our best efforts, most of Eridu has been overcome by shadow. Do you not feel the change? The uneasy rumblings in Tiamat's Sibittum?"

A loud gasp from the assembly interrupted Inanna's recount of her memory. Everyone looked over at a terrified Maahes. "Wait, wait, wait, wait! Are you saying that Tiamat, the goddess of chaos and the primordial waters escaped her prison? How? That can't be possible. Isn't she still imprisoned to this day? We didn't learn about any of this in Bit Nisirtisu. I thought the escape of Tiamat meant the apocalypse, end of times, the destruction of the known Universe!" Maahes was beginning to hyperventilate. Ninimma approached him and licked his head to calm him down. "Deep breaths kitten. How about we listen and give the Queen of Heaven a chance to complete her story before we panic. Obviously, there is much we do not know that the masters now see fit to educate us on. I'm sure things will make sense soon." Inanna nodded to Ninimma and closed her eyes to once again gather her thoughts. "Where was I... Ah yes. Utu had brought to our awareness the weakening of Tiamat's Sibittum."

Utu's rebuke had refocused his companions' attention. Inanna looked at the image of Earth and watched the fading lights. As they watched, three lights dimmed and then disappeared. Utu continued. "If we do not act swiftly, we will no longer be able to contain Tiamat. We must focus our energies on protecting the few Ni left and abandon the cause of rehabilitating the Halqu." Inanna didn't want to hear him. "You are suggesting that we sacrifice souls to the Darkness? We vowed to protect Ni. If we fail and allow them to become Halqu, it is our responsibility to bring them back to the light. We cannot just abandon them." Ereshkigal groaned. "As much as it pains me, I agree with Inanna. Without the protection of Ni, normal souls will be consumed by the Darkness making it impossible for them to enter the Hall of Maat and pass their final judgment. I will not have my domain overrun by lost souls searching for atonement." Utu was determined. "I, above all, do not wish to abandon the Ni. I believe in loyalty above all else, but if Tiamat escapes, all will be lost. Everything we have built since the beginning of time would be destroyed and pain and devastation would rule. We must all agree to a course of action so there can be no blame later. We must choose those in the Eridu quadrant to save. My greatest concern lies with my pack with a tribe of Yeniseian people in Barskoon on lake Issyk Kul. A seed of the Dalkhu has taken over a missionary who was sent to the east via the silk road. On the trip, the Darkness infected many, but most worrying, an innkeeper in Barskoon. The more the Darkness grows in him, the more he is attacking the Ni protected by my pack." While they spoke the image of Earth faded and the face of a white wolf-dog appeared. "Utu, Forgive me for interrupting your high counsel, but the circumstances are dire. Our pack in Barskoon is losing their Ni. The shadow influenced human has deceived the group of Ni and caused them to be in his debt. He had agreed to trade a number of pelts for food. He provided the food first but before the Ni could deliver him the pelts, the shadow man sent bandits to steal the pelts. When the Ni could not deliver the merchandise, he involved the local authorities who have taken the tribe's children as payment. The pack had done all they could but in their attempt to free the children, many of the pack were killed. The grief of having their children stolen and that of the children being ripped from their families and being sold into slavery is rapidly diminishing their light. We must act now or they will be Halqu." Utu acknowledged the message and turned to Inanna and Ereshkigal. "We must see to this ourselves. If we lose this group of Ni to the darkness, there will not be enough light to keep Tiamat fully contained." The women nodded and in a flash they were gone.

***

The trio appeared in their human form just outside the settlement at Barskoon. Ereshkigal covered her wings with a large cloak. A cream colored dog with a brown head and large brown patches on its body approached them and communicated using telepathy. "Lord Utu. We have failed. I am the last of my pack. Three of us were killed by the bandits. Two more were killed and one gravely wounded trying to save the children from the slave market. Vuk succumbed to his injuries this morning. The innkeeper has sold most of the tribe's children, but he keeps the leader's daughter for himself as a way to continually torture them. Many dark thought forms have been plaguing my master Ni and I fear he plans to act on them, which will surely surrender his soul to the Darkness." Utu spoke for the group. "Show us the way." As they approached the inn, a large commotion could be heard from inside. A man ran from the entrance of the inn but before he could escape, a Mongol spear flew through the air and impaled the man, pinning him to the ground. The dog howled but the trio heard her scream in words. "*No*! We are too late!" The Kahu felt a deep rumbling that was too deep for the humans to notice, but the people in Barskoon did notice the sudden wind and clouds moving in to darken the sun. Lake Issyk-Kul was shrouded in darkness and parts of it began to bubble. The humans near the lake saw the disturbed water but could not see the shadow rising from its depths. Utu, Ereshkigal, and Inanna watched in horror at the scene unfolding. Their power and connection with all matter allowed them to see things on all planes of existence, even down to their atomic structure, but only in their higher form. Since they had traveled to Barskoon in their true form of spirit and did not enter via Babu to be incarnated, they could see the full scope of the disaster. Some of the Darkness of Tiamat had escaped her prison deep in the Earth and was grasping to infect the first living thing it came across. Utu commanded his Canine Kahu to herd the humans near the lake as far away as she could, but it mattered little. Tiamat's shadow had found a host, a small bacterium called Yersinia pseudotuberculosis. Once infected with Tiamat's shadow the microscopic creature began to change and evolve. Many years later this new species would be named Yersinia pestis or more commonly known as the Black Death. Even with all their power, the trio could do nothing to prevent the spread of this disease without first replenishing the light to hold fast the containment of Tiamat. Inanna was the first to speak. "We must return to Barag and change our strategy. Kahu on earth must be given reinforcements and we must speak with the seers to determine which Halqu will be most responsive to rehabilitation. More light must be added to Tiamat's prison immediately." Solemnly the others agreed and they retreated to their respective domains.

Inanna paused her story to let it sink into the assembly. "Each division of Kahu worked tirelessly to stave off destruction. All but a few Halqu were abandoned to the darkness so that their Kahu could be assigned to a more strategic position. It took us fifteen Earth years, but we were able to reclaim enough Halqu back into Ni in order to contain Tiamat and send her back into her eternal rest." Maahes was listening so intently that his gaping mouth dropped a bit of drool onto his fur. He quickly closed his mouth and licked his lips. "Master, what happened to the bacteria that you saw change?" Inanna looked to Ninimma to answer the kitten's question. Ninimma, equally shocked by the story, recounted the history of the Black Death. "The bacteria infected many around lake Issyk-Kul. Being that Barskoon was a popular stop over of the Silk Road, the disease, spread by fleas that infested rats, was able to proliferate across Western Eurasia and North Africa. It killed anywhere from seventy-five to two hundred million people in Eurasia, approximately half the population." Maahes sniffed back tears. "But what happened to all the souls that were sacrificed to the Darkness?" "That is beyond my purview. You would have to ask the Keeper of Zikru in Kur." Inanna looked down in shame. "Those of us who knew the cause of the plague were too ashamed to speak of it. This experience is how I can confidently advise you to find a solution that does not include killing the Dalkhu. We must do what we can to return the human host to the light. If this is not possible, we must prepare for the fallout of dispersing the seeds of darkness from the annihilation of the Dalkhu's host. We must not repeat the mistakes of the past. The immense suffering brought on by the Black Death fed the Darkness until it reproduced so much, that it destroyed all the available hosts. The defensive strategy adopted by the Kahu saved some, but so many perished. We cannot allow the humans to suffer through such darkness again. I will summon an assembly of the quadrant leaders from all three branches of the Kahu. We will work together to decide how to handle this Dalkhu. Until then, I advise that you listen to Ama-gi and follow her orders. Additional Kahu will be assigned to all Ni that may come in contact with this creature. If Ama-gi agrees, we will dismiss." Ama-gi nodded and the Kahu retreated to their individual tasks.

Maahes did not leave the Ziana Giš. He lay on his belly with his legs tucked beneath him, his claws out, gripping the tree for support. He did not know what to think. He was questioning everything he had learned in his training at Bit Nisiritsu. Lady Inanna, Lady Ereshkigal, and Lord Utu were the pillars of the Kahu. It was the three of them that formed their respective branches of the Kahu. There had been the incident between the three that caused the Great War of the Kahu, but apart from that all three were considered beyond reproach. To hear Lady Inanna speak of their multiple mistakes and see her hang her head in shame was devastating for Maahes. He now understood how children on Earth must feel when they learn that Santa Claus isn't real. Ki-Ang noticed the distress in Maahes's body language and plopped down beside him. "That was a wild story, wasn't it." Maahes didn't even look at Ki-Ang. "I can't believe it. I finally meet the Great Queen of Heaven and I learn that she and the other Masters of the Kahu were partially responsible for one of the worst disasters in recorded history. They were supposed to be perfect." Ki-Ang laughed. "No one is perfect. Not even the so-called gods. Sure, they are powerful higher beings, but that still leaves them far from perfection. Did you not study the other stories about Inanna or the stories when she was referred to as Ishtar? She was volatile. Apart from the Queen of Heaven, she was known as the Goddess of Fearsome Powers. She was, and still is, a great warrior, but I don't recall any story, poem, or epic that described her or the others as perfect." Maahes sighed. He didn't know how to explain how he was feeling. "I guess you're right. I just always thought that they were these brilliant heroes. I don't like the idea that they don't know what they are doing. I thought that when you get older and wiser that there comes a point when things aren't difficult anymore and you just know stuff. But if someone as timeless and powerful as Lady Inanna can make mistakes, then what hope does someone like me have?" Ki-Ang understood how Maahes felt. He too wanted to believe that there was a being in the Universe who truly was omnipotent, omniscient, and omnipresent. He just was wise enough to know that this being was not so easily understood and named like humans seemed to think it was. "Maahes, I know you are feeling a bit of cognitive dissonance, but try to look at the bigger picture. They didn't really make a mistake. A mistake means that you know better but you act in the wrong way anyway and regret it later. Kind of like having a big meal of canned chicken and then sneaking in and eating the entire box of treats. You know you shouldn't but you do it anyway and get a stomachache. That would be a mistake. If you make the best decision that you can with the information that you have at the time, it really isn't a mistake. Sure it is a learning experience, but not a mistake. Lady Ereshkigal acted with the information she had when she chose to order the death of the Dalkhu. They were up against a strong and seemingly crafty enemy and they were momentarily bested." Maahes sat up in objection. "But half the population of Europe Asia, or whatever Master Ninimma said, died!" Ki-Ang held back his smile at Maahes gaff. "That's true and had the Masters known that, they would have chosen differently, but what happened after?" Maahes thought hard but couldn't come up with an answer. "I- I was more interested in Greek, Roman, and Egyptian Human historical events." Ki-Ang sat up to be at eye level with Maahes. "The tragedy gave way to a socioeconomic evolution for Europe, and a large part of the rest of the world, that changed the course of history. It destroyed old labor hierarchies and gave those that survived a new admiration of life. The Black Death led to the Renaissance, which promoted the rediscovery of classical philosophy, literature, and art. Quality of life improved and though society was far from perfect, the tribulation definitely helped nudge it in a better direction." Ki-Ang could tell that Maahes was still struggling with his emotions. Ki-Ang was never one for bright shining words of wisdom. He much preferred sarcasm or dark comedy to deflect negative emotions. "Though if you still feel that the Masters could have done better, you could always march down to Kur and give Lady Ereshkigal a piece of your mind." Maahes jumped and stared at Ki-Ang with wide eyes. "Are you crazy?! Once in Kur no one is allowed to leave unless they are servants of the underworld! I'd be trapped!" This time Ki-Ang could not contain his laughter at Maahes's response. Maahes, realizing he was being teased, snorted and gave Ki-Ang a dirty look. "*Ha*. Very funny Master Ki-Ang but you know-" Ninlil's approach cut Maahes off. He closed his mouth and shrunk in the powerful seers presence. Ninlil was soft spoken but had a calmness that demanded respect. "My apologies for interrupting. May I borrow Ki-Ang for a moment?" Maahes couldn't find the voice to speak so he just nodded and backed away quickly. Ninlil turned to Ki-Ang. "Come with me."

***

Ninlil and Ki-Ang traveled to É. Simtum. "Dingir mentioned that you spent a Ti on Earth with a little girl named Asha. Did you enjoy it?" Ki-Ang closed his eyes to allow the warm wave of memories flow over him. "Yes. It helped me to remember why I became Kahu. Her love was so pure that it helped me to reconnect with the love I feel for humans. I miss her sometimes." Ninlil eyes, crossed as they were, betrayed a hint of a smile. "How would you feel about going back?" Ki-

Ang stopped walking. "What do you mean? I have learned my lesson. I have come to terms with my Girru with Gideon. I am ready to continue to fight for the wellbeing of our Ni. I am needed here." Ninlil turned to face him. "I believe you are. That is why I mentioned it. Asha is a Ni. Like all Ni, she has a great purpose to spark light in other human souls, but additionally, she helps Kahu." Ki-Ang was confused. It had been millennia since humans worked with Kahu openly. Not since the fourth century had he known of humans working with Kahu. "What do you mean?" "She is not aware of it yet, but part of her purpose is to rescue and rehome animals on earth. Keepers of Zikru use people like her to place Kahu in their Girru. Not only that, like you experienced, when Kahu reach a point of fatigue or are touched by the Darkness, the pure love of a rescuer can help to reignite their light and heal their spiritual wounds. As you felt, Asha has a strong light, but she hasn't fully realized her path yet and the journey is riddled with darkness and obstacles. She needs an experienced Kahu to help guide her through these formative years. If you are willing, I would like to recommend you for the assignment." The idea of seeing his girl again made his heart sing, but now was not a time for him to be selfish. He would go where Ama-gi needed him. "I am certainly willing, but I am just a humble warrior. I will go where I am sent. The decision belongs to Ama-gi." Ninlil had already made up her mind, but she was glad that he was willing to go. Ninlil saw much darkness in the Ni's future and her heart told her that out of all the Kahu, only Ki-Ang would be able to help her overcome it.

    Ninlil made the suggestion to Ama-gi, who agreed to consider the idea. At first, Ama-gi was not sure a basic guardian role would be a good use of Ki-Ang's talents, but the thing she was sure of was that he must be kept away from Gideon at any cost. Ki-Ang was far too emotionally invested to have a paw in the strategies against the Dalkhu. In fact, all the Feline Kahu had such strong opinions that she had allowed the Canine Kahu to take the lead. She didn't like handing over the reins to the dogs, but at least it wasn't to the birds. Ama-gi had eagerly awaited Ki-Ang's return from his Ti so she could assign him to a Girru that would secure a strong defensive position for the Kahu. Ninlil assured her that the Ni she wanted to assign Ki-Ang to would play an important role in defeating the Dalkhu, but she wasn't entirely sure how. Ninlil's advice was good enough for her. Ama-gi sent a message to Ninimma to send Ki-Ang to the Girru as

Ninlil suggested. Ama-gi had no time to rethink her decision. She was kept too busy by moving Kahu around like chess pieces. The leaders of the four quadrants from each of the three divisions of Kahu had met and argued until they decided on a strategy that all could accept. Now they just had to hope that their experience would lead to their vastly different styles complimenting each other instead of causing their downfall.

Ama-gi approached a large scrying mirror to await a check in from one of her Kahua. Before she could connect with him, a guard of Saa Barag approached her. "Ensi, Lady Gula of the Canine Kahu wishes to see you. Shall I let her into our sanctum?" Ama-gi, even after centuries, was still uncomfortable with the title Ensi. It meant righteous ruler and was the title bestowed upon the acting leader of each Kahu division, but she didn't yet feel worthy of it. To her the title of 'Ensi' would always belong to her predecessor, Inanna. "Yes. Thank you. Allow her passage. She must have something important to discuss if she came here from Urgi Barag herself." The guard disappeared and returned with a Sulki trailing behind. The dog was large but skinny. She had a broad chest that tapered significantly at the base of her ribs. Her legs were extremely long and lean and her hip bones were prominent. The color of her coat appeared white at a distance, but up close, it had a deeper cream color on the back and framing the face, with a thin stripe running down the bridge of her nose. The nose was the largest feature on her face that sat at the end of an extremely long snout. Her ears looked like human hair that flowed freely next to her giraffe-like neck. When she saw Ama-gi, the Sulki left the guard behind and approached on her own. Ama-gi greeted her guest. "Ensi Gula, Silim! Welcome to Saa Barag." But Gula had no time for pleasantries. "Ensi Ama-gi. Apologies for barging in like this. There has been a development with the Dalkhu that is in need of attention. As discussed, I sent one of my Kahu to Gideon in an attempt to herd him back to the light, but things did not go as planned. I think it is something that you should see." Gula rummaged through a bag hanging around her neck and retrieved a crystal ball. She placed the ball on the ground and used her nose to roll it towards Ama-gi. Ama-gi peered into the ball. Through the slobber bubbles, an image began to take shape.

CHAPTER TWENTY-THREE
Get to the Pointer

Gideon sat alone in his small apartment. Eight months ago his mother had died and without her, his father would have nothing to do with him. It had been three years since Cassandra left him and his fall into alcoholism and general disregard for everything in his life had cost him his job. He spent a good amount of time on the internet, even though the sound of his dial-up modem gave him a migraine. He spent most of his time in chat rooms where he and other men talked about the women in their lives who had wronged them. Gideon found it comforting to know that it wasn't just him who had been in love with a soul-sucking banshee. It made him feel good to revel in the pain of the other chat room members in a sort of sick camaraderie. While on one of his female hating rants, Gideon began to list all the times he could think of in history when women messed everything up. As it happened, one of the other members of the chat published a 'men only' magazine that specialized in misogynistic rhetoric. He was impressed with Gideon's knowledge of 'masculine' history and hired him to write a column for his publication. It wasn't a high paying job, but it paid the bills and Gideon got to stay home and wallow in his female-hating self-pity. The problem with staying at home and only interacting with dialogue boxes is that one can get very lonely. Gideon did try to get out every now and again, but being around happy, smiling people enraged him. How dare the strangers he come across display such flagrant happiness while he felt so phenomenally miserable? Besides, after he was banned from multiple coffee shops, the library, and two supermarkets for his angry outburst, he didn't see much point in leaving the house. His chat room buddies said he needed a dog, but warned not to get a small dog because that would bring his masculinity into question, but Gideon didn't have space in his small apartment for a big dog. As fate would have it, a solution appeared in the form of an advertisement in the local paper. Gideon, while browsing the personal ads, came across a section selling German Shorthaired Pointers. Gideon deliberated on the idea. A pointer was not a big dog, but it wasn't small by any means. Also, pointers were hunting dogs so he was sure his machismo chat buddies would approve. It used to be that Gideon wouldn't care what a bunch of anonymous, ego-obsessed jerks thought about him, but since Cassandra left his self-hatred had sky-rocketed.

The men in these chatrooms convinced him that his divorce wasn't his fault, that it was Cassandra's fault. They validated his contempt and venerated hatred. Without their hostility to feed off of, Gideon would be left with his own thoughts and memories of a now unobtainable happiness. He needed that cesspit of masculine facade to avoid any accountability for his descent into contempt for life. As Gideon stared at the ad, he felt conflicted. He desperately wanted a companion, but something in his gut felt repulsed. A voice told him that it would just be another thing that would use him, suck up his money, and probably end up hating him, just like every other being in his past. He crumpled up the newspaper page and threw it at the trash can. It hit the rim and rolled back to his feet, the square of the ad facing straight up at him. The title 'Man's Best Friend' burned into his brain. He picked it up and walked over to the phone.

***

Gideon placed the young dog on the carpet in front of the couch and sat down. This dog was already six months old. When Gideon went to look at the litter advertised in the paper, this pup was also there. He was from a previous litter, and because he was all black, no one had wanted to buy him. The breeder offered the older dog to Gideon at a discount when he complained about the price of the younger pups. Gideon had felt an instant kinship with the unwanted older puppy and after talking the breeder into a larger discount than originally offered, he took the dog home. The dog was elated to be receiving all the attention. In Gideon's living room, he ran around frantically sniffing the carpet and flinching at every encounter with the furniture. He made his way around the entire area and eventually made it back to where Gideon's feet were. The pup sniffed the feet and got very excited. It was like he had forgotten that Gideon was there and was now happy to have a friend. The pup wagged his tail so hard and fast that his entire rear end shook back and forth like a springing door stopper. Gideon reached down to scratch the pup's head. The little dog was so excited he enthusiastically licked Gideon's hand as he rubbed his head, causing him to tilt his head backwards until he did an ungraceful backflip. Gideon laughed out loud. It was the first time he had felt any kind of joy in three years. The foreign feeling made him uncomfortable. The smile hurt his jaw muscles and he began to feel sick to his stomach. He stood to detach himself from the situation and sought out an old comforter that he could put on the floor for a makeshift dog bed. The pup eagerly followed in Gideon's every step while simultaneously sniffing around. The pup was so caught up in his sniffing, that he didn't notice when Gideon stopped at the closet, colliding with the back of Gideon's legs. The impact knocked Gideon's knees forward into the closet door. The sharp pain caused him to cry out and he reached back to the offending animal and smacked it on the nose. "Watch it. Stupid animal!" The puppy tucked its tail between its legs and cowered on the ground by Gideon's feet. He looked up at the angry man with his head tilted down and his big brown puppy eyes looking up. Gideon felt conflicted. He was angry and everything in him wanted to smack the dog again. He even considered taking the dog back and admitting it had been a mistake, but the love and sadness in the puppy's eyes stirred a feeling of compassion that was buried deep in his soul. He gritted his teeth and let out a string of curses. With one hand grabbing a blanket and the other scooping the dog up from the floor, Gideon headed back to the living room. The entire walk back, the puppy was wagging its tail, hitting Gideon in the ribs with each swing. The impact stung, but the pain triggered a feeling of contentment that Gideon thought he was no longer capable of feeling. When Gideon shook out the blanket, something went flying across the living room. The pup shot after it, proudly returning it to Gideon's feet. It was one of Silvestr's old toys. One of the ones that Cassandra had bought him before they were together. Gideon picked up the toy and squeezed it in his hands as he collapsed onto the couch. His whole body tensed up as he dropped his arms into his lap, still squeezing the toy. The pup's eyes went wide and with a high pitched bark, the pup attacked the toy and started a one-sided game of tug-of-war. At first Gideon was angry and tried to take the toy away from the puppy, but the inherent joy of the game got to him and he caught himself laughing again. He snatched the toy out of the pup's mouth and looked down in triumph. The expression of pure joy in the dog's eyes made him sigh. He looked at the old toy with so many painful memories, snorted, and threw it onto the blanket on the floor. "Fine. Take it. I hope you tear it to pieces." The pup chased after its first possession and after throwing it in the air a few times brought it back to Gideon expectantly. The two passed the next twenty-five minutes playing fetch in the small apartment. When the pup was finally out of energy and had plopped on the blanket to rest, Gideon considered a name. "What am I going to call you? You're a German Pointer, so I think a German name would be fitting. Adolf means 'wolf' and 'noble' but I would probably catch flack if I name you after a fascist dictator. Hmmm, let's see. I could call you Wolfgang, but that's not particularly masculine, I don't think the guys would approve. What else? Oppenheimer was of German descent, but that is a mouthful. There's Levi Strauss, inventor of blue jeans. Or August Ferdinand Möbius who discovered the Möbius strip. Martin Luther?" The pup didn't stir. Gideon sat in silent contemplation. The lack of noise from his human roused the pup and he picked up his head to make sure his human was still there. The fur and whiskers on his muzzle were disheveled from the slobber he drooled during his playtime. Gideon chuckled at the funny look and a light bulb popped on in his head. "That's it. Otto von Bismarck. The Iron Chancellor of Germany. It's a good, strong historical character and you two share the same scruffy whiskers. What do you think? Otto?" The direct attention excited the pup and he started wagging his tail. "Ok. Otto. Your name is Otto."

***

The next six months were very rough for Otto. He learned quickly that Gideon had a very short temper. Adjusting to an apartment was difficult as he had been used to a house with a yard and doggie door. The puppy was not accustomed to holding his bladder. Only being allowed to relieve himself twice a day during walks was a hard concept to grasp, but he was forced to catch on quickly. When he messed in the apartment, Gideon would beat him with a rolled up newspaper and shove his nose in the mess. Otto would be forced to hide behind the couch while Gideon yelled at him for the duration of the clean up. Despite the cruel training methods, Otto loved Gideon. The first week, Gideon had tried to force him to sleep on the ground next to his bed, but Otto's incessant whining and barking eventually broke Gideon's resolve and he let Otto on the bed with him. That had been their routine for a week until Gideon got frustrated enough to put a box by the bed so Otto could hop up on his own and sleep there every night. As much as Gideon grumbled about having a dog on the bed, he was secretly thrilled. It touched his heart that this living creature loved him so unconditionally. Gideon was not delusional. He knew he was mean to the puppy and reacted harshly from anger, but still Otto loved him. Even when Gideon was hitting him, Otto still looked at him with such love in his eyes that it made Gideon feel sick and happy all at the same time. Once they got a routine down, things were smoother. Otto learned to hold his business until they went on their walks. Gideon bought some more toys to keep Otto entertained during the day. They both enjoyed resting on the couch at the end of the day watching tv while Gideon drank enough to lull him into a dreamless sleep. Gideon found himself feeling lighter. The knots of hate he had been cultivating in his gut didn't feel as heavy as they did previously. The pain was still there, but he found himself focusing more on Otto and job hunting that the weight of that pain was not as prevalent. As Gideon sat on the couch watching an evening game show, Otto relaxed near his feet. Otto was never more than a few paces from Gideon, even when he was getting yelled at. An empty bottle of beer dropped from Gideon's hand to the floor by Otto's head. Otto looked up to see his master passed out on the couch. He watched Gideon's rhythmic breathing to be sure he was fast asleep. When Otto was sure that his friend would not be waking up any time soon, he made his way to the bathroom. Otto nosed open the slightly ajar door. The bathroom was dark, but as the door swung open, light poured in from the living room. Otto approached the toilet. Thankfully, Gideon never put the toilet seat down, so Otto wouldn't have to worry about waking Gideon by trying to flip open the lid. Otto stared into the toilet bowl, waiting for a reply. The Ensi herself responded. The image of her long face barely fit in the round toilet bowl and the white of her coat blended with the white of the porcelain, making her look a bit like floating eyes and a nose. Otto held his amusement in. This was serious business. Gula spoke first. "Damu, I'm glad to see that you are safe and seem unaffected by your proximity to the Darkness." Otto looked back over his shoulder. Even from such a distance, he could still see the shadow emanating from the sleeping Gideon. "This is by far the most difficult Girru I have been on. The Darkness is fighting tooth and nail to rid itself of my presence. Luckily, I avoided having my tail cropped, so it gives me a greater range to keep the darkness out of my energy, but my muscles hurt from the constant wagging. I have even had to resort to biting the shadows, but Gideon seems to find the sight of me chomping the air amusing." Gula looked compassionately at her brave Kahu. "How are you holding up, with the beatings? Has it gotten any better?" Otto looked down but tried to reassure his superior. "They still happen from time to time. It is easy to forget myself on the earth plane and I have chewed some things I shouldn't have, which resulted in rather harsh discipline. The Darkness really comes alive during the beatings. It appears to wave and crackle like flames being fed fresh tinder, but I have been able to avoid any contact with the resulting shadow ash. The work I did with Lord Utu has really helped strengthen my aura and I am confident that the Darkness will not be able to penetrate my defenses. I admit that I have felt a creeping sorrow from the assaults, but my loyalty and love for Gideon helps offset the feeling. He usually gets it out of his system quickly and we can return to being friends. I really feel that I am making a difference. From what I can see, the Darkness has retreated deeper inside Gideon. I just know that there is a sliver of decency left in him and that sliver of light is fighting with all its might to be the stronger force and repel the Darkness. I just hope that my continued loyalty will feed that light enough to give it the edge it needs." Gula's joy showed on her delicate features. "That is wonderful. I won't lie. If we are able to reclaim the Ni from the Darkness, it would give me great pleasure to have that to throw into those snooty felines' faces. Don't get me wrong. I am happy that relations between our factions have improved, but even after millennia of restitution, those cats still have a holier than thou demeanor. That would certainly change if we were able to fix one of their biggest mistakes. I get the bum wiggles just thinking about the bragging rights. But I dogress. My main concern is for your safety and the integrity of the mission. If anything changes for the worse, you let us know immediately and we will extract you. You are already a hero, so don't make any stupid, self-sacrificing decisions. Understood?" Otto wasn't about to give up if things got tough, but he knew what Gula wanted to hear. "Understood Ensi." Gula nodded her satisfaction. "I regret that these more modern times do not allow for the placement of a pack, but we have positioned additional Kahu nearby to protect innocents from the Dalkhu and offer back-up should you require it. Keep up the good work. Good dog." Otto wagged his tail and lapped from the clean toilet water to end the connection. Gideon, hearing the slurping sound, awoke. "*No! No! No!* Bad dog. Drink from your bowl! *Disgusting!*" Otto returned to the living room but was pushed away by a repulsed Gideon.

***

Otto and Gideon went out for their evening walk. Gideon complained about the monotony of twice daily walks, but under the surface griping, he was really beginning to enjoy the exercise. He was drinking less and Otto's high energy walks were helping Gideon lose the beer belly that he had packed on. Feeling healthier led to Gideon feeling happier. He even started saying hello to people they passed on their walks. Every day Otto was feeling more and more confident about his mission. Gideon had not been as violent as he had been in the past and Otto had noticed a significant decrease in the amount of shadow projectiles being loosed by Gideon's darkness. Otto couldn't be sure, but it appeared to him that Gideon's darkness was shrinking. Before he entered his Girru, Otto was trained by many masters of the Kahu in Urgi Barag. Utu helped him learn how to strengthen his energy so the outer layer of his aura acted like armor that could not be penetrated by even the strongest shadow. He used the power of the vortex to continually renew his energy. To Gideon it looked like Otto was obsessed with chasing his own tail or that he was circling to find a comfy sleeping position, but Utu had taught him how to use this motion to absorb energy from the surrounding area like doggie tai chi. Utchitel had taught him how to stay centered and not open himself up to darkness in times of despair. Vuk taught him to be an efficient predator. How to keep his instincts sharp so he could rip to shreds anything that the Darkness threw at him. All his training had been valuable, but the thing that stuck with him the most was the story that Sunka had shared with him.

Sunka and Damu plopped down in the grass. They had just finished defensive tail training and needed the break. Sunka decided to use the time to educate in a technique that she thought might be useful in defeating the great Darkness in the Dalhku. "Damu, I want to tell you a story from the Ani'-Yun'wiya'. A young one was brought before Grandfather for starting a fight. The boy apologized to Grandfather and confessed he did not know exactly why he attacked the other child. Grandfather told the boy that he was experiencing this inner conflict because of his two wolves. The boy was confused. Grandfather said 'Inside every man lives two wolves, a white wolf and a black wolf. Every day the wolves fight for dominance, causing conflict for the soul.' The boy asked Grandfather, 'which wolf wins?'

Grandfather smiled and said, 'whichever wolf you feed.'. I believe that this is true for the Dalkhu. As long as a piece of Gideon survives, it means that somewhere buried deep inside is the white wolf. In order to bring him back to Ni, you must find that white wolf and feed it." Damu thought about his master's words. "But Sunka, how will I find the white wolf? And how do I feed it?" Sunka stood and then jumped and landed with her butt up in the air and her front paws stretched so her chest was near the ground. She let out a playful yip and Damu jumped up with his tail wagging. "Damu, you can summon the white wolf through joyous laughter." Sunka then approached Damu and started licking his muzzle. Damu bowed his head and accepted the affection. "You feed the white wolf with the bright light of loyalty, acceptance, and unconditional love."

As Otto sniffed the grass for a good bathroom spot, he thought about Sunka's advice. It certainly did seem to him that the more he was able to make Gideon laugh, the more the 'white wolf' was visible. The more Otto loved and accepted Gideon, in spite of the sometimes cruel treatment, the more the 'white wolf' gained strength and put down the 'black wolf'. Since it seemed like the tactic was working, Otto vowed to feed the 'white wolf' a never ending buffet if it meant saving Gideon from the sad fate of a Dalkhu. Suddenly, something caught Otto's attention and he tilted his head to hear better. No sooner had he turned himself towards the sound than he was buzzed by a furry bullet train. The dog turned around and ran up to Otto with her ears back in a playful mood, jumping up on her hind legs. He heard her voice in his mind. "Quick. Sniff my behind so we can have a chat without making the humans suspicious." They began circling each other, noses to butts. A task that proved more difficult for Otto since his new companion was much smaller than he was. "I have been assigned to help you. Barag warns that the Darkness in the Dalkhu is emanating a strange frequency. They don't know what it means, but they are concerned." A woman came running up calling a name and Gideon noticed the strange dog and grabbed its trailing leash. The other dog continued. "I am here to help however you need. I think our owners could be friends and our combined strength might be what is needed to ignite a spark to banish his darkness." The woman approached. Her hair was in braids but pulled back into a bun. Her features were strong and striking, especially her high, defined cheekbones. Her smile was large and welcoming. Gideon's voice caught in his throat. The anger he had felt about the loose dog evaporated from his mind. He didn't know what to say. He hadn't spoken to a woman one on one since Cassandra left and he wasn't that good at it before. Now not only did he have to battle his shyness, he had to sift through odious one liners implanted in his mind from the female-hating chat rooms. "This thing belong to you?" He held out the leash of the little dog but didn't bother to get up from his spot on the bench. "Yes. That one's mine. Thanks. She shot off like the bottle cap of a shook up soda pop. I can't hardly catch my breath." The woman huffed and puffed. Gideon looked at the open seat next to him. He thought about scooting to the middle of the bench in hopes that she would go away, but he surprised himself by squishing to the far end of the bench. "Maybe you should sit down before you pass out." The flash of emotions on the woman's face made Gideon instantly regret his offer. "Or don't. Just trying to be nice." The woman felt bad for hurting his feelings. "Sorry. You caught me off my guard. Thanks." She sat down. Gideon reached into his satchel and pulled out one of his 'travel beers' and offered it to his bench buddy. "Sometimes Otto here takes his sweet time doing his business, so I come prepared for the wait." The woman laughed and accepted the beer. "I admire your foresight. Sometimes I get so frazzled I even forget to bring the dog. I'm Jackie by the way." Gideon looked at Jackie and then looked at the little terrier playing with Otto. "Jackie, please don't tell me that is a Jack Russell Terrier. I'd have to audibly groan." Jackie bit her bottom lip and made a face. "She is." Gideon groaned. "I might have to take that beer back." Jackie quickly opened and chugged some of the can. "Oops, too late now. I know it is cheesy. So I probably shouldn't tell you her name." Gideon looked at the dog and back at her owner. "Oh god. I am afraid to ask, but go ahead, tell me." Jackie started laughing and snorted before she could say the name, but took a deep breath and answered. "Crowe." Gideon thought for a moment. "Oh my god. A Jack Russell, Crowe?" Jackie cracked up laughing again. Gideon shook his head. Her laugh had a snake-like quality about it and it should have annoyed him, but he found himself smiling like an idiot. "I guess I really can't say anything. I have a German Short-haired Pointer named Otto." The woman stopped laughing. "Oh, like Otto Frank?" Gideon was a bit taken back that Jackie would get the joke at all, even if she did think of the wrong Otto. "You like history?" Jackie shrugged. "I can't say I'm a huge history buff, but I'm a teacher and my sixth grade students are reading 'The Diary of Anne Frank'. I just figured since Otto Frank was a German businessman and your dog is German…" Gideon smiled. "You are almost right. He's named after Otto von Bismarck." Jackie snapped her fingers. "Darn. That was gonna be my second guess." The dogs continued to play while watching their owners. Otto noticed something strange. No tendrils of darkness were extending towards Gideon's companion. In fact, the aura of the woman seemed to be sending sporadic zaps of white light at any exposed shadow, so the shadow had completely retreated into its host. An excitement flooded Otto. Maybe, just maybe, this plan might work.

***

Gideon, against his better judgement, actually started growing fond of Jackie and Crowe. The four of them would meet up for their evening walk and Gideon and Jackie would chat while Crowe and Otto would play. They talked about history, science, current events, but never their private lives. Jackie would pick Gideon's brain about cool history facts that she could use with her students. She always praised him for his ability to make obscure or ancient historical facts more accessible and relatable. Gideon would play down her compliments, but she insisted that he had a talent for teaching. Her words got Gideon thinking. Perhaps he could look into getting a teaching job. Not with young children of course, he couldn't stand to be around little kids, but he would make a decent college professor. Months had passed and Gideon was feeling less lonely. He stopped visiting his regular internet chat rooms as much, and he felt less comfortable writing seething chauvinism articles for the magazine. His latest story had been rejected because the editor thought the article was too judgmental about Thomas Jefferson's sexual exploits and didn't highlight his masculine accomplishments enough. The editor was threatening that if Gideon couldn't get the article correct and submitted by the print deadline, that he would start looking for a replacement. "You see Otto, it isn't just women. Everyone sucks. They are selfish and stupid. This jerk can't even recognize genius when he has it working for him. At the first sign of trouble, people abandon you. It's just human nature." Otto looked at Gideon sitting at his typewriter fuming. He could see the swell of darkness creeping above his shoulders. Otto barked a warning to the emerging shadow, which quivered at the canine's incantation. Gideon shushed Otto and stared at the keys. The shadow began to emerge again and once again Otto yelled "Wasu!" Which meant 'Leave!' in Sumerian, but Gideon just heard a 'Woof!'. Otto could see Gideon's battle with the Darkness and he knew he had to distract him quickly. Otto ran and got his leash and ran back to Gideon, dropped the leash at his feet, and yipped. Just a few months ago, such a forward demand from Otto would have been rewarded with a kick or swat with a newspaper and the instruction to "shut the hell up." but the work that Otto and Crowe had been doing in an attempt to feed Gideon's 'white wolf' had been paying off. He was slower to anger and had even managed to fight back his own darkness on an occasion or two. Gideon looked at the leash and then back at the typewriter. "To hell with it. Let's go for a walk." Otto jumped around in excitement. This could work. His Kahu could be the ones to save the world from another catastrophic evil.

Gideon knocked on Jackie's door. She peeked out the window and then swung open the door, hurrying back to the kitchen. "Come on in. I'm fixing to set this kitchen on fire, so bear with me." Gideon walked into a smoke filled living room. "You need any help?" Gideon heard a loud laugh from the kitchen. "Nah. I just successfully tested a thesis. Conclusion is that buying fast food is significantly less dangerous than trying to fry your own special recipe chicken." Gideon felt uncomfortable standing in the living room holding his dog's leash while Crowe bounced around like a pinball and smoke and curse words billowed in from the kitchen. "Hey, I don't want to impose. I stopped by because Otto and I are going out early for our walk and I wanted to see if you still wanted to join us. I didn't mean to interrupt your cremation." A loud hissing laugh roared over the sound of clanging pans. "Cremation, that's funny. Let me just say my final goodbyes and I'll grab Crowe's leash. Gideon heard the sizzle and bang as something hot was thrown in the sink. Crowe was already sitting by the door when Jackie finally came back with the leash. "Ok, let's get some fresh air. And maybe some dinner."

***

Gideon and Jackie sat at the dog park eating hot dogs. It was late enough that the only two dogs staring at them, begging for them to drop a piece, were Crowe and Otto. Jackie finished off the rest of her hot dog, split the remaining bun in two, and threw the pieces as far as she could manage. Both dogs shot off like rockets. "Thanks for agreeing to get dinner. I was starving. I mean, I love me some blackened chicken, but the Pompeii style thighs I had going on tonight were somethin' else. There is only so much char that one can consume." Gideon, slightly buzzed from the bottle of bourbon they got to accompany the hot dogs, let himself talk without his usual censorship. "Yeah. I agree. My ex could burn water. I hardly ever ate anything home cooked that didn't have a layer of char." Jackie looked over at Gideon. As much as they had chatted, he had never spoken of his personal life. Gideon realized what he said and clamped his mouth shut. There was a bit of an awkward silence until the dogs returned. "Hey Gideon, I have a favor to ask. I have to go out of town for a school thing in a week. I know it's last minute, but would you be able to dog sit Crowe while I am gone? It's only for a few days. I usually ask my sister to watch her, but she has a cat that doesn't care much for poor little Crowe. I know she would prefer hanging with Otto and you." Gideon was grateful for the change in subject and would have agreed to rob a bank with Jackie if it had meant not saying anything else about Cassandra. "Yeah sure. That shouldn't be a problem." Jackie started listing off Crowe's schedule, diet, and favorite toys. Gideon turned back to the concealed bottle of bourbon and clenched his jaw as his thoughts uncontrollably focused on memories of Cassandra.

Jackie had dropped Crowe off in a rush. Gideon didn't mind though, because he still wasn't finished with his article and he was beginning to get stressed. The two dogs lay by the couch, silently watching the human at his typewriter. To Gideon, they looked to be resting, but they were deep in discussion about him. "You weren't kidding about how scary that darkness gets when he is upset." Otto put his chin on the floor. "Yeah. I've been with him for over three years. He seems to be getting better, but then something upsets him and the Darkness emerges like a bear after hibernation, hungrier than ever." The two dogs watched the pattern of shadow change with every rogue thought that popped into Gideon's mind "You never do anything right." "You know this one won't be good enough either." " A real man would have his life in order and not be struggling to keep a second rate job."

"A competent writer would have this done by now." "It's no wonder no one wants anything to do with you." "You are such a loser." Every negative thought bubble grew and then burst, just to give birth to another dark thought bubble. It was like watching a tar pit. The more negative thought bubbles that burst, the more stuck Gideon became, sinking ever deeper into his own darkness. The more frantic Gideon got, the bigger the shadow seeping from his shoulders became. Both dogs let out a quiet rumbling growl. There was nothing they could do. Otto had tried putting his head in Gideon's lap to remind him of his support, but it was just met with an angry shove. Gideon's taps on the typewriter grew evermore aggressive until he was practically hammering each key. "We have to do something or it's going to consume him. Sunka said that joyful laughter summoned the 'white wolf'. Maybe if we can make him laugh with some silly antics, then we can reverse this." Crowe agreed and they started trying different behaviors and watching Gideon's response. Crowe tried standing on her back legs and making a downward sweeping motion with her front paws. Gideon didn't even look up. Otto chased his tail around until he fell down. Nothing. Crowe rolled on her back and wiggled back and forth making happy growling noises. Gideon cursed and pulled the paper from the typewriter. Otto went and grabbed a toy and playfully tossed it in the air and tried to catch it, over and over until the toy fell and landed on his face. Gideon rapidly retyped the article, muttering to himself. The dogs were running out of ideas. Otto retrieved his blanket and tossed it over his head. Crowe jumped up and grabbed the blanket, attempting to run off. Otto snatched the blanket back and the two played tug-of-war, Otto flinging the smaller Crowe back and forth. Gideon glanced up and a small smile crossed his face. "Yes! I think it is working. Keep going!" To the dogs' surprise, Gideon stood up and shouted. "Yes! Done!" He pulled the finished paper from the typewriter and set it on the table. He went to the kitchen and returned with a beer. Opening the can and taking a long swig, Gideon belched in accomplishment. The dogs continued their playful antics, scooting closer to Gideon in an attempt to capture his attention. Gideon set his beer on the table and walked to the bookcase to retrieve an envelope. Crowe used all her strength to pull the blanket out of Otto's mouth. He lost his grip on it and Crowe went tumbling backwards into the table leg. The impact shook the table, knocking the beer can over onto the finished article. Gideon yelled and rushed over to the table to try and save his paper, but the ink was already running down the page. Crowe ran over to help lick up the disgusting liquid. Otto yelled at her to keep her distance, but she wasn't listening. A furious Gideon almost tripped over the small dog trying to rush for a towel. His anger at the obstacle was amplified by the circumstances and he kicked Crowe like a donkey. Crowe, not weighing more than twenty-five pounds, went flying into the book case. It teetered and a large bronze replica of the Sutton Hoo Helmet fell from an upper shelf. Otto was frozen. He could see what was going to happen, but his legs couldn't carry him over to Crowe in time. The sculpture fell on her, making a horrible crunching sound. Crowe yelped a long cry of pain. Gideon realized what he had done and his panic returned. "Not again. I can't be responsible for something like this again. Gideon rushed into the kitchen to find the number Jackie had left for her vet. Otto rushed to Crowe's side and pushed the large sculpture off her. She was breathing funny. Otto felt responsible. "I'm so sorry. This is all my fault. I should have warned you sooner to keep your distance when he is mad. He gets so violent. Talk to me." Crowe didn't say anything. She only whimpered. Otto could see her light beginning to fade. He was absolutely devastated. He didn't want her to leave so quickly. He needed her help. He didn't want her to suffer or return to Barag with a broken spirit. He had to do something. He looked around for Gideon, but he was still in the kitchen yelling into the phone. There was only one way he could save his friend. He would have to transfer his protective energy to her. He had worked hard to cultivate the strong shielding aura, but she needed it more than him at the moment. Without it he would be exposed, but without it she would die. The choice was clear. He lay down next to Crowe and put his chin on her chest, resting the full weight of his head on her little body. He closed his eyes and imagined his bright, golden armor leaking from his aura to hers. With every moment, her breathing got a bit better and her whimpering tapered off. Otto felt very weak without the defensive armor but he was happy to see the brightness return to Crowe. Gideon rushed back in and kicked Otto's head off of the smaller dog and scooped her up. Otto followed them to the door, but Gideon yelled at him. "No Otto. Stay!" Slamming the door, they were gone.

Otto paced nervously around the house. He was too weak to contact Barag and Gideon had not returned with Crowe. He heard a car pull up to the apartment and the smell told him it was Gideon. Otto ran to the door, barking and jumping up. Gideon pushed past the concerned dog. He paused by the table. With a frustrated scream he threw his keys across the room and kicked the chair, dropping to the floor. Otto cowered, but he could see that Gideon was hurting. Gathering his strength he cautiously approached Gideon. He placed his paw in his lap and nudged his arm with his nose, trying to stick his head under Gideon's arm. Out of character, Gideon grabbed the dog and pulled him into his lap. Gideon hugged Otto and Otto tried to lick his face. For a moment Gideon sat in the embrace, but the air changed. Otto felt the atmosphere go from sadness to anger like someone flipped a switch. Gideon's grip started to get tighter and tighter. Otto squirmed to get away but Gideon had him in a chokehold. Fear started to permeate Otto's consciousness. It was not a feeling he was accustomed to. The Darkness started seeping out of Gideon to form a giant bat with wings spread behind him. Gideon lifted his fist and as he brought it down, the bat creature swooped through Otto's chest. The attack continued. With every kick and punch, the shadow creature penetrated and slashed Otto's weakened defenses. Otto lay helpless on the hard floor. Was this how humans experienced death? A lonely, cold seeping in like water to a sinking boat? He had failed. In his attempt to save his friend, he had made himself vulnerable and the Darkness had known exactly when to attack. When would the Kahu stop underestimating their foe? Gideon looked at the dog. All he felt was hatred. "Get rid of it." Gideon didn't even know where the thought came from, but now that it was out, he had to obey. He picked up Otto and threw him in the car. Gideon drove far from his home and dropped the dog on the side of the road. When he sat back in his car, he paused. He couldn't do this. He had to go back and get his dog, but a voice in his head screamed "*No*! Leave!" He obeyed.

    Otto lay alone. Pain shooting to every part of his body. His fear began to fade. Apart from the pain he could only feel one emotion. **_Hate_**.

CHAPTER TWENTY-FOUR
Moving Fur-ward

"Asha Lee Vardan! Are you in that bathroom with those kittens again?" Cassidy was exacerbated. She had told Asha to finish her homework over an hour ago and her math pages were still sitting on the table, blank. Cassidy opened the bathroom door to find Asha sitting against the sink cabinet, covered in kittens, reading a book out loud. All the bathroom's occupants looked up at the intruder. "I am doing my homework. I have to read this for my book report. They like listening." Cassidy tried to stay strict, but the scene was too cute to not smile at. All she could do was sigh and give in. "Ok. You can finish one more chapter, but then you have to take a break from reading and do your math pages. Once those are done you can play with the kittens all you want." Asha groaned but agreed. She hated math but she would get her multiplication and division tables done if it meant more time with her furry new friends. Cassidy and her daughters, Asha and Lily, had been volunteering as a foster family for local animal rescues and the humane society for the past three years. Asha adored it. It was hard to let the kittens go when they were old enough to be adopted, but she liked being able to help animals and her mother Cassidy felt the same. Asha's dad, on the other hand, was not a fan of having his home taken over by litters of stray kittens, but he preferred fostering to the alternative of his wife and children adopting a slew of pets. They already owned two dogs and two cats, he didn't understand why the girls felt like they needed more, but Cassidy was going to do what she wanted with or without his blessing. The litter they were caring for currently had been given names from one of Asha's books. If there was anything that rivaled Asha's love for animals, it was her love for reading. Asha adored reading to the animals and the animals seemed to like it too. Cassidy always encouraged it. Asha was dyslexic and reading was difficult for her, but reading aloud helped her practice. Becoming more familiar with common words made it easier to read and less embarrassing when she had to read aloud in school. Asha finished her math as quickly as her brain would allow and rushed back into the bathroom to read another chapter or two to the kittens. Her little sister Lily also pushed into the kitten room. While Asha read, Lily started playing with a string. Most of the kittens ran over to play, except one. A fluffy little male kitten named Luke. While all the other kittens rambunctiously attacked the string, Luke sat in Asha's lap and lovingly stared at her as she read. It was the beginning of a beautiful friendship.

***

When the kittens got to the age where they could be adopted, Luke and Asha's bond had grown and Asha couldn't bear the thought of parting with him. It took a while for her to convince her mom and even longer for her mom to convince her dad, but they eventually agreed that they would adopt Luke. Luke did everything with Asha. He listened to her read and make up her own weird songs, played the villain or sidekick to her superhero, and he even tolerated her attempts to dress him up in doll clothes. Whenever Asha suffered an asthma attack, Luke would lie on her chest and purr. Having a friend that was always there for her helped Asha to feel confident, even in the face of relentless bullies. The worst of these bullies was her own father, Doyle Vardan. Asha was desperate for his love and affection, but he made no secret of the fact that he did not like his daughter in the least. This rejection would have been hurtful in and of itself, but Doyle took it a step further and used every opportunity he could to tell Asha how stupid or ugly or annoying she was. His mean comments hurt, but with Luke there, Asha always had a fluffy shoulder to cry on. The fact that Luke chose her to love, unconditionally, helped to make up for the paternal spurning. Every time Doyle pushed Asha away, Luke was there with open paws and a rumbling purr to convince her that she was lovable and she was enough. With the love and companionship they shared, the years passed quickly. In the place of the adorable little poof ball that stole her heart, Asha had a strong, beautiful house lion. His coat was long and silky and resembled the color of coal on his back and charred coal on his stomach. Luke's MaineCoon lineage gave him a large physique and subtle tiger stripes on his side, as well as a boxy face and ear tufts. The Angora side of his mix gave him a smooth coat with a fluffy flared tail. However, it was his Kahu heritage that gave him the love, wisdom, and strength to protect her spirit from the constant attacks. Luke made sure to check in with Barag regularly. It was easy to do, because Asha loved shiny things. His favorite spot was the gaming television she had in her room. Whenever Asha had an asthma attack, the medicine would make her very jittery, but she had to stay in bed to rest. The best way to reconcile the two states was by playing video games. It kept her mind active, gave her shaky hands something to do, but was restful enough not to trigger another attack. This television was the perfect size for scrying and the shiny black screen reflected his image handsomely. He had plenty of time everyday when Cassidy took Asha and Lily to school to check in with Maahes, but this Girru was different in many ways from previous Girru Ki-Ang had accepted. With the level of danger, the Feline Kahu had adopted a protocol from the Canine Kahn's playbook and assigned multiple Kahu to each Ni within Gideon's reach. Some were placed directly with the Ni, others were placed in homes near the Ni or connected to the Ni somehow, and others entered temporarily in either human or cat form to check in. Luke was never alone. He liked the change, but it had taken some getting used to. As a cat in more modern times and living with animal rescuers, it was not simple for Luke to get outside to confer with his colleagues. However, today was his lucky day. The previous night had been cool, and Cassidy had opened the window to enjoy the fresh, cool air, but had forgotten to close it. All Luke had to do was make sure he was back in before they got home. It was a good day to be outside. The sun was shining but it wasn't too hot. Luke had to be very careful. The Vardan family lived near a busy street. Kahu or not he had learned the hard way that cars are dangerous. When he heard the roar of an accelerating car, his body still tensed up from the traumatic memory of his previous Girru. Luke made his way over the fence to the front yard. In the middle of the yard there was a giant swamp white oak tree. Luke liked to meet near this tree because it reminded him of Ziana Giš. He plopped under the shade of the tree and rolled on his back, wiggling in the fragrant grass. Looking up into the tree he saw two familiar faces. Lumma and Maahes hopped from branch to branch until they could crawl down the trunk to Luke. Both bobtail kitties looked the same as they did in Barag. When Kahu entered the Earth realm for short durations as a messenger or missions not related to directly guarding a Ni, they could choose their own form. Most chose to keep the image consistent to how they looked in the spirit realm. Apart from Inanna, the Kahu preferred to stay in feline form. Lumma greeted Luke. "Sup Ki-Ang? I learned that greeting in my last Girru." Lumma beamed with pride in her use of the colloquialism. Maahes cleared his throat and spoke up. "Master Lumma, papyrus three twenty-three, line thirteen, hieroglyphs four through ten of the Miu text suggests that when conversing with a Kahu in Girru, one should always use their Girru name to enhance familiarity." Lumma and Luke stared at Maahes. Lumma was not amused. "Zip it Heads. When you reach your hundredth century as a field guardian, then you can lecture newbies about protocol. Ki-Ang is not some rookie who is gonna forget his name if we don't drill it into him. Just chill kitten." Luke chuckled. If Maahes didn't have the cover of his fur, Luke was sure he would be blushing like a boiled lobster. "You are both right. Lumma, you can call me whatever you'd like, but Bob, you better stick to using my Girru name." Maahes nodded. "Yes sir Master Luke." Luke chuckled again but knew that Maahes would never understand the reference if he told him why that was funny. "I know that it isn't my mission, but are there any new developments with Gideon? Any breakthroughs?" Lumma just shook her head. "I wish I had better news for you, but despite the Canine Kahu's best efforts, he remains a Dalhku. Last I heard, they had made enough progress to assign a second Kahu. I know it doesn't sound like a huge development, but before, Master Utu was leery about risking the light of more than one Kahu by exposing them to the Dalkhu. The fact that they now feel comfortable enough to have two, I take to mean that they are at least making progress. But you know how dogs are. Informing us about their progress isn't a priority for them. How is your Ni doing? Ninlil told me that there is a source of darkness that swirls around her in the visions. Have you identified it?" "The source of darkness is the same as previously reported. The Ni's father is sinking further and further into his own darkness and that shadow is being drawn to the Ni's light. I have been keeping any shadow forms from attaching to Asha, the Ni, but I feel an odd sense of impending doom. I can't be sure if it is a warning that the father's darkness is getting worse or that something else is on the horizon. Please inform me if anything changes with Gideon. I fear that the more Asha becomes connected with her light, the more the Darkness will be drawn to her. Until Ama-gi and the others can decide how to deal with Gideon, I want to make sure he doesn't get anywhere near my girl, I mean, the Ni." Lumma looked at Maahes. "Uh Ki-Ang, there is just one more thing. Ama-gi wants us to help strengthen your aura. We will be visiting once a month to deliver energy we absorbed from Grandmother Zinana Giš. So don't argue and just accept it gracefully." Luke felt the urge to argue, but he had learned his lesson from his time with Gideon. There was no room for ego when others might get hurt. He rolled onto his side "Fine. Let's get this over with. The family could be back at any moment." Maahes and Lumma placed both front paws onto Luke and began pressing his body with alternating feet. Luke's girl had called this 'making bread' or 'kneading'. Kahu used it as a method to transfer energy. If the kneader focused, they could send light energy through their toe beans while focusing it to a specific area with the placement of their paws. The energy transfer was cut short by a van pulling into the driveway. As the family got out all three cats began to bolt until a small voice yelled *"Luke freeze*!" As Maahes and Lumma made their escape, Luke froze and sat back on his haunches with a cheeky "meow". Under his breath he cursed. Now he was going to be under tighter security.

***

A few years had passed since Luke had started his Girru. Things had been going well. Most of his time was spent protecting Asha from the emotional abuse of her father. Every cruel word or thoughtless action sent daggers of darkness into Asha's aura. Despite the constant attacks, Luke was proud that the emotional wounds never festered. He could see how every cutdown hurt the girl, but she never dwelled on it for long. A song, a book, a stint of playing make believe always help to rejuvenate her spirit. She was lucky to have a loving mother and the support of her Kahu guardian to always keep her head above the tumultuous waters of paternal emotional abuse. Luke was sleeping soundly on the couch. The family had been gone all day. Something roused Luke from his dream. His nose twitched and his body felt like it was vibrating. The feeling was familiar, but something that he had not experienced since Barag. Someone powerful was approaching, but Luke was not expecting anyone, so it put him on edge. His fur began to fluff up and his eyes darted around the room in vigilance. Keys rattled in the doors and Asha came bursting through holding a small puppy. Luke arched up in surprise. "Luke! Look! We got you a little sister!" The puppy squirmed in the girl's arms trying to lick her face. The pair bounded up to Luke and the puppy's eyes locked with his. He heard her voice in his head. "Hi. Hi. Hi. Hi. Hello! Oh my dog! I completely forgot how much fun the Earth plane was! There are so many smells and tastes and feelings and smells. I love this girl! I just met her, but I love her soooooooo much! Do you love her? I just met you but I think I love you too. Want to be best friends? Ok, we are now best friends. Ooh I know you.

You are Kahu so we are friends already, but now we are double friends because we are Kahu friends and Girru friends." The pup's tail was wagging faster than a pinwheel in a hurricane. Asha looked back at her mom. "Look mom! She likes him." Cassidy agreed but saved Luke from further smothering. "It looks like it, but let's bring her back here away from him until he can get used to her. We don't want to stress Luke out." The group went into the backyard, leaving Luke to catch up to what just happened. "Did that thing just say she was Kahu?" He was not informed that a Canine Kahu was being assigned. He would have to have words with Maahes as soon as possible.

Luke's tail was already in full swing before Maahes even answered his summons. Maahes looked guilty and apologized before Luke could say anything. "Sorry Master Luke, Master Ama-gi just told us. We didn't know that Master Ama-gi and Ensi Gula were assigning a Canine Kahu to your Ni. I don't know exactly why they chose to do that, but they said that she was experienced and the seers insisted that Ensi Gula send another strong Kahu." Luke flipped his ears back. "Do they think I am going to fail again? If Ama-gi didn't think I could do this, then why did she assign me." Luke heard a loud sniffing from under the door. A voice rang through from the other side. "Hi! Are you talking to Saa Barag? Tell them to tell Gula I said hi!" Luke glared at Maahes. "How is *that* supposed to help me?" A tiny wrinkled face poked over Maahes's shoulder. "Now, now. Don't be rude. Shasta is a well respected Canine Kahu in Urgi Barag. You should be grateful for her help. She, and her pack, used to protect the Shasta people before they were forcibly removed from their lands." Luke made a confused face. "That is who Ama-gi sent. There is no way that ditsy thing is Coyote of Shasta. I always imagined her more, well, dignified." Ninimma rolled her eyes. "For goodness sake! She is three months into her Girru. Even Kahu must go through the adolescent stage on the Earth plane. You would be the last cat I would expect to dismiss the influence of physicality on the soul. You have been incarnated enough to know that physical conditions such as age, hunger, sickness, etc can affect the manifestation of the soul on the Earth plane. That is Shasta and as soon as her body and brain develop fully, you will be grateful for her presence." Luke hated it when Ninimma was right. "Ok, but right now she is annoying." A loud snort and "Hey!" was heard from the other side of the door. Ninimma gave Luke a dirty look. "For fluff's sake! She is young, not deaf. Now you are going to go and apologize. No more complaints from you. You two will be working together, so you better be nice!" Without another word, Ninimma and Maahes were gone. Luke grumbled to himself, but made his way to the door and stuck his paws out underneath. "Hey doggo. Come back. I'm sorry. You're a good dog." Before Luke could pull his paw back, the bouncy puppy had her face pressed up against the crack under the door. "It's ok best friend. I *love* you. We're gonna be the bestest team!"

***

Ninimma had been spot on. As the puppy matured into a dog, the refinement of a seasoned Kahu began manifesting more in the dog. Now that she was a year and a half old, her wisdom and power was apparent. Gone was the high energy, fluffy puppy with oversized ears. In its place was a dignified, white shepherd with the patience of a guru and grace that Luke might have even classified as semi cat-like. Shasta was all white with medium length fur. Her snout was long, but rectangular. Her ears were large and stood straight up. Contrary to her large size and apparent power, she had a humbleness to her that made her approachable. Asha was on cloud nine everyday from the love she received from her two guardians. This day, as Asha quickly ran up to Luke and Shasta to give them goodbye kisses and bid them farewell by name, Luke's curiosity began to get the better of him. When Cassidy and her daughters left, Luke couldn't hold in his question any longer. "Shasta, I have to know. Your name. I know it from Barag, is 'Shasta' and in this Girru, Asha has named you 'Shasta'. Is that just a huge coincidence or did your Keeper of Zikru set that up?" Shasta nonchalantly lifted her back leg to scratch her ear. "Oh, I almost always use my name in Girru. During the time I spent with the Shasta people, I learned a lot about dream quests and dream walking. Now, before I step into a Girru, I meet the Ni in their dreams. Here I provide the suggestion for my name so when I enter the Girru, they always end up giving me the name I suggested. I can also use dream walking within the Girru to help the Ni confront things that they cannot understand or cope with during their waking hours. I find that humans are more connected with their soul during dreamtime as compared to their waking hours. I suppose it seems silly to use such a sacred process for something as trivial as a name, but I believe that a name holds special power. The right name can enhance one's natural abilities and aid in success. A mismatched name can block certain skills and hinder the mission. Our Keeper of Zikru believes that words are magic. If that is so, then names must hold power as well." Luke was impressed. As much as he tried to push aside his prejudice, Luke still saw Canine Kahu as stubborn, simple-minded lackeys. Feline Kahu considered themselves to be much better strategists than their Canine counterparts. The Canine obsession over loyalty and their abhorrence of manipulation was in direct opposition to the Feline ideals of strategy and adherence to the mission. However, working with Shasta had opened his eyes to the value of the Canine ideals. He still couldn't help but feel that felines were superior, but he had a new appreciation for the Canine Kahu.

***

Shasta was enjoying her Girru, but she knew not to let her guard down for a moment. Her and Luke had Asha well protected from her father's darkness, but neither her nor Luke had any intention of becoming complacent. The looming threat of the nearby Dalkhu was always on their minds. Shasta knew Luke's history with the Dalkhu, so she tried not to bring it up often. She could tell that the memory was still painful for him. She admired Luke's loyalty to his former human. She had assumed all Feline Kahu were cold, indifferent, and just a bit lazy. Most of her fellow Canine Kahu believed that a Feline Kahu would abandon their Ni at the first sign of infection and that the cats despised a Ni that would succumb to the Darkness and preferred to leave such Ni to their fate with no interest in bringing them back to the light. Her time with Luke had helped her to realize that she still had lingering bias from the Kahu conflict. Perhaps when she returned to Barag, she would suggest more pairings of Canine and Feline Kahu for future Girru. The sound of Cassidy returning from dropping the girls off at school let Shasta know it was time for her to check in with Barag. She ran out the dog door to the kiddie pool in the backyard. She used her mouth to remove a few fallen leaves from the surface of the water and stared at her reflection. The image that appeared surprised her. "Gula. I was not expecting you. I would think you have your paws full with matters concerning the Dalkhu." Gula didn't waste any time. "It is precisely that reason that I need to speak with you. As you know, Damu was given the Girru with the Dalkhu. He had undergone intense training with Master Utu, myself, and others to help him strengthen his light as much as possible. It seemed to be working. Despite the evil treatment of Damu by the Dalkhu, Damu was able to retain strong defenses against the darkness, never allowing any shadow to pierce his aura. Unfortunately, due to unforeseen circumstances, that didn't last. In trying to protect the light of one of his pack, he left himself open to the Darkness, who pounced on the opportunity Damu's weakened state provided. The good news is that Damu has survived the physical attack and was not sent to Barag with darkness in his soul. The bad news is that the Darkness has infected him. We can no longer contact him and he is deep within a personal battle for his soul. Inari has arranged that Damu, or Otto as the Dalkhu called him, will cross your Ni's path. He is in desperate need of healing and Inari believes that your Ni, with your help, can provide that. We would like you to speak to the Ni's mother in her dreams to convince her to bring Damu into the pack." Shasta agreed, but had her concerns. "I will do as you ask, but does Hemsut not have any concerns as to how the presence of the Dalkhu's darkness within Damu might affect the Ni? Is it worth the risk to expose the Ni to even a fragment of that darkness?" Gula was steadfast. "I understand your concerns, but the risk to the Ni is less than the risk of abandoning Damu to the Darkness. I have faith that you and the Feline Kahu can protect the Ni while helping Damu to regain his hold on his light. If something goes wrong-" Shasta heard the sound of the back door opening. Without hesitation, she started biting the water in the kiddie pool and jumped in to play in the shallow water, erasing any hint of the previous image. Cassidy looked at the wet dog and shook her head. "Shasta, you are going to make the entire house smell like wet dog. Get over here so I can dry you off."

***

That night Shasta left Asha's room to go sleep on Asha's mom, Cassidy. Shasta needed a physical connection with the human in order to ensure that the dream work was as potent as it could be. Once she was sure Cassidy was deep in slumber, Shasta placed her head on Cassidy's thigh. Shasta closed her eyes and drifted off to sleep.

Cassidy was walking down the street with her two girls and their dog. Asha held the dog's leash but when Lily went to grab it, her hand passed right through it. Lily began to cry but nothing Cassidy did could soothe the child. A bright light appeared at their side and the dog's shadow grew to the same size as the dog. Like a balloon filling with air, the shadow rose from the ground into a three dimensional thing. The shadow dog looked back at Lily and a pink tongue flopped out of its mouth. Lily stopped crying and took the shadow leash.

The next day Cassidy had a vague memory of her dream. She usually didn't remember her dreams, so the fact that the memory was clear seemed odd to her. As she folded the washing, she heard a high pitched cry from the backyard. Moments later Lily came running in the house. "Mommy! Asha won't let me hold Shasta's leash! She's not shaywing! I wanna play with Shasta too! It's not faiw!" As the girl bawled, Asha came in to defend herself. "Mom, I am trying to teach Shasta a trick and Lily keeps getting in the way. I told her she can't hold the leash because I want Shasta to pay attention to the trick." Lily started stomping her feet. "I wanna teach a twick to Shasta too!" To add to the chaos, the phone began to ring. Cassidy shushed both the girls and told them to wait on the couch. "Hello?" A woman's voice was on the line. "Hello. May I speak to Cassidy Vardan?" "Speaking." "My name is Ruth with animal control. I'm calling because I have you on a list of fosters. We are currently looking for a foster family for a male, medium sized adult dog. This poor baby was found severely beaten and close to death. The vet has fixed him up, but he needs to go to a foster until he is healed and can be put up for adoption. Is there any chance that you might be able to help us out?" Cassidy should have said 'no'. They already had a full house and she knew that Doyle, her husband, would not be happy if she took in another animal, but something in the woman's voice tugged at her heart strings. Worried that the pause in conversation would lead to another rejection, Ruth continued. "We're having a really tough time placing this poor little guy because he is all black and already a few years old. We don't have the staff at the kennel to care for his medical needs, so if we can't find him a foster, we may be forced to euthanize him." The guilt tactic was low, but effective. Cassidy didn't have the heart to say no and possibly condemn a dog to death. Her dream randomly popped into her mind and she looked over at her two girls still quietly arguing on the couch. No more convincing was necessary. "Well, I certainly don't want you guys to have to put the poor baby down. I have two girls. I will come by later with them, and if they all get along, we can help foster him." Both girls heard what their mom said and stopped arguing in favor of listening to the conversation. Both were excited to possibly be getting another dog.

***

After only a week of having their new foster, it was apparent that Lily adored him. She had always felt that, even though Shasta was supposed to be a family dog, she loved Asha more than she loved her. Now with the foster, whom they had named Shadow, Lily felt that she had her own dog. She begged her mom and dad to keep him. Doyle, though he openly despised his older daughter, actually seemed to like the younger one. He gave her anything she wanted. He was not amused with the idea of another animal, but gave in to Lily's demands after about a week. While Shadow was healing, he was kept isolated from the other animals. Shasta and Luke would try to peek in when the humans entered or exited the laundry room, but it was difficult to assess how their fellow Kahu was doing. Luke was steadfast in his patrols. He wasn't going to allow any darkness to get close to his girl. Shasta would stay near the door and try to speak with Shadow, but she never got an answer. Finally, after a few weeks of healing, Shadow was introduced to the other animals. At first glance, everything seemed normal with their new companion. His aura didn't seem overrun with darkness as Luke was expecting. In fact, Shadow came out of the laundry room wagging his tail and playing with Lily. If they had not been warned beforehand, they might have never known that Shadow had been infected with such strong darkness. Luke was the first to see it. He watched Shadow like a puma stalking its prey. At first Shadow's light seemed to be shining, but occasionally as Luke watched, the light seemed to experience interruption like static on an old television. It appeared like a glitch that quickly remedied itself, but would recur over and over again. During these phases, the light around Shadow would swirl with darkness that would quickly disappear like coffee sediment being kicked up by a spoon that quickly sinks back below the surface. As the dogs and children played, Shasta tried to communicate with Shadow. Initially he ignored her, but she persisted. "Damu,

Hemsut arranged for you to be here so we could help you. We can't help if you won't let us in. Luke knows what you are going through. He was also assigned to that human. He is called Ki-Ang in Saa Barag." This got Shadow's attention. "I don't want to talk about it." He looked directly at Luke. "If you were with him, you know. I don't want to think about it." Luke jumped to the back of the couch. "So don't talk about it. After I left my Girru with Gideo-" Shadow barked, startling the girls. "Don't say his name!" Luke smoothed out his fur and continued. "Ok. After I left that Girru, our Teacher sent me to be with that Ni there. Her love helped me to remember who I was and regain my strength. We want you to do the same. We don't need to know what happened, but if you allow us to help, we will do what we can to strengthen your energy so you can defeat whatever darkness broke through your defenses." Shadow went back to ignoring the two Kahu and focusing only on the girls. Luke didn't push. After all, it was the love of a child that helped him, so perhaps it would help Shadow the same way. Still, he wouldn't allow Shadow to be around his girl unsupervised.

***

Things remained consistent for weeks. There was disturbance within Shadow's light, but those disturbances remained confined within Shadow. Asha mostly spent her time with Shasta and Lily interacted with Shadow. Luke preferred this. Shadow was calm and gentle, but Luke didn't trust him. Every now and again, Shadow would get a distant look in his eyes and jump when something in the present forcefully brought his attention back. Shadow was having one of those moments. His mind slipped back to his time with Gideon and he lost track of where he was. Mindlessly, he tried to hop over the gate to go into Lily's room, but he misjudged his distance and his back foot got caught in the gate. His horrid yelp captured everyone's attention. The pain in his back legs triggered the panic he felt during the last beating from Gideon. Doyle rushed up to grab Shadow and free him from the gate, but Shadow was stuck in the past and could not separate the two. Shasta watched in horror as a chute of darkness shot from Shadow's back. The form resembled a jellyfish with the numerous tentacles encasing Shadow as he struggled against the fence and Doyle's grip. In his panic, Shadow bit Doyle's arm. The Darkness around Shadow began to pour into Doyle's wound like water being pulled down a drain. The more he cursed and let his anger flare, the faster the Darkness seeped into him. Shasta tried her best to counteract the attack with a howl, speaking the incantation "Wasu" repeatedly, but it happened too fast and the word was spoken to late. Doyle's own darkness flared and popped with the infusion of the new power. The fusion settled onto Doyle's shoulders like 80's shoulder pads and haloed his head in the style of a heavy metal hairband. It pooled in dark patches on his eyes and mouth. Doyle threw Shadow into the room. Asha started yelling. "Don't be mean to him!" Lily cried while Doyle yelled back at Asha. "You need to shut up Asha Lee! I will handle the dog. Stop being a bossy little brat and get out of here." Asha started crying and ran to her room. Luke was right on her heels. Shasta positioned herself at the door of Asha's room and continued to howl to keep the hateful projectiles being fired by Doyle away from Asha. Cassidy came running into the scene and was able to calm things down. After checking the dog and sending Doyle to clean up his wound, she settled Lily and finally went to check on Asha. Luke was curled up in her lap as she hugged him. When Doyle had gone, Shasta joined them and licked Asha until she laughed. Everyone was traumatized, but thankfully it appeared as if none of the darkness was able to harm the Ni. Asha was taking her father's cuts in stride and chose to focus on the love of her furry friends rather than the words spoken out of anger by her father.

***

The damage to Doyle by Shadow's attack was far from harmless. The new infusion of darkness increased his emotional attacks on his daughter. Asha could do nothing right. He walked in on her making up a song and told her how bad her voice was and that she shouldn't sing. She came out to show her parents her makeover of her little sister with their dress up clothes and Doyle told her it looked stupid and she should never be a fashion designer. Asha made sandwiches for lunch and Doyle spit his bite out saying it was too gross to eat. Each little dig took its toll, but every time Shasta and Luke were there to counteract the hit. Asha didn't understand why her dad didn't like her, but she squared her shoulders and hoped that one day she would be able to earn his affection. Instead of allowing herself to be swallowed by the pain, she chose to focus on doing better in school. If she could be the best in her class and make the honor roll, then maybe her father would see that she had worth and deserved his love. Her effort was cut short. On a Thursday in the fall, Asha had a severe asthma attack. She was sent to the nurse's office, but the school 'nurse' was just an office worker with first aid training and didn't know how to treat asthma. She gave Asha some hot Tang and sent her back to class. Asha continued to struggle to breath for the rest of the day. When her dad picked her and her sister up that afternoon, Asha was pale and queasy. She tried to tell her dad that she couldn't breathe and didn't feel well, but he was more interested in listening to her sister's excited ramblings. She crawled in the backseat of her dad's car as her sister quickly filled him in about every minute aspect of her day. Asha tried to interrupt and tell her dad that she needed help, but Doyle snapped at Asha for being a spoilsport for not being as excited as her sister. When they turned a corner, the movement overwhelmed Asha's resolve and she vomited all over the backseat. Lily screamed and Doyle went off on an angry tirade. Between the curse words and cut downs, Asha's vomit began to mix with tears. She probably would have cried harder if her lungs could have taken in the oxygen. When they got home, Asha tried to go inside to clean herself up but her dad locked her outside with a rag and bucket. He told her she would not be coming inside until his car was spotless. Luke sat at the window, pawing at the glass. Asha's light was fading, not just from the attacks of her father, but because her little body was starting to shut down. Shasta could sense it too and sat at the door howling. Doyle threw a shoe at the dog and yelled "Shut up!" Asha grabbed the rag and went to the car. Through each strained inhale, she tried to find the strength to wipe the throw up out of the car. She could hardly lift the rag, but she was too afraid to go knock on the front door. She was terrified and alone. She took in a wheezing breath and laid her head on the vomit covered seat cushion. Her chest felt like an elephant was balancing on it. Just when she thought she was going to die, a van pulled into the carport. Cassidy stepped out of the van, confused by the panic barking of the dogs inside. "Asha, what are you doing?" Asha picked her head up and backed out of the car. One look at her daughter's blue lips and Cassidy knew that they had to go right now. There was no time to call an ambulance. She screamed for Doyle and in a panic tried to ascertain what had happened as she strapped Asha in her van. The more she learned the angrier she was. As fast as she could, she hopped in the car and they raced to the emergency room.

As it turned out, the asthma attack was not just an asthma attack but pneumonia and a collapsed lung. After a week's stay in the hospital, Asha was released for home rest. She was happy to be feeling better, but what hurt the most was not the bruised feeling in her chest but the pain that her father cared more about the backseat fabric in his car than he did for her. Cassidy was livid and she and Doyle had a huge fight about it. He didn't believe he had done anything wrong. As Asha settled in her bed, she could hear her parents arguing. "You didn't think it was a big deal?! She was BLUE! Why didn't you call me? What if I had hit traffic?" Doyle was defensive and overflowing with excuses. "She didn't even say anything about not being able to breathe." Cassidy was not calming down. "Maybe she didn't say anything because she couldn't breathe!" Asha pulled the pillow around her ears. She was glad that her mom cared about her, but it made her feel guilty that she was the reason that her parents were fighting. Luke jumped onto the bed and head-butted Asha. His purr was so loud that it almost drowned out the fighting in the background. Shasta stuck her head up on the bed and gave her signature 'woo woo woooo'. It wasn't quite a bark or a howl but it always made Asha smile. Luke was concerned for his girl. There were places where small shards of darkness were trying to drill through her outer light. Luke went to work with his kneading. Every place he saw a sliver of shadow he would knead until the Darkness was dissolved by healing light. When Luke was too exhausted to continue, Shasta crawled up on the bed. She plopped her large front paws up one by one, then in an ungraceful pull and hop, she flung her back end on the twin bed. There was barely enough room for one and a few stuffed animals were forced to abandon ship to accommodate Shasta's large frame, but Asha loved it. The dog placed her head directly on the girl's stomach. Asha was calmed by the action of stroking Shasta's head and was asleep after only a few moments. Shadow nosed the door open and slinked inside. The argument was still raging and Shadow felt responsible. "I did this. I am so sorry. I failed Gideon and now something inside of me has poisoned the Ni's father. How could I have allowed the Darkness to gain such a strong ally?" He hung his head in shame and whimpered. Shasta left her head on Asha's stomach but shifted her eyes to look at Shadow. "Don't worry about the girl. This experience has only served to increase her compassion. Darkness was in her father long before you came here and it will continue when you are well enough to leave. My concern is for you. You continue to feed the Darkness with your fear and guilt." Her words made him think of Sunka's story. He wished he could stop feeling afraid and guilty. He knew he should be strong and brave and focus on moving forward, but all he could think of was the look on Gideon's face as he kicked him. The twisted smile that proved that the human he dedicated this life to save, derived pleasure from causing pain. Knowing that he shouldn't be feeling guilty when he did, only increased the feeling. Luke's words surprised Shadow. "I was afraid. When I tried to return to Gideon and discovered just how far gone he was, I was terrified. I was the one who failed. You were brave and tried to help someone who has been consumed by darkness. When I first met Gideon, he was full of light and compassion. He had his weak spots, but he was not consumed. That happened on my watch. I didn't believe that I deserved to be a Kahu any longer. Our Teacher Dingir, sent me here to live with Asha. I came here powerless. She loved me anyway. I came here afraid. She comforted me. I came here ignorant of everything that was really important and Asha and I learned together. I was mistaken before. I thought I had to do something to be a good Kahu. I thought I had to change my human's experiences to ensure that all they experienced was happiness and simplicity. I was wrong. Asha taught me that. When I came here the first time, she was so frail. She could hardly breathe, but she used the breath she had to sing to me, to comfort me. Just now, I thought she would come home from the hospital broken by the Darkness, but here she is, stronger than ever. Sure she was wounded and did not escape unscathed, but look how much stronger her defenses are now. I still wonder, if I would have allowed Gideon to be exposed to more attacks, but stayed by his side and helped him pick up the pieces instead of trying to shield him completely, would we be in the situation we are today? I could dwell on that thought and let it poison me, but I have a new mission. I must support this Ni. I can learn from the past and try something new this time. So far it seems to be working. If you continue to beat yourself up, you are practically doing the work of the Gaudium Cleptes for them." Shadow hacked to clear his throat. "I am so disappointed in myself." Luke agreed. "Yeah. That doesn't go away, but it just means you cared. The trick is to have those feelings, but continue to move forward despite them." Shasta could see a pulsating light within Shadow. "Courage is not the absence of fear, but the strength to move forward dragging the fear along, kicking and screaming. It can be a slow process, but we are here for you. Puppy steps."

Asha coughed and shifted her weight. Shadow looked up at her with his eyes, his eyebrows took turns bouncing as his eyes shifted. "You are right. I need to feed my 'white wolf' and get on with my mission." Luke looked at Shasta to see if she understood the wolf feeding comment. She didn't look confused so he wasn't going to ask. He assumed it was just a dog thing. Luke was glad Shadow seemed to be healing, even if it was little by little. As Shadow turned to leave, Luke noticed a dark form that looked like a spider near Shadow's heart. He moved to stand and pursue, but Asha reached her arm over and pinned him to the bed. Looking at his girl distracted him and he fell happily asleep.

***

Luke hid under the bed. Cassidy had said the horrid 'V' word and he wasn't going to submit to the ordeal with any grace whatsoever. He heard her approach and he squeezed closer to the wall, but she passed him by to retrieve the harness. Luke exhaled and emerged just in time to see Cassidy, the girls, and Shasta load into the van. Asha was reassuring Shasta. "Don't worry. It is just a couple of shots and we can get a treat after." Luke looked over at Shadow. Something was off. His light seemed to have returned, but there was something odd about how it pulsated. When the van pulled away, Shadow headed directly to the back door. He pushed up on the lock on the dog door and slid the metal sheet out. Luke followed him into the yard. Shadow ran back and forth by the fence. It looked like he was searching for something. Luke couldn't stand it anymore. "Whatcha doin?" Shadow looked up with a bit of a start. "Oh, good it's only you. I am looking for a way out of here." Luke watched him rummage around a bit more. "Why?" Shadow looked back and forth to clear the area of any eavesdroppers. "I have been thinking about what you said. About finding a new mission." Luke squinted his eyes at the dog. "And?" Shadow stopped what he was doing and approached the cat. "You were right. I just needed to find a new purpose. I know what I need to do. I accepted this Girru to stop the Dalkhu and that is what I need to do." Luke's eyes got wide. "No, you misunderstood me. You will find a new mission, but what you should do now is focus on healing. Your energy is still fractured. You shouldn't try to protect Gideon and bring him to the light until Gula clears you." Shadow looked at Luke and tilted his head to the side. "Oh no. I failed in bringing him to the light. Like you said, the more I tried to help, the more the

Darkness controlled him. I'm not going to try to fix him." Luke sighed in relief. "Oh good I thought-" Shadow interrupted. "I'm going to kill him." Luke arched his back. "What?! *No!* You can't kill him." Shadow went back to hunting for a way out of the yard. "Why not? You saw what just a tiny bit of his darkness did to Asha's dad. Can you imagine what will happen if other dark souls are exposed to that kind of power? Doyle almost let his own daughter die. If that spread we would have no chance in protecting Ni." Luke didn't know what to do. "*No.* You have to stop. Didn't Lord Utu tell you what happened last time they killed a Dalkhu? It will spread the Darkness faster." Shadow shook his head. "I was there last time. I was part of the pack near Issyk-Kul. The birds made a mistake. They didn't contain the Darkness before they killed the Dalkhu. I have a plan." Luke knew he had to stop this. "Ok, but if you have a plan, you should talk to Shasta and Gula or even the Avian Ensi. You shouldn't act alone." "Why? You cats do it all the time. I think you have it right. The Canine Kahu believe in loyalty to the Ni no matter what, but I didn't sign up to be loyal to the Gaudium Cleptes." Luke didn't know what he could say to talk sense into the determined canine. "You have to stop this. Gideon isn't the Gaudium Cleptes. He was a Ni. I have to believe he can come back. We can't give up on him!" Shadow twisted around to face Luke with a vicious growl. "He gave up on me! I loved him and he left me for dead! He killed you. He destroys everyone he comes in contact with and must be stopped!" Luke flinched at what he saw. A multitude of tiny shadow spiders were crawling over Shadow's bright energy field. Luke could see their sticky webs sticking to and manipulating his energy. Luke was confused. He knew that the goal of the Darkness was to spread, so why would this bit of the Gaudium Cleptes be set on manipulating Shadow to kill Gideon, one who was actively helping the Darkness spread? Shadow found a loose board in the fence and started chewing it. Luke tried to reason with him, but it wasn't working. Luke tried to block his way. "Please stop. I want to stop the Gaudium Cleptes as much, if not more than you, but this isn't the right way. You are letting yourself be controlled by your darkness! Stop! I won't let you kill Gideon. I know there is good left in him." Shadow stopped and glared at Luke. "Why are you protecting him? I am finally following a purpose again. I am right! I am going to stop evil, using force if I have to. If you aren't with me, you are against me!" Before Luke knew what was happening, Shadow lunged at the defenseless cat.

***

Luke blinked open his eyes and saw blue sky. He turned his head and saw a few sparrows hopping around by him. A shiny crow landed in the center of the sparrows, scattering them. "Hey. You. Bird. I can't move. I need you to take a message to Saa Barag or to Lady Ereshkigal if you must. It is an emergency. Damu is going after the Dalhku and intends to kill him." The bird twitched its head back and forth and hopped towards Luke. "Stupid bird! Did you hear what I said?! Go! Now. It's urgent." The bird pecked him on the head. "I heard you cat. Don't worry about the urgency. You'll be headed back to Saa Barag yourself in three, two, one-" Everything went black.

CHAPTER TWENTY-FIVE
Let Sleeping Dogs Lie

Shadow found a spot near his old apartment to wait for Gideon. He was prepared to wait as long as it took. He sat in the bushes thinking about an attack strategy. He had lied to Luke about having a plan. He just knew that he had to have a purpose or the emptiness inside of him was going to swallow him whole. The more he waited, the greater his guilt became. He had attacked a fellow Kahu. How far had he fallen into darkness to be able to harm another guardian? Sorrow knotted his stomach. This was wrong. What he had done was wrong. Clarity began to return to his thoughts and he considered abandoning this stupid plot, but then he saw Gideon. Rage filled him. Shadow crouched and prepared to lunge. The only thought that occupied his mind was hurting the man who had hurt him. He started moving forward when Gideon waved. Shadow froze. Jackie came trotting up with Crowe in tow. She was ok. Crowe was ok. Joy flooded his soul, drowning the Darkness. His sacrifice had worked. The energy protected her enough to save her life and her light. She was wagging her tail and walking just fine, though he did notice a bit of a limp. The relief he felt was greater than the hatred he was consumed by just moments earlier. Crowe paused and sniffed the air. Her tail began to wag faster and she looked around, sniffing in Shadow's direction. Shadow hid himself deeper in the bush. Shadow reprimanded himself for allowing things to come this far. He had no choice but to return to Shasta and submit to any punishment they saw fit to give him. He was ready to retreat, when Gideon knelt down and rubbed Crowe's ears. He laughed as she licked his face. Gideon pulled a treat from his pocket and hand fed it to Crowe. A voice whispered in Shadow's mind. "He was never that affectionate with you. He hated you. He beat you. How dare he pretend to be so loving now. He almost killed her. You sacrificed yourself for her and how does she repay you? She replaced you. She took your home, your human, your mission. Gideon prefers her." The hackles on the back of Shadow's neck raised. All he could see was red. All he could think of was revenge. Gideon must die. Now was not the time. He must wait until they were alone so no one could come to Gideon's aid. The shadow spiders weaving darkness around Shadow multiplied. Each spoke thoughts of hate. The sound consumed him and drove him insane.

***

Damu felt himself falling. He wanted to cry out but the descent stole his voice and all he could do was fall in the Darkness. Damu contorted his body, chomped at the air, clawed in the Darkness in a desperate attempt to stop the plunge. Nothing worked. Abruptly, he stopped moving. He couldn't see anything. He was no longer falling, but he was not on the ground. He was suspended in nothingness. Trapped in a void. He saw himself, like he was looking through the large end of binoculars. He could hear the hateful thoughts echoing through the void. He tried to scream rebuttals, but no sound escaped his mouth. He was no longer in control of his body or his mind. The void was cold and lonely. He could see Gideon, Jackie, and Crowe leaving for their walk. He so desperately wanted the help of his friend, but try as he may, he couldn't ask for help. He couldn't reach out. He was trapped within himself. He searched around for an escape, but he could see no end to the heavy darkness that encapsulated him. Damu felt numb. Waves of fleeting emotion crashed over him like violent waves against a rocky shore. Frustration, guilt, helplessness, restlessness, worthlessness. Each torrent knocked him further from himself until he felt unable to move. He wanted the release that crying might bring, but even that was beyond his reach. He was stone. Cold. Hard. Immovable. All he could do was watch in horror as the Darkness that had him trapped destroyed the world that he loved.

***

Shadow waited in ambush. Gideon returned to his apartment. Shadow was willing to wait all night and day if he had to, but Gideon saved him the vigil. He quickly exited the apartment and hopped in his car. He backed out of his space and approached the busy road. He flipped his blinker on, opened the moonroof to let the cool evening air in, and waited for the light to change and pause the heavy evening traffic. This street was dangerous because it always had lots of cars and the opposite side of the road to Gideon's apartments had a steep embankment that led down to a small lake. Gideon chose the apartments specifically for the view, but exiting the complex with the drop off and semi-blind curve was dangerous. Gideon looked down at the radio. A loud thump caused him to jerk his head back up.

Standing in attack position on the hood of Gideon's car was his dog Otto. Otto's eyes were red and his teeth were bared. Slobber dripped from Otto's gums and frothy saliva shot at the windshield as he barked at the driver. Gideon was frozen with fear. He watched his old dog as he slowly raised his gaze and settled on the open moonroof and then slowly lowered his head to meet Gideon's gaze. Gideon thought he saw an evil smile on the deranged dog's face. Realizing what the dog was about to do, Gideon floored the gas as Otto made a leap for the open moonroof. The acceleration caused Otto to overshoot the opening and flip over the moving car. Gideon's car flew into traffic. A giant tractor trailer swerved to avoid the car that unexpectedly appeared in front of him, but its speed was too great to stop or change direction in time. The truck clipped the back end of Gideon's car, sending it into a spin. The truck took over the right lane and ran another car off the road into the parking lot of the apartment complex. The rogue car just missed Otto as it slammed into the row of parked cars behind him. Gideon tried to hold the wheel and control his vehicle, but it was in vain. An SUV coming the opposite way crashed into the spinning car and pushed it into the curb. Gideon's car flipped up onto two wheels then rolled backwards over the metal guardrail, sending the car bouncing down the hill. When Gideon's car hit the water, his head bounced off the steering wheel and knocked him unconscious. The cabin of Gideon's car began to fill up with water as it sank below the surface.

***

Crowe wiggled her way out of a semi-open window as Jackie showered. She knew that she had smelled Otto and she had to find him. He had saved her life, but more than that he had saved her soul. The Darkness that had been seeping into her as she lay dying was worse than the pain her broken body felt. Physical death did not scare her, but losing herself in such hopeless despair was the most frightening thing she had ever felt. Before she could make her way to the place she thought Otto was hiding, she heard the sound of screeching tires. A car barreled into the parked cars in front of her and over the damage, she saw Otto standing in the parking lot. She was horrified by what she saw. The black dog she used to know was transformed. He had a spine-chilling shadow dog with red eyes draped over his body like a skinwalker in a wolf pelt. The shadow's hackles were like spikes and its back was arched. This couldn't be her friend. From the corner of her eye, she saw Gideon's car go over the side of the hill. She turned her attention back to Otto. Moments after Gideon's car disappeared from view, Otto collapsed and the sinister shadow completely vanished.

Damu watched as his shadow self stared down Gideon. He screamed and screamed in silent protest. "*No! Leave him alone!*". Damu knew what his body was doing was wrong but he had no power to stop himself. He ran around the dark void barking and digging, trying anything he could think of to get out, but nothing escaped this vacuum. He felt his body lunge forward, but thankfully it didn't find its mark. His body hit the top of the car and rolled onto the asphalt. When he saw the car barreling towards him, he wanted nothing more than to will himself in front of it. He wanted this nightmare to end, even if it meant servitude in Kur. He didn't want to hurt anyone else. His body stood on shaking legs. Damu knew that the Darkness would go after Gideon again if he didn't stop it, somehow. Out of the corner of his eye, Damu saw Crowe. He willed her to run away, leave him be. He couldn't control himself and the last thing he wanted was for her to get hurt trying to help him. Just as his body became aware of Crowe's presence, everything went dark. After a moment of spinning in pitch black, he felt a surge of warmth. Damu slowly opened his eyes. He was no longer trapped in the void seeing the world from that skewed perspective, he was in his body. More importantly, he was in control of his body. That heavy, disabling darkness was gone. Crowe was lying beside him with her head on his chest, staring at him. Her tail began to wag as he looked around. The destruction of the previous five minutes was still fresh. Sirens could be heard in the distance, as well as an approaching helicopter. A police officer had been sitting at the market down the street for a speed trap and had radioed in the accident as it happened. Police and good samaritans were negotiating their way down the hill to rescue the unconscious Gideon from the car. Damu scanned his body. He felt nothing but relief and happiness. He was free. Crowe picked up her head and scanned him. "Are you ok?" Damu was a bit stunned. "I feel like me again. I think the darkness is gone. I don't understand what happened." Crowe walked around him, slowly looking him over. "I can't explain it either. Just a moment ago, you were more darkness than dog, but now you are shining like a brand new dog tag." Crowe heard Jackie's voice calling her. "You better hide. Gideon told Jackie that you died in the accident that hurt me. If she finds out he lied, she won't have anything to do with him and I won't be able to complete my mission. Though, I'm not even sure if he is alive after that crash." Damu felt ashamed. He ran to the bushes and Crowe started barking. Jackie ran to her dog and surveyed the scene. She kissed Crowe and hugged her tight. "Don't sneak out like that. You could have died!" Damu watched from his hiding place. A pungent smell overwhelmed him. It was a smell he was familiar with and though his instinct told him to growl and try to scare off the annoying messenger, he knew that he deserved the punishment. Tree dogs were always the harbinger of bad news, whether it be a reprimand, sanction, or counsel summons. Tree dogs were the MPs or Internal Affairs of Barag. They were made up of dogs who did not follow Lord Utu in the Kahu conflict. They were rewarded by the counsel for not participating in the insurrection, but punished by Utu for their disloyalty. No loyal canine could stomach the presence of the tree dogs. A tiny voice squeaked, "Greetings Damu." Damu controlled his lips so as to not bare his teeth, but it was a struggle. "Squirrel." The tree dog twitched its long fluffy tail. "You have been summoned by the counsel. Come with me please." Damu hated to be subjected to the presence of such a traitorous creature, but he had given into the Darkness, killed a fellow Kahu, and tried to kill his human. He deserved punishment. He tucked his tail between his legs and followed the messenger.

***

Ki-Ang sat at the scrying mirror. He watched the moment that Asha returned home to find his body. She had been devastated. He had watched her everyday that had passed as she cried herself to sleep. He was given leave to visit her in spirit. She couldn't see him, but a part of her sensed his presence and was calmed by it. Shasta stayed by her side and for that he was grateful. He wanted nothing more than to rush back into another Girru, but Ama-gi told him to wait. The last time he defied her ended in tragedy, so he chose to listen to her this time. Knowing that Asha was not alone helped his patience. He had grown to admire Shasta and trusted her with his girl. He was confident that Asha was protected, but it didn't change the fact that he missed her dearly. Ki-Ang stepped away from the mirror and sat down.

He sensed someone approaching and turned to see Ama-gi gracefully striding up. "I assure you that the Ni is safe. All the Darkness that had been enhanced by Gideon's darkness has returned to its previous state. We can't seem to track what happened to it. When Gideon crashed, it all vanished." Ki-Ang had been made aware of what happened. Damu had returned to Urgi Barag and had been debriefed and sentenced by the counsel. No one really understood what had happened to the Darkness. Apart from being told about the accident, Ki-Ang was not informed of Gideon's condition. "Can I ask about Gideon? Is he dead?" Ama-gi still was leery about letting Ki-Ang be too involved in anything related to Gideon, but she felt he at least had the right to know. "Gideon is not dead. He is in a coma. The humans were able to rescue him, but the head trauma and near-drowning proved too much for him to wake from. He is currently on life support and not anticipated to wake any time soon, if at all. Our best guess is that because the darkness requires a host to survive, that when Gideon became trapped in the coma, that the darkness was trapped with him. It also seems that all the darkness connected to the Dalkhu was neutralized as a result of being cut off from its source. We've never seen anything like this, but it appears to be the solution we have been searching for." It was not the ending Ki-Ang had hoped for. Ki-Ang longed for Gideon's redemption and along with it, redemption for himself, but at least no one else would be hurt and humanity was safe for the time being. "What happens when Gideon wakes up?" Ama-gi shook her head. "We don't think he will wake up. Multiple seers have looked into his destiny, and they see nothing. Not death. Not recovery. Only nothingness." Ki-Ang felt sad, even though it meant that the Darkness would be trapped along with him. "So he is stuck in a living death until his body gives out? Then what?" "No one can say. We hope that because his soul was so integrated with the Darkness, that it will pass to Kur along with the soul. We are preparing for multiple scenarios. In the event of Gideon's death, multiple Avian Kahu will be assigned to his journey to Kur. If the Darkness should separate from Gideon before he is judged, we will have Kahu ready to track and neutralize anything that escapes. We will continue to have Kahu assigned to Gideon, even in his current state, but it appears that the danger to humanity has passed, for now." Ki-Ang should have felt relief, but a nagging feeling wouldn't let him embrace this as an ending. "What about Asha? Can I return to my mission with her?" Ama-gi saw the pleading in Ki-Ang's eyes, but could not give in. "I'm sorry Ki-Ang. We need you elsewhere. Without the threat of the Dalkhu, it is not necessary for one Ni to be guarded by two strong Kahu. We think it is best to leave the young Ni in Shasta's care and assign you to a different Girru." Ki-Ang wanted to object, but she was right. Asha was safe and there were others who needed his protection. He looked at the scrying mirror, said one last silent goodbye, and exhaled. "I understand. Where do you need me?"

EPILOGUE
CAT-atonic

The nurse entered the room for her morning routine. She brought in a fresh vase of flowers and some balloons. "Good morning Gideon. Guess what today is. It's your anniversary! Happy six years. I know what you are thinking. It is messed up that we are celebrating six years in a coma, but you are still here. That means you are a fighter and that *is* something to celebrate!" She placed the flowers by his bed and tied the balloons to a chair. They always kept at least one chair in the room for visitors, but the lonely chair in Gideon's room never saw one behind. No one came to visit him anymore. Jackie visited a few times for the first year, but she started dating someone, got married, and moved to the west coast. No one else cared that Gideon was no longer around. His nurses felt bad for him and were convinced that the lack of visitors was a huge part of why he wasn't waking up. They tried to talk to him as much as they could during their shifts, but most of the time, Gideon was alone. As she went about her duties, his nurse rattled on about her kids and workplace gossip. A few pigeons sat on the outside of his window, melodically cooing to the sound of the life-support machines. The nurse finished her work, patted Gideon on the arm, and left. The steady beep from the heart monitor and the rhythmic hissing of the ventilator provided the only soundtrack for Gideon's sad existence. A loud beep sounded from the hall and a muffled announcement followed. Then, in perfect clarity, a voice rang out in Gideon's room. "Gideon…. Gideon.Wake up!" The beeping of the heart monitor quickened and alarms started to ring. Gideon's eyes opened wide then turned black.

THE END…

Made in the USA
Monee, IL
06 March 2025

f3f2a2a3-62bb-43f9-a3bc-0f792816b015R01